Blessing in Disguise

Blessing
in
Disguise

Eileen Goudge

VIKING

VIKING
Published by the Penguin Group
Penguin Books USA Inc., 375 Hudson Street, New York,
New York 10014, U.S.A.
Penguin Books Ltd, 27 Wrights Lane, London W8 5TZ, England
Penguin Books Australia Ltd, Ringwood, Victoria, Australia
Penguin Books Canada Ltd, 10 Alcorn Avenue, Toronto,
Ontario, Canada M4V 3B2
Penguin Books (N.Z.) Ltd, 182–190 Wairau Road,
Auckland 10, New Zealand

Penguin Books Ltd, Registered Offices:
Harmondsworth, Middlesex, England

First published in 1994 by Viking Penguin,
a division of Penguin Books USA Inc.

10 9 8 7 6 5 4 3 2 1

PUBLISHER'S NOTE
This is a work of fiction. Names, characters, places, and
incidents either are the product of the author's imagination or
are used fictitiously, and any resemblance to actual persons,
living or dead, events, or locales is entirely coincidental.

LIBRARY OF CONGRESS CATALOGING IN PUBLICATION DATA
Goudge, Eileen.
Blessing in disguise / Eileen Goudge.
p.   cm.
ISBN 0-670-84961-8
1. Fathers and daughters—United States—Fiction.   2. Women
biographers—United States—Fiction.   3. Remarriage—New York
(N.Y.)—Fiction.   4. Family—Georgia—Fiction.   I. Title.
PS3557.O838B58   1994
813'.54—dc20   93-50238

Printed in the United States of America
Set in Sabon
Designed by Ann Gold

FOR MY CHILDREN, MICHAEL AND MARY,

AND MY STEPCHILDREN,

AARON, JONAH, AND KATE

I would like to thank several people who assisted me in getting this book off the ground, from the "blueprint" to its final unveiling.

First and foremost, my wonderful husband and agent, Al Zuckerman of Writer's House, for his keen eye in helping me shape my story, and his insider's knowledge of the publishing world.

Jonah Zuckerman, my equally wonderful stepson, and a recent graduate of Harvard architectural school, who helped me with the architectural details and assisted me in designing a building that, if built, would actually stand up.

Catherine Jacobes, my former assistant and forever friend, not only for her constructive criticism, but her hand-holding during times of crisis.

Pamela Dorman, my editor, and Audrey LaFehr, for their helpful comments.

Blessing
in
Disguise

Prologue

Washington, D.C.
1964

It had to be some kind of emergency, Grace thought.

Why else would Daddy be driving so fast? She looked over at his tightly clenched mouth, at the creases in his cheeks like long cracks in a boulder. Most of the time Daddy laughed a lot, and when he did the lines in his cheeks swooped up in a way that always made her think of ribbons on a wonderful big present.

But he wasn't laughing now. When his secretary called a little while ago Grace had heard him talking in a low rumbling voice, as if he were trying to calm Margaret down and at the same time keep her and Sissy from overhearing. But what could have gotten Margaret so upset? At her desk in the front room of Daddy's big paneled office, she always looked so smooth and sensible. Daddy's favorite joke about his secretary was that she ought to be in charge over at the Pentagon instead of merely running his office in the Senate building.

Margaret almost never phoned Daddy at home, and when she did it usually had to do with important papers needing to be dropped off, or an urgent message. It was *her* job, Margaret had once told Grace, to keep people from pestering Daddy.

Especially on weekends. Lots of times when he couldn't come home to New York, Grace and Sissy (escorted by Nanny if Mother was too busy) took the train to Washington to stay with Daddy at his apartment on P Street. And if someone who'd managed to get past Margaret called, Daddy would get off the phone as quickly as possible, then give Grace his special it's-nothing-that-can't-wait-till-Monday wink.

People were always calling or writing her daddy. People who were broke, and needed a job. People who wanted his help getting laws passed. Black people came to him, some with angry demands, some with tears streaming down their faces to thank him for everything he'd done for their cause.

And now, strangely, it was Margaret who needed Daddy. As soon as he'd hung up, Daddy had hurried them out to the car, without even waiting until Nanny got back from church.

The townhouses and crowded sidewalks of Old Town Alexandria were giving way to the lawns and tree-shaded houses of Mount Vernon. Grace clutched the Buick's shiny handle. Suppose they got into an accident, and she had to jump out quickly? The way Daddy was driving had pushed her stomach up into her throat, where it felt like a wad of swallowed bubblegum.

"Daddy, why are we . . ." Her voice was pinched off by a sudden sharp turn that sent them squealing around a corner.

"Not now, Grace," Daddy said a little irritably, keeping his eyes on the road. His graying red hair looked wilder than usual, crinkling away from his ears and forehead.

Beside her, Sissy sat peacefully sucking on a rope of red licorice. At five years old, she minded better than Grace, who was nearly ten and Ought to Know Better. In her pink dotted-swiss sun dress and white Mary Janes, Sissy reminded Grace of a plump, ruffled cushion. Except a cushion didn't whine and whimper the way Sissy did when Mother and Daddy weren't around to see what a pain she could be.

"What a *sweet* child," people were always saying about Sissy. No one ever said such things about Grace, with her perennially scabby knees and the look on her face of always wanting to know more than she was being told.

When Grace had once asked her mother why they couldn't all move to Washington to live with Daddy, why they had to wait in case he didn't get elected to another term, Mother had snapped, "You ask too many questions."

According to Mother, it wasn't exactly *polite* to ask so many questions.

Now Grace was silent as Daddy pulled up at the curb in front of a small, shabby yellow house tucked back behind some overgrown shrubs and low-hanging trees. She watched him as he threw open his door, turning to her only after he had one leg out.

"Look after your sister, hear? I won't be long." Daddy sounded out of breath as he stretched out his big red-knuckled hand to pat Grace's knee.

Grace didn't understand why they couldn't come inside with him. At the office, Margaret always greeted them with a smile. Sometimes she had a package of lemon wafers hidden in a desk drawer, and she'd make a great show of letting Grace and Sissy each have one while pretending to keep it a secret from Daddy. Why wouldn't Margaret want to see them now?

Grace wanted to say something about how scared and worried she felt. But she nodded and said, "Okay, Daddy."

"That's my good girl."

He'd called her that ever since she could remember, his good girl. But she wasn't always good. And she seldom minded. It wasn't that she didn't *try*. It was just that she was so curious. When told to stay put, she couldn't help poking her head around a doorway or tiptoeing to the top of the stairs to hear or see what it was the grownups wanted to shut her out of. Like the time Daddy objected because Mother's sister, Selma, got married and Gemma and Charles weren't invited to the wedding.

"Blessing is the deep *South,* Gene. You and your committee have done wonders as far as the Negroes are concerned, but you can't expect things to change overnight." Mother's voice came drifting up the stairs of their Park Avenue prewar, where Grace sat crouched behind the carved newel post. "Of *course* I agree they should have been invited. They've been with our family since I was in diapers. But you know Mother. She would have had another stroke if I insisted."

Daddy muttered something that sounded like Grandma's having another stroke might not be such a bad idea as far as he was concerned. Then, as if to show Mother he hadn't meant it, he said teasingly, "Cordelia, I sometimes think you married me just to shock your mother." Grace had known then, by the rich, booming sound of his laughter as it swelled up and out like a great balloon, that he wasn't blaming Mother for Grandma Clayborn's stubbornness.

Now, as Grace watched her father's broad, sloping back disappear up the shaded front path, she itched to run after him. She wondered what Margaret's house was like inside. She'd never thought of her as being anywhere but behind the front desk in Daddy's office, with its big black typewriter and neat stacks of papers.

But she couldn't follow Daddy. She'd *promised.*

She fished in the pocket of her jumper for her own red licorice. She wasn't like Sissy, who gobbled up treats as if she were a fat little goldfish. She liked to save things for later. It was more fun that way, looking forward to something for hours, sometimes a whole day. But when she pulled out the licorice Daddy had given her this morning, she saw that it had gotten all sticky and was covered in little flecks of lint.

She chewed on it anyway, mad at herself, and mad at Sissy, who was too young to know what was going on.

"I'm hot," Sissy whined.

Grace rolled both front windows all the way down. "There," she said, trying to sound the way Mother did when she meant for a subject to be closed, once and for all.

"I'm *still* hot." Sissy squirmed beside her.

The sun beating in through the windshield made the shade-drenched trees alongside the house look like a cool creek daring Grace to roll up her pant legs and wade in.

Grace, hot and irritable herself, snapped, "You're *not*. And if you don't leave those shoes on, I'll slap you."

Sissy stopped trying to unbuckle her shoe and started to cry, a low aimless noise like a fly buzzing against a windowpane. Her licorice slipped out of her hand onto the hump in the floor, where it stuck in a fat, gooey squiggle.

Grace tried to wipe Sissy's sticky hand with a crumpled Kleenex, but that only seemed to make it worse. Sissy's round muffin of a face got all scrunched up, and tears rolled down her cheeks.

"I want Mommy!" she wailed.

"You mean Daddy," Grace corrected her. "You want *Daddy*."

"No, *Mommy*."

"Mother's in New York," Grace snapped. "Here"—she shoved her licorice at Sissy—"you can have mine."

"I don't want it!" Sissy threw it down on the seat.

Grace felt like crying herself. She itched all over from the heat, and wished she hadn't snapped at Sissy, because now she wanted to take her shoes off as well. On top of everything else, she had to go to the bathroom.

"I'll be right back," she told Sissy. "Don't move." That was like telling a fish not to fly away, she thought. Sissy whined a lot, but she never *did* anything.

Walking up the front path, Grace forgot how annoyed she was at her sister and began feeling scared again. Sounds drifted toward her from inside the house—*bad* sounds. Shouting. A voice that sounded like Margaret's, shrill, pleading. And a man's, but not Daddy's—it was husky and mean. Mr. Emory? Grace had never thought of the photo on Margaret's desk, of a brown-faced man in some kind of uniform, as a real person.

Now she felt her arms go tight with goosebumps.

She quickly told herself that the noise was probably just the TV turned up too loud. Inside, the house would be cool and calm. Margaret would be wearing a crisply ironed skirt and blouse, and she'd smile and sort of scoot herself down so she could look directly into Grace's eyes, and say, "My, aren't you growing up so fast I can hardly keep up with you!"

Margaret Emory was a Negro, but she didn't look or act anything like Gemma or Old Charles. For one thing, she wasn't very dark. Her skin was more the color of the beige face powder Mother kept in her purse to pat over her nose. She wore silk stockings, and high-heeled shoes like Mother's. Her hair was smooth, and tucked under at the ends. When she talked on the phone, arranging Daddy's appointments, she sounded very businesslike. Most people called her Mrs. Emory, but she'd told Grace it would be okay to call her Margaret, the way Daddy did.

"Who are *you?*"

Grace was brought up short by the throaty voice that seemed to jump out at her from the shadows surrounding the tree-shaded porch.

"I . . . I'm looking for my daddy." Grace squinted, letting her eyes adjust to the sudden shift from brightness.

Seated on the top step was a skinny girl in pedal pushers and a too-big T-shirt. Grace recognized her at once from the framed photo that sat on Margaret's desk next to the one of Mr. Emory. She had her mother's light skin and pale-green eyes. Her hair stuck out in stubby braids on either side of her long face with its queer, slanted cheekbones.

"That's not what I asked you."

Once again Grace was startled by that foggy, nearly grown-up-sounding voice. She was reminded of her homeroom teacher, Miss March, who wore dark-red lipstick and always smelled of cigarettes.

Grace felt herself getting annoyed. "I'm Grace Truscott," she answered. "Who are you?"

"Nola." She spoke offhandedly, almost rudely.

"Oh."

Grace glanced at the front door, with its oval of glass that seemed to wink at her like a merry eye. The need to pee had become desperate. She planted one foot on the bottom step of the porch.

"You can't go in there," Nola informed Grace in her homeroom-teacher voice.

"Why?"

She rolled her eyes. " '*Cause*." As if Grace were a two-year-old who needed to have it spelled out, she added, "They're talking."

"Who?"

"Mama and Daddy and Uncle Gene."

But it was more than just talking. Even from far away, Mr. Emory's voice seemed to punch out into the tree-shaded stillness like a fist about to smash something. Grace felt hot and shaky. She was afraid she might wet her pants.

She felt angry, too. At this surly girl who acted as if she had a perfect right to call Daddy "Uncle Gene." Then she remembered Daddy telling her that, whenever Margaret had to work after hours, Nola would come to the office to do her homework. It was because Nola's father, a merchant marine, was away a lot, and there was no one at home to watch her. Grace could imagine Daddy inviting Nola into his office, helping her with a math problem, maybe letting her curl up on the deep-cushioned sofa with a book the way *she* liked to do. Because Nola was so strange, he would be extra nice to her. Daddy had a soft spot for oddballs—they made the world more interesting, he said.

Then Grace forgot Nola as the voices inside rose to a furious pitch.

"They sound *mad*," Grace said, alarmed.

"That's just Daddy. He gets that way sometimes." Nola tried to shrug, but Grace could see the pinched spots on either side of her mouth where the skin had gone white. She noticed that Nola was sitting with her knees all scrunched in against her chest, her lanky arms wrapped tightly about her shins. *She's scared, too,* Grace realized.

But as soon as Grace had climbed the steps and started to brush past her, Nola was on her feet, bristling like a cat. She was several inches taller than Grace, with long knobby arms and legs and big padding feet.

"You can't go in there," she said, more forcefully this time.

"I have to go to the bathroom," Grace informed her haughtily.

"Mama said to stay outside." Nola looked at her that way Miss March did when Grace spoke out in class without raising her hand first. Those queer green eyes of hers narrowed almost shut, as if she were about to pounce.

Grace marched past her anyway. She felt Nola grab her arm, but she shook it off and walked right up to the front door.

"It's not your house," Nola hissed.

"I don't care whose house it is," Grace told her.

She was shaking, and her underpants felt a little damp already. But she wasn't going to let this bully of a girl see how scared she was. She pushed open the door, and slipped inside.

"Daddy!" she cried, but the sound she heard herself make was no louder than a whisper.

Darting through Margaret's small, neat living room, she followed the shouting voices that grew louder and louder as she made her way toward the back of the house. Her heart was pounding. At the end of a narrow, dimly lit hallway, she spotted an open door. From where she was standing, she could just make out the back of a chair with a man's jacket thrown across it. She crept closer, edging around so she could peek in without anyone's noticing.

The blinds were drawn, but thin bands of light leaked through, throwing stripy shadows over a neatly made double bed and a dresser that looked strange until Grace realized why: unlike the dresser in her mother's room, with its lacy scarf and Limoges vanity set and silver-backed combs and brushes, there were no knickknacks cluttering its surface, no perfume bottles, no jars of face cream or tubes of lipstick, nothing but a plain wooden hairbrush.

Margaret, dressed in a limp blue housecoat that was nothing like the crisp suits she wore to work, stood with her back up against the dresser, one hand pressed to her mouth, her eyes round with panic. Across from her, on the other side of the bed, stood a big man in navy trousers and a white shirt rolled up at the sleeves. In the dim light, his forearms looked dark and shiny.

Daddy hovered in the doorway, his back to Grace. She could see his reflection in the mirror behind Margaret, huge and wild-haired, making her think of the story of Sampson that Sister Boniface had told in Catechism. She remembered another story, one Daddy had told about when he'd been a fireman, long before he was a senator, and even before he got elected to Congress. How he'd once dashed into a burning tenement that was about to collapse, and carried a three-year-old boy who'd been hiding under the bed to safety. A window had exploded in his face as he was climbing down the ladder, and if it hadn't been for his helmet and mask Daddy might have been killed. He still had a faint purplish scar above one eye that Grace loved to run her finger over. The skin was soft, almost silky, not like the roughness of the rest of his face.

Now, with his reflection mostly hidden in shadow, all she could see was Daddy's scar, standing out vividly in a slash of light.

"Put it down, Ned, before someone gets hurt." His voice rolled down like thunder from a mountaintop.

That was when Grace saw the gun that Margaret's husband was holding. Suddenly she couldn't breathe. She tried to suck air into her lungs, but it was as if they were packed with cotton. She ducked down lower, too scared to run.

"Who the hell you think you *are*, waltzin' into a man's house, telling him what to do?" Ned waved the gun in Daddy's direction. "Yeah, I know, you the big hero got every black man bending down to kiss his shoes. Out there marching with Dr. King for the black man's rights. Yeah, well, what about *this* black man's rights, huh?" His voice was choked off by a sob. The gun wobbled alarmingly in his grip. "What about a man who comes home to a wife who ain't his wife no more?"

"You don't know what you're talking about, Ned," Daddy said, trying to sound reasonable. His voice wasn't scared, just sorrowful, like when he'd spoken into the microphones at President Kennedy's funeral.

"God's sake, man, don't tell me I don't know!" Ned was nearly screaming. "You think just 'cause you the boss man that mean you payin' the bills round here and sayin' what's what? You don't know a damn thing what goes on outside that fancy office of yours. . . ." Grace realized suddenly that he'd been crying, his cheeks wet and his hand unsteady as he raised the gun, aiming it at Margaret.

"Put it down, Ned." Daddy spoke more sternly this time. "Whatever the misunderstanding between you and Margaret is, I'm sure—"

"Ain't *no* misunderstandin'!" Ned shouted. "I seen what I seen!" He was looking straight at Margaret now, and squeezing the gun to make it stop wobbling. "You . . . you . . . *bitch*. Always thinkin' you better than the rest of us black folk. Even *talk* like a white lady. And now you takin' away what little I got left. Jesus God, I oughta k——"

"No, Gene!" Margaret's voice rose to a shriek as Daddy lunged forward, throwing himself at Ned.

Grace, crouched in the hallway outside, felt herself grow very still. There was only the wild pumping of her heart, which had suddenly grown too large for her body. Something warm and wet dribbled down the inside of her leg, and she dimly realized that she'd wet herself. But it was as if this were happening to someone else. She watched helplessly as her daddy and Ned struggled across the room. Daddy was bigger, but Mr. Emory was wild, crazy. Strange gargling noises erupted from his throat as he twisted the arm Daddy held pinned, struggling to free himself.

As if hypnotized, Grace stared in horror at the gun, caught in a band of dusty sunlight that fell across Ned's straining knuckles, a deadly jewel turning this way and that, twinkling with menace.

Suddenly there was a deafening crack—as if the room

were being ripped in two—that brought a swift, jabbing ache to her ears, and jerked her legs out from under her. She landed on her tailbone with a jolt.

Through the buzzing cloud that seemed to be wrapped around her head, she watched Ned topple onto the bed. A huge red flower was blossoming at his throat, spreading across the white bedspread.

Blood. It was *blood.*

She clapped her hands over her ears, and began to scream. Or at least she *felt* as if she were screaming. But the only sound that came out of her mouth was a shrill gasping noise.

The floor beneath her spun and tilted. Her fear was huge, like some great monster that had gobbled her up, leaving no part of her to feel anything else. But then the numbness began to fade. Inside her underpants, she stung where she'd wet herself. Her bottom hurt where she'd landed hard on the floor. But when she tried to stand up, her legs folded under like a paper doll's.

Finally, bracing herself against the wall, she managed to push herself to her feet. Grace was backing away when she bumped up against somebody. She let out a strangled yelp, and spun around. The lanky girl stood there, frozen in her path, her eyes no longer slanted, but round and silvery-pale as nickels. She had seen it, too. She had seen everything.

They both turned to stare as Margaret let out a wild shriek. Watching the gun fall from Daddy's hand to the floor with a hollow *thonk,* and Margaret sink to her knees before the bloodied bed where Ned lay, Grace wanted to take an eraser and rub everything out, like when she messed up on her times tables. She wanted to make this not have happened. For her and Daddy and Sissy to be in his car, driving to the Maryland shore, where he would buy them lobster rolls and she would run along the pier, feeling the spongy old boards beneath her feet and collecting fishhooks in the heels of her Keds.

But, turning back to Nola, seeing her ashen face, Grace knew that there was no taking it back. Whatever happened next, Grace would never ever forget this. Neither, she felt sure, would the girl standing beside her, stiff and unmoving, her face expressionless except for those queer eyes that were like two holes burned in a blanket.

If a house is divided against itself, that house cannot stand.

St. Mark 3:25

Chapter 1

Grace was reaching behind herself to button her dress when she noticed the spot—just over her right breast, a tiny watermark shaped like a Rorschach blot.

She felt a flicker of annoyance. Silk. It ought to have been outlawed, she thought, along with asbestos and No. 2 red dye. When was the last time she'd worn silk without having to run straight to the dry cleaner? When was the last time she'd worn silk, period?

An image from long ago flitted across her mind—swirls of taffeta the color of raspberry sherbert, an orchid corsage on her wrist. Some awful country-club affair that Grandma had insisted she attend. By evening's end, she recalled, the orchid looked as if it had been trampled by Sherman's army, which, the way people in Blessing talked, you'd have thought had scorched its way through Georgia the week before.

Staring into her closet, Grace thought of the evening stretching before her like a battlefield. *What does it matter what I'm wearing?*

Hannah would probably be thrilled if she showed up at the door in her underwear. All the more reason to find fault with her father's girlfriend.

Girlfriend. The word stuck in her mind like something scrawled in her Robert E. Lee High yearbook, adolescent, transitory, inconsequential somehow. My God, she was thirty-seven years old, and someone's *girlfriend*.

It would be different if we were married.

But was that really what she wanted—to be a wife again, and play stepmother to Ben and Hannah? Didn't she have enough to handle just being the *mother* of a teenager? Besides, Jack hadn't even *asked* her to marry him. Whenever the subject came up, he adroitly managed to skirt it.

Grace felt a knot form in her stomach, and along with it came the sudden certainty that *nothing* about this evening was going to turn out okay. But she quickly filed that thought away, under "Pending" (on the mental shelf below "Maybe It'll Work Out on Its Own" and just above "You're Wasting Your Time"). Right. Just because this was their first dinner together, all five of them, was no reason to panic. There would be enough of that after Hannah arrived.

She peeled her dress over her head, inside out, experiencing the same relief she felt each time she shucked off a pair of pantyhose at the end of a day of talk shows and interviews and book signings. Tossing it onto the floor of her closet, she plucked a pair of Levi's from a hanger. Softened by many washings, they slid on over her legs and hips like lotion. Next, she pulled on the fifties men's pajama top she'd bought at Canal Jean—aubergine satin worn to the texture of chamois, with black piping and an unreadable monogram. Tucked in, with its sleeves rolled up four times, it fit her just fine. Now her Navajo conch belt threaded through the loops of her jeans. There.

Caught in the sepia glow of the late-afternoon sunshine angling down from the loft's bedroom skylight, she examined herself in the full-length closet mirror as if studying the photograph of someone she had not yet gotten to know. Hazel eyes in a heart-shaped face no longer girlish, but shot with tiny crinkles, like a delicate tissuey valentine that's been crushed then pressed nearly smooth again. Dark straight hair brushing the knobs of her too-thin shoulders—no gray yet, but maybe she wasn't looking hard enough.

Was this the face of a likable person? A woman you would welcome as a friend? A wife? A stepmother?

Bong.

In the living area, down the hall, Grandma Clayborn's pendulum clock marked the hour in what Grace had always thought of as a somewhat ominous tone. She counted six chimes. God, Jack and his kids would be here in less than half an hour, and she hadn't cleaned up or even put the water on to boil for the rice.

Briefly, she considered phoning Jack and telling him she was sick, a sudden attack of the flu. No, that wouldn't work. He'd be over like a shot, toting a plastic tub of chicken soup with matzoh balls from Lou Siegel, like that time when she really *was* sick with the flu.

All the stress she'd been under? He'd buy that. He was her publisher after all, he knew how crazy her schedule had been lately with this book—all the shuttles to Washington, the interviews with ex–staff members, friends, legislators and former legislators, longtime bureaucrats, anyone who'd known Eugene Truscott. And as if writing a biography of her famous father wasn't enough of an undertaking, someone at Cadogan had stolen a look at her most recent draft and leaked the story of the senator's being involved in the shooting death of Ned Emory. It had appeared in yesterday's *Times,* and for the past two days the phone had been ringing practically nonstop—mostly reporters. Jack, though not denying the publicity value for the book, was as angry as she was. Plucked out of context, the story had come off as lurid, sensational, possibly even criminal.

But Jack, damnit, he'd be so nice if she were to duck out of this dinner, so sympathetic, that she'd be plagued with guilt for days afterwards.

Besides, Jack wasn't the problem. *He* wasn't why she had

heartburn, and her stomach felt as if something she'd swallowed hadn't quite gone down.

It was Hannah.

Tonight's menu wasn't chicken cacciatore over rice, as she'd planned. No way, José. It was going to be Grace Truscott, skewered and roasted over hot coals.

Grace jammed her bare feet into antique crocodile pumps—a pair that had belonged to her grandmother back in the days when size-six shoes were what most ladies wore, and everyone took it for granted that crocodiles had been placed on this earth to be worn—and dashed down the hall into the huge, airy space that encompassed the kitchen, living room, and office. If Mother were making this dinner party, she thought, there'd be ivory-colored place-cards inscribed in copperplate and Grandma Clayborn's good Havilland china, and an uncorked bottle of Châteauneuf-du-Pape breathing on the sideboard. For her mother, letting even a small thing like the rice go till the last minute would be a sacrilege.

In the kitchen, tiled in cloudy sky blue and open on three sides, Grace peeked in the oven at the chicken supposedly cacciatore bubbling inside. Her heart sank. The clotted mess—chicken legs and breasts dissolved into stringy clumps—looked more like last week's thrice-reheated leftovers than the glossy photo in her *Better Homes & Gardens* cookbook.

She realized that she'd forgotten to cover the dish for the last half-hour, as the recipe had called for. And that, actually, it had been more like forty-five minutes. She'd been so busy helping Chris with that essay of his on the Spanish Inquisition she'd lost track of time. God, what on earth was she going to do *now?*

After thirty years with a Martha Stewart clone, Jack

would expect a woman who could at least get an ordinary dinner on the table without screwing it up.

"What's that?"

Grace turned to find her thirteen-year-old son slouched in the doorway like a haphazardly parked bicycle—all shank and bone and jutting angles, head cocked so that his silky brown hair fell across his eyes. Love, helpless and yearning, swept over her on a tide of annoyance. Chris was at a stage where everything, however obvious, was stated in the form of a question. If she told him to put his jacket on as he was going out, he'd look at it and say, "What *for?*"

Right now, Grace didn't want a scene. "It was supposed to be chicken cacciatore," she said with a laugh. "But your guess is as good as mine."

Chris shrugged, locking his arms across his skinny chest. She had to search his face for the last traces of babyhood—the round chin she'd so often wiped clean, the pale freckles dusting his snub nose, his soft, almost unfocused-looking blue eyes. He was so vulnerable, standing at the crossroads of adulthood, not knowing where to turn, everything about him declaring his uncertainty, even the way his voice had begun to crack.

"I'm not hungry anyway. I'm going over to Scully's," he said. "We'll get some pizza later on."

"Hold on there, pardner." She hadn't realized she was holding a serving fork, until she looked down and saw that it was pointed straight at Chris. *En garde,* she thought. "Have you forgotten we're having company for dinner?"

"You mean Jack?" The way he said it sounded almost like a sneer.

Grace decided to play dumb.

"Yes, Jack. And Hannah. And Ben. You haven't met him. He's older than Hannah. Closer to my . . . Well, anyway, he's a good guy. You'll like him." She lowered the fork, and felt her mouth form a rueful smile. "Look, don't jump up and down too much. I wouldn't want people to get the wrong idea and think I was going out of my way to make a good impression here."

Chris cracked his own upside-down version of a smile as he cast his deadpan gaze on the casserole dish containing the earthly remains of the chicken cacciatore. "You could always call 911."

"Thanks, you're a real help."

"Hannah's nice, but . . ." Chris shrugged.

He didn't have to say it—she knew what he was thinking. He'd rather contract Lyme disease than see her marry Jack. On that subject, her son's feelings were no more a secret than Hannah's.

She watched as he tossed his hair back with a sharp jerk of his head. His eyes made a brief appearance, naked and somehow too bright. They were the exact shade of Win's, grayish blue, the color of the ocean off Long Island Sound.

Poor Chris. In some ways the divorce had been hardest on him. Even though he saw Win nearly every weekend, she knew how much Chris missed having him around.

"Look, Mom, I promised Scully I'd check out this new Mario Brothers game of his." Chris spoke in a flat voice. "Don't worry, I'll be back in time for dinner."

"You'll be back *before* then. So you can change." She took in his torn jeans and the Metallica T-shirt that was sizes too big.

"What's wrong with what I'm wearing?"

"You look . . ."

"Like you. I look like *you*, you mean." Chris shot her a scornful glance that said he wasn't fooled by what she'd thought an artful outfit—in his eyes, it was just jeans and an old pajama top. He snatched a handful of crackers from the assortment she'd carefully arranged on a tray alongside a wedge of Brie, and was gone.

I miss him, she thought.

Not that silent, skulking teenager, but her funny, bright little boy, with his silly elephant jokes and eager laugh, and the way he used to burrow under the covers when she came in to kiss him good night. Most of all, she missed holding him on her lap, his small body heavy with sleep, his head blindly butting her breast in search of a comfortable spot to roost.

When had he begun to change? Had it started even before the divorce? Should she put his sullen rebelliousness in the same category as the faint shadow that had recently begun to make an appearance on his upper lip, and the sheets she found hastily stuffed into the hamper some mornings?

Grace felt suddenly tiny and inadequate, a dust mote adrift in this enormous, soaring space. A row of tall windows made it seem even bigger, providing a truncated view of the skyline, above which she could just see the tip of the Empire State's spire—lit orange and yellow for Halloween next week. Below the windows stood the pine harvest table she'd set with such care. Her colorful Quimper plates and Mexican embroidered cloth napkins, the mismatched silver she'd collected over the years at flea markets and rummage sales.

Chris's therapist, Dr. Shapiro, said he would need time to get over the divorce. But how much longer would it take? And what was she supposed to do about it in the meantime?

The intercom buzzed, startling her into nearly knocking over the wineglass, set amid a drift of cucumber peels, that she'd been about to pick up. She hurried to answer it.

It was only Jack, thank heavens. He'd promised to get here early, before Ben and Hannah, and he had. A show of solidarity? *United we stand, divided we fall.* A minute later, she watched him sail through the doorway in his rumpled

Burberry raincoat—a tall, heavyset man with an open smile and dark curly hair shot with gray—and she could feel all her unraveling ends strangely—magically, even—becoming whole.

Now Jack was scooping her against him, smothering her with his hugeness, his happiness at seeing her. His embrace released some charge in her, making her limbs tingle, her belly loosen and grow heavy, expectant. She felt as if she could never get enough of him—his tweedy smell, or his thickly muscled arms holding her tight. She imagined that inside Jack his blood ran faster, surer, redder than any other man's, a vein of rich ore that if tapped would yield up incalculable treasures. Her own blood raced at the thought of what lay ahead, the bed in which he would take her, later, when the kids were safely home or asleep. . . .

"Do I smell something burning?" Jack ruffled her hair lightly.

Grace groaned.

"Uh-oh. Anything I can do to help?" He pulled back, smiling, his deepset navy eyes crinkling.

"A priest would be nice. I think last rites may be in order. Do rabbis do that kind of thing, too?" She was reminded of the old joke—guilt: the Jews invented it, and the Catholics perfected it. *Does Jack feel guilty about marrying a Catholic? Is that what's holding him back?*

Jack crossed the vestibule in several long strides. To his left was the grouping of furniture that defined her living room—a deep sofa upholstered in Sea Island cotton, an old Morris recliner she'd re-covered in dark-green corduroy, scattered armchairs, a glass coffee table with wrought-iron legs twining up like vines. Jack shrugged off his raincoat and tossed it in a long free throw over the back of the sofa, heading toward the kitchen. A moment later, he was examining the chicken and rolling his eyes.

The great thing about Jack was, he never lied to her. When he told her something she'd written was good, or that she looked terrific, she knew it was the truth. Because he'd just as easily tell her that what she'd written was awful, or that she looked like ten nights of missed sleep.

"I have a confession to make," she said. "I don't come with a *Good Housekeeping* Seal of Approval."

"I didn't fall in love with you for your cooking," he said, dropping the lid back on the casserole dish with the finality of someone nailing down a coffin lid.

"Flattery will get you nowhere," she warned. "I want to feel miserable for at least five more minutes."

"Can I kiss your neck while you're at it?" He bent and began to nibble her ear. His lips were shockingly warm, especially considering how overcooked she herself felt.

"Jack." She glanced up at her Felix the Cat clock flicking its tail above the sink full of pots and pans she hadn't gotten around to washing. "It's almost six-thirty. Your kids will be here any minute." She tried to sound like no more than a normally frazzled hostess, but inside her panic was mounting.

He straightened, his blue eyes serious now. "I'll tell you what," he said. "You finish up whatever's left to do, and I'll take care of the main course."

"What are you talking about? There isn't time!"

"Look." He took hold of her, turning her gently so she was facing him. "I'd gladly eat stewed cardboard if it'd make you happy, and I wouldn't mind a bit. But I know how much you've been looking forward to making this a nice evening for Hannah and Ben. Not," he added sternly, "that they'll like you any less if it doesn't work out exactly the way you planned."

No, she wanted to say, *Hannah will only hate me more.*

Before she could speak, he held up one hand—large and

long-fingered, the hand of a carpenter, not an executive. "Just give me five minutes, okay? Trust me. I'll be back before you know it." He jogged over to the living-room sofa and grabbed his coat.

Ten minutes later, he was back, gingerly carrying a large, grease-stained paper sack as if it were the Holy Grail. He set the bag down on the kitchen counter and opened it, letting loose a heady garlic aroma. "Lasagne," he said. "Cesare makes the best there is."

"I get pizza at Cesare's all the time," Grace said, mystified. "I didn't know he made anything else."

Jack winked. "The best-kept secret in Chelsea—he keeps a limited supply in back. You just have to know to ask."

Grace stared at him. How was it that Jack—from Park, way up on the East Side, who published first-rate books out of a landmark building on Fifth Avenue—knew more about the back rooms of greasy Eighth Avenue pizza parlors than she did?

I can't even do *takeout* right, she thought.

Grace caught a glimpse of herself in the mirrored wall opposite the kitchen counter wearing the ruffled apron she'd hastily thrown on just before Jack arrived. She began to laugh. This is ridiculous, she thought. This isn't me. What is going *on* here?

But she knew. Oh my, yes, she knew exactly what she was doing.

Instead of catching that new play Lila had an extra ticket for, you're running around in circles, hoping to impress the hell out of some guy, show him what a great wife you'd make.

Not some *guy*. Jack. Jack Gold, who loved her at three in the morning, hunched over in front of her computer screen, wearing her oldest terry robe with Wheat Thins crumbs caught in its folds.

And after she'd won the Pulitzer for *Bridge over Troubled Waters,* and felt that if one more person phoned supposedly to congratulate her and then tried to sell her something or offer her some kind of deal she'd lose what was left of her shell-shocked mind, who but Jack had materialized on her doorstep with a bottle of chilled Moët and two tickets to Bermuda?

Now, watching Jack unearth a Pyrex dish from a cupboard, into which he began deftly transferring the lasagne from three aluminum-foil containers, she thought, *I could be happy with this man.*

"Have I told you lately that I love you?" she asked.

"Not for at least eight hours. I was beginning to feel deprived."

Expertly, as if he did this for a living, he sprinkled extra cheese over the top and popped the lasagne into the oven. While it was heating, he came over and wrapped his arms around her, nearly engulfing her with the sheer solidness of him—like a tree that appears tallest when you're standing directly underneath it, looking straight up. Her head resting against his collarbone, she caught the smell of his sweat and felt the dampness of his shirt—he must have run all the way to Cesare's and back. A deep tenderness welled up in her.

"How did it go today?" he asked cautiously.

"You mean, in between phone calls from reporters? All I can say is, thank heaven for answering machines."

"A couple of days ago you were wishing they'd never been invented."

"That was *before* I got through to Nola."

"You talked to her?" Jack's eyes widened.

"This afternoon. I would have told you sooner if you hadn't gone flying out the door practically the minute you got here, but, yes—would you believe it?—Nola Emory actually picked up what must have been my sixteenth call."

Grace sighed. "She was so impersonal, Jack. Like I'd dialed the wrong number. She said she had nothing more to say about her father's suicide than what had been in the news-papers. *Suicide.* Jack, that's *not* what happened."

"What did you expect her to say?"

"The truth. That it was an accident. Jack, she was *there,* and so was I. We saw them struggle. The gun . . ." She shut her eyes, feeling a sharp pain behind her forehead. All those years ago, Daddy—Margaret, too—had suppressed the truth for the sake of his political career. And hadn't Mother, after Grace had sobbed out the whole story to her, made sure she kept silent, too? Still, it wouldn't let go of her. Maybe that was the reason she'd finally gotten up the courage to put it all down on paper, to wrest those rattling bones out of the closet and into the light. "My father was simply *protecting* Margaret. What I want to know now is, who does Nola think she's protecting?"

"Herself probably. Look at what's happened already—the press is having a field day with this story. Those calls you've been getting, that could be exactly the kind of thing this Nola Emory wants to avoid."

As if on cue, the phone rang. Grace heard her machine, behind the wall of bookcases that that enclosed her office space, pick up. "Nancy Wyman from Associated Press . . ." came the tinny response to her own message. Though prom-ising to call back later, Nancy left both her office and home phone numbers.

Grace looked at Jack, who offered her a grim smile.

"Looks like you've opened a Pandora's box," he commented.

"I just want to set the record straight! Of course I knew there would be questions raised, but once people have read the book . . ."

"You were nine and a half," he reminded her. "Are you

certain of what you saw? Memory sometimes exaggerates. And even if it happened the way you say it did, why did your father tell the police he arrived on the scene *after* Ned was shot? And why was his good friend Mulhaney put in charge of the investigation? Grace, *those* are the questions people will be asking. They'll want to know just what your father was hiding."

"He wasn't hiding anything," she protested. "He was just protecting himself. His position, his whole career, was at stake. And he was so close to pulling a majority his way on the Civil Rights Act. A thing like this would have . . ."

Grace pulled free of Jack and went over to her desk, snugged in behind a high bookcase crammed with books and magazines. She found what she was looking for atop a pile of pages from a transcribed interview, and brought it over to Jack.

It was a newspaper photo of her father standing behind Lyndon Johnson as he sat at a table, pen in hand. The caption underneath read: *LBJ Signs Civil Rights Act.*

"It was Daddy who made it happen, who pushed it through," Grace said, her voice rising. "He risked his career, the favor of his constituency, for what he believed in." She thought of the stories Daddy used to tell, about the years before his family moved to New York, growing up in Tennessee, where blacks were treated like farm animals, sometimes worse. And about when he was stationed in Okinawa during the war, captain of an all-black quartermaster company, how the system that made heroes of white soldiers only served to crush and humiliate men of color. Daddy had sworn he would never stop trying to right those injustices. "Do you know what my father told me once? He said he thought it was *luck* that he'd ruined his lungs fighting fires. Otherwise he might never have run for office."

Jack put his arms around her. "Grace, you don't have to

convince me your father was a great man. But even more than it loves its heroes, the public loves a scandal. Look at Chappaquiddick. Who knows what really happened? All we can be sure of is that it ruined any chance Teddy Kennedy might have had to become president."

"That's why I need Nola to back me up."

"But she's not talking."

"She will," Grace said with more conviction than she actually felt. She couldn't help remembering the hostile little girl who'd tried to prevent her from going inside Margaret's house that day.

"I hope you're right." Jack looked thoughtful. "It would certainly strengthen our position from a legal point of view."

"Jack, you're not afraid of some kind of libel suit! Who would—?" She stopped, realizing at once what he was getting at. "Oh, Jack, you *can't* think my mother would do such a thing. What would she have to gain from it?" Then Grace remembered Mother's current crusade, for which she'd been soliciting funds since God knows when: the Eugene Truscott Memorial Library.

Mother could move mountains if she had to . . . or *become* one.

Like after Daddy died, transplanting the three of them to Blessing so she could take care of impossible, bedridden Grandma Clayborn, then raising two daughters alone in that big old house.

One whiff of scandal concerning Daddy and she *would* put up a fight. No one had ever been able even to *disagree* with him without Mother's jumping to his defense.

Wasn't that what her mother had done with Win, too? Closing her ears to the truth about her precious son-in-law. Even, in her own charming way, trying to bully Grace into staying with him. Pushing and prodding until Grace finally had blown up at her. Since then she and Mother hadn't spoken except to exchange forced pleasantries over the phone.

"Talk to her," Jack urged softly, as if echoing her thoughts. "Explain why you're doing this, and see if you can get her on your side."

"I'll try," she told him, placing her palms against his chest, hoping some of his calm and sureness would somehow flow through to her. "But after all this time, she's probably convinced herself that *her* version—the one she and Daddy cooked up—is the true one."

"I'll bet she hasn't forgotten that you're her daughter."

"Maybe, but I'm not exactly high on Mother's list right now."

"Nobody could ever accuse you of being a quitter," Jack said with a teasing smile. "Anything you want, you go after with a howitzer."

Including you? Is that what it'll take to pin you down, Jack?

But she didn't say the words; they remained lumped in her throat as she went about tearing apart lettuce leaves and tossing them into the monkey-pod bowl that had been Sissy's wedding present to her when she married Win.

Sissy—with her husband of nearly ten years, and her two boys—who had once gushed that *nothing* could be more fulfilling for a woman than marriage and motherhood. At the time, Grace had been in the midst of a divorce, with an eleven-year-old son who was barely speaking to her, a grand total of four hundred dollars and eighteen cents in her savings account to tide her over until Win's settlement check arrived, a beat-up Honda with eighty thousand miles on it, and four silver chafing dishes, wedding presents she'd never gotten around to exchanging, going black in her closet.

The last thing she'd wanted then—and she'd vowed to herself that it would be forever—was to get married again.

So what happened? Grace wondered now.

"Delicious," Hannah said, delicately bringing her fork to her lips. "Honestly, Grace, it's the best lasagne I've ever tasted."

Grace glowed, feeling a surge of gratitude that she knew had to be vastly out of proportion to what had been merely a polite remark . . . and certainly no reflection on her talent as a cook. Then she noticed the tiny smirk prying at the corners of Hannah's mouth as she chewed, and her heart lurched. Could Hannah have guessed somehow . . . or had Chris spilled the beans?

She glanced over at Chris, head down, shoveling food in like there was no tomorrow. No, Chris probably hadn't even noticed that the stuff on his plate wasn't what she'd cooked.

Grace wanted to feel kindly toward Hannah. It was hard to picture this lanky girl with her heavy black hair tied back in a loose ponytail, wearing a baggy sweatshirt over even baggier jeans, as the enemy. At sixteen, Hannah still carried herself with the round-shouldered awkwardness of a young woman not yet accustomed to her height. But, like the breasts Grace could just barely make out beneath the folds of her oversized sweatshirt, there was more to Hannah than what was on the surface.

I'm exaggerating this whole thing, Grace thought. *She just needs time to get used to me.* In a rosy flush of sentimentality, Grace imagined what it would be like having a daughter, if only a borrowed one, arranging that marvelous hair of Hannah's, and having Hannah come to her for advice about boys and clothes and schoolwork.

She looked across the table at Jack, who sat beaming at her. Just for a moment, she allowed some of his optimism to rub off on her. Maybe everything *would* be okay after all.

". . . So I told Conrad, if you're going to *act* like a Republican, the least you can do is *dress* like a Democrat," Hannah was saying. "Daddy, you should see the way he dresses, it's practically obscene. I mean, whoever heard of argyle socks in *high school?* It's not even as if he's president of the debating team or anything."

"It's not his clothes, we've established that. . . ." Jack met Grace's eyes. ". . . So what is it about the guy you're so crazy about?"

"Daddy!" Hannah, blushing furiously, rolled her expressive eyes.

"You men are so literal," Grace said, feeling allied with Hannah at that moment, despite her having monopolized the conversation so far this evening. "You think that, just because some woman pays attention to the way you look, or how you're dressed, she must be head over heels."

Jack smiled at her. "Oh? Just what *would* it take?"

"A man who can cook," she told him with a laugh.

Jack chuckled, raising his wineglass. "On that note, I'd like to offer a toast . . . to our hostess. And to a memorable meal."

Grace cringed inwardly, wishing she'd kept her mouth shut. She watched Hannah join in, but for once Hannah didn't appear to be mocking her. She sipped her wine, and then surprised Grace by picking up the bottle and pouring an inch or so into Chris's empty water glass. Chris looked up at her, startled. Clearly, he hadn't expected to be included among the adults, but was pleased that Hannah, at least, thought of him that way. Grace, touched by the unexpected thoughtfulness of Hannah's gesture, began to feel that maybe there was hope of Hannah's warming to her as well.

"More wine for you, Ben?" Jack turned to his son, seated on his left, between Chris and Grace.

"Thanks, no, Dad. I'm driving, remember?"

Grace looked over at the tall, strikingly handsome young man seated beside her. There was some resemblance to his father, sure, but mostly it was hard to believe that someone as vital and youthful as Jack could be old enough to have fathered someone almost thirty—only seven years younger than she. Never mind that Jack had married young, while still in college, with a son in kindergarten by the time he'd been made editor at Cadogan. When she looked at Ben, who had followed in his father's footsteps and was himself an editor at Cadogan the arithmetic didn't seem possible.

Ben had Jack's height and his curly dark-brown hair, worn long, brushing the collar of his navy blazer. But his features were more refined—the high forehead, tapered nose, and chiseled mouth of a nineteenth-century aristocrat. Grace imagined the unmarried editorial assistants up at Cadogan growing weak-kneed at a warm glance from those sea-green eyes. It was a wonder that Ben didn't have a girlfriend.

"Ben is nuts," Hannah commented to no one in particular. "He parks his stupid Beamer on the *street* and doesn't care if it gets ripped off or not."

Ben laughed, a rich, warm laugh. "If it's stolen," Ben reasoned, "my insurance will cover it. If some hopped-up parking attendant puts a dent in it, I'm stuck with a five-hundred-dollar deductible."

"For that, I sent you to college?" Jack laughed.

"I remember my first car, when I was seventeen." Grace smiled. "It was—"

"Speaking of college," Hannah cut her off, "I've been talking to my adviser about it, and he thinks I should definitely consider UC Berkeley. What do you think, Daddy?"

Grace shot a glance at Jack—was he even *aware* that Hannah was once again pre-empting her? She found herself remembering the way Hannah always zipped into the front seat of the Volvo, next to Jack, whenever they were going somewhere, leaving Good Old Grace to sit in back, smiling gamely, like a hitchhiker who ought to consider herself lucky to have snagged a ride at all. Jack never seemed to notice.

"Berkeley's a fine school," he was saying now. "So are Columbia and Georgetown, and they're a hell of a lot closer. You keep writing papers like the one on Dr. Freestone and you'll be able to take your pick."

Grace saw Hannah flash her a guilty glance, as if she were waiting for Grace to remind her that *she* was the one who had set up the interview with Laslo Freestone, whom Grace herself had interviewed three years ago for a *New Yorker* profile.

"Hey, Chris, I hope they haven't started stuffing your head with all this mumbo-jumbo about college at your school yet." Jack jumped in before Hannah could thank her, if that's what she'd been about to do.

"I'm only in the eighth grade." Chris lifted his head from his plate to give Jack a look that would have stopped a rhino in mid-charge. Grace was sure he knew Jack had only been trying to draw him into the conversation, and she burned at Chris's rudeness.

"Daddy, remember that ski trip to Vail when *I* was in the eighth grade?" Hannah piped up. "I was thinking maybe we could all go again this Christmas break. I mean, the three of us. Like the old days . . . except for Mom." She looked about her brightly, as if expecting her suggestion to be met with enthusiasm all around.

Struggling to keep her smile pinned in place, Grace became suddenly absorbed in spearing a particularly slippery chunk of tomato on her plate. Out of the corner of her eye, she caught Jack looking at her protectively, and she thought, *Don't. Don't say anything. Please. Just let it go.*

"What I had in mind was *all* of us going somewhere together over the holiday," Jack said mildly. "That is, if you don't have any other plans, Ben. There should be plenty of snow up at the cabin, good for cross-country. How would you feel about that, Grace? Chris?"

What Grace felt at that moment was a sudden chill, as if the room's temperature had dropped twenty degrees. Silence, thick as frost, settled over the table.

When it became more than she could bear, Grace said lightly, "Actually, I barely know how to ski. Years ago, when Chris was little, I tried learning, but it turns out I'm completely hopeless."

"Maybe you didn't have the right teacher," Ben suggested kindly.

Grace had to lower her eyes so he wouldn't see the gratitude she was sure was written all over her face.

"God, Daddy," Hannah said, blowing her lips out in a sigh of disdain. "Sometimes you can be so *dense*. Don't you get it?"

"Get what?"

"Christmas. It's *Christmas* we're talking about. You know, like jingle bells and Santa Claus." Hannah turned to Grace, and gently, apologetically, explained, "We don't celebrate Christmas, but Daddy sometimes forgets that not *everybody* is Jewish."

Two can play at this game, Grace thought, and plunged in. "In my family, Christmas wasn't really about jingle bells and Santa Claus. My mother headed a church drive to collect food and clothing for the poor."

Now it was Hannah's turn to look uncomfortable. Clearly aware that she'd been one-upped, she lowered her eyes.

"Dad wants me to spend Christmas with him in Macon," Chris blurted. He addressed Grace's reflection in the darkened window at her back, his expression flat. "So, whatever, you know. Do what you want."

Et tu, Brute? Now, when she could have used Chris's support, he'd chosen to spring this on her. And the worst part was, she couldn't show it. She wouldn't. Not in front of Hannah.

"Coffee, anyone?" she asked with forced brightness, feeling like an actress in a Folger's commercial. She rose and began clearing the plates. "I hope you all saved some room, because I have the most decadent chocolate dessert, and I refuse to get stuck with leftovers."

"I'll give you a hand." Jack got up, deftly scooping up plates and silverware and glasses.

A few minutes later, coffee and dessert served, she felt herself relax a bit. Hannah was clearly enjoying the cake, which Grace had picked up at Cafe Bondi. Chris was on his second piece, and had even thought to ask if anyone else wanted more before cutting his. Ben was telling his father about the great reorders they were getting for one of his books, Will Harrigan's behind-the-screen memoir of his years as a network newscaster.

Grace thought they were nearly out of the woods when Hannah announced suddenly, "Daddy, I don't feel so good."

"What is it, pumpkin?" Jack reached across to cover her hand with his, his forehead crinkling with concern. "You do look a little green around the gills."

Grace saw it, too. Hannah's normally porcelain complexion had gone a greenish gray, and there was sweat beading on her forehead and upper lip. This had to be just another of Hannah's ploys, she thought, then felt ashamed of herself.

She rose and went over to where Hannah sat shivering, her arms wrapped tightly across her chest. "Oh, sweetie . . . can I get you anything? Aspirin, some water?"

Hannah shook her head so hard her ponytail went flying up to flick the back of Grace's wrist. "My . . . stomach . . . Oh, God . . . oh, I think I'm going to be sick."

Then Jack was helping his daughter to her feet, steering her down the hallway in the direction of the bathroom. He returned a moment later, looking both concerned and vaguely sheepish. She knew how he felt, the way every parent does sometimes, half responsible for things their kids do that nobody could have helped.

"Must've been something she ate," he said. "She's allergic to practically everything. She'll be all right once I get her home."

"Look, Dad, there's no reason for you to run out on Grace," Ben said. "I can drop Hannah off on my way home."

"If you're sure . . ."

"Dad, I said I'd take care of it." For an instant, Grace caught a glimpse of something tight and barbed behind his Ralph Lauren–model's face.

Hannah emerged a few minutes later, pale and a bit shaky, but calm. "I'll walk you two to the car," he said, hugging her against him while she buried her face briefly in the creamy folds of his sweater.

"You just want to make sure I still have one," Ben laughed. "Grace, sorry we couldn't hang around to help with the dishes. Dinner was great, and I love your place." He rabbit-punched Chris's shoulder. "Hey, bud, hang in there. Don't spend it all in one place."

"Uh . . . mmmm," Chris muttered, shifting his stance ever so slightly so as to distance himself from the group gathered near the door.

"Better now?" Grace asked as she was helping Hannah on with her coat. "I can't help feeling responsible. The torte was probably a mistake, too rich on top of all that other stuff. All those nuts."

"Did you say *nuts?*" Hannah wheeled around to stare at her, one sleeve hanging empty at her side.

"Well, yes, that's what a torte—"

"God, I can't believe it. I'm *allergic* to nuts. I thought you knew."

Watching as Hannah, looking somehow small and defenseless, was bundled out the door between the tall forms of her father and brother, Grace had a terrible stab of guilt, thinking surely Hannah or Jack *had* told her and she'd forgotten.

She felt suddenly tired, too exhausted to stand. A hot bath, then bed. When he got back from seeing the kids off, she'd send Jack home, too. Leave the dishes until the morning. Leave everything.

Chris, sensing her mood, sidled past her, silent as an undertaker, snagging his jacket from the Victorian hall stand by the door. "I'll be at Scully's," he muttered.

"You were just over there." She didn't care if his best friend lived downstairs; it was the principle of the thing. Besides, Petie Scully was only eleven. Why didn't Chris have any friends his own age?

"*You* were the one who said I had to come back for dinner," he reminded her with an air of strained patience.

Grace watched him go, feeling too depleted to stop him, or even to scold the son who she knew wanted—no, *needed*—some sort of limits drawn.

But it wasn't until she'd headed into the bathroom for an aspirin to relieve her head, which was suddenly pounding, that Grace discovered how bad things could get just when you think you've had all you can take.

On the floor, like an awful metaphor for this whole disastrous evening, was a small puddle of vomit.

She was on her knees cleaning it up, wearing fat rubber gloves, fighting to keep from crying or getting sick herself, when Jack walked in. He stared down at her for a moment, then pulled her to her feet.

"You shouldn't be doing this," he said gently. "I'll take care of it."

"Why shouldn't I?" she snapped. "Because she's your daughter? Because we could never possibly come close to *sharing* responsibility for things that happen with your kids or mine?" Tears stung her eyes.

"No, Grace, that's not it at all," he said, his mouth—oddly vulnerable in a face strong and creased with living—turning up in an ironic half-smile. "I was just thinking how tonight you've had enough of Hannah as it is."

"It wasn't so bad." Then she caught herself, admitting, "Okay, so maybe it wasn't a bed of roses."

"No, but you handled it like a pro." He put his big hands on her shoulders, his smile fading, giving way to apology, and maybe a touch of regret.

"Jack, is this how it's going to be with us from now on?" Grace felt herself begin to tremble.

"I love you," he said, his voice grave. "And I don't want to let you down." He looked uncomfortable now, his eyes sliding away from hers.

"But you're not ready for anything more than this?" she blurted. "Sleeping over at each other's places? Family get-togethers now and then when we're feeling especially masochistic?"

He was silent, his eyes troubled. When he did speak, his voice was measured, thoughtful. "I wish I could tell you what you want to hear. But you're right about its being more complicated than just the two of us. Let's take it one step at a time."

Jack yearned to offer her more . . . so much more. Would he have, *could* he have, if only she was closer to his age? If their children—Chris and Hannah—weren't so violently opposed to their union?

Minutes before, waiting downstairs with Hannah while

Ben brought his car around, Jack had caught a glimpse, possibly for the first time—or maybe it was just the first time he'd allowed himself to see it—into the dark heart of his daughter's unhappiness. Yes, she was impossible at times. Yes, she'd been hard on Grace. But underneath her rudeness was a little girl who felt so lonely and abandoned she couldn't help striking out at the person she saw as the cause of it all.

He closed his eyes for a moment, seeing the scene downstairs with Hannah, as if it were a home video of her that he'd rewound.

"You don't have to, Daddy. Really, I'm okay." She shifted her weight subtly but oh so meaningfully, drawing away from him and his clumsy attempt to console her.

She wouldn't cry, he knew that—she was stubborn, like him. But if ever misery wore a face, it was Hannah's at that moment. He longed for the old days, when he could scoop her up and hold her against his chest, safe from harm. Now she was a tall reed facing into the wind, close to breaking.

"Feel better," he called to her as she stepped off the curb, moving in the direction of Ben's car.

She just looked at him . . . a long over-the-shoulder glance that cut to his heart's quick. A look that told him that feeling better wasn't an option for her right now. And he knew that Grace was inevitably tangled in all this. Because his life was not an egg to be easily separated, yolk from white. He'd have to tread carefully now rather than take yet another drastic step. . . .

"Oh, Jack, I don't know if I'm cut out for this." Grace sighed. "The waiting, the wondering. I'm too old to be chasing after some fantasy."

"Me, too." Jack lifted her chin with his finger to meet his steadfast gaze. All of a sudden he looked every day his age, older and more weary than she had ever seen him.

Grace saw herself then, as if through Jack's eyes: a small woman in blue jeans damp at the knees, wearing big yellow rubber gloves and standing in front of a toilet with tears pouring down her face.

A woman madly in love with this big, wonderful man who held out no promises, only his arms spread wide to engulf her. A woman who wondered where this treacherous, uncharted road was taking them, if one day she'd be stuck cleaning up a different sort of mess.

Chapter 2

Hannah felt sick.

Not like she had to throw up again. No, this was different . . . in a way, worse. By the time Ben was parking his Beamer in front of her building on Gramercy Park, Hannah was thoroughly disgusted with herself. Why had she carried on like such a jerk at Grace's? Horrid and nasty, like snotty Corinne Cavanaugh, always making digs at poor, fat Francie Boyle.

Except, she reminded herself, there was nothing fat or pathetic about Grace. Maybe, if Grace were homely, or had bad skin, or even bad *breath,* it wouldn't be so awful. Then she could at least feel sorry for Grace, maybe even just a little superior. The trouble was, Grace was so damn . . . perfect. Not a bad cook, either. Next to her, Hannah felt so awkward—horsy, clumsy, oily. Just looking at Grace's Dove-commercial complexion, she could almost *feel* the blackheads popping out over her nose and chin.

"You don't have to come up with me," she told her brother, who, after walking her to the elevator, now stood waiting for it to arrive. "I'm *sixteen,* you know, not six." She was immediately sorry she'd snapped at him.

But Ben only gave her his usual water-off-a-duck's-back shrug. "It's no big deal. I'll keep you company till Mom gets home."

Nothing new about Mom being out, Hannah thought. But this time she kept it to herself.

On the fourth floor, as she and Ben made their way down

the cavernous hallway, Hannah found herself walking softly so as not to disturb any of the neighbors. Ever since she was little, for some reason, this place, with its dimly lit art-glass fixtures, ceiling coves, and heavy paneled doors, had reminded her of a corridor in some huge mausoleum. The kind of place where you felt you had to whisper. She remembered, a year or two ago, when some of the co-op members had wanted to cover the hallway's old Victorian tile floor with carpeting. There was a big skirmish, spearheaded by her mother, as chairperson of the preservation committee. And since Mom usually got what she wanted, Hannah now, despite her best efforts, didn't succeed in keeping her movements from sending old Mrs. Vandervoort's Rottweiler, in 4C, into a frenzy of barking.

She unlocked her front door quickly, before Mrs. Vandervoort could poke her head out and give them one of her scowls. Ben followed her inside, where instantly their footsteps were muffled by a Chinese runner so well padded it felt like walking on a foam mattress.

"Sounds like Mom is back," Ben whispered.

Music trickled in from the living room, soft and forgettable . . . one of those New Age CDs Mom liked. Music for when you were in a bad mood and needed cheering up, or when you were a good mood and needed *affirmation* of it; music to put you to sleep, or wake you up, or, for all she knew, to take a crap by.

It was like everything else in this apartment—the watered-silk walls and Aubusson carpets, the English hunting prints and needlepoint pillows, the fringed shawl draped over the back of the antique sofa—artful and *coordinated.* Yet somehow not quite real, like a Ralph Lauren showroom. Shrugging her coat off, Hannah felt its hem catch against the bundle of dried grass sticking up out of the antique umbrella-stand next to the front hall closet. Watching bits of fuzz and broken stem drift onto the carpet, she felt a dart of panic. God, Mom was going to *kill* her. She usually tried to be so careful . . . only, damnit, why couldn't there be *umbrellas* in the stand instead of some stupid arrangement you had to tiptoe around?

"*Ben* . . . darling, is that you?" Mom's voice drifted toward them, hopeful and lighthearted.

Hannah winced. Why did Mom just assume it was *Ben?* Ben had moved out *ages* ago—Mom only liked to pretend he still lived here. It should have been the other way around, Hannah thought. If Hannah had her own apartment, Mom wouldn't even notice she was gone. Hannah Gold, the Amazing Invisible Daughter. She hadn't minded so much when Daddy was here, because he'd always been so *happy* to see her, as if there was nobody on earth he'd rather be with.

But now Daddy had Grace.

And she had . . . *who?* Conrad?

All her talk at dinner, but she still wasn't so sure how Conrad felt about her. Oh, he was big on all the stuff that *went* with liking someone; he could go on for hours about all the reasons they should go to bed together. But that was just sex. Not necessarily the same as wanting to *be* with her.

"Tell her I just dropped you off, that I couldn't come up," Ben said in a low voice against her ear. Hannah saw that he wasn't taking his coat off.

"Tell her yourself," she said. He was getting all the attention, and he didn't even *want* it.

"Han, give me a break. . . ." In the dim hallway, she could see Ben's eyes narrowing. He darted an anxious glance at the track-lit entrance to the living room.

Hannah fought back her resentment. Yeah, okay, so Ben didn't have it that easy, either. Mom leaning on him all the time, refusing to give up her subscriptions to the Met, her chamber music series, ABT, and just expecting Ben—no, *pressuring* him—into escorting her to every opera, concert, ballet. Not to mention the charity affairs and dinner parties. Sometimes, Mom didn't even tell people he was her son, Ben had confided to her. Almost as if she *wanted* everyone to think he was her date.

"It's me, Mom!" Hannah called out, adding *sotto voce* to her brother, "You're off the hook."

"Thanks," he mouthed, backing out the door.

In the living room, Hannah found her mother, dressed in a black wool-crepe sheath with an Hermès scarf swirled over one shoulder, sunk into the overstuffed chair by the fireplace. She was balancing an open book of upholstery samples across her smoke-stockinged knees. As she glanced up, the light from the cloisonné floor lamp beside her made her hair glow, a blend of honey and buttered maple. Hannah knew that it cost her maybe a hundred and fifty dollars a month at Recine to make it look like she'd been born with it.

"Hi, sweetie," Mom said distractedly as she went back to poring over her samples. "How was your evening?"

"Fine," Hannah lied. "How was yours?"

"Good. Did I tell you who I was having dinner with? He's a client, a divorced investment banker with *loads* of money and, better yet, absolutely *no* idea what he wants. I'm doing his entire apartment, Sixties off Fifth prewar. Lots of paneling, zero light, so I was thinking . . ." She flipped a page, fingering a square of cabbage-rose chintz.

Hannah waited, hoping against hope that this time would be different. *Just once, why don't you ask me what I think?* Not just about upholstery samples, but how she felt about the divorce, and Daddy having a girlfriend, and . . . oh, school, and what college she might want to go to, and even Con, *especially* Con.

More than anything, Hannah longed for her mother simply to hold out her arms to her, and hug her the way Grace was always hugging Chris—whenever he would let her, that is.

But what did she know about Grace and Chris, *really?* Aside from tonight's dinner, she'd only been dragged along on a handful of so-called family outings—apple-picking up in Pawling, and the few times they'd gone to the movies and caught a bite to eat afterwards. And, yeah, the night Daddy had gotten them all tickets to a Mets game. That time, even Ben had come along.

She saw her mother look up sharply, as if she'd read her thoughts. Hannah knew what that particular gleam in Mom's eye meant, and she felt herself shrink from it.

"How did it go tonight?" Mom was keeping her voice light, the right note of mild interest, but Hannah could see the tightness in her neck.

The room felt like a stage set, with Mom at the center, spotlit for effect. Behind her, the tall glass-front bookcase lined with leather-bound sets of Dickens and Thackeray and Mark Twain that these days no one ever looked at. On the small piecrust table beside her mother, a collection of antique snuffboxes left no room for a book, if you happened to be reading one.

"I told you." Hannah dropped to her knees in front of the teak cabinet which held the stereo, and began searching for her Chris Isak CD. "We had dinner, Ben drove me home. That's about it."

She thought about telling her mother that she'd gotten sick. Mother would be sympathetic . . . for about five seconds. Then she'd want to know *how* she'd gotten sick, and why on earth her father hadn't *told* Grace beforehand that she was allergic to nuts.

Why don't you ask me how I feel about Daddy and Grace instead of pumping me for info? she wanted to ask.

"That's not an answer—that's *haiku*," Mom said with a brittle laugh. "Where *is* Ben, anyway?" She looked over Hannah's shoulder, as if still expecting him to appear.

Hannah felt herself go cold inside. "He couldn't find a parking space. He said to tell you hi."

"Oh dear, and I wanted to remind him about the Philharmonic tomorrow. I was thinking we could have supper at the Russian Tea Room with the Minkins afterwards."

Hannah found the CD she was looking for. "Do you mind if I put on something else?" To hell with whatever stupid tête-à-tête Mom had planned for her and Ben. Besides, this drippy New Age stuff was really getting to her.

"You haven't *really* told me anything about how it went tonight," Mom said as if she hadn't heard Hannah's question.

"It was okay." Hannah felt the coldness inside her begin to spread.

She could hear her mother sigh. "Really, Hannah, you act as if I *care* what your father and his . . . that *girl* he's seeing . . . are up to. I was *only* asking out of politeness."

Sure, Hannah thought, *and I'm Paula Abdul.*

"Okay, we had lasagne," she said, keeping her back turned and her voice neutral. "And chocolate cake for dessert." No, she wouldn't tell her mother about getting sick. Much as she disliked Grace, she found herself feeling strangely protective of her all of a sudden.

Anyway, her mother didn't need to know everything.

"Comfort food," Mom said a little too sweetly. "How *cozy*. I suppose you all gathered around the TV afterwards to watch an old episode of *The Waltons*."

"Mom, come on. It was no big deal."

"I did a loft in that building once. Horrible place—the elevator always breaking down, no security whatsoever."

"The elevator works fine now."

"I suppose you'd know better than I would, spending so much time over there."

"I've only been at Grace's once before, and that was just for a few minutes. Usually we go to a movie or something. Or hang out at Dad's."

"I see. You mean she spends the night. You don't have to protect your father, Hannah. It's not as if it's any of *my* business . . . though I would have thought he would at least have enough sense to know what's appropriate for his sixteen-year-old daughter."

"They don't do it in front of me, if that's what you mean!" Hannah whipped around, accidentally knocking over a stack of CDs on the low lacquered table beside her. They clattered to the floor with a sound like breaking glass.

Mom squeezed her eyes shut, her fingers tightening about the vinyl edges of her sample book. "You don't have to shout. I'm only expressing concern over your welfare. And will you *please* try to be a little more careful."

Hannah's stomach clenched into a hard fist. Now she *did* want to scream, and *really* break something. What would Mom do if she smashed one of her precious porcelain candlesticks, or that dainty French clock on the mantel? Have her sent off to a school for the incorrigible? Or lobotomized?

"Mom, I wasn't shouting." Hannah forced herself to lower her voice, then scooped up the CDs, wincing when she saw the scratch she'd left on one of the polished parquet floor tiles. She set them on the table and took a deep breath, rocking back on her heels. "I just hate it when you put me in the middle—you know, like getting me to say stuff about Daddy."

"You don't think I should have the right to know what kinds of situations you are being thrown into?"

"Look, why don't you just ask Daddy?"

Mom slapped her sample book shut. "Do you think he

would tell me anything? If you had any idea what I've been through, you wouldn't suggest that I . . ." Her eyes glittered, and her lower lip began to tremble. "Do you know what it's like, to be fifty years old and simply cast aside like a . . . a worn-out sofa? After all the years of putting *my* needs on hold so your father could finish school, and then staying home with Ben . . ."

I don't count, Hannah thought, *because she had me after they could afford a nanny.* She thought of cocoa-skinned Suzette, who had taught her to sing Jamaican nursery rhymes, and had bandaged her skinned knees, even come to see her in school plays. In those days Mom was just getting her business started, and was almost always wrapped up in a business meeting or running around to antique auctions. Daddy had been the one who showed up at parent conferences, and helped out at her school's annual Christmas fair.

But Suzette was long gone, and now so was Daddy. Mom was all she had left, and Hannah, if she'd been small enough, would have crawled into her lap and laid her head against Mom's heart. She'd heard this particular speech about Dad often enough to be able to mouth the words along with Mom; still, Hannah knew her mother was hurting, and she wanted to be able to make her feel better.

Kneeling on the floor in front of her, Hannah took her mother's cool, slender hand in her own. "Mom . . . I'm really sorry about what happened, the divorce and everything. But you're not the only one. I feel like Daddy left me, too."

For a moment, Mom's expression softened, as if she were on the verge of saying something sympathetic. But then she withdrew her hand and pressed it to one temple, her eyes tightly shut, as if she were suddenly getting a headache.

"Oh, Hannah, *really.* Your father would walk over hot coals for you. I *don't* think you can compare my situation with yours."

Maybe if you'd been a little nicer to him he wouldn't have left you! Hannah felt like shouting. Why couldn't Mom just once admit that she might have had something to do with their splitting up?

Holding her frustration in, Hannah pleaded, "Mom, please, can't you just let go? You have a great career, this apartment, friends who love you." *A daughter who wants to love you, too.*

"Easy for you to say," Mom snapped. "You have your whole life ahead of you."

Hannah hated it when anyone told her that—as if she were a stick of Wrigley's Spearmint just waiting to be chewed. Just because she had a whole lifetime to be miserable, did that mean she had no right to be miserable now?

She fought back the sharp words on the tip of her tongue, and said softly, "But *right now* I feel like . . . like all this stuff with Dad is really messing things up with *us*."

"What do you *want* from me?" Mom asked, sounding irritable.

Hannah struggled to find words to fit this great booming hollowness inside her. "I just want . . ." she stopped. Exactly what *did* she want? For her mother and her suddenly to be best friends, like Kath and her mother, who did practically everything together and sometimes even wore each other's clothes? No, she decided. What she wanted was just to feel needed. She sucked in a deep breath. "I was wondering if maybe you and I could go out sometime. You know, to one of your concerts or something."

"Oh, that. Sure, anytime, sweetie." Mom seemed a bit relieved as she waved a hand airily, and went back to poring over her samples. Hannah knew that would be the end of it, because that's what Mom always said when she had no intention of following through.

Tears filled her eyes. If only she had someone to be

with—someone who loved her and wanted her just for herself.

She thought of Conrad, and remembered his telling her that his parents were away for the weekend, and what a bummer it was that he had to stay home and babysit for his little brother. At this moment she didn't care where it might lead; all she could think of was having his arms around her, holding her tight . . . so she could *feel* that she was real, that she wasn't invisible.

"I'm going out." Hannah stood abruptly, and retraced her steps to the coat closet. All of a sudden her stomach didn't hurt anymore.

"Hannah, just *where* do you think you're going? For heaven's sake, you just got here!"

She could hear the clicking of her mother's high heels against the floor, then only a muffled tapping. Grabbing her coat, Hannah made a dash for the front door, yelling over her shoulder, "I'll be at Kath's." Her best friend lived only a block away, on Irving Place, so it was no big deal for her to go over there at ten o'clock at night.

"Are you nuts?" Kath squealed when Hannah called from a phone booth to ask Kath to cover for her. She dropped her voice to a throaty God-forbid-my-parents-should-overhear-this whisper. "I mean, come on, Hannah, Con's been after you for weeks to . . . well, *you* know. What's he going to think, you showing up this time of night, with his parents away for the weekend?"

"I don't *care* what happens," Hannah said, fiercely blowing her nose into the crumpled Kleenex she'd fished out of her coat pocket. "I need to see him."

Deep sigh. "Okay, I just hope you know what you're doing."

"I don't know if I'm really going to . . . well, you know. I haven't made up my mind about that part."

"Okay, but, if you do, promise you won't let me in on the juicy details. I'd be too jealous." Kath, who was sure she was going to end up a nun if she didn't find a boyfriend in the next twenty-four hours, sighed again.

Five minutes later, after phoning Conrad, Hannah was on a train heading uptown to his apartment. Daddy would have a fit if he knew she was riding the subway this time of night, she thought. But, if he cared so much, he'd be around to *see* where she was going and what she was doing, instead of just hearing about it two or three days later. Or, in this case, *not* hearing about it.

Hannah started feeling sick to her stomach again. Then she remembered what Grace had said about her parents.

While Daddy was helping Grace put dinner on the table, she'd heard them talking about the book Grace was writing. Something about her father and mother having what Grace called an "unusual" marriage. The two of them never fought, she claimed, never even exchanged a harsh word. They were really crazy about each other . . . except for one thing.

Most of the time they didn't live together.

All the years Grace's father was away in Washington being a senator, her mother lived with Grace and her sister in their apartment in New York. According to Grace, the arrangement had worked out perfectly. Her mother had had her charitable work and her positions on various boards to keep her occupied. Her parents saw each other on weekends and holidays, when Grace's father came home or they took the train to Washington to be with him. And whenever it looked as if he might be coming home for good, he'd get elected to another term.

Grace told Daddy that *she* was the only one who hadn't been happy about it. But maybe that had been the secret to her parents' success, Hannah thought. Maybe the real truth was that people weren't meant to be together all the time. If families didn't spend so much time around each other, they wouldn't get so attached.

Hannah thought about Grace's father dying when Grace was almost fourteen, and decided that, as tough as it must have been for Grace and her mother and sister, the fact was that, in a way, he'd already left them. Because, whether it was a father being buried or merely walking out the door, it boiled down to the same thing: your dad not being around when you needed him.

Chapter 3

"There's just one little problem." Dan Killian leaned back in his swivel chair, his hands forming a steeple over his bulging purse of a belly. "To be perfectly honest, it *could* be a rather sizable problem. Now, don't get excited, Dellie, not till you've heard me out."

"I'm listening, Dan."

Cordelia Clayborn Truscott did not allow herself to wilt back into the masculine leather embrace of the wing chair opposite Dan Killian's scrolled walnut desk, nor did she give in to the urge to toy with the rope of pearls that hung straight as a hangman's noose down her bosom. *I won't let him see me squirm,* she thought. Instead, she sat up even straighter, fixing Dan with a pleasant, attentive gaze that was in direct defiance of the wild hammering of her heart.

Don't you dare back out on me, Dan Killian . . . not YOU, of all people. Dan, with whom she'd hunted tadpoles in the creek below her house when they were both young enough to run about half naked without anyone's batting an eye. And who, by the time they were sixteen, had become downright *fascinated* with the hidden fruits of her formerly flat chest, even going so far, one moonlit April evening in the greenhouse, as to unhook her brassiere. To this day, she couldn't smell peat moss without recalling the guilty thrill of Dan Killian's pale, trembling hand on her breast. She'd loved him then, as much as any sixteen-year-old can, which, she realized now, was about as close to true love as their wading in the creek at age five was to swimming.

Was he going to renege on his promise simply because she'd refused to lie down with him all those years ago? Was this brought on by some long-simmering resentment of his?

Cordelia caught herself smiling at the thought. Heavens, the very idea! Dan, with his three chins and five grown children, married forty-odd years to the Robert E. Lee High Dixie Queen of 1948.

No, his abrupt about-face had to have been spurred by something far more recent. She could sense what he was about to say, and she had to fight to keep from jamming the heels of her hands against her ears. To be so close to having her dream realized, only to have the rug pulled out from under her—oh, how could she bear it?

She could see it in her mind so *clearly:* Gene's library, a cathedrallike building filled with sunlight and books, and with his speeches, letters, articles, the laws he'd stayed up to all hours drafting. An image so real to her that she could almost envision it springing full-blown onto the lovely grassy rise at the south end of the Latham campus, where the old Henley dorm had burned down several years back.

Cordelia could think of no stone she'd left unturned in attempting to raise the six million or so it would cost. As chairwoman of the Eugene Truscott Memorial committee, she had approached more foundations than the Lord knew existed and had gotten money from dozens of them, had even managed to wrangle a small federal grant. She'd been to banks, oil companies, gotten a nice little gift from Gene's old fireman union. But she was still short more than a million—eight hundred and fifty thousand of which had been promised to her by Dan Killian—and she was tired. Lately, she'd been at meetings like this where she momentarily forgot what she was going to say. She didn't know how much longer she could keep it up.

Cordelia adjusted her ivory gabardine skirt, lining up its

pleats with the same care with which, each spring, she marked with string the rows of tiny seedlings to be planted in her herb garden. For a delicious second, she let her mind drift ahead to thoughts of the mild fall afternoon that awaited her at the end of her present ordeal. She imagined herself, in her gardening pants and floppy straw hat, kneeling in the rich soil of her garden, working side by side with Gabe as they harvested the last of the summer's herbs.

Gabe . . .

In Dan's darkly masculine office with its faint but pervasive odor of cigar smoke, Cordelia nevertheless felt as if a fierce sun were burning her face, heating her whole body. She willed herself not to think about Gabe. She must concentrate on what was happening here, *now;* on Dan Killian and the nasty little bomb she could sense he was about to drop. . . .

She watched Dan's meaty hand stir among the papers on his desk and finally haul up a newspaper clipping that fluttered restlessly in the tepid air from the ancient air-conditioner.

"Right out of the *Constitution,*" he pronounced, as if it were the founding fathers' great document instead of just a silly newspaper. "Says here, Dellie, that your Grace—who you know we're all just so proud of she might just as well be right smack in the middle of Jackson Park, bronzed and with a plaque at her feet—says here that Grace is writing a book, a bi-*o*-graphy," he added sententiously, drawing one word out into three. "About her daddy. About Eugene."

"This is hardly news to me, Dan," interrupted Cordelia. She'd known about the book long before Grace had ever set a word down on paper, had been *excited* about it even, until this . . . this . . . Oh, the unfairness, the cruelty of it!

"Most of it complimentary, from what I understand," he went on. "But there is some stuff that's downright disturb-

ing. Something about—hell, I'll come right out and say it—
Gene being involved in a man's killing. A *black* man." He
kept his head low, tucked into the loose chins wattling his
neck, his pale eyes peering mournfully above the gold rims
of his spectacles. "Excuse me, Dellie, but that's just what it
says."

"I *know* what it says, Dan." She immediately regretted
letting her impatience show. She heard her mother's voice in
her head: *A lady is polite and well mannered at all times,
even when subjected to undue pressure.* "I get the *Constitution,* too, delivered right to my doorstep. Though, if you
ask me, with half what's in it these days, they might as well
just toss it straight into the trash can."

"But surely—"

"I have discussed this with Grace, and have given her my
thoughts on the subject," Cordelia said, her tone as precise
as the snipping of secateurs on a particularly thorny bush.

Inside, though, she could feel her heart slipping like new
shoes on icy pavement, and with it her careful composure.
She steeled herself. No, she *wasn't* going to let Dan Killian,
who had once felt her breast in a hothouse, see her fall apart
now. Instead, she replayed in her mind last week's phone
call from Grace. The outrageousness of her dragging that
long-ago tragedy into the light again! And now the newspapers making Gene out to be some kind of . . . of murderer.
Or, at very best, a liar.

Oh, yes, she knew what had really happened that day.
Gene had confided in her immediately afterwards. How
could he not? They'd shared everything. She alone knew how
tortured he'd been, for months on end, wracked with misery
and self-doubt. But she didn't have to have been there to
know he hadn't murdered that poor man . . . that he'd only
done what she, or anyone, would have expected of him.
Why, he'd risked his own life to save Margaret's!

But if he'd told the truth? With Gene's integrity in question, his enemies on Capitol Hill would have snatched at the excuse to kill the Civil Rights Act he'd been pushing for. The press, too, would have been on him like jackals. And the public? Come election day, even his staunchest supporters would have thought twice about punching a hole in the ballot beside Gene's name.

And where, Cordelia wondered, would this country be today if Gene had allowed that to happen?

"The *truth* is," she went on, struggling to control the quaver she could feel building at the back of her throat, "that Gene was the finest man I've ever known." She fixed Dan with an unwavering gaze as she said it. "And I'm confident that when Grace comes to her senses she'll set the record straight."

"Are you saying that Grace didn't actually *see* this killing, like it says here?"

"I'm saying that Grace always was prone to exaggeration. And in this case . . . why, she wasn't much more than nine years old at the time. I'm choosing to believe her imagination simply became *overheated*." By no means was that an excuse for her daughter's present lack of discretion, but Dan Killian didn't have to know *everything* that went on in her family.

Cordelia squeezed her hands together in her lap, feeling overheated herself and even a bit faint, though no doubt it was a good deal cooler in here than it seemed. Her pulse stepped up its shallow, flighty rhythm.

She wanted to scream at Dan, force him to end this torturous foot-dragging and say whatever it was he planned on saying. But then, when he finally *did* speak, she longed to run from the room, slam the door on him.

"Well, now, Dellie, I wish I could believe all this was going to blow over. But it's not as simple as all that." *At least he has the decency to look ashamed,* she thought. Watching him heave his bulk from his chair, Cordelia felt acutely aware of her own diminutiveness—what others, she knew, often mistakenly perceived as fragility. "I phoned this reporter fellow in Atlanta, and he says he got it from a reliable source. Not only that, but the wire services have picked it up. By tomorrow, people all over the country are going to be talking about this over breakfast. Shoot, Dellie, you know how I felt about Gene. He was a fine man, a *great* man. But this . . ."

"Why, Dan Killian, if I didn't know better, I'd think you *believed* that vicious gossip!" cried Cordelia, no longer able to contain the hot fury rising in her.

"'Course not, 'course I don't." Groping in his back pocket for a handkerchief and mopping his shiny forehead, Dan moved around his desk and paced over to a row of shelves where the half-dozen trophies from that silly golf club of his were displayed. Hackers and Slicers, they called themselves. And how fitting. Because that's how she felt now, as if he were hacking at her, slicing her dream to bits. "It's these times we're living in, Dellie. These damn prickly times. Why, at the mill alone I employ more than eight hundred men and women—more than three-quarters of them black or brown or something in between. We've had affirmative action groups, the NAACP, you name it, stirring up trouble wherever they can. You know I'm a fair-minded man . . . always have been. But just how do you think they-all'd react if Killian Textiles were to donate close to a million dollars toward a memorial for a senator who'd supposedly had a hand, however accidental it might have been, in killing a black man?"

Cordelia felt like shouting out the truth, asking Dan what *he* would have done in Gene's place. But she already knew the answer. Dan was a coward. She wondered now, as she often did, what would have happened if Gene *hadn't* gone to Margaret's rescue that day. Might Margaret, or even her little girl, have gotten hurt or, worse, killed? Ned Emory, she'd learned after his death, had been unstable, even violent. Forever accusing his wife of things she hadn't done, affairs with other men. Dear, plain, sensible Margaret, of all people!

Cordelia forced herself to speak in the voice, soft-edged and honeyed, that she used to cloak her emotions whenever they threatened to run away with her. "I was just remembering that nasty union business some years back, all your people on strike, and the scabs you trucked in. One of them got killed, didn't he? Shot right through the head, God rest his soul. I most particularly remember you calling Gene in a panic, saying that, if somebody didn't bail you out real quick, you'd have a dozen killed and your precious mill going up in flames."

"Dellie, you don't have to remind me," Dan groaned. "I know there probably wouldn't *be* a Killian Textiles today if Gene hadn't gone out on a limb for me, if he hadn't leaned on the union bosses, gotten them to sit down and hammer out something we could all live with. Hell, you think I'm not *grateful?* There's not a thing I wouldn't do for Gene if he were standing right here in front of me now asking me."

And because he's not here to ask, you stick a knife in his back.

A wave of regret swept over her—strangely, not for what Dan was robbing her of now, but for the youth they'd left behind, along with everything they'd once foolishly, blindly believed possible. . . .

"Well, Dan, I don't honestly know what to say. I never in a million years would have believed that you would back out on your promise." Cordelia adjusted her cream hat with its navy-on-white polka-dot ribbon, pulling its brim down in the hope of partially masking the scorched tightness of her face. "It grieves me, too, that people would be ready to tar and feather a man who is practically a saint to them, merely on account of some misinformed article about some silly book."

"Dellie, it's your own *daughter* who's writing it!"

"Have you considered that she might be acting out of some childhood grudge against her father and me? You know children these days, a chip on their shoulder the size of the national debt. All those talk shows on TV, people going on about how their mothers were too strict or too bossy, and how their fathers were too wrapped up in their work to toss them a ball or play checkers with them. And those audiences just egging them on. I hate to say this, but Grace was always like that, making a mountain out of every molehill."

"You have a point there." He sighed, replacing the trophy on its shelf. "Maybe that's why I hate this job so much sometimes, because it reminds me of being a parent, of the decisions you have to make that always seem to end up hurting one child or another." Dan walked over and stood looking mournfully down at Cordelia. He made her think of that toy her girls had played with when they were little, a set of plastic eyes and mouth that you stuck into a raw potato. In spite of herself, pity welled up in her. For, buried beneath the pouches of flesh, she had just then caught a glimpse, like the face of a drowned person floating just below the surface, of the sweetly rounded features of the boy she'd once loved.

She pictured Gene then, not particularly handsome, but he had the kind of face—afire with the intelligence behind it—that you saw once and never forgot. Clever caricaturists could capture it in three or four swiftly sketched lines—the hawkish nose, the deepset eyes, the thatch of hair that didn't quite hide the jagged scar over his brow.

Oh, how she missed him still! She remembered as if it were yesterday that terrible night—young Tommy Pettit, one of Gene's top aides, standing at her door, his eyes bloodshot, his doorknob of an Adam's apple working as he told her of the helicopter crash half a world away. First had come the shock, but then how furious she'd been! At the self-serving Pentagon officials who'd allowed Gene to go off to that war zone and then had not protected him. And, yes, at Gene himself, who had placed himself in jeopardy over something as nebulous, as *meaningless* as a "fact-finding mission." It was her fury that had given her the strength to cope that first day, and the one after. She had run on empty, without food, drink, sleep, sustained only by the great buzzing wall of red behind her eyes.

But by the morning of Gene's funeral, she'd had to drag herself out of bed to wake the girls . . . and then had crumpled to the floor, crushed by grief. Even now, she could feel its weight pressing down on her. The years had only served to wear it down, smoothing it like a stone at the bottom of a riverbed, which anchored her even while it dragged at her.

"So where does that leave us, Dan?" she asked him, keeping her voice soft, but taking little care to round its sharp corners.

"I'm going to have to hold off writing that check," she heard Dan say through the rushing of blood in her ears. "Until this whole thing blows over . . . or until . . . well, we'll see. I know you had your heart set on this, Dellie, but Gene, I think, would have been the first to agree with me that you don't pick up a hot potato unless you want to get your fingers burned."

How dare you? she wanted to cry out. *How dare you use Gene against me?* This is for him, not for me. For him!

And the deadline for the architects' competition was less

than eight weeks away. Six carefully selected firms at which talented people were slaving away, building models, preparing drawings on great sheets of paper . . .

Cordelia felt an urge to slap Dan Killian's mealy potato face. But she immediately shook it off. After all, he wasn't at fault, not really.

It was Grace who deserved to be slapped.

Cordelia had to draw on every last bit of willpower to rise from her chair and hold out her small hand to be swallowed up by Dan's huge, cushiony one.

"I was just thinking, Dan, that if all those years ago you had asserted yourself a bit more, the night of our junior prom, we might not be having this discussion today. I might even have married you. I'm glad for both our sakes that I didn't." Hearing the words escape her, she felt shocked. And saw that Dan was, too, judging from the scarlet flush spreading upward from the folds of his neck. She drew herself up to her full five feet two inches and added, "If there's one thing I've learned in fifty-nine years, it's that we all do what's best for ourselves in the end. That's what made Gene so extraordinary, don't you think? He always put his own needs last. But I don't want that to be his monument—a memorial to him that didn't get built because the concerns of others came before his."

"Dellie, I—"

"Don't apologize." She stopped him. "Nothing has changed as far as I'm concerned. I'm sure that once this bit of gossip has died down you'll see your way clear to doing the right thing. Oh, and Dan"—she put out a small, coral-nailed hand that didn't quite meet his sagging shoulder, and allowed a sad smile to surface—"the creek's high from all that rain we had this summer. Lots of tadpoles. Come on by one of these days, bring the grandkids."

Dan nodded sheepishly.

As he ushered her to the door, obsequious as a maître d'
at one of those overpriced restaurants that were springing
up like toadstools around Blessing, Cordelia remembered her
lunch date with Sissy. Oh, how she wished she could go
straight home instead, to her garden . . . and to Gabe.

Sissy was also insisting they stop afterwards at that
dreadful new shopping mall near Mulberry Acres, out on
what, in her day, had been the old Fullerton estate. Her
daughter was still looking for the perfect dress to wear to
her tenth-anniversary party. The trouble was, she'd been
looking for that dress since September, and here it was almost November, and she still hadn't found it.

With a sigh, Cordelia made her way out of the plush-
carpeted hallway above the First Citizens Bank of Blessing
—which her grandfather had founded, and her father had
managed until the day he died—then down a flight of stairs
that led to a brass-fitted plate-glass door onto Main Street.
Her heart was still beating too quickly, and the thudding in
her breast had spread up into her temples, but she was almost certain no one passing by would notice. All anyone
would see was a slim, middle-aged woman in a cream-
colored linen suit and matching hat, walking briskly toward
the meter in front of Thompson's Drugs where her silver
Town Car was parked.

Driving along the Interstate, the dwindling cow pastures
and peach orchards of her childhood giving way to the strip
malls that clustered like horseflies about the grander Mulberry Acres shopping complex she was now approaching,
Cordelia remembered the unpleasant duty that lay ahead—
the whole reason she'd invited Sissy to lunch in the first
place.

She had to find some way of gently letting Sissy know

what half the town of Blessing would soon be privy to, if they weren't already: that Beech was cheating on her.

The crust of that man! He no doubt believed that Sissy was too devoted to suspect . . . and that even if she did catch wind of it she would just shovel it under the rug. But there was one thing Beech, with his jacked-up ego, hadn't counted on—that Sissy, if she didn't love herself enough to do something about this, fortunately had a mother who cared enough about her for both of them.

Her daughter would not take the news well, she knew. Sissy might even accuse her of meddling, of trying to break up her marriage, which admittedly Cordelia had been opposed to from the start.

But was a mother who loved her daughter supposed to keep quiet while her double-talking son-in-law made a fool of the girl? It wasn't, after all, as if she'd had to go sniffing around to ferret out Beech's slimy peccadillo. Emily Bowles down at Whipple's Bakery said she'd seen the two of them holding hands *in broad daylight.* And just last week Cordelia herself had accidentally picked up the phone and heard him cooing over the bedroom extension. It was only a matter of time before Sissy caught on, or one of her busybody friends put a bug in her ear. Wouldn't it be better for her to hear it from someone who had only her best interests at heart? Didn't Sissy have a right to know, so she could either put a stop to it or, better yet, divorce the loudmouthed piece of trash?

On the other hand, Cordelia reflected, look at the wedge that had been driven between her and Grace when she'd interfered with Grace's marital problems. . . .

By the time she'd parked her car behind the restaurant, a brand-new brick affair with white collonades that overlooked the manicured green of the Mulberry Acres golf course, Cordelia was having second thoughts about breaking the bad news to Sissy.

How strange! she thought. Usually she couldn't bear dithering. *Any* course of action, in her opinion, was better than none. Hadn't it been her suggestion, all those years ago, that Gene call in his old friend Pat Mulhaney at the FBI to handle the Emory mess as discreetly as possible?

Darling Gene, I helped save you from scandal then . . . and I'll do everything I can to save you now.

As she spotted her daughter at a table by the window, Cordelia's thoughts abruptly returned to the business at hand. If *she* didn't look after Sissy's best interests, who would? Even before Gene died—with Grace a precocious fourteen, and Sissy still a baby at ten—the burden of raising her daughters had fallen mainly on her shoulders. Those early years, with Gene away in Washington or traipsing over the countryside raising funds and drumming up votes, she had been mostly alone with the girls. It was merely owing to the strange and wonderful spell Gene had cast over her, she decided, that she had somehow never *felt* alone. No matter where he was, he called her every day, and flew home most weekends, his pockets full of little gifts for them—paper dolls and tin frog noisemakers from the five-and-dime for the girls, a pretty pair of earrings for her or maybe a jar of her favorite piccalilli.

She wanted that for Grace and Sissy both. A marriage like the one she had had—rich, unconventional, exciting. Perhaps hers had been *too* exciting at times, like the hornet's nest Gene had stirred up down here when he came out in strong support of the civil-rights movement. But never, ever had it been boring.

Winding her way over to the table where Sissy sat, Cordelia wondered which was worse—Beech's utter lack of both decency and discretion, or the mere fact that he was so un-utterably, irredeemably pedestrian.

The trouble was that in many ways, though Cordelia hated admitting it even to herself, so was Sissy.

After half an hour of listening to Sissy prattle on throughout lunch about her ridiculous anniversary party, how quickly people had accepted her invitation, the wildly talented pianist she was thinking of hiring, the sumptuous flowers and cake she'd ordered, Cordelia began to feel a headache coming on.

Shifting in her white wicker chair under a false arbor drooping with silk lilacs that was supposed to give the feel of a veranda (but only succeeded in making her feel claustrophobic), Cordelia felt the throbbing in her head quicken. *This party means everything to her. How can I tell her that her husband of ten years is cheating on her?*

Instead, over coffee and dessert, she told Sissy what had happened at Dan Killian's office, expounding as little as possible on the long-ago "suicide" of Margaret Emory's husband. Luckily, all Sissy seemed to remember about that day was her father and sister being horribly upset, and then policemen arriving on the scene. At the time, Cordelia had pacified her by explaining that Mr. Emory had had an accident, and Daddy had gone there to see if he could help. Even now, Cordelia didn't elaborate . . . partly because Sissy didn't seem particularly interested in the details, but mostly because she herself believed that what was buried was best left that way.

"I think it's just spiteful," Sissy broke in, her cheeks flushed with outrage, stabbing a forkful of her Black Forest cake. "Grace is doing this out of meanness, pure and simple. I remember, when we were young, and . . ."

Sissy was off and running on one of her numerous tales of How I Was Mistreated by Big Sister. Cordelia felt a flash of impatience toward her daughter, remembering why she normally *didn't* confide in Sissy. No matter whose problem it was, Sissy always somehow managed to turn it into her own little drama.

Cordelia only wished she'd learn when enough was enough. Yet, even so, she took a breath and forced herself to focus on what her daughter was saying.

". . . and then, when I slipped and fell in the creek and was practically drowning, she just stood there laughing. *Laughing,* like my pain was for no other purpose than to amuse her!"

Sissy's rosebud mouth was pursed in a beleaguered expression, the effect of which was spoiled by the cake she was chewing on. Her dear face, once so pretty, was clearly paying the price of too many such mouthfuls, Cordelia thought sadly. If Sissy were to spend half as much time in that Lucille Roberts figure salon she'd recently joined as she did rooting around for a dress that would hide her figure flaws, she'd be so much happier with herself she might forget about rehashing her childhood grievances.

At the same time, Cordelia felt a rush of affection for Sissy—the child who had clung to her and tagged after her while her oldest was off with a gaggle of hippie friends, or buried in books down at the library. Good, thoughtful Sissy, who called every day just to see how she was doing. Sissy didn't hold her mother responsible for her own life's maybe not turning out quite as she'd expected it to. And so what if she was on the plump side . . . or if those spoiled-rotten boys of hers hadn't the manners of a chimpanzee? They'd grow out of it, and Sissy could lose the weight if she put her mind to it.

"There wasn't but two feet of water in that creek, hardly enough to drown a mosquito," Cordelia recalled with a laugh, hoping to get Sissy to see the humor in the situation. But, watching her daughter's face crumple, she immediately wished she'd kept quiet.

"Why is it," Sissy demanded, "that, whenever you're mad at Grace and I take your side, you turn right around and defend her?"

"I am not defending anyone. I was merely pointing out—"

"Tell me, Mother, if Grace is such a wonderful daughter, why is she spreading that lie about Daddy?"

Cordelia felt the blood drain from her face. Sissy was right, of course . . . but hearing it from her only made it worse. She felt caught between her two daughters, itching to knock some sense into one and to throttle the other.

Then, inside her mind, soothing as a glass of Netta's iced sun-tea on a hot day, she heard Gabe's voice say, *It isn't the muddle you're in that matters, but what you make of it.* How simple he made things seem! But he was right.

"I don't know why your sister is doing this," Cordelia told Sissy. "But I intend to put a stop to it. You can be certain of that."

She watched Sissy chase the last maraschino about her plate before finally spearing it with her fork. "Oh, Mother, let's face it, when has Grace ever once listened to you, or to anyone? Did she listen when you pleaded with her not to toss away twelve years of marriage? Really, the way she acted you'd have thought Win had been fooling around on her with half the women in New York. And I've never seen a man cry so, he was that broken up about it. Why, if I hadn't been there to console him, Lord knows what he would have done!"

"I don't see Win as the suicidal type," observed Cordelia crisply.

"Really, Mother, it was just a figure of speech." Sissy

had her purse open now, and was peering into her compact mirror as she applied a fresh layer of strawberry pink to her lips. "What I meant was—oh, damn, don't you hate it when this happens? You'd think somebody could invent a lipstick that didn't break apart like it was made of butter."

"If you didn't roll it up so far, that wouldn't happen," Cordelia pointed out. "Just about halfway is best."

Sissy tossed the broken end of the lipstick onto her plate, and glowered at her mother. "Well, *you're* in a fine mood this afternoon." Then she caught herself and sighed, "Oh, Mother, I'm sorry. You have a perfect right to be upset. And if it makes you feel any better, I'd like to give Uncle Dan a good sharp boot in the behind."

"You could boot him from hell to breakfast, but I doubt that would solve anything." Even so, the thought of it coaxed a tiny smile from Cordelia.

"I'll bet if you flirted with him he'd come around." Sissy gave her a coy sideways glance as she peered once again into her pocket mirror, fluffing her hair.

"Sissy!" Cordelia pretended to be shocked, but was unable to keep a startled laugh from escaping her.

"Oh, Mother, I was only teasing." Sissy was giggling, too, her face, as she dropped the mirror back into her purse, no longer tense and puffy-looking, but softly rounded and even lovely. "You know, I always *did* think Uncle Dan had a crush on you. Didn't you two use to go out in high school?"

"Back when dinosaurs roamed the earth," Cordelia said with a snort, then added quickly, "Anyway, even if he were free and I was interested in him, I'm too old for that kind of thing."

"*Are* you?" Sissy stared at her, her smile fading.

Cordelia experienced an uncomfortable prickling at the base of her spine.

She knew what Sissy was getting at, and cursed herself for having inadvertently walked into a trap. "Goodness, what a question!" she hedged with a breathless little laugh.

"Oh, it's not *you* I'm worried about," Sissy went on in that same slyly innocent tone. "It's just that you can't be too careful about what some men will think. You wouldn't want to be giving anybody any *ideas,* that's all. I mean, Mother, it's one thing to be polite to a man who works for you, and it's another to be asking him in for tea."

Cordelia felt herself growing hot, her cheeks glowing. "Well, if I don't have a perfect right to be talking about my own roses with my own gardener, then I don't know what the world is coming to!"

"He's not just a gardener, and you know it. I had him for English my sophomore year in high school. He was my *teacher,* for heaven's sake. And even then we all thought he was loony, going on and on about Sir Gawain and Ivanhoe and Beowulf like they really existed, like they were his personal friends he was going bowling with that night. Then him chucking it all over to become a *gardener,* of all things. And now look at him, acting like he'd move in tomorrow if you so much as crooked a finger at him. It's . . . it's not right!"

Cordelia planted both hands firmly on the table, on either side of her frilly chintz place mat, like a passenger aboard a ship bracing herself for a squall. Barely trusting herself to speak, yet conscious that a woman at the next table was looking their way, she managed a grim smile.

"Caroline." She only called Sissy that when she was very upset with her, or around someone she knew Sissy was trying to impress. "I think I'm qualified to tell the difference between what's right and what isn't."

Sissy's pink cheeks flared, and her sly look instantly dissolved into a sheepish one. "I'm sorry, Mother, I was only trying . . ."

"Gabe and I are *friends*," Cordelia emphasized icily. "Now, are you quite finished? Because, if you still want to go shopping, I don't have all day."

"I have the dress all picked out," Sissy gushed, nearly stumbling over herself in an obvious effort to smooth things over. "I had them put it on hold for me over at Foxmore's. I can't wait to show it to you. Oh, I *do* hope Beech likes it."

Cordelia plucked her napkin from her lap and carefully folded it before placing it to one side of her cup and saucer. *Now,* she thought, *say something about how it'd be a pity to waste time worrying about what Beech will think, when it's clear as the nose on your face that his mind—not to mention another part of his anatomy—is elsewhere.*

But just then their waitress appeared to ask if they'd like anything else. Cordelia shook her head and asked for the check.

While Cordelia was signing her credit-card slip, Sissy blurted out, "What are you going to do about Grace?"

Cordelia visualized a knob, like the one on a television set that controls the volume, and she was turning it, turning it down, until the hurt and anger booming in her chest were reduced to a whisper.

At the same time, a soft voice in the back of her head was also murmuring, *True, it's all true, she's only telling the truth*.

But she wouldn't listen to that voice, because, even if it *was* the truth, Grace had no business spilling it to the whole world, especially *now,* with the fate of the library hanging by a mere thread.

"I'll set her straight, that's what," Cordelia replied with more determination than she felt. "She mustn't be allowed to *publish* this . . . this ugliness. There are too many people who believe whatever they see in print." She thought of Dan Killian, and felt a fresh spurt of anger. "Once I explain it all very reasonably to her, I'm sure she'll see how wrong it would be."

"You and Mahatma Gandhi."

"There's no need to get smart-mouthed with me, Caroline Ann."

"What I meant was, it won't do any good *your* talking to Her Royal Highness," Sissy said with a sniff. "Why, just the other night, Beech was saying wasn't it a shame that Win and Grace were divorced, because that Win, he had such a *way* with her. He could convince anyone a dollar bill was pea soup, and they'd eat it. Ha! If Beech ever tried that with me, I'd have the dollar spent before he could get the words out of his mouth."

I doubt Beech Beecham would know how to hang on to a dollar bill if it bit him in the behind, Cordelia thought. *Lucky for Sissy and the boys I made that trust airtight so he couldn't get his sticky fingers on it.*

"Dear, have you ever thought that maybe Beech isn't—" she started to say, but Sissy cut her off with an impatient wave.

"Listen, Mother, about Win? I have an idea. What I was thinking was, you could talk to Win yourself. Get him on your side, so to speak. He's still the father of your grandson, isn't he? You've a perfect right to be involving him in this. And he *is* a lawyer, after all."

"Are you saying . . . ?" All thoughts of Beech vanished.

"I'm not saying anything. Just *suggesting,* is all." Sissy's blue eyes were round and innocent as a baby's. "Win could try to reason with her on your behalf. As your attorney."

Cordelia, numb for a moment, felt Sissy's words wash

over her like icewater. Some kind of *legal* action? Against her own daughter? The very idea!

"About that dress," she said, unable to consider such an awful possibility another moment. "If you don't want to be late picking the boys up from school, we ought to go over and have a look at it while there's still time."

"Oh, never mind about the boys, Beech is picking them up," Sissy informed her with an airy wave that set the charm bracelet squeezing her plump wrist to tinkling.

"Doesn't he have to be at work?" Cordelia asked, her tone guarded.

"Why, sure, but he's got this meeting not too far from school, where they're building that hotel—some kind of big rental-car deal he's helping put together. It's keeping him pretty busy these days, I can tell you. . . ."

I'll just bet.

It was on the tip of Cordelia's tongue to tell Sissy just *how* busy Beech was, but then she stopped herself. Sissy's remarks about Gabe made it clear that she thought her mother had lost all perspective—and probably her marbles as well—where men were concerned. Besides, Sissy was so looking forward to this party. How could she spoil it for her?

"Why don't we stop in at Joan & David afterwards?" she said brightly to Sissy as they crossed the parking lot. "I'll bet you could use a new pair of high heels to go with that dress. My treat."

She'd been intending to stop in at the Book Nook instead, to pick up a book on heritage roses that she'd ordered for Gabe, but maybe Sissy was right. Even if she didn't intend it as such, he might get the idea that she was interested in something more than friendship.

And if he did? Would he merely smile to himself, no

more than mildly flattered by the infatuation of a woman ten years older than he—a woman who occupied a social realm that was a whole other world from his?

Nonetheless, Cordelia felt her face grow warm, ashamed of the thought that rose in her now like a tulip's first green blade pushing its way up through frozen ground—the thought that Gabe Ross was just the sort of man a woman would *want* to be taken seriously by. . . .

"Lobelias, they'd be just the thing for that spot. Don't you think so, Gabe?"

Cordelia squinted against the late-afternoon sunlight as she surveyed the newly mulched area under the hundred-year-old pecan tree where a colony of bleeding hearts had recently been uprooted.

Gabe Ross, kneeling in the soft earth of the perennial bed below the porch, set aside his thinning shears and stood up—slowly, stretching his arms and his back as he did so, clearly reveling in the pure pleasure of the movement. Remembering Sissy's cutting remarks, Cordelia took in Gabe's sweat-stained canvas hat and the crumbs of peat moss clinging to the soiled knees of his khaki trousers, and wondered if perhaps there *was* something not quite normal about a man who would toss away a respectable teaching position to become a gardener.

But under his hat's dog-eared brim, Gabe's brown eyes, the color of strong brewed tea, were so bright and lively with intelligence—no, more than that, a kind of wisdom that didn't come from books or teaching *Beowulf*—that she immediately felt guilty.

After all, *she* loved to garden—at times, it seemed the only thing that kept her sane.

"Not enough sun," he told her, shaking his head. "Lobelias need some light, or they get leggy and don't bloom the way they should." She loved the deliberate way he spoke, and the way his brown hands cupped the air in front of him as if he could somehow make *it* bloom. "There's something in the soil, too—that's what killed the bleeding hearts. Too much acidity, is my guess."

"There's always something killing off the bleeding hearts," Cordelia sighed, thinking of Dan Killian. Then, seeing the quizzical look on Gabe's sun-cured face with its slightly crooked nose—broken years ago, he'd told her, in a schoolyard fight he'd attempted to stop—she added quickly, "What do you recommend?"

"I've mixed some lime in with the mulch, but that won't cure whatever is bothering you." Gabe's eyes crinkled and his mouth stretched in a wide and disconcertingly boyish grin. She watched him pull a neatly folded handkerchief from his back pocket, and the thought stole into her mind —*Somebody's looking after him, ironing for him.* Her heart catching just the tiniest bit, she watched him mop his brow, then tuck the handkerchief, still folded, back into his pocket. He glanced upward at the cloudless sky. "It's going to rain. See that red rim around the sun? That means a wet day tomorrow."

Wasn't that just like him? she thought. Asking a question, or making a remark, that cut right to the heart of things . . . then, just as quick as you please, switching over to an entirely different subject so as not to crowd you too close.

"Well, thank goodness, with this heat I feel like I'm melting right down into my shoes," she replied, fanning herself with the straw hat she held in one hand. "This is the hottest Indian summer since I can remember."

It felt good to have changed out of her gabardine suit into a pair of soft old chinos and a cotton blouse still smell-

ing of Netta's ironing board. She thought ahead to the cool
shower she would take after she'd finished harvesting the
herbs. But the truth was, she didn't mind getting dirty working in her garden.

Cordelia gazed around her, remembering what this place
had looked like in the last years of her mother's illness—the
rose beds half eaten away by Japanese beetles, the hollyhocks
alongside the garage like rangy scarecrows, the orchard of
dwarf peaches and plums overgrown and matted with
weeds. Even the tulips and crocuses and snowdrops had
stopped coming up each spring, as if the effort was simply
too much. And the peonies, why, they'd hung their heads in
shame. It seemed as though the word had been passed
among them that there was no point in their trying to look
good, because no one cared.

People are like that, too, she thought. *If you're not loved,
then you have no love to give.* Maybe the only thing sadder
than a weed-choked garden was a barren heart. With Gene,
she had basked in the sunlight of a good man's love. Now
all she had was memory. But was that enough?

She thought of Gabe's callused palm against the handle
of a trowel, the deft way he plucked away dead leaves. All
around, she saw the evidence of the care that she and
Gabe—mostly Gabe—had lavished on this old place, bringing it back to life in some areas, replanting altogether in
others. The Old English rock garden where the dilapidated
toolshed had once stood, with its trailing ferns and clumps
of sweet William and violets starting to die back with Indian
summer's end. The begonia arbor along the shady side of
the garage, with its hanging wire baskets of plump fleshy
hybrids—Ruffled Double, Sensations, Crispa Marginata.
And the raised herb garden, for which Gabe had laboriously
hauled the stones up from the creek, one wheelbarrow load
at a time.

Right now the forsythia hedge lay dormant, but come April the whole south flank of the stone wall that surrounded her two acres would be a cloud of yellow. Then there would be tulips and narcissi strung like bright beads linking the rows of sweet-magnolia and crepe-myrtle trees. By summer, the roses would be blooming—the trellis of tea roses that arched over the gate leading to the orchard, the shrub roses high and wide as hedges, the grandifloras and floribundas that grew on either side of the curving front walk. Roses with names like Prosperity and Moonlight, Peace and White Dawn. And the fragrance—oh, you could almost sip it, like the sweet wine Gabe made from the elderberries that smothered the wall facing the kitchen garden.

Her garden had perhaps fared better than she had, Cordelia thought. She had nourished it, while her own heart echoed like an empty house.

Is it too late? she wondered, her gaze falling on Gabe. *Could he possibly be interested in me that way?* Yesterday, she might not have dared to imagine so, but since Sissy had planted the idea in her head, it seemed to be growing.

I could ask him to supper, she thought. What would be so terrible about that? She knew that he'd gotten divorced around the same time that he'd left teaching. He seldom talked about his ex-wife, but Cordelia remembered having seen her around from time to time, shopping in the Piggly Wiggly or trying on shoes at Rambling Rose. Attractive, slender, dark-haired, and *young.* No more than thirty-eight or -nine. No children, and she suspected Gabe had wanted them, the way he'd spend hours with the Burgess girls next door to her, teaching the names of all the roses, and showing them how to plant bulbs and prune shrubs.

But what would he think? A woman with silver hair, who took pills for her blood pressure and, each time she grew dizzy, feared she might be having a stroke—not like the mild one she'd had last summer, but one that would leave her unable to move or speak?

As she pulled a pair of secateurs from the basket looped over her arm, Cordelia caught him looking at her. He was in the midst of staking a droopy hydrangea branch, his forearms corded, a length of raffia twine clamped between his even white teeth. He straightened, at the same time breaking into a smile that pulled at her heart like the twine that was now being tightened about the stake.

"I think this is my favorite time of year," he said. "Maybe because we tend to appreciate most that which is in dwindling supply. I think it was Thoreau who said that life near the bone is the sweetest."

"Right now I'd be a lot happier with more rather than less." She sighed, thinking of the money still to be raised for Gene's library. "Sometimes I feel like Sisyphus, pushing that boulder up the mountain and having it roll right back down to the bottom."

It had been like this all her life, it seemed, starting with her being born south of the Mason-Dixon Line. When she was a teenager, all those squabbles she and Mother used to have about her being too rambunctious and opinionated. And, worse, harboring ideas that weren't minted in the South, like her views on integration, and women doing more with their lives than having babies and organizing bake sales. Why, hadn't Mother become positively apoplectic when, instead of following her family's well-trodden path to Duke, she'd announced her decision to attend George Washington University instead?

Years later, of course, she'd come to appreciate what she'd been too much of a firebrand to see when she was young: the wealth that life in Blessing had to offer. The richness of its earth and the bounty of its rolling green hills. Its unhurried pace that allowed for an occasional misstep. Its people, maddening at times in their antediluvian beliefs, but as true as a plumb line and as steadfast as the levee down at Brinker's Creek.

And with Grace, she'd also gained a new appreciation of her own mother's trials, trying to tame a daughter whose every action and opinion seemed to fly in the face of good sense.

Yet, at times like these, she wondered if living here all these years had taken some of the edge off her spirit, the way a piano goes out of tune when it's not being played enough. Despite her position on the boards of Latham University and Hilldale Hospital, she'd grown somewhat . . . complacent. She needed the bracing confidence of people like Gabe, who believed she was still capable of more than warming a chair in some boardroom.

"You'll get your library, Cordelia." He said it as if it were a simple truth of nature he was observing—the fact that lilies grow from tubers, or that the section of branch from which a peach has been picked won't bear again.

Hearing him, his calm assured tone, and feeling a touch as light as rain against her arm, she felt her battered sense of purpose begin to revive.

A memory came to her, of the time she'd been summoned to school for a conference with Sissy's sophomore English teacher, Mr. Ross. She recalled how apprehensive she'd felt, meeting for the first time the man Sissy and her friends were constantly making fun of, nearly choking with laughter over the fact that he'd had tears, actual *tears* in his eyes when he read a Dylan Thomas poem aloud to them in class. Cordelia had anticipated a fussy man of uncertain masculinity, with weak eyes and asthma—like Mr. Denniston, who ran the only haberdashery in town and was rumored to be a homosexual.

And hadn't she been stunned to encounter the actual Mr.

Ross? Ruddy-faced and outdoorsy-looking, with his crinkly brown hair and equally rumpled seersucker jacket that made her think of a young boy lying in the grass, flushed from turning cartwheels. And that slightly flattened nose, which looked odd next to cheekbones as sharply defined as a Comanche's.

"I'm honored to make your acquaintance, Mrs. Truscott," he'd introduced himself. His almost quaint formality, and the way he'd wasted no time in ushering her to the chair beside his desk, had impressed her at once. "I was a great admirer of your husband's, you know. A truly courageous man. I heard him speak once . . . on the steps of the Supreme Court, after the decision was handed down on *Sullivan* versus *New York Times*. It was an experience I'll never forget. Your daughter, she's very much like him—that same fire, that sense of commitment."

"Sis . . . you mean, Caroline?" Cordelia couldn't contain her surprise. Even she, who loved Sissy no end, could not imagine those qualities in her soft, placid daughter.

He blinked, then smiled. "Actually, it was Grace I was thinking of. I taught her, too. Let me see, it must be four, five years."

"But you hardly seem . . ." Cordelia caught herself on the brink of rudeness.

"Old enough?" he finished for her, smiling. "I'm thirty-two, Mrs. Truscott. I believe it was my first year at this school—before that I taught in Atlanta. If it hadn't been for Grace, and a handful of students like her, it might well have been my last. Now, Caroline . . ." He paused, and she saw him scratch behind his ear, a habit she would come to know in later years as a signal of mild distress.

Cordelia felt herself growing tense. "She's doing her homework, isn't she? She's not failing, I mean?" Truth to tell, Cordelia rarely saw Sissy read anything unless it was one of those magazines that told you how, if you fixed your hair a certain way, or showed a flair for accessorizing, boys would be falling all over themselves to date you. Most of her time she seemed to spend giggling over the phone with that pimple-faced Beech Beecham.

"No, no, not failing," he was quick to reassure her. "Though," he added with a rueful smile, "I won't deny there is room for improvement. Actually, Mrs.—"

"Cordelia. Please call me Cordelia." For some reason, she felt safe—comfortable, even—in allowing the familiarity with this boyish man who spoke with such polish.

He gave her a level look, his eyes dark with seriousness. "There was an incident the other day, involving Caroline and another girl. It wasn't reported, but I thought you should know . . ."

Cordelia squeezed her eyes shut, imagining Sissy cringing in a corner, the object of torment by some smarter, prettier, more popular girl.

". . . It wasn't what she did so much as what she said," she heard him continue. "Caroline called her a nigger. 'Stupid, monkey-faced nigger' were her exact words, I believe. After Marvella accidentally knocked a book off her desk."

Cordelia felt his words hit her like a stinging slap. Sissy? *Her* Sissy, who'd come home from grade school in tears almost every day over some classmate who'd called her fat or stupid? She, of all people, ought to have known how something like that would hurt.

Deep shame flooded through Cordelia. Thank heaven Eugene wouldn't have to hear this.

"I'll speak to her," she said stiffly to this teacher who sat looking at her with such compassion she could hardly bear it. She felt as if he were seeing right through her, and knew exactly how awful she felt. "It won't happen again." She started to rise.

Gabriel Ross put out a hand to stop her. "Wait. I wish you wouldn't. Speak to her, that is. I didn't ask you here to tell tales, or to have Caroline punished. She punishes herself, far too much. That's where it comes from, this lashing out, from her feeling she can't be like the others, that she'll never measure up."

"She's . . . a good girl." Cordelia wanted desperately to smooth things over, to make everything all right.

"She is," Gabriel agreed. Then he smiled, that heart-warming, luminous smile of his that said, somehow, against all her worst fears, everything *would* turn out all right. "It's the hurt ones we have to look out for in this world, Cordelia, because, if we don't stop it where it lives, the hurt, it spreads, like a pebble dropped in a pond, to hurt others."

Looking at him now, in his battered hat and dirt-stained trousers, seventeen years later, the laugh lines around his mouth and eyes visible against the deeper brown of his tanned cheeks, she was once again filled with a sense of his goodness, of the sureness of his footing . . . and, at the same time, of her own helplessness ever to bridge the gap between them.

What would it look like—never mind to the small minds around here, but to her friends in New York, Washington, her colleagues on the boards on which she served—if she, the widow of the great Eugene Truscott, were to take up with a gardener? Not to mention the disparity in their life-styles. Gabe, with his modest little house down on Oakview Avenue by the Kmart, how would *he* feel about sharing in all this—her enormous house, her generous income from the wise investments she and Gene had made? Knowing him, he'd want no part of it.

Still, what would be the harm in merely asking him to supper? She could use the company. It was as simple as that.

"Gabe, I . . . ." she started to say, but something made

her change her mind—maybe it was the unsuspecting look on his face. "Shall we get to those herbs before it gets dark?"

Walking around the house toward the kitchen garden in back, Gabe pointed out where the paint was flaking off one of the dormers. "I'll get up on a ladder and give it a lick with the paintbrush," he offered, though, strictly speaking, his job didn't extend to house repairs.

"Oh, this old place is practically falling down around my ears," Cordelia sighed. "Sometimes I think the best thing would be just to sell it. Even the new dishwasher—Netta's been complaining that it makes the most unearthly clattering noise."

She looked up, taking in the two-story Victorian with its gables and turret and white-columned porch. The truth was, for all her complaining, the old place, even with its miles of trim and fussy gingerbread forever in need of paint, was more solid that those spanking-new Mulberry Acres townhouses Sissy had dragged her over to look at the other day, their walls so thin you could hear someone sneeze on the other side.

"I could take a look at that dishwasher for you, if you'd like," Gabe offered.

"Really, Gabe, you're far too kind. . . ." She paused, thinking, *Don't be a fool, it'd be the perfect excuse to ask him to stay for supper.* But what about after that?

Rushing ahead before she could change her mind, she finished, ". . . but I wouldn't dream of it. Really, I can have that nice Mr. Crockett look at it, and it won't cost me a cent. It's still under warranty."

Cordelia felt weak and cowardly. How could she expect to fight the likes of Dan Killian, and her own stiff-necked daughter, when she couldn't even get up the nerve to invite Gabe Ross to supper?

She felt a stab of misgiving . . . and of longing, too, for

the company of a man across from her at the kitchen table. A man whose talk went far beyond whether the Robert E. Lee Rebels stood a chance of beating the Wilston Wildcats this year, or what business Corky Oakes had displaying those condoms right up next to the cash register in his drugstore for any five-year-old to see.

Stooped side by side in the herb garden, they worked their way up the narrow gravel pathway between the rows, snipping and tying the last of summer's bounty—miniature chives, winter savory, golden oregano, lemon thyme, bee balm, purple basil. The scent, like the most heavenly potpourri, drifted up around Cordelia, and she thought of the little net bags of verbena she would make up for Netta to put at the back of every drawer. Tonight, she would chop and store the basil in olive oil, and hang the rest of the herbs to dry in the attic. And tomorrow, she and Netta would make up quarts of tarragon and rosemary vinegars.

It was dusk by the time they finished, the last of the sun's rays skimming the top of the weeping willow that overhung the gazebo. An ache had crept into her back, and her hands stung with tiny cuts caused by the prickly herbs. But she didn't mind; in fact, she felt better than she had all day.

Gabe, with a flourish, handed her a bouquet of mint. "For Netta's sun-tea," he said, "which I wouldn't say no to a glass of right now."

And if I asked you to stay for a plate of Netta's good chicken stew, what would you say to that?

But just then the distant trilling of the phone reached her ears.

Dashing back through the kitchen door, Cordelia headed for the heavy black telephone that had stood on the cherry stand in the hallway for nearly fifty years. Could it be Dan, calling to say he'd decided to give her the money after all? Her heart was pounding so hard she could feel it in the back of her teeth. *Silly,* she told herself. *It's probably nothing— Dr. Bridges' office calling to confirm my appointment next week, or Nat Duffy down at the Sunrise Nursery letting me know the seed catalogues I ordered have come in.*

Cordelia snatched up the receiver and heard the crackling of long-distance, then a man's voice, deep yet oddly musical.

"Cordelia? It's Win. Listen, I just got a call from Sissy. She sounded pretty upset, so I thought I'd better see how you were doing. I've seen the newspapers, and she filled me in on the rest. . . ."

Cordelia felt her panic subside. It was only Win, dear thoughtful Win, who still called her every birthday and Mother's Day. And who besides Win ever bothered to send her snapshots of Chris, like the one she'd gotten just last week—a photo of the two of them at East Hampton, Win, tall and blond and tanned, his arm slung about the awkward-looking boy at his side.

It had been wrong of Sissy to call him, of course. Involving Win would only make this whole thing worse. But, even so, how good to hear his voice! Win, she remembered, had always been clever at fixing things; he even settled most of his cases out of court. And before her mother had passed on, back when he and Grace were newly engaged, who but Win had ever been able to charm a smile out of the old dragon?

Yes, maybe he *could* fix this. Already, in one day, she'd kept her mouth shut too many times when perhaps she should have spoken out. And where had that gotten her? What could be the harm in at least asking Win's advice?

"Win, what a nice surprise!" she cried, then dropped her voice. "Why, yes, all this publicity about Grace's book *has* been rather upsetting. Actually, I'm glad you called, because I was hoping you might be able to help."

In spite of herself, the story came tumbling out—how

hard it was for her to talk to Grace, the article in the *Con-stitution,* her meeting with Dan Killian this morning. She wondered, even as she was telling it, how much he already knew about Ned Emory's death. It would only have been natural, when they were married, for Grace to have told him the whole story. But if Win was aware that Cordelia was concealing anything, he didn't let on.

After a moment of silence, he said, "I could file an injunction to try and put off publication." Smooth, commanding, speaking to her as if she were his client, as if she'd agreed to hire him as her attorney. "From what I understand, this story's got no corroboration. Just Grace's say-so, and she was a young child at the time. Unless you think someone might be able to back her up."

Cordelia was about to remind him, in case he didn't already know, that Margaret was dead. Then she remembered that Margaret had had a daughter, a little girl—oh, no, she'd be a grown woman now—named . . .

"Nola," she heard herself say aloud. "Margaret had a daughter named Nola. But I don't know if she was there, if she saw . . . anything. Gene might have said something about it—I just can't remember." She sighed. "It was all so long ago." She didn't add that, when little Grace had come to her, white-faced and babbling hysterically, she'd simply hushed her up, as she would have a crying baby.

But now Cordelia wondered if Margaret's daughter might be involved in this somehow. If she *were* to back up Grace's story, then people would *really* talk and make heaven knows what kind of awful assumptions. There'd be no point in still trying to get that money out of Dan Killian, or any of those foundations. In fact, the library might turn out to be nothing more than one big pipe dream.

And even if she managed to pull off a small miracle and it did get built, without her beloved Gene's unsullied reputation, his place in history, his library would be just another pile of bricks and stone.

She had to fight this, even if it meant risking the thing she held most dear: her own integrity. She wouldn't be lying, she told herself, only protecting what deserved to be protected. Gene had done no wrong. That was the truth—the *only* truth she would permit herself.

"I could speak to this Nola if you like . . ." Win started to say, but Cordelia cut him off.

"Do whatever you have to, Win." She clutched the receiver tighter to her ear, the smell of crushed chives that clung to her fingers making her eyes water and her nose sting. "Whatever will stop this from going any further."

Chapter 4

Nola stared at the sheet of vellum trace taped to her drafting table. She'd been slaving over this elevation for weeks, and it *still* wasn't right. Loose ends jumped out at her: a pair of columns that appeared too slender in contrast to the massive pediment above . . . a window that seemed ill-proportioned . . . a shed dormer that awkwardly interrupted the elegance of the gently sloping roof. . . .

She felt her head begin to swim as the spidery graphite lines melted into a gray blur. Damn. She rubbed her temples with her knuckles.

It was late; everybody in the office had gone home hours ago. She was tired, was all. She just could not *concentrate.*

Her thoughts wandered to the phone call she'd gotten last night, some WASP lawyer—had to be, with a name like Winston Bishop, probably with a Roman numeral or a "Junior" attached to it that he neglected to mention. Nice and friendly, none of that legalese shit. Inviting her to lunch, or, if she was too busy, maybe a drink at the Union Square Cafe, which he knew wasn't too far from her office. (And how the hell did he know where she worked?) Saying he had some questions concerning her father's death.

You and every damn Tom, Dick, or Harry who reads the newspapers, she'd almost blurted. Then he'd told her who his client was: Mrs. Eugene Truscott. Good God, as if she wasn't already on overload with *Grace* Truscott calling her every other day. Now she'd have the widow trying to tug her in the opposite direction, begging her to keep her mouth shut.

Well, the old lady wouldn't have to bother. She'd told that fancy lawyer there was no point in wasting a meal or even a drink on her—she had nothing to say on that subject other than what had been reported at the time, which had been merely a paragraph on the obituary page concerning the suicide of a black man whose only claim to fame was his wife being the secretary of a famous senator. She could sense the relief in Winston Bishop's voice just before he hung up.

Now she wondered if she was going about this the right way. Should she at least meet with Grace Truscott, find out how much she remembered or knew . . . and if that was *all* she knew?

Nola closed her eyes, rubbing her thumbs lightly over work-swollen eyelids.

"Man cain't get a thing done with folks hangin' round till all hours. . . ."

Her head snapped up. Only the custodian, old Leroy, muttering outside the door to the office she shared with the firm's eight other project architects. She waited to see if he was going to barge in, the way he sometimes did when he caught her working late, but then she heard the muffled squeak-rattle of his janitor's trolley as it moved on down the hallway.

Time to move on myself. She had to get home, back to her girls. And sleep . . . she *had* to get some sleep or tomorrow she'd be prying herself out of bed, her eyelids fastened shut with Velcro. God would probably forgive her for another frantic morning of inside-out T-shirts and Cheerios hastily sloshed with milk, she thought, but would Tasha and Dani?

Shit. She hadn't even called home to see if Tasha had

come out okay on that math test she'd been worrying over all week. And Dani, whimpery from her sore throat, she'd have worn out Florene right down to the soles of her shoes. How many times can a babysitter be coerced into reading *Green Eggs and Ham* out loud before going completely bonkers . . . or, worse, throwing in the towel?

But just then, as Nola was tearing off a sheet of trace to tape over her drawing, she saw it as if for the first time, not as it was, but how it *must* be. It was as if she'd been struggling with a too-tight jar lid, and now it was suddenly giving way. *Yes . . . oh, yes.* In minutes of working furiously—five, twenty, she didn't know how long—she'd sketched a new front façade.

Then she sat back and looked at it. This time she was seeing it as clearly as if it were framed and spotlit, a Jacques-Louis David Roman interior hanging in a museum. Nothing like the cerebral, cutting-edge designs that had earned her the Carnegie Prize at Cooper Union. This drawing's neoclassical features went *against* everything she'd been taught to admire. But that was what made it so right. . . .

It'll never get built, warned a cynical voice in the back of her head. With six other firms vying for this commission, another design was sure to be chosen. Even here at Maguire, Chang & Foster, she had major competition. She thought of Randy Craig, who occupied the cubicle alongside hers. She'd been positively blown away by that Horatio Street town house remodel of his. And with this design competition, she hadn't missed the lustful look on his face when Maguire, too swamped with paid commissions to give time to what was little more than a bird in the bush, had handed them each a rough sketch he'd dashed off of two different approaches he wanted to see developed. Randy had tried to act cool, yeah, one more pain-in-the-butt assignment, but ever since he sure had been logging in the extra hours.

Having caught a glimpse over Randy's shoulder the other day at the design he'd been slaving over—stark, streamlined, reminiscent of Erik Gunnar Asplund's famous library in Stockholm—she'd wanted to shout in his ear, *No, no! You don't understand! That's not how it should look!*

But he only would have wanted to know what made *her* such an expert.

Straightening on her high stool, Nola arched her back and pushed her fist into the throbbing curve of her spine. Shoving aside plastic triangles, Mayline, leadholder, she looked down at her drawing, envisioning it as solid and somehow three-dimensional, thrusting outward from the flat surface of the paper like real granite and brick and steel girders.

The Eugene Truscott Memorial Library.

She saw its interior coming together in one seamless whole—the wide entrance vestibule opening onto a short hallway, then a flight of steps descending a half-level down into a second anteroom, walled in glass on all sides, through which light would sluice like water from a diverted stream. In the main reading room, three huge frosted skylights along a ceiling that curved graciously but didn't soar into outer space, and bookshelves arranged in a pattern that echoed the geometry of the recessed metal columns in the wall and the ribs in the barrel vault above. Floors that made you think of the earth they were built on, gently sloping and stepping to create spaces in which people would gather away from the formality of the tables and chairs.

She thought of Irving Gill's comparing his buildings to boulders that nature would chisel with storms and decorate with lichen and vines. This one would be like that—smooth to the eye, rough to the touch, but never static.

Not a lifeless monument to a glorified dead man—a Lincoln Memorial, a Widener Library—but the kind of place that would draw people in.

The way *he* would have wanted, she thought.

She felt a catch in her throat. Would she ever see it, ever stand in its shadow, or walk through its doors? Or would it end up just as more lines on paper, another "interesting" exercise, like design reviews at Cooper Union, when her projects had routinely been torn to shreds by her professors? Except this time, even if she could get her bosses to run with it, it would be the Eugene Truscott Memorial committee doing the judging.

But what if they do choose it? Are you prepared for what might come out if this thing actually does get built?

Anxiety stirred in the hollow space just above her solar plexus—a low dangerous thrumming like a hornet's nest under an eave.

Hey, Nola cautioned herself. *One step at a time. First, Maguire. Get it past him, then you can worry about the rest.* She hoped that Maguire wouldn't be annoyed that she'd scrapped his sketch. If he liked her design, there might even be a bonus in it for her, or, better yet, a raise. Damn, she could sure use one!

After all, it had been *she,* not Randy Craig, who had gotten them the Petrossian commission after Maguire nearly blew it with his overwrought design for the Easthampton beach house. Petrossian—*Andres* Petrossian, whose Carnegie Hall concerts were always sold out months in advance —almost walked, *would* have walked, if she hadn't taken a chance, jumped in with her own two cents, pointing out how they could knock out a wall and pitch the roof, add skylights, make the living and dining rooms a single cathedral-ceilinged space with a wraparound deck overlooking the ocean. Just last summer, the violinist's weekend getaway, with its soaring central space, had been featured in *The New York Times Magazine.*

Remembering that article, Nola saw in her mind another, more recent headline: DEAD SENATOR IMPLICATED IN DECADES-OLD KILLING.

Damn you, Grace Truscott, for raking all this up. Nola itched suddenly to pick up the phone. But she held herself back. What would she accomplish by telling the woman off?

Stowing her things on the shelf above her table, she grabbed her coat and purse and was out the door, waving to Leroy, who was busy emptying a wastebasket into a garbage bag. The old man merely grunted.

Waiting for the crosstown bus on Fourteenth Street, which after nine ran once in a millennium, Nola found herself longing for the luxury of a seat-sprung, smelly taxi. But she let the Yellow Cabs with lit-up for-hire signs just whiz on by. Every dollar she saved was money she could squirrel away for later, for the private school she wanted for Tasha and Dani.

By the time she'd transferred to a bus going up Eighth, and had walked the long block to her building—on Twenty-second just off Ninth—Nola was so tired she could hardly see straight. A blind man finds his way home by counting the number of steps, and that was how she'd felt, gliding from one circle of lamplit sidewalk to the next as if by memory alone, hardly noticing the Federal-style row houses and Italianate brownstones wedged together on either side of the street.

Step on a crack, break your mother's back.

The thought jumped into her head, uninvited, all those cracks she'd jumped over when she was a child. Now, even dead and buried, Mama still wasn't safe.

Can't think about that right now. Just get home. . . .

Florene greeted her at the door of her floor-through, wearing a wide, welcoming smile. "Lord, girl, you look like something got run over crossing the street. You okay or do I call the paramedics?"

"I'm just beat, is all," she sighed. "Nothing a good night's sleep won't cure." She dropped her bag by the wildly futuristic Pucci de Rossi hall table that she had splurged on back when she was married, when Marcus was raking it in at Salomon Brothers—before he lost his job and wound up knee-deep in debt.

"Or a good man," Florene interjected with a laugh that rumbled through her massive body. "Honey, if you ask me, you could use both. There's nothin' like some lovin' between the sheets to put the spring in a woman's step."

Florene ought to know, Nola thought with a surge of affection. She claimed to be fifty-eight, but Nola thought sixty-three or -four was more like it. And in her time, she'd had three husbands, not to mention several boyfriends who kept her plenty busy in between baby-sitting stints. Florene —who once told her that the day she retired from her clerking job at Macy's was the day she'd cracked out the Reese's Pieces and said to hell with being a size ten—was living proof that bigger was better.

"If you find one, be sure and give him my number," Nola joked. "Seems like the only men who get close to me are the ones on the street looking for a handout." She smoothed a peeling edge of wallpaper on her way into the kitchen. "How'd everything go tonight?"

"Fine, 'cept the TV's on the fritz again. Left me high and dry, right smack in the middle of *L.A. Law*." Florene bent over with a whoosh of exhaled breath to retrieve a balled-up candy wrapper that had rolled under the kitchen table. "That woman called again, too, didn't leave her name, but I recognized her voice—same one been callin' you all week.

Oh, yeah, and Tasha said she was sick, but I figured it musta been all those cookies she ate. Let me tell you, that girl can out–Peak Frean me any day of the week."

Ignoring the fresh reminder of Grace's persistence, Nola said, "Tasha's sick?"

"Nothin' to get all riled up about. Tummyache is all. If I had a nickel for each time one of my kids'd had a bellyache, right now I'd have my butt parked like Ivana Trump up at the Plaza Hotel, all kind of gorgeous men just beggin' to make my acquaintance."

"They don't seem to be having any trouble finding you right where you are." Nola couldn't help laughing as she poured herself a glass of orange juice, looking about the tiny, cluttered kitchen and thinking that, if Florene watched less TV and put in some more time cleaning up after herself and the kids, there wouldn't be this mess to come home to every night. But that was nothing compared with how much the girls adored her. Florene was Big Bird with an attitude.

"Do like me, and put some miles on that tired ass of yours." Florene shot her a wicked grin as she gathered up a bulging satchel from which Nola could see, poking up over the top, a ball of unraveling yarn, a half-eaten bag of Doritos, a dog-eared Harlequin paperback, and one of Dani's vivid drawings. "You'll feel better and live longer. Beats Geritol every time."

Yeah, sure, maybe I'll get real lucky and wind up with another guy like Marcus.

"No thanks, Florene," she said. "After what I went through the last time, I'm keeping my ass up on blocks until I find a man who knows what else I'm good for."

"You do that, girl . . . but don't wait *too* long, or all the good ones'll be taken. Skinny thing like you don't have the pick of the litter the way us big gals do."

Florene let loose one of her rumbling belly laughs, and

Nola laughed with her, deeply and fully, feeling better than she had all day. All *week*, for that matter. Florene was good medicine . . . even if she gave lousy advice.

She reminded herself, for the umpteenth time, how lucky she was to have Florene, not only as a babysitter, but as her landlady as well. And Florene thought *she* was the lucky one, not only that Nola's rent money enabled her to keep up the mortgage payments and repairs on this ever so slightly run-down place she'd inherited from her first husband, but that she got to play grandma to boot. Not to mention Ann Landers.

Nola told Florene good night and hurried down the hall to the bedroom Tasha and Dani shared.

She found Dani asleep on her stomach, with her little butt making a mound under her Winnie the Pooh comforter, and her thumb propped against her half-open mouth. Nola felt tenderness well up in her.

"Mommy?" Tasha called over to her from the other bed. She sounded stuffed up, as if she had a cold . . . or had been crying.

She was sitting bolt upright, not even leaning back against the wicker headboard. Her face, polished by the yellow glow of the nightlight, looked small and pinched. An old woman's face on an eleven-year-old's body. Only her hair, a softly waving brown, looked unruffled. Tasha had been waiting up for her all this time.

"Hey, sugarpie . . . what's happening?" Nola sat on the edge of Tasha's bed, and without thinking put a hand to her forehead to see if she was running a fever. It felt cool as marble.

"Dani makes bougary noises when she sleeps. Just listen to her." Tasha wrinkled her nose primly at the soft, snuffly snores coming from Dani's side of the room.

"Is that what's keeping you awake?" Nola scooted over

to wrap an arm about Tasha's thin shoulders, which were pinched tight as a clothespin.

"No."

"Something at school?"

"Uh-huh."

"Not Jamal again?"

"He *always* sucks." Her voice dropped to a pained whisper. "My teacher doesn't like me."

Nola's heart lurched. What could have happened to make Tasha think that? Something in particular . . . or the same old don't-give-a-shit attitude her teacher had been coasting by on since the beginning of the year? Mrs. Millner struck her as a real burn-out case. Probably been at it too long, though she didn't look much older than Nola's own thirty-seven. She remembered that stupid and probably dangerous tinfoil business—assigning a bunch of eleven-year-olds the at-home science experiment of melting tinfoil. You bet she'd raised hell. So would any other mother with her head screwed on.

"She on your case about those times tables you were having trouble with?"

Tasha shook her head, her shoulders corkscrewing violently within the crook of Nola's arm; finally, she blurted tearfully, "Sh-she's making me be in the puh-play!"

The play? It must have been announced in one of those mimeographed sheets the school was always sending home with the girls—PTA meetings, and field trips, and what to do about head lice. Oh, right. Something about it being Black Pride Week, and the fifth-graders putting on a play about the civil-rights movement.

"She give you one of those crummy parts where you don't get to say anything?" Nola spoke lightly, hoping that was all it was.

Tasha broke into a fresh torrent of sobs.

"I huh-have to be the b-bad lady who yells at Rosa Parks for sitting duh-down on the b-bus!"

Nola felt something heave over inside her, slowly, like a large flat rock. Feelings tumbled through her that she'd thought she had buried with her mother . . . of not fitting in, of not being black enough . . . or white enough.

She felt a bolt of anger. She wanted to strangle Tasha's teacher.

"Did she tell you why she picked you?" Nola asked gently, working to hold back her rage. She patted Tasha's shoulders until they stopped hitching and her sobbing subsided.

"She didn't say, but *I* know," Tasha lashed out. "Jamal says it's 'cause I'm a honky!"

A honky? Nola felt a bubble of hysteria rising in her, and had to clamp her teeth over her tongue to stop it from erupting. Oh, that was rich. How Mama would have appreciated that joke. Mama, who'd been turned away from three different motels once on a trip to Mobile. And Mama had been light-skinned, Nola herself nearly white enough to "pass," if that antiquated notion still applied. Even though Marcus's complexion had been somewhat darker than hers, both girls were on the fair side. She should hardly be shocked that Tasha and Dani stood out among even their Hispanic classmates.

"Oh, sugar." She sighed, suddenly too weary to move, except to rest her cheek against the top of Tasha's head, which felt soft and silky as new grass. "I'll talk to her. Tomorrow."

Nola felt her relax a bit, and saw Tasha bring her thumb to her mouth before the child realized what she was doing. Catching herself, she ran her thumb back and forth over her lower lip.

"You won't say it was me who told?" she asked.

"I'll say I heard it from one of the other mothers."

"Then Mrs. Millner won't be mad at me?"

She sounded, just then, like little Dani, asking for assurances where there were none to be had—as if Nola could somehow keep a skinned knee from hurting when the Band-Aid was pulled off, or make Marcus show up when he'd forgotten it was his weekend with the girls.

Nola pulled Tasha close, squeezing her tightly. She'd sent away for the applications, and had stored them in the top drawer of her desk—Grace Church, St. Luke's, Little Red School House, Friends. Next year maybe . . . oh, but it *had* to be next year. For Tasha, especially. Bright and sensitive, but too high-strung for those damned IQ tests that would have gotten her into one of the "special" public schools, like Hunter.

But private-school tuitions were so high—ten thousand a year, *double* if she were to send Dani, too (and how could she not?). Though they weren't exactly *poor*, unless she got herself bumped up to associate or project manager, private school was not going to be an option.

"I'm going to sleep now." Tasha yawned, and slithered from under Nola's arm, curling up under the covers with a corner of her pillow tucked tight against her cheek, her thumb playing across her lower lip. In that instant, she and Dani could have been twins. " 'Night, Mommy."

" 'Night, Tash." Nola bent to kiss her daughter's cool forehead. Her own face felt flushed and achy, and a pulse in her temple leaped close to the surface.

Back in the kitchen, Nola thought about eating something, but the idea of going to the trouble of fixing even a sandwich was more than she could manage. Instead, she poured herself what was left of the coffee, and helped herself to a stale-looking Danish from the Entenmann's box Florene had left on the counter. Dinner *chez* Nola, she laughed to herself as she made her way down the hall to her bedroom, behind the stairs.

But instead of getting undressed and climbing right into bed, Nola found herself sinking onto the low ottoman in front of her dressing table as she remembered Florene telling her that Grace had called. Again.

What did the woman want? *Really?* Would Grace try to pry out of her the thing Mama had made her promise never to tell?

Nola looked around her, at the walls papered in an extravagant design of birds and trellises twined with leaves, and at the starkly modern bed with its hand-rubbed mahogany-and-black-lacquer finish. The whole room, this whole apartment, was like that, like *her,* a study in sharp contrasts—like that turn-of-the-century oil of a woman sewing by lamplight, which she and Marcus had gotten at a terrific price at an auction at Lubin's—hung next to the Matisse print that Tasha said looked like an upside-down Gumby. And the ancient, balding Turkish rug on which sat a stack of oval Shaker boxes, a halogen floor lamp of green oxidized brass, a vaguely Arts and Crafts dresser she'd found at a flea market.

Leftovers from another life, she thought. Once upon a time, when he'd been trading Government-backed mortgage bonds, Marcus's commissions had made it possible for her to go back to school *and* for them to buy all this nice stuff. Now it served as a vivid reminder of a time when, instead of conning herself into believing the money would keep on coming, she ought to have been socking it under her mattress.

This unfinished business with Grace—it was a reminder, too. Of long-ago promises that should never have been made. Of childhood years when Mama had often worn the anxious look of someone running scared—which, in a lot of ways, she had been.

She'd been fooling herself, thinking that if she ignored her Grace Truscott would eventually go away. Now Nola was remembering the little girl who had forced her way into Mama's house that day. No. Grace Truscott was not going to just fade away.

Suddenly it hit Nola, as if she'd been slapped. It was as clear as if she'd glimpsed into a crystal ball. The time had come to stop playing hide-and-seek. She had to face up to this. Look Grace Truscott in the eye and beg her, if she had to, to back off, for the love of God, *just back off.*

It was late—after eleven—but Nola knew that, if she allowed herself to sleep on this, by tomorrow she might chicken out. And maybe this was one time when gut instinct had to prevail. She picked up the phone and quickly punched in Grace's number. She didn't have to look it up. Grace had left it on her answering machine so many times, she knew it by heart.

Nola chose Colombe d'Or on Twenty-sixth Street, just off Lexington. It was chic, and too pricy for her, but she was sure she'd never be spotted here by anyone she knew.

Stepping out of a brisk wind into the garden-floor restaurant's burrowlike warmth, ducking slightly to clear the low entrance, she felt an odd mix of cozy familiarity coupled with mounting dread. She scanned the tables along the exposed-brick wall beyond the bar, and immediately spotted a woman sitting by herself who looked somewhat familiar.

Yes, it *was* her. All grown up, yet the features Nola remembered from so many years ago were clearly recognizable. She had known Grace was pretty. But, Lord, so *tiny.* Even seated, she looked as if she couldn't be much more than five feet. A doll-sized woman, wearing a filmy white aviator's blouse tucked into close-fitting black jeans, with a chic little tapestry vest and jangly gold necklace like a Brobdingnagian charm bracelet. Nola, in her tailored camel slacks and blocky houndstooth jacket, felt like an NFL linebacker by comparison.

She checked her coat and started over toward the table, savoring these few moments of being able to observe without being observed. Grace's hair was dark and silky, she saw, whereas hers had to be raked into a knot at the back of her neck to keep it from frizzing. And Grace's hands—so small they made her silver rings look absurd somehow, like a child playing dress-up.

But despite her size, everything about Grace, even the way she sat—insouciantly slouched back on her tailbone, one foot in an impossibly tiny suede boot balanced across her opposite knee—seemed to give off the message: *I know what I want, and how to get it.*

Watching Grace casually take a sip from the goblet of Perrier and lime in front of her, Nola felt a tug in the pit of her stomach, as if she were being pulled toward Grace against her will. *Damn her. Damn her to hell for dragging me into this.*

Could Grace possibly know how shaken she'd been? All those messages that she couldn't bring herself to answer, Nola had played them back, over and over. Searching . . . for what? Some clue that would tip her off to the trap Grace might be setting?

Wondering now if she *were* walking into a trap, Nola paused a moment in the midst of winding her way among the packed tables and adjusted the front of her jacket. Then she stepped into full view.

"Hello. You must be Grace."

Nola took a grim sort of pleasure in watching Grace start in surprise, nearly knocking over her drink as she rose to shake Nola's hand. Nola slipped into the empty chair across the table, feeling Grace's eyes on her, taking inventory.

She wasn't uncomfortable being stared at. People had been staring at her since she was twelve, a scrawny kid as tall as some men, with legs up to her navel and dresses that were always a few inches too short. Not that Mama, with her needle and thread, didn't always pretty much keep up with her; but Mama swore that, every night she stayed up late to take a hem down, Nola would be an inch taller by morning.

Gone now was the slouch she'd affected as a teenager to look shorter. Nola sat straight as a T-square, neck extended, her gaze as level as a surveyor's line.

"I was so afraid I'd be late that I got here ten minutes early," Grace said with a nervous laugh that made Nola want to like her in spite of herself. "If I'd somehow missed you, after all this, I'd have kicked myself from here to kingdom come." Just a trace of a Southern accent, like a pinch of sugar in a cup of strong, brewed coffee.

"And here *I* am . . . late." Nola managed a small, tight smile.

Don't apologize. Don't explain. Nola willed away the usual half-assed excuses that sprang to mind. *Let Grace do the explaining.*

"Nice place," Grace commented, looking about her. "I read somewhere that the food is good."

"I don't know, I've never eaten here," Nola replied with the wry half-smile of a working woman on a tight budget who scarcely has time to scan the morning paper, much less bother with reviews of pricey restaurants. She settled her handbag squarely on her lap, noting with disdain Grace's oversized leather tote, slung haphazardly over the back of her chair for any pickpocket to come along and help himself to. Only someone born into money would be so careless.

Nola watched Grace take another sip of Perrier. "Oh. Well . . . the truth is, anything would taste good to me right now. Last night, after you called"—again, that disarming smile that made Nola, against every instinct, want to like her—"I guess I didn't get much sleep. All I could manage for breakfast was black coffee."

"Join the club. Uninterrupted nights of sleep are definitely a thing of the past for me."

Grace looked at her blankly.

"I have two girls," Nola explained. "Tasha's ten, and Dani just turned six."

"I remember when my son was six." Grace sounded wistful. "I wish I'd found some way to bottle that age and store it up for later."

"Teenager?" It wasn't such a wild guess—Grace's expression suggested that she'd recently weathered a few storms on that front.

"And how!" Grace laughed, but Nola detected a note of tension there. "Chris is at that *age.* I'm not sure whether it's him being thirteen, or me being over thirty. Either way, there are days when I think I'm going to go right through the roof."

"Mine has a few of those holes in it," Nola sympathized, rolling her eyes. "And Tasha's still got a ways to go before she really hits her stride."

"I hope I get a chance to meet your girls someday," Grace said.

Nola could feel herself withdrawing from the spontaneous warmth that had sprung up between them as if from a fire that had gotten too cozy. She had to stay alert, on edge, none of this we're-in-the-same-boat bullshit.

Leveling her gaze at Grace, she said, "I'm not sure what the point would be."

Grace abruptly leaned forward on her elbows, fixing Nola with a clear, knowing gaze. In a low voice, all pretense at polite banter laid aside, she said, "I know what you're thinking. You didn't come here to listen to me make small talk." She was the first to look away, toying with the red plastic straws from her drink, rolling them absently between her palms, hard and fast, like a determined Girl Scout trying to make a fire with two sticks. "God, I can't believe you're here! We were just kids, I know, but I remember absolutely everything about you . . . and about . . ." She faltered, then picked up: ". . . that day."

Now Nola was leaning forward, too. "Why can't you just let it be? Why drag it out in the open after all these years? For God's sake, they're *dead,* both our fathers. My mother, too. They're not here to defend themselves."

Grace was shaking her head, flinging down her straw. "I'm not *accusing* anyone."

"Maybe not, but you're making him look bad all the same."

"*My* father . . . or yours?" Grace asked softly.

Nola could hear a humming deep in her eardrums, like a steel cable stretched too taut.

"This isn't about them," she shot back. "What it's about is *you.* Why the sudden compelling need to rake it all up?"

"I had to," Grace replied simply. "This thing, it's been in my head all these years, like a bad movie that keeps re-playing over and over. I can't believe a tragedy as awful as that didn't affect my father the same way. And how can I write about his life with any kind of honesty if I leave out something so important?"

"Okay, but what do you need me for?" Nola sat back and crossed her arms over her chest. "You already know everything there is to know." Her heart stepped up its frenzied beat, and she had a sudden, unwanted vision of herself being given a lie-detector test, her arm cuffed and wired, the needle on the graph fluctuating wildly.

"Who are you protecting, Nola?" Grace pressed, leaning closer. "*Is* it your father? The fact that he might have ended up a murderer if he hadn't been stopped?"

Nola suddenly felt as if she couldn't get enough air into her lungs. Her head grew light, and black specks floated across her field of vision.

Then she reminded herself, *The best defense is a good offense*. Gripping the edge of the table, she demanded, "What right do you have to come barging into my life, asking questions that are none of your damn business?"

"She made you promise, didn't she? Just the way Mother and Daddy made *me* promise."

"I don't know what you're talk——"

"Oh, yes, you do. I can see it in your face. You're afraid to talk about it, even to someone who was there. Someone, I'm guessing your mother, drilled it into you that you had to keep quiet or something really terrible would happen." The smile on Grace's pretty, heart-shaped face was grim. "I know because they did it to me, too. Only they didn't exactly *say* I wasn't supposed to tell. My mother . . . she has a way of just *looking* at you where you know you'd rather walk over hot coals in your bare feet than have her come out with what she's thinking."

"It wasn't that way with me. Mama, she—" Nola stopped herself. "Look, this isn't going to get us anywhere. I'm all grown up now. I make my own decisions. Doing show-and-tell for a bunch of reporters doesn't happen to be one of them." She brought a cool, trembling hand to a cheek that felt as if it had been scalded.

She was glad for the distraction when their waiter brought the ginger ale she'd ordered.

"*Not* a bunch of reporters," Grace corrected her. "Me, just me. I want to be able to explain so people will truly understand."

"It's not that simple."

"Then that's what I need to know. *Why* it's not simple."

"What about what *I* need?" Nola felt something hard and bright flash inside her.

Grace sat back suddenly, her face pale and earnest. Then, pressing forward again, she touched the back of Nola's hand, lightly. "I know you'll probably find this hard to believe, but all these years . . . I've wondered about you. Even before I started the book, I thought about calling you, just to . . . well, so I'd have someone to talk to about this."

Nola felt the same tug as before, pulling her toward Grace against every instinct that was telling her to resist. *Admit it—you've felt the same way.* Longing for someone to confide in, share this awful burden with, a burden far greater than Grace could begin to imagine . . .

Careful, she warned herself.

"You want the truth?" She spoke with the cold precision of a cleaver thudding into butcher block. "I was *glad* when my father died."

Nola could see that Grace was taken aback—more than that, actually *shocked*—and she felt a strange sort of triumph.

"My God," Grace said in a soft rush, almost an exhalation.

"Before Dad died, the only good times Mama and I had were when he was away at sea," Nola went on. "He'd be gone for weeks, months sometimes. When he got back, it'd be okay for a little while . . . but then he'd get these crazy ideas in his head, and start acting ugly, accusing Mama of things."

"What things?" Grace asked.

"Most of the time it was little stuff," Nola continued, almost as if she were talking to herself, or dreaming aloud. "Dad yelling that she'd gotten 'uppity' working up there on Capitol Hill, that he didn't know anymore if she was black or white. Then he'd get it into his head that she was cheating on him. Oh, the men! Once, it was supposed to have been nice Mr. Crosley, who worked at the market where Mama shopped. Another time it was Uncle Lester, Dad's own *brother*."

"What did your mother do about it?"

Nola shook her head, remembering. "Mama would get real quiet, and then Dad, he'd . . ." She stopped herself, suddenly reluctant to go on.

But Grace, without saying a word, wouldn't let go. She leaned in so close that Nola could feel Grace's breath on her face, like a faint summer breeze. Her hazel eyes were bright as sunlight on water.

"Sometimes he'd hit her," Nola finished in a flat voice.

Grace was silent for a moment, her expression grave. "I'm sorry," she said at last. "It must have been awful for you."

"Why should you care?" A bitterness rose in Nola's throat like the aftertaste of sour, unripe fruit. "You don't even *know* me."

"No," Grace acknowledged, "but I always wondered if you felt as bottled up as I did. After all, our parents never asked *us* if we minded going along with their glossed-over version of the truth."

"So why *didn't* you call me ten years ago?"

"I don't know. Something always stopped me at the last

minute. I was afraid you'd be like *them,* acting like it never happened."

Nola felt the cold from the icy glass in her hand spread up through her arm, across her chest. "It happened," she said, the words working loose like rusty nails from a door long ago hammered shut. "My dad . . . he went off the deep end. Mama got scared and called your father. She was always going on about how Eugene Truscott could fix just about any kind of trouble there was. Oh, yeah, I know it was an accident, but the fact is, he *did* fix it. Lucky for Mama and me, unlucky for Dad. End of story."

"Nothing that ends that badly is ever really over." Grace spoke quietly, but Nola shuddered at the truth in her words.

Abruptly, she said, "Look, this is just between you and me. Beyond that, I really can't help you."

"Even now that the cat's out of the bag, and your backing me up can only *salvage* my father's reputation?" Grace pressed.

Nola felt as if she were tottering on some incredibly steep precipice, about to tumble into a bottomless void. "I . . . can't," she repeated feebly.

"Why not? He was good to you, wasn't he? I know that when your father died he looked after you and your mother. He put aside money for you to go to college."

Nola found herself nodding. "Yes, he was good to us. He kept Mama on salary even after she got too sick to work."

"Then think of this as a way of repaying him!"

"Please," Nola begged. "You don't know what you're asking."

But Grace wouldn't stop, wouldn't let go. "Nola, there's no one else. You've *got* to help."

Nola felt her rigid control snap suddenly. "You're used

to getting your way, aren't you? Grace Truscott, the great senator's *privileged* daughter. Well, let me tell you—"

"Grace!" a deep voice interrupted from above.

Nola looked up into a pair of the greenest eyes she'd ever seen, in a face that was almost frighteningly handsome. She had a fleeting impression of curly dark-brown hair, a mouth full and sensuous, before she was able to focus on the man who stood over their table. Impossible for a male in New York City in the nineties to look like that and not be either married, gay, or terminally narcissistic. Even so, he was smiling at her with what appeared to be genuine interest.

"Ben Gold," he introduced himself, putting out his hand. A good handshake, firm and dry without being too aggressive.

"Nola Emory," she responded. The little smile playing at his lips and the way he was staring at her prompted her to ask, "Do I know you from somewhere?" The name *was* familiar.

"We haven't actually met, but I've heard all about you." Ben gave a disarming laugh, then, noting her puzzled expression, he added, "I work for my dad at Cadogan."

"Your dad is . . . ?" She raised an eyebrow.

"Jack Gold." When Nola didn't react, Ben turned to Grace with an amused look. "You haven't told her you're dating your publisher?"

Nola watched Grace give an awkward little shrug, and look down at the table.

Sidestepping that subject, Nola remarked lightly, "Must be interesting, having your father for a boss. I'll bet it sometimes feels like you never left home."

She saw Ben's expression darken, then a split second later he was joking, "Except that, when I ask for a bigger allowance, we're talking a lot more money."

Nola found a corner of her mouth turning up. Then it

came to her why his name had rung a bell—hadn't that
novel she'd finally managed to finish been dedicated to a Ben
Gold?

"You're Roger Young's editor, aren't you?" she asked.

He nodded, obviously pleased that she'd made the connection. "But I don't mind saying I wish I was Grace's editor
as well. . . . At the very least, I'd have be having lunch right
now with two beautiful women instead of one very pedantic
old man."

Nola broke the awkward stillness that fell over the table
with a laugh that surprised her as much as it obviously did
Grace. She wasn't sure why she was laughing, whether it was
from pleasure at this young man's candidness, or from relief
that he'd rescued her, for the moment at least, from Grace's
probing.

"I'm sorry you can't join us," Grace told him.

"Me, too, but duty calls. He's an author of mine, a doctor I'm hoping will be the next Pritikin." He switched his
attaché case to his other hand. He was wearing a navy corduroy sport jacket and a knitted tie that looked almost stud-
iedly casual, along with his brushed suede oxfords and the
Oliver Peoples sunglasses pushed up into his dark curls. "He
claims old age is cultural. That, under ideal circumstances,
the human body is designed to last for a hundred and twenty
years. I suppose that must mean, on Dr. Dorfmeyer's scale,
that the three of us have yet to hit puberty."

Nola felt absurdly flattered by Ben's including her in his
"us," and by the way he was looking at her—a second too
long each time their eyes made contact. How long since she'd
been so acutely aware of a man's attention?

Not that she went out of her way to notice such things.
Once burned, twice shy, she thought. What was it Marcus,
red-eyed and furious, had said to her as he was packing up
his things? *No one will ever love you the way I do.* And she

remembered thinking, *Thank God. I couldn't bear to be loved that way by anyone, ever again.* Since he'd moved out, she'd reveled in having their king-sized bed all to herself. It was only lately she had begun to feel as if she were sleeping on an ice floe.

Nola met Ben's eyes as he turned to go, and felt her face grow warmer. As he disappeared around the arch into the next room, she found herself wondering if she would ever see him again.

"He seems like a nice guy," she told Grace. The anger she'd felt just minutes earlier was gone. In its place, there was only a heavy tiredness.

"He is." Grace sighed, and once again began tearing off little pieces of her napkin. "I'm just not sure I'm ready to be the stepmother of a thirty-year-old."

"You're engaged?"

"No." Grace's eyes slid away.

Nola could see she'd hit a nerve. Quickly she changed the subject.

"I saw your name in the paper the other day. Not in connection with any of this." She spread her hands. "Something about a circus?"

"Oh, sure, that." Grace, who appeared to be scattered like the pieces of her napkin, seemed to pull herself together. She smiled vaguely. "The Big Apple Circus. It's a benefit for PEN. A bunch of authors making fools of ourselves in front of an audience. Should be a hoot, if I don't fall flat on my face. I'm doing a trapeze act."

"Sounds dangerous."

"There's a net." Grace shrugged. "Besides, in college I was on the gymnastics team. I was actually pretty good. The balance beam was my best event."

"Well, good luck." Nola heard the note of bitterness in her voice, and saw that it hadn't escaped Grace, either.

"I'll need it," she said, and added with a sigh, "Oh, Nola, I'm still not getting through to you, am I? Has *anything* I've said made the slightest bit of difference?"

After an awkward silence, Nola answered softly, "I understand where you're coming from. I just don't feel like going along for the ride."

Grace suddenly twisted around, fumbling for something in the large leather tote that was slung over the back of her chair. Pulling out a manuscript box, she thrust it at Nola. "Please," she whispered with tears in her eyes, "read it. It won't hurt you to at least *read* what I've written. You might change your mind."

Nola stood abruptly. "My mind is made up." But somehow she was taking the manuscript, grasping it with both hands as if it might somehow anchor her against the wave of vertigo engulfing her. "Excuse me, but I have to go. I'm sorry about lunch."

Grace reached out and grasped Nola's hand, pressing it between her child-sized palms a beat longer than a handshake. But she made no effort to stop her from leaving.

Nola, as she headed for the exit, stumbling a bit where the floor gave way to a slight incline, felt sick, as if she *had* eaten a huge lunch.

Had Grace sensed her holding back?

Had she guessed what it was that Nola couldn't bring herself to tell: a truth more shocking than any Grace could imagine?

An hour later, Nola sat with her boss at the large table in the conference room, her drawings spread out before them. She could see the surprise on his thin, rather pointed face as he studied them. Even knowing she'd won both the Carnegie

Prize and the coveted AIA award at Cooper Union could never have prepared him for this.

She felt a little incredulous, actually. A design as assured as this, with such ingenuity—it was like that fairy tale about the shoemaker's elves, a thing that seemed to have been magically drafted while she slept.

But Ken wasn't jumping up and down. . . . Damn, the man wasn't even *smiling*.

"It's nothing like what I had in mind," he said.

Her boss was blunt, and she admired that in him, even when it made her squirm. Right now, she was fighting to keep her butt nailed to the padded leather seat of her swivel chair. When he looked up at her, the puzzled expression in his close-set blue eyes, behind their tortoiseshell spectacles, was like sandpaper against her already raw nerves.

"If someone had left these on my desk, I never would have guessed they were yours," he went on. "Not your style."

Nola watched him shift his attention back to her drawings and stare intently at the vellum sheets, which seemed to her to float atop the highly polished rosewood conference table.

"Yeah, but do you *like* it?" Nola blurted. She had to know. Now. Before she snapped in two with the strain.

Ken looked up, as if surprised she'd have to ask. "I'd be crazy not to."

"Then it's yours." She swallowed hard against the excitement she could feel pushing its way up her throat. "I mean, not just the firm's. But you, personally."

"Well, sure, but there's no question you'd be getting a good deal of the credit. . . ."

"What I'm trying to say, Ken," she broke in, "is that I'd prefer my name not appear anywhere in connection with this design. If it *should* get selected—and I know that's a big if

—I'd work my tail off to get it finished. But I'd want to stay out of the spotlight." She pulled out the frayed clipping from yesterday's *Times* and extended it to him. "Maybe this will explain it."

Ken scanned the bit of paper, then looked back up at Nola with a bewildered frown.

"Ned Emory was my father," she told him. "My mother worked for Senator Truscott."

Ken scrubbed his narrow face—which had always made her think of an alert greyhound's—with a pale, hairless hand. "Okay, but I'm still not sure what you're getting at."

"Let's just say that it would be better if I weren't involved. It might look like favoritism. That, or just the opposite. Mrs. Truscott might not want any association with me. I'd probably remind her of something she'd rather not dwell on."

Ken rubbed his chin thoughtfully. "You may have a point. I know a few of the people on that committee, and they sure as hell wouldn't want to risk alienating Cordelia Truscott. Still . . ." He spread his hands in an outer-borough shrug, still the cop's son from Flushing. "I'll be honest with you, Nola. I like you. I like your work. And *this*"—he tapped the presentation drawing—"is fucking brilliant."

She allowed herself an instant to glow, and quickly asked, "But?"

"I'll have to run it by the guys. See what they think."

"When?"

"Hey, keep your shirt on. Tomorrow. I'll let you know soon as I can."

Nola fought back her impatience and said, "I guess I can wait that long."

Most of her life, she'd been putting a lid on her emotions; she ought to be used to it by now.

When she returned to her work station, Nola's gaze was

drawn to the shelf above her drafting table, to the boxed manuscript crammed between rolls of blueprints. Slowly, she reached up and pulled it down, its weight seeming to drag at her arms.

So much to tell . . .

She couldn't shake the awful certainty that Grace was not going to let up, that she would keep hammering and hammering until she got all the answers she needed.

Forgetting the elevation for Chang that she'd promised to have finished by the end of the day, for a moment forgetting even her own design that right now was making its way down the hall to the executive offices, Nola opened the box and began to read.

Chapter 5

. . . There's a story Eugene Truscott liked to tell, about how he helped Lyndon Johnson cattle-prod Congress into passing the Civil Rights Act. He let the President in on a little trick that had worked for him in the years when he was running for re-election: One day a week, between the hours of nine and ten in the morning, his Elmhurst office door stood open to local party loyalists and businessmen who wanted their photo taken with Representative Truscott, then House Majority Whip. Of course, every Democrat worth a lick of salt wanted his handshake with the big guy recorded for posterity and for his own political enhancement . . . and in this way, in the few minutes it took for the photographer to frame his shot, while the representative from Queens chatted amiably with his admirer, he gained more information and influence than he could have in days of stumping the campaign trail.

Johnson liked the idea, and wasted no time in instituting it. Every Monday, between the hours of nine and ten in the morning, the Oval Office stood open to members of the House and Senate who wanted their picture taken with the President. . . .

Grace stopped typing, and stared at the words glowing on the computer monitor in front of her. There was a tightness in the back of her neck, and behind her eyes. She felt as if she were slogging her way through wet cement. It shouldn't be like this, she thought. The hardest part was behind her—the endless research, then pushing herself through the first draft. The stage she was at now—going over her manuscript, rearranging paragraphs and sentences, weaving in bits of fresh new information—was a process she'd always enjoyed.

Why was she feeling so wound up?

Maybe because she'd been at it continuously since eight this morning, with only a slapped-together sandwich for lunch, gobbled at her keyboard. Time for a break, she told herself.

She saved the file she'd been working on and switched off the computer. But still the book wouldn't let go of her.

She thought about her lunch with Nola Emory, a week ago today. Something had been nagging at her ever since. Was it something Nola had said? Or what she *hadn't* said? Grace couldn't shake the feeling that Nola had been withholding something. . . .

But maybe she was just being paranoid. Lately, thanks to Hannah, her antennae had been tuned in to every word, every little gesture and facial expression that might mean the opposite of what it seemed.

Hannah. Thinking of her reminded Grace that, despite having done all her Christmas shopping early (just the *thought* of plowing through the post-Thanksgiving crush made her claustrophobic), she still hadn't found a gift for Hannah. Later this afternoon, after her Big Apple dress rehearsal, she and Lila and Chris were going shopping. Maybe Lila would come up with an idea for Hannah. Lila, in her own offbeat way, was great at knowing exactly the right thing for every occasion. Like the time Grace had broken her toe, and Lila had presented her with a single handknit sock.

Grace was heading toward the kitchen to make herself a cup of tea before Chris got home from school when the phone rang. She dashed back to pick it up in her office.

"Ms. Truscott? This is Mrs. Ellerby at St. Andrew's. I'm afraid there's a bit of a problem with Chris." Hearing the unfamiliar voice with its ring of authority, Grace collapsed into the chair in front of her desk.

"Did something happen to him? Is he all right?" She heard her own voice rising in concern. "He didn't . . . he's not in any kind of trouble, is he?"

Her thoughts flew back to that scare he'd given her shortly after she and Win had separated, not showing up after school for hours and hours while she frantically phoned every one of his friends and classmates—and then the call from the precinct house saying they were holding him for shoplifting. Torn between anger and relief that at least he was okay, she hadn't known whether to throttle him or to hug him.

"Nothing to get overly alarmed about," Mrs. Ellerby said quickly. "But I'd feel more comfortable if you would stop by the office so we could discuss this in person."

With a single stroke, Nola, her book, Hannah were all wiped away. Grabbing her coat and purse, and flying out the door, all she could think about was that Chris, her un-happy son, was once again in some kind of trouble.

With her blunt gray hair and plain scrubbed-looking face, Mrs. Ellerby reminded Grace of the nuns who'd taught her catechism at Our Lady of the Scapular: imperturbable, with a gaze that, though not unkind, had been sharpened by dec-ades of being on the lookout for gum chewers, slackers, and troublemakers. At the moment, she looked apologetic for having dragged Grace down here. But then she said, "Really, there's no need to panic. Not *yet,* anyway . . ."

Grace felt something in her gut downshift suddenly, like a four-wheel drive hitting a rocky stretch of road. She felt guilty somehow, as if *she* were the one being called on the carpet. And maybe it *was* partly her fault, whatever Chris was in trouble for.

She looked about the small, glass-walled office with its lumpy couch scattered with stuffed animals. On the wall above the desk, a corkboard message center was dotted with colored pushpins and crammed with children's bright-colored drawings, thank-you notes from mothers, Xeroxes and memos about faculty meetings, PTA events, upcoming field trips.

". . . a few of the eighth-graders get like this," Mrs. Ellerby was saying. "A bit early in the year for Chris to be chafing at the bit, but you never know. At any rate, there have been only two incidents." Grace watched the school counselor shuffle among the neat stacks of paper on her desk and pull out a manila folder from which she extracted two slightly crumpled notes scrawled on yellow lined notepaper. "Is this your handwriting, Ms. Truscott?"

The notes were identical. *Please excuse Chris for yesterday's absence. He wasn't feeling well.* They were signed, *Grace Truscott.*

Hot fury at Chris rose in her, shocking in its intensity. How *dare* he!

One teacher, on his last report card, had cheerfully described him as "uncooperative at times, but we're working on it!" She could deal with uncooperative. She *had* been dealing with it for months, years. But *this* . . .

She handed the notes back to Mrs. Ellerby.

"No," she said crisply, dismayed to see that her hand was trembling. "I didn't write these."

"I thought not." Mrs. Ellerby sighed. "Oh dear . . . and I'm afraid we can expect another one tomorrow morning as well."

"Then he's not in school today?" A pulse leaped in one temple.

"I would have called you sooner, but I was just now going through some of these files and it wasn't until I saw a release form with *your* signature on it that it dawned on me." Mrs. Ellerby reached over to pat her hand kindly. "There's no cause for any *real* worry. He's always gotten home on time, hasn't he? We can assume he will this time, too. He's probably just sneaked off to a movie, or one of those video parlors the boys, especially, can't seem to get enough of."

Grace tried to absorb Mrs. Ellerby's reassurances, but her mind was running in frantic circles. Suppose Chris hadn't gone to a movie, or some video parlor? In this city, with its muggers and drive-by shootings, he could be in danger, maybe even hurt.

She had to fight to keep from jumping up, racing off in search of her son. No, Mrs. Ellerby was right. He'd always come home before, and he would this time. But what then? The problem wouldn't be solved by her reading him the riot act.

Grace stared out at the now-empty corridor. "Miss Longacre's Third Grade Class," read the sign tacked on the wall above a collection of wildly colorful drawings. Pilgrims with their muskets, smiling turkeys, Native Americans bearing baskets of corn. Thanksgiving in just two weeks, a time when families reunited, when people who didn't see each other often and who might not have a whole lot in common joined hands around the table.

She thought of their being invited to spend Thanksgiving with Jack's brother in New Rochelle, and suddenly she wanted to cry. Aaron, the insurance broker, whose speech was peppered with Yiddish, with his collection of antique

Judaica that he liked to show off. And wide-hipped Dora, mother of their five bright-eyed, impossibly well-behaved children.

"What are you going to do?" Grace asked, feeling something close to hatred toward this kind-faced woman who had been the unfortunate messenger of today's bad news. She twisted at the straps on the canvas tote bag balanced across her blue-jeaned knees.

"Actually, I was hoping *you* might have a suggestion. If there's some kind of problem at home, I could recommend someone. I have several names, therapists I've referred students to in the past." Mrs. Ellerby leaned forward, dropping her voice. "All of this would be completely confidential, of course."

"Chris is already seeing someone," Grace told her. "He has been for two years now."

She felt a sinking despair, as if she'd followed all the road signs only to end up nowhere near where she wanted to be. Where should she turn now? To Win? He'd claim that Chris was a different kid around him: happy, outgoing, talkative. And it was *true,* damnit. She'd seen them together, how Chris's face lit up when his father walked into a room.

Dr. Shapiro? He was doing his best, judging from the sessions she'd participated in. Chris would at least *talk* to him . . . though Grace couldn't help feeling at times that it was like prying nails out of a board with nothing but your fingers.

"Well, then . . ." The counselor appeared at a loss.

Grace stood up. "I'll speak to Chris," she said, hoping she sounded confident, in control, when in fact she felt as if she were fishtailing all over the road. "I'll make sure this doesn't happen again."

No guarantee, they both knew that, but what else could she say?

The final bell rang, and as she made her way down the path that cut across the small lawn tucked between the school and St. Andrew's small quarry-stone chapel, Grace felt herself caught up in the stampede. Books and backpacks, pigtails and earrings, jeans and T-shirts emblazoned with rock stars' logos went hurtling past in a burst of laughing, shouting, shrieking cacophony. Instinctively, her head whipped about, searching for Chris.

But, of course, Chris wasn't there. Tears welled, and she felt her hands knotting into fists at her sides. On impulse, she stopped at a pay phone on the corner of Hudson and Christopher.

Grace went through a receptionist, a secretary, and a frustrating minute of being on hold before Jack picked up. "Grace!" His deep, hearty voice seemed to flood her like the cup of tea she'd missed having back home. "I was on the other line with London, but when I heard it was you—"

"Jack, I'm sorry to bother you at work," she broke in. "But something's come up." She told him about Chris.

She half-dreaded hearing him say, with a chuckle, something like, *Boys will be boys*. As Win would have. But she could almost see Jack wincing as he said, "Jesus, just what you need right now. Anything I can do to help?"

"I'm on my way home," she told him. "If he's not there . . ." She left her worst fears unspoken.

"Listen, I'll meet you at your place. Ten minutes, fifteen at the most if I can't snag a cab."

"Jack, you don't have t——" she started to tell him, but he'd already hung up.

How could she ever have doubted his love? Grace wondered as she hurried out to the sidewalk to catch a cab. Even with his blind spot about Hannah, maybe in some ways *because* of it, he was the most caring man she'd ever known.

She was climbing out of the taxi in front of her building

when she spotted him rounding the corner. He quickened his step, hurrying over to meet her.

"You didn't have to come," she told him, "but I'm glad you did."

He wrapped his arms around her, and she buried her face in the folds of his overcoat. Though he didn't appear out of breath from the two long and three short blocks he had to have run to get here so quickly, she could hear the muffled thudding of his heartbeat.

"Don't worry," he told her. "He'll be okay."

"Oh, Jack, I know there's no reason to think he won't be back. That's not what I'm afraid of. It's just . . . it feels like I'm losing him, like he's slipping away from me."

As she drew back, he brushed a stray hair from her cheek, his fingers warm despite the chill wind that was sending leaves scudding along the sidewalk where they stood. It was one of the things she loved best about Jack—he gave off a heat that was palpable, like one of those old-fashioned wood-burning stoves set in the corner of a drafty cabin.

"He'll grow out of it," Jack said. Then, as if realizing it was just the sort of glib reassurance she might have gotten from a magazine article, he added with a sigh, "But in the meantime it's tough, I know."

"At least Hannah doesn't play hooky."

"Sometimes I almost wish she would. Hannah takes everything so seriously."

"I wish I could believe Chris was out there having a grand old time. But, Jack, it's like he's trying to tell me something . . . only he doesn't know how. Is it my fault?"

"Chris is a good kid," Jack said, and from the thoughtful way he spoke she knew he meant it. "And you're a terrific mother. Don't be so hard on yourself."

Tears stung her eyes. "Thanks, I guess I needed to hear

you say that." She blinked, and smiled up at him. "But you could have told me over the phone."

"Isn't it better hearing it in person?"

She nodded. "Now I know why I fell for you."

"You mean it wasn't my suave charm and my sex appeal?" He grinned, his navy eyes crinkling.

"That, too."

"I'd ask you in," she told him, "but Chris should be turning up any minute, if he's not here already. I think I'd better handle this on my own."

At the same time, a part of her longed for Jack to say, *Grace, you've handled this on your own long enough. It's time someone else stepped in.*

If only Chris were her and Jack's son, then it would be natural for Jack to talk to Chris. And afterwards she and Jack would discuss it quietly in the bedroom, sharing their frustration, trying to come up with a solution.

But all Jack said was, "Good idea."

A wave of loneliness swept over Grace. She felt suddenly, and quite inexplicably, abandoned. But that was silly. Jack had rushed away from his desk to come to her aid—how many men would do that? What more could she reasonably expect? Anyway, Chris would sooner listen to a street-corner evangelist than take advice from Jack.

"We still on for dinner?" Jack asked.

She nodded distractedly.

"Why don't we meet after work at Balducci's, pick up a few things? Save you from having to try to cook," he added, looking devilish.

"Sounds good," she told him, trying to muster an enthusiasm she didn't feel. "I'll phone you when I get back from shopping with Lila."

Riding the elevator up to her floor, Grace, oddly, felt

worse than she had before Jack arrived to console her. But as she let herself into her loft, she was met by the throbbing beat of Chris's stereo. The wave of relief that crashed over her left her weak-kneed.

She found him in his room, lying on his bed with one arm flung over his eyes as if even the anemic glow from around the edges of the closed Levolors was too much light. Stepping over a crumpled heap of clothes, a slew of audio cassettes, a plate littered with sandwich crusts, she gave the volume knob on the stereo a hard wrench.

The noise ended with a dying squeal, and Chris bolted upright as if he'd been stuck with a pin. "Hey!"

Grace sat down on his bed, her ears ringing, anger making her heart thud. She opened her mouth to light into him; then something stopped her. As if she'd stepped outside of herself, and a kinder, wiser twin were taking over.

She took a deep breath.

"Chris," she said gently. "Let's go. Come on, get your jacket."

"Where?" His eyes narrowed.

"Out."

"Mom, I have *homework*," he protested.

She started to say something about how you only have *homework* when you've attended *school*, but she managed, just barely, to keep her mouth shut.

"I'll help you with it later on. Come on, it's a beautiful day out there, and it's just going to waste."

He looked at her like she'd lost her mind. "What about you? How come you're not working?"

Was that how Chris saw her? Always too busy to spend time with him? And now, with Jack, even more unavailable. Grace felt a swift jab, like a hypodermic needle piercing her. A syringe filled with something more powerful than any drug: the truth.

"I *am* working," she told him, attempting to drag his limp form off the bed. "If you don't call hauling a hundred and twenty pounds of dead weight work, I don't know what is."

Chris cracked a tiny smile. He swung his legs over the side of the mattress, and his sneakers landed with a thump on the scuffed floor beside the bed.

"Does this have something to do with Jack?" he asked, a suspicious look dawning on his pale, thin face.

"Jack who?"

"Mom, get real."

"I am. You're the only man I want to spend the afternoon with." He didn't have to be told that Jack was coming over for dinner tonight; that was still hours away.

"You're acting goofy. Where are we going?" It seemed to dawn on him that her unexpected behavior might have something to do with his cutting school, because she saw him flush suddenly, streaks of color shooting up from the collar of his rumpled blue jersey.

Grace took his limp hand in hers, and squeezed it. His gray-blue eyes regarded her with a new expression, one of wariness mingled with yearning.

"The circus," she told him.

Grace, poised on a narrow steel platform high above the circus ring, thought about the imprisoned writers in China they'd be raising money for at this benefit and wondered if it wouldn't have been wiser simply to give a large donation. But right now she was trembling so hard she couldn't have written a check if she'd tried.

Looking down, she could just make out the slim, athletic figure dropping into the seat next to Chris in the front row below. Even from this distance, she recognized the loose-limbed elegance with which he sat, the way the light shone against his thatch of golden hair. Win. What was *he* doing here? How had he even known about this dress rehearsal?

Her nervousness about her trapeze act faded as another kind of anxiety took hold. What did he want? And why, when he could have just picked up the phone to reach her, had he bothered to come uptown to Lincoln Center? On a weekday, no less, when he was always buried in meetings, court appearances, briefs, depositions, every billable minute crammed with work.

It had to be about Chris—Win planning to sweet-talk her into letting Chris spend Christmas with him.

She felt her breath coming in short bursts, her anger rising. Chris had spent *last* Christmas with his dad and grandparents in Macon. This year it was her turn. Of course he'd be *sorry,* he'd say he hadn't meant to spoil anything. Mr. Who-Me?-I'm-Completely-Innocent. So typical of him, never meaning any harm, never aware of when he *did* hurt people.

Like last May, when she'd told him she was getting Chris a skateboard for his birthday, and Win had gone out and bought him a damn *bicycle.* Of course, once he laid eyes on that Raleigh ten-speed, Chris hardly even *looked* at his skateboard.

To hell with Win, she thought.

Grace tore her gaze away from her ex-husband and tightened her grip on the trapeze bar. Win, Chris—everything dissolved as she took a deep breath and prepared to swing out, her heart hammering, the muscles in her arms and legs so tight they were almost cramping. Though she'd practiced this move dozens of times, she felt her armpits, her whole body, go sticky with panic. But she'd be damned if she'd let Win see how scared she felt.

She gave a little nod to Emilio, who stood poised on the opposite platform alongside his brother—the two of them, both so swarthy and hairy-chested, they might have been twins. Then she pushed off with the balls of her ballet-slippered feet.

It was as if she were being catapulted into the sun . . . blinding spotlights rushing at her, the net below a rippling meridian. At the highest point of the arc made by her swoop-ing body, she seemed to halt in mid-air, suspended motion-less for a single heart-stopping moment before Emilio, hanging by his knees from his trapeze bar, reached up to snare her ankles.

And then she was upside down and flying backward with only those hands, like steel manacles encircling her ankles, preventing her from plunging downward. Blood bucketed into her face with the suddenness of a slap, and she felt her spine contracting against the sharp yank of gravity, the ends of her hair whipping up to sting her cheeks. The dense, yeasty odor of animal dung and sawdust swelled up at her like an incoming tide.

Then a second pair of viselike hands caught hold of her and steadied her as she landed on the opposite platform.

Grace felt hot lights on the back of her neck, and looked down at the net suspended not more than a dozen feet above the ring. Would it really have supported her if she'd fallen? And what had made her think that the ease with which she'd tumbled and spun and flipped as a high-school and college gymnast would carry her through into middle age?

All at once, she *felt* every day of her thirty-seven years. Her knees buckled. Tiny white fireflies swarmed at the pe-riphery of her vision. She clutched Emilio's brother, Ramón, who seemed as relaxed as a cat.

"Much better that time," he told her. "Not so . . . like wood." He made a swift chopping gesture with his right hand, then smiled so brilliantly she could see the reflection of the spotlights twinkling on his perfect teeth.

She found her gaze wandering downward, looking to see if Win was still watching her.

He was. Stretched comfortably in the first row, an expensive calfskin loafer balanced atop his opposite knee, smiling as if the thought of anything bad happening was the furthest thing from his mind. That was Win. Phi Beta, crew captain at Harvard, top 10 percent at Columbia Law, partner at Horowith, Aikens & Fine after only five years. He *expected* good things to come his way, and he was seldom disappointed.

Maybe he *had* loved her, she thought. As much as he'd been capable of loving. And despite everything, she'd certainly loved him—blindly, naïvely, stupidly believing he would never hurt her.

But that was all ancient history, she told herself firmly.

A ladder plumbed straight down off the platform, and now Grace was backing down it, her feet easily finding the rungs. Below her, a crew of workmen was assembling some sort of elaborate seesaw, and the sounds of electric drills and hammering ricocheted in the vast, tented space. Out of the corner of her eye, she caught a glimpse of an older, heavyset man in a rumpled gray sweatsuit trying desperately to hold his balance atop a rolling seesaw. Norman Mailer? She turned and waved at him, relieved that she wasn't the only author crazy enough to go out on a limb for the sake of PEN.

Moments later, blessedly earthbound, she found the opening in the shallow wooden barrier that enclosed the ring, and made her way over to Win.

"Hey, what are you doing here?" she greeted him, feeling an odd, spiraling dizziness not unlike the vertigo she'd experienced up on the trapeze.

Her former husband rose to greet her, a tentative smile making him look hardly older than Chris himself—a fair-haired boy hoping to wrangle a special favor from his teacher. He even looked like a collegiate—gray worsted slacks, starched button-down shirt open at the collar, a Fair Isle vest of subtle, overlapping shades of blue.

"I spotted your name in the *Times* among the list of luminaries performing for the PEN benefit. When I called, someone told me about this dress rehearsal." He smiled. "I didn't want to miss the opportunity of seeing you in action."

"You mean, you're not here about Chris? I thought—" Then she looked around, discovering their son was nowhere in sight. "Where *is* Chris?"

"He said he wanted to have a peek backstage, but I think he was aiming to give us some time alone. Do you have a minute?" Win's voice, with its faint Southern overtones, soothed her like a remembered melody . . . and at the same time alarmed her, because it always seemed to promise more than she knew Win was capable of delivering.

She paused, just long enough to let him know his wish wasn't necessarily her command, then said, "Sure. Okay. Just let me throw something on."

"Here." He snatched up the charcoal cashmere blazer that had been folded over the arm of his seat, offering it to her with a little shrug no doubt meant to disarm her.

Grace hesitated, not wanting to take it. But wouldn't that make it seem as if she *cared?*

She put it on.

Custom-tailored to fit Win's six-foot frame, it came halfway down to her knees, and smelled endearingly of the Old Spice he'd worn since they were in college together. For some reason, she felt vaguely annoyed by his courtesy, and by the way his eyes kept stopping just north of her collarbone. Too much of a gentleman to gape at her next-to-nakedness, she supposed. Or had her body lost all its appeal as far as he was concerned?

Damn him. Weren't ex-husbands supposed to be bas-
tards? Well, sure, he was . . . only a well-bred one.

"Look, if this is about Christmas," she blurted, "I don't
think you should have made plans before talking to me."

"Chris told you that?" Win pushed a hand through his
hair—thick, ripely golden, as if he had spent all last summer
on a yacht.

Grace was swept with an odd sort of longing . . . only
she couldn't decide whether she wanted to be *with* Win, or
simply *be* him, eternally young and golden and charmed. So
effortlessly was he clearing the hurdle of this unexpected—
and uncalled-for—appearance that she found it hard to mind
the ease with which he was dodging her question now.

"Hey, I'm really sorry, Grace. It was nothing definite.
We just talked about it, that's all. I thought I'd made it clear
to him I'd have to speak with you first." He gave her that
ingratiatingly boyish half-smile that had once melted her
heart.

"I think he wanted to get back at me." She sighed, letting
her guard down an inch or so. "God only knows why. All I
do these days is look at him and I rub him the wrong way."

"I know what you mean," Win said with a wry laugh.

But, damnit, he *didn't* know. . . .

It was like when they were married, his being so cavalier
about their vows, as if the rules and conventions of others
didn't apply to him.

It all came rushing back to her. Two years ago, that writers' conference in New Orleans. She'd been so damned eager
to get home to Win and Chris, she'd grabbed an earlier flight
back to La Guardia, skipping the Paul Prudhomme faculty
banquet. Hadn't even thought to call Win, let him know she
was on her way. As she crawled along the Long Island Ex-
pressway in a cab with a caved-in seat, all she could think
of was how she needed to be with Win, and that all the

idiotic things they'd been arguing about lately—like his forever standing her up at the very last minute, claiming too
much work at the office and leaving her with an extra ticket,
or a canceled dinner reservation—weren't really so important. They'd work it out somehow, take a long vacation, get
counseling, something.

And then home, dashing up three flights rather than waiting for the elevator to appear, which, like everything about
their Central Park West prewar, was prone to breakdowns.
To someone else it would have seemed funny, like something
out of a Feydeau farce, her bursting in, breathless, calling
out, "Win! Chris! I'm home! Where is everybody?" . . . and
Win appearing at the door to their bedroom, ashen-faced,
frantically clutching his bathrobe about him, stammering a
strained greeting.

It took a moment to hit her. Even while she could see
quite clearly, through the partially open bedroom door, a
flurry of blond hair, white panties, clothes being thrown over
pale limbs, she remembered thinking quite calmly, *It's awfully early for him to be in bed, not quite nine. He must be
really wiped out from this Hashimoto case.* . . .

Then suddenly she thought: *Nancy.* There could be no
mistaking her, the woman she'd half-glimpsed through the
bedroom door. Her dear friend, Nancy Jerace, wife of Sam
Jerace—their next-door neighbor from way back when she
and Win had lived in that dreadful sixth-floor walk-up on
East Seventy-eighth. Nancy had been the matron of honor
at her wedding (much to Sissy's annoyance); Grace and Win
had been named godparents of Nancy and Sam's firstborn,
Jess. And every August since Chris's birth, they'd rented the
same beach house on Fire Island, sharing each other's kids,
washing each other's sandy clothes, taking turns riding their
bikes to the market. . . .

The pain had come crashing in. Fierce, pitiless, slamming

down on her head, her chest, so she had to grab hold of a table to keep from losing her balance. *Oh, God . . . oh God oh God . . .*

A cheap one-nighter, that she might have been able to forgive. A brief affair with one of the long-legged, narrow-hipped secretaries that seemed to populate Win's offices. But Nancy? All at once she'd been struck by the enormity of it, the intricacy, the lies piled one atop another, months', maybe even years' worth.

Things that had hardly seemed worth commenting on at the time suddenly clicked into place. The way Nancy, when talking to Win, would bring her hand to rest against his shoulder. How she always seemed to laugh loudest when it was Win telling a joke. And that dinner party when she'd made such a point of telling Grace not to dress up, and then had greeted them at the door in an amber silk sarong that perfectly matched her eyes, her strawberry-blond hair arranged in a topknot from which ringlets spilled down around her elegant long neck.

But it wasn't just Nancy. It had to have been Win, too. . . .

Grace was jerked from her reverie by the sudden flurry of a chicken as it rose, squawking, into the air while being pursued by a red-wigged clown. She took a deep breath, picturing a balloon being filled with calm, sweet air. She willed herself to remain perfectly civil—lighthearted, even.

"Poor Chris . . . He'd probably be happier with a mom who stayed home and baked cookies than one who's swinging on a trapeze," she said with a laugh.

"You were wonderful up there," Win told her. "Reminds me of those gymnastic meets you used to compete in back at Wellesley. You always made it look so easy."

"What I remember is a lot of twisted ankles and pulled muscles."

"Don't tell me you're not enjoying this," he said with a laugh. "I know you—you're not happy unless you're on the edge."

But she didn't want to talk about the old days with Win . . . or what would or wouldn't make her happy.

She glanced at her watch. "Look, Win, I'm in sort of a rush. I was going to throw something on; then Chris and I are meeting Lila. *Is* there something you needed to talk to me about?"

"Actually, there is." He motioned toward the pair of seats he and Chris had vacated. "Can we sit down? It'll only take a minute. It's about your mother."

"Mother?"

Grace abruptly sank down into the nearest seat, watching as a yellow plastic hoop that had escaped from one of the animal trainers rolled to a stop against the barrier in front of her. An author she recognized as Roger Young, Cadogan's best-selling techno-thriller writer, darted after the hoop and hooked it deftly with one finger. She remembered Jack telling her how imperiously demanding Young was, and how everyone at Cadogan—with the exception of Ben, his editor—hated dealing with him.

"I talked to her last week." Win's voice was soft. "Grace, she's really upset about this book. I've never heard her so . . . Well, it was the first time I've known her to let her guard down. Has she spoken to you about it?"

"Not exactly." Grace tried to remember what *had* been said the last time she'd spoken with her mother. "She told me about the drapes she was having the drawing room measured for . . . and—oh, yes—something about the hospital. Some new piece of radiology equipment for the children's wing at Hilldale she was all excited about."

"Nothing about the book?"

"That was the whole reason I *called*—to tell her what I

was doing, and why—but she just cut me off. Said it'd be nice if Daddy's own *daughter* would keep in mind that people read a book and they believe any sort of nonsense. And in case I needed to be reminded, bad taste was simply bad taste, whether it was in writing or otherwise."

"I see." Win looked a bit awkward—embarrassed, even. "Well, I'm afraid it may be more serious than she has let on to you. She asked for my advice . . . my *legal* advice. Grace, if you go ahead with this, your mother means to apply for an injunction to stop publication."

Grace felt suddenly disoriented. What was Win saying? He knew what had really happened with Daddy and Ned Emory. She'd *told* him, years ago, when they were first married. Could it be that Win had never believed her in the first place . . . and that Mother, over the years, had somehow convinced herself that the accident never took place?

"She *can't.*" Grace shot up from her seat.

"This is the United States, Grace." He took hold of her wrist and drew her back down, his fingers warm and oddly comforting. "Anyone can sue anyone for anything . . . and in this day and age, they generally do."

"Oh, God, I should have known." She pulled her knees up, slippered heels balanced on the edge of the chair.

"Frankly, I'm a little surprised you didn't consider your mother's feelings when you undertook this book." His words, though brutally direct, were softened by the gentleness of his tone.

"Never mind what I've written, she's never really forgiven me for who I *am.* The one thing I ever did *right* in her eyes was to marry you, and look how it turned out."

When they were getting divorced, her mother had been relentless. *Win loves you,* she'd reasoned. *He's assured me it was never serious with this woman.* Finally, Mother berating her, actually *scolding* her, as if she were some two-year-old throwing a tantrum. And Grace at last *had* lost her temper, shouting, saying maybe *she* ought to marry Win, if she thought he was so wonderful.

"I still don't think she was so wrong about us," Win said, his smile carrying more than a trace of wistfulness.

"You're on her side, I suppose." She searched his face for confirmation. "Win, this is crazy. You *know* I'm telling the truth."

"I know what you *believe* you saw." Win's slate-blue eyes were clear and maddeningly guileless.

"In other words, I imagined the whole thing," she said flatly.

"I didn't say that."

"You didn't have to."

Win sighed, and suddenly she *felt* nine years old again. "Grace, I didn't come here to argue with you. Honestly."

"What are you going to do?" she asked, hugging herself to stop the shiver she could feel spiraling up from her tailbone.

"Do? Nothing. I gave her the name of another attorney, of course."

"Why?"

Now he was looking surprised, and pained. "I'd say it's pretty obvious, wouldn't you?"

"Win, if you agreed to represent her, isn't there a good chance you could head her off at the pass, so to speak?" Grace felt her heartbeat slowing as she grappled her way toward a solution. "As far as she's concerned, *you* can do no wrong. You could convince her that a red light means go."

Win shook his head. "I don't want to see her hurt. I don't want to see either of you hurt by this."

If you cared so much about my feelings, wouldn't you have thought twice before jumping into bed with Nancy? Not just any woman, but *Nancy*. Her closest friend, to

whom she'd once confided, at a party when she'd had a bit
too much to drink, that she wasn't wearing any panties under her dress. Win liked it when she did that, Grace had
whispered. It made him hot, thinking of her that way.

Had Nancy been wearing panties that night? Grace
wondered.

And for Win . . . was it just the sex, or had he actually
loved Nancy?

Oh, Win . . .

Winston Conover Bishop. She'd met him at a Kappa Alpha mixer when they were both freshmen, she at Wellseley,
he at Harvard. Somehow, she hadn't been all that surprised
when she learned he'd grown up in Macon, just over the
mountain from Blessing—his was a name you'd expect to
stumble across on a tombstone in a Civil War–era graveyard.

They'd had everything in common—they both loved
Faulkner, loathed Nixon, and reveled in anything that involved the outdoors. Coincidentally, both their mothers had
been Chi Delt sisters at George Washington University. It
was almost as if they shared the same family tree, as well as
all the same traditions.

She thought of Christmases after they were married, how
every December they would drive up to Brewster, to a tree
farm where they would comb the aisles of spruces and firs
and pines planted in rows like corn, searching for the one
perfect tree. And the parties, that silly Santa Claus tie she'd
given Win that he actually wore; the annual caroling excur-
sion through their building, followed by Win's famous eggnog spiked with Amaretto. And Christmas Eve, when they
would bundle their sleepy son in his snowsuit for midnight
mass at St. Patrick's, kneeling beside Win in that glorious
space with the choir's music soaring about them, the weight
of their baby son warm against her chest. . . .

Stop this, she commanded herself. What was the point of dredging up the past?

"Look, I don't want this blown out of proportion any more than Mother does," Grace said, pulling herself back into the present. "It's just that she and I don't exactly agree on what to do about it."

"Come on, Grace. What you're doing may be perfectly ethical as journalism . . . but the fallout here won't be happening on some island out in the middle of the Pacific." He fixed her with that disconcerting gaze of his. "What I need to know, before I'll agree even to *consider* getting involved, is if you can honestly say to me this has nothing to do with your wanting to get back at your mother."

"For *what?* Do the two of you think I'm holding some kind of grudge against her? Win, it's nothing like that with Mother and me. We're just not . . . We don't see eye to eye on most things, that's all. But she's still my mother. I would never intentionally hurt her."

"She might need some convincing of that."

Grace could feel tears coming on. "You *are* on her side!" she cried, swiping at her nose with the heel of her palm.

"Grace, I'm sorry. I didn't meant to upset you." Win was offering her his handkerchief, but she shook her head violently, pushing his hand away.

She blinked, and saw a too-thin, concave-chested boy threading his way toward them through a thicket of chairs. From a distance, she might have been able to fool herself into believing he was someone else's son—the way he walked so carefully on the balls of his feet, as if he were afraid of making too much of an impact; the way he kept his head lowered so that his silky brown hair covered most of his face. Her heart caught.

"Chris!" she called out.

He ground to a halt a few feet short of her, his gaze flicking from her to Win, giving his normally closed face an odd alertness. He half-lifted his arm in a limp wave. "Hey, sorry if I kept you guys waiting."

"C'mere, buddy." Win rose and stepped forward. He looped an arm about Chris's shoulders, pulling him so close that Chris seemed to fold in on himself. Chris beamed up at him, and Grace felt her heart constrict with envy. Win grinned at him and said, "I hear you and your mom are going shopping."

Chris's smile faded. He looked down at his feet and mumbled, "Yeah, I guess so."

"Too bad. I was hoping you and I could catch a quick bite, then maybe an early movie."

Chris looked at Grace with mute appeal, and she couldn't help feeling manipulated, though it may not have been intentional. Now, once again, it had come down to a genteel tug-of-war between Win and her, with Chris in the middle.

"Mom . . ." Chris started to say.

"Hey, no problemo, some other time." Win stepped in quickly to rescue Grace from playing the heavy. "We still on for the weekend?"

"Sure, Dad."

"Better be. I got a tennis court all lined up for us." He swung an invisible racket. "Ready to slaughter your old man?"

Chris looked up, once again smiling at his father with an openness and acceptance that made her ache with jealous longing.

Where's my big guy? Win used to call out, returning home from work. And there would be five-year-old Chris hurtling at him like a small missile, smashing into him and wrapping both arms about Win's knees. After Win was assigned to the Pan Am bankruptcy and his hours became interminable, Chris would wait up for the sound of Win's key in the lock. Even now, it sometimes seemed as if Chris were lying in wait, holding an ear cocked for the snick of a door that wasn't going to open, the sound of a footfall that was passing through another doorway half a city away.

It wasn't Win's fault that Chris worshipped him. And Win was reasonable at least. She knew him well enough to predict that there wouldn't be a battle over her plans to spend Christmas in the Berkshires with Jack and Hannah.

"You'll call me?" she said to Win.

Win nodded. "As soon as I've spoken to your mother."

Grace felt herself tense. "What are you going to tell her?"

He paused, then said, "That, as her lawyer, I'd advise her to try and work this out with you before taking any kind of action."

"Win?" she said softly as he was turning to go. "Thanks."

"Hey, what are friends for?" His eyes were soft, full of regret . . . and something else. Yearning? She wondered briefly if his becoming involved in this thing with her mother would really be such a good idea after all.

Win was halfway toward the exit when she turned to her son. "Go on," she said, placing a hand between Chris's jutting shoulder blades and giving him a little push. "You know how Lila and I get, once we start yakking—you'd probably be bored stiff. Just tell your dad not to keep you *too* late."

She watched Chris run to catch up with his father, and Win delightedly sling an arm about their son's shoulders. Suddenly she was swept with an aching nostalgia for the days when they'd been a family, complete and untouched by all that had happened.

   She was surprised now to find a spark glowing in her chest where a moment ago there had been nothing but ashes, its heat pushing her to run, run fast, in any direction that would take her far away from Win.

Chapter 6

In the Juniors Department at Saks, as she and Lila made their way through a maze of acid-washed jeans and oversized sweatshirts and rhinestone-studded denim jackets, Grace thought, *It won't make any difference what I get Hannah. She'll hate it, and she'll hate me for trying to win her over.*

What do you get a sixteen-year-old Lizzie Borden for Hanukkah when you don't even *celebrate* Hanukkah? A set of Ginsu knives? A chain saw? A one-way ticket to Botswana?

"What do you think . . . the green or the blue?" Lila held up the same blouse in two colors.

"Honestly?" Grace asked.

"Hey, do I look like the kind of person who wants to be lied to? With the exception, of course, of guys who are terminally terrified of commitment but have to pretend they want to get married so they can sleep with me. If he's cute enough, I'd believe it if he told me the Pope was Jewish. So?"

Grace laughed. "In that case . . . neither."

Both colors clashed with Lila's nuclear-flash hair, all three inches of it, white-blond and standing up in moussed spikes all over her head. Lila's birth certificate might give her away as thirty-six, but in her black tights and cowboy boots, with her leather bomber jacket slung over a chartreuse silk bodysuit and black jersey miniskirt, she looked like someone who did all her shopping in Juniors. Only if you looked closely would you see the lines around her eyes and mouth, as nearly indetectable as the sprinkling of dog hairs that covered her from the neck down.

Lila Nyland, Punk Pet Groomer of the Stars. Grace smiled to herself, thinking of her best friend's Decoesque dog-grooming salon on Perry Street. Tall Tails had somehow become chic . . . lots of actors, musicians, and fashion people went there, partly, Grace suspected, because Lila cared a lot more about the dogs than who was at the other end of their leashes.

She'd seen Lila grab hold of a snarling Doberman, letting him know through the palms of her hands who was boss, then soothing him, sweet-talking him until he was licking her face, gentle as a lapdog. She had that effect on people, too—she'd jerk your chain while she was giving you the shirt off her back.

She'd first met Lila ten years ago, when she'd brought in her collie, Harley, to be groomed. Lila had noticed her sneezing, and seen how red and puffy her eyes were. "Hay fever," Grace had explained. Lila had shaken her head, *Uh-uh,* and pointed a finger at Harley. Lila, as it turned out, was right. She was allergic to *dogs.* And hadn't Lila proved to be an angel of mercy, keeping Harley with her, at no charge, until all the allergy tests had been run and the results were in? And then, when Grace was agonizing over what to do about the dog, it was Lila to the rescue once again, offering to adopt Harley, with generous visitation rights.

And now she was praying Lila could help her, not only in finding something that would be right for Hannah, but with the big picture—how she was going to sort out the jumble her life had become.

"What about for Hannah, then?" Lila wanted to know, waving the blouse in front of her.

"Oh, God, you've got to be kidding."

"What's wrong with it?"

"Nothing. If you like acid rain and toxic waste. Look, Lila, I think we're on the wrong track here. Bottom line, I doubt if Hannah would want *anything* that had my finger- prints on it."

"That bad, huh?"

"Get this. Last night, we're having dinner at Michael's, and just as the main course is being served, she bolts for the ladies' room. Doesn't come out until it's time for the check. What am I supposed to do, *apologize* for how I feel about her father?" Grace sighed. "This thing with Jack, I don't know whether I'm crazy in love . . . or just plain crazy."

"Come with me, let's try this on." Lila grabbed a differ- ent shirt off the rack, and steered her in the direction of the fitting room.

"But I don't . . ." she started to protest, then realized this was Lila's way of calling time out. And, after all, weren't fitting rooms the female equivalent of the confessional?

Suddenly Grace longed to unburden herself. Lila could be blunt and outspoken, but she had a good heart and more sense than most shrinks. And Grace felt so weary with going it alone.

"Did you know that more people commit suicide around Christmas than any other time of the year?" Lila observed when they were alone in the tiny Formica cubicle barely big enough for one.

"Thanks, now I *really* feel better." Grace squinted at her reflection in the mirror. "Speaking of which, do they *pur- posely* design these mirrors to make you want to jump off a bridge?"

"Yeah." Lila laughed. "There's some guy in Quality Control saying, 'Hey, Henry, not enough flab showing, send it back!' " She grabbed Grace's shoulders, hard, as if Grace were a stubborn terrier trying to wriggle from her grasp. "Now. What gives? I thought you were head over heels."

"I was. I am." She sighed. "It's complicated."

"Hannah, right?" Lila raised a plucked brow.

"Oh, Lila." She longed to sink right to the floor among the discarded tags and staples and bits of string. *Bless me, Father, for I have sinned. . . .*

But what sin? What had she done other than fall for a man who, like herself, came as a package deal?

Lila nodded knowingly. "What did you say to her the other night, after the dinner from hell?"

"What *could* I say? I wanted to strangle her. But I'm the adult, aren't I? I'm supposed to be reasonable, the one to make peace."

"Fuck that." Lila's words echoed in the small space, shocking her. "Look, Grace, *stop* with the Melanie Wilkes routine. Just be yourself. Give her what she's got coming."

"And what, exactly, is that?"

"A piece of your mind."

"I'd like to give her more than that." Grace, out of the corner of her eye, saw her reflection in the mirror. A small woman in a yellow knitted silk turtleneck, and chocolate stirrup pants, her cheeks striped with hectic color, her hand held up, palm out, as if she were about to slap someone. Instantly, she felt ashamed.

Here's another option, she told herself. *You could walk out of here, and go straight to the nearest phone booth. Call Jack, and cancel our plans for this evening. Thanksgiving and Christmas, too. In fact, cancel everything.*

Life would be so much simpler. No feeling bad about each other's kids. No hassles from Hannah and Chris about the time she and Jack spent together *away* from them. No worrying whether or not Jack would ever get around to making a commitment.

But the thought of mornings and evenings and weekends

without Jack hit her like icewater gulped down on an empty stomach.

"At least it'd be honest," she heard Lila saying, as if from a distance.

Grace looked at her. "Then Hannah would *really* hate me."

"Sounds like you couldn't do any worse than you already have. And when you and Jack get married—"

"He hasn't asked me," Grace cut her off. "And if he's smart, he won't."

"Grace, what are you so afraid of? Hannah's going to grow up and go away. So will Chris, one of these days. What else, that you'll *fight,* that he'll lay into you, that you'll lay into him? There's a name for it, kiddo. It's called *marriage.*"

"Hey, I've been there."

"Win?" Lila waved a hand dismissively. "You and Win never fought. That's like saying you went ice-skating without skates. Win just never saw the point. He didn't *get* it. You. It. Marriage."

"And Jack does?"

"I don't know. And neither will you, until he's put to the test." She gave Grace a sly look. "I *do* know that Jack is one of the best guys I've come across in this age of pinstripe Neanderthals, and if *you* don't take him I just may try and give him a spin."

Grace felt some of her misery begin to dissolve. It was hard to be depressed around Lila. She had so much damn enthusiasm for life. And for her fellow creatures, both the two-legged and four-legged kinds.

"Let's get out of this hamster cage," she told her friend. "I still have that present to buy."

"Boy, you really believe in doing your Christmas shopping early, don't you? Me, I always wait until the last possible moment. You ever want to see true insanity, try Macy's an hour before closing on Christmas Eve."

On their way down in an elevator crowded with women in minks, Lila muttered, "I'm having an allergic reaction to fur."

Grace turned to her, laughing. "You?"

"Oh, it's not what you think. It's this overwhelming urge to get down on all fours and snarl at anyone who happens to be wearing one. You know what I did this one time?" She picked a strand of what looked like collie hair from her jacket, and held it up for inspection, her elfin face lighting up with a slow, wicked smile. "I was passing one of those salons in the fur district, Twenty-eighth or Twenty-ninth Street, and I saw this woman trying on a full-length silver-fox coat. It looked awful on her . . . really hideous. And suddenly I couldn't bear the thought of those beautiful animals giving their lives for something so ugly that someone was going to spend a fortune on. So I—"

"Don't tell me," Grace broke in with a laugh. "You barged in there and strafed the joint with a can of spray paint."

"Better. I walked to a phone booth across the street . . . and I called her."

"You didn't!"

"I just asked for the lady trying on the fox. I could see through the window when the salesman handed her the phone. I told her that if she bought that coat she'd be making one of the biggest mistakes of her life."

"Didn't she want to know who you were?"

"Yeah. I told her, 'The voice of your conscience.' " Lila grinned. "She didn't buy the coat. I saw her sort of shove it at the salesman, and then she stalked out, all red-faced."

"You're evil, you know that?"

"I know, that's why we get along so well."

They got off at the main floor, emerging into a gaggle of grim-faced shoppers loaded down with Saks' signature crimson shopping bags. Moving through the accessories aisles, Lila was off and running with one of her Tall Tails stories, about some hotshot film producer who'd brought in this beautiful golden retriever with a bald spot on its rump that some vet had said would never grow in. The guy wanted to know if there was such a thing as hair transplants for dogs.

"I told him to buy a hamster and teach it to ride piggyback." She laughed at her own retort. Her voice husky, robust, and somehow sexy, Lila laughed the way Tanya Tucker sang. She didn't need mirrors—she saw her reflection in the people around her, everywhere she went, who turned to smile at her, wanting to be in on the joke, whatever it was.

Then they were edging their way through the crowds congregating at the cosmetics counters, ducking human mannequins armed with perfume atomizers. Finally, when they had pushed their way out onto Fifth Avenue, Grace shoved a couple of dollars into a Salvation Army bucket, half in gratitude for being allowed to flee the crowded store.

She felt even better after they'd looked at the spectacular store windows. This year's theme was *The Velveteen Rabbit*—the story of the stuffed rabbit that came to life because it was truly loved. Each display more enchanting than the next, with its exquisitely dressed mechanical figurines moving about in picture-book settings.

Grace had a sudden inspiration. A doll. What if she gave Hannah one of those wonderful handcrafted dolls like the ones her aunt Selma used to collect? More decoration than plaything, and not at all babyish. Probably wildly expensive, too, but so what?

"Come on," she said, grabbing Lila's arm. "I just thought of something."

"I hope it has to do with food. I'm starving."

"Afterwards. This is important."

"More important than a kosher hot dog with mustard and sauerkraut? You heard of a place where I can buy Manolo Blahnik shoes at half-price?"

"Manolo Blahnik? Forget it. Anyhow, I'm talking toys, not shoes." She started pulling Lila down the sidewalk.

At F A O Schwarz, it was even more crowded than Saks, but Grace hardly noticed. Bypassing a menagerie of giant stuffed animals corralled at one end of the main floor, they rode the escalator to the second floor, where they found the section featuring collectors' dolls. Row upon row, little princesses with porcelain faces and rosebud mouths, dressed in crinolines and leghorn hats and sausage curls. Victorian, Regency, turn of the century—every era's fashions.

"I think I'm going to be sick," Lila muttered.

Grace glared at her. *"You're* a big help."

"That's exactly right." Lila abruptly turned to face her, and Grace noticed for the first time the silver earring in the shape of a Keith Haring dog that dangled from her right ear, while an emerald stud twinkled in the other. "Grace, are you insane? This is a sixteen-year-old girl we're talking about here. When I was that age, if someone had given me a doll, she would have become an enemy for life. What exactly is it you're after—a meaningful relationship with your stepdaughter . . . or *Return of the Exorcist?*"

Grace felt her enthusiasm wither. Lila was right. What could she have been thinking?

She saw Lila glance over at a preschooler not three feet away, spread-eagled on the floor, flailing his arms and legs and screaming while his red-faced mother crouched over him, desperately trying to calm him. Lila accidentally-on-purpose brushed up against the mother, causing her to turn away, and at the same time she leveled an index finger at the kid, staring down it as if it were the barrel of a gun. He stopped screaming and gaped at her, his eyes wide, his mouth drooping open. The mother, who hadn't noticed Lila standing there, scooped him up, cooing, "You can have any stuffed animal you want, Thatcher. That's for being such a good boy, and doing what Mommy says."

"How did you do that?" Grace whispered in amazement.

Lila shrugged. "Dogs and kids. They're not so different. You've got to let them know who's boss. The minute they see a chink in your armor, they're at your throat. Like this thing with Hannah. The way I see it, you're giving her too much control. Letting her throw all the punches."

"You're saying I should hit her right back?"

"No, but you should stand up for yourself. She'll respect you all the more for it, believe me."

"I respect Sugar Ray Leonard. It doesn't mean I'd want to live with him." She stopped. "Hey, what are you doing?"

Lila had taken off her leather jacket with the brass studs in the shape of a musical staff; she was stuffing it into the shopping bag with the jeans and flannel shirt Grace had bought for Chris. The leather jacket she swore had been given to her years ago by none other than Bruce Springsteen himself, right off his back—supposedly out of gratitude for her having saved his then girlfriend's (or was it his sister's?) Labrador retriever.

"I'm saving your ass," Lila replied matter-of-factly. "Don't tell her it's from me. Say it came from the Boss. She can get down on her knees and kiss his CDs . . . but, whenever she puts it on, it's you she'll think of."

Grace stared at Lila, then started to laugh. Soon she was laughing so hard she was crying. She felt like that kid throwing the tantrum—she couldn't seem to help herself, even while she could see shoppers casting curious glances at her as they wandered past.

In the next moment, she found herself in Lila's arms. Lila

smelled a bit doggy, but it was a nice, comforting smell. Her friend gave her a quick, hard squeeze, and pushed her away.

"It's no big deal, okay?" Lila's voice was huskier than usual. "So I don't want to hear another word about it."

"Lila . . ."

"Shut up, and get moving. I didn't fuck Bruce, if that's what you're thinking."

"I never . . ." When she turned, she saw that Lila was grinning. Clearly, the subject was closed.

Grace carried the shopping bag as if it contained the Holy Grail. Hannah would flip when she saw the jacket. But it couldn't fix everything, could it?

Because, even if she could somehow win over Hannah, what if Jack stayed on the fence forever? She'd heard all the horror stories from her unmarried girlfriends—guys who were quite content to date them for years on end, until the woman finally threw in the towel.

But Jack wasn't like that, she told herself firmly. He loved her.

Oh, yeah? a voice inside her scoffed. *That's what you thought about Win.*

Balducci's, at ten past six, was a madhouse.

As Grace and Jack squeezed their way past rush-hour shoppers lined up at the deli counters, clutching their waiting-list numbers as if they were winning lottery tickets, Grace almost wished they'd opted for Campbell's soup and saltines. But, at the same time, the aromas were intoxicating—imported cheeses, huge coils of sausage, crocks of glistening olives, exotic coffees being ground. There were platters heaped with pasta salads, grilled vegetables, risotto, veal scallopini. And at the front of the store, bins of such out-of-season delicacies as fresh figs from Turkey, bright-red

Israeli tomatoes, peaches that looked as if they'd been plucked off a tree minutes before.

"Do you want to stand in line for cheese while I do the bread counter?" she asked Jack, who carried a shopping basket piled with produce and takeout containers as if it were a child's lunchbox.

Jack didn't look the least bit impatient or frazzled. He smiled at her, taking the package of fresh pasta she was holding and dropping it in the basket.

"At your service, madam," he teased. "Though, if it gets any more crowded, I think they're officially going to have to declare it a war zone."

She stood up on tiptoes to kiss him lightly on the lips. "Just in case you get captured behind enemy lines and I never see you again." Then she was off, sidling past a fat woman in a fur coat pushing a cart loaded to the brim.

Minutes later, carrying several loaves of bread and a bag of *pain au chocolat* for tomorrow morning, she caught up with Jack at the checkout counter, where she found him chatting animatedly with a white-haired man wearing a yarmulke.

Seeing Grace, Jack slipped an arm about her shoulders. "Grace, this is Lenny. Remember I told you about my cousin, Leonard? From Borough Park?"

"His *kosher* cousin." Lenny laughed, showing a mouthful of teeth too even and white to be anything but dentures. "I only come here for the fish, but don't tell my wife's family. To them, it's *trayf* just setting foot in a place that sells sausages." He rabbit-punched Jack's arm. "What about you— where you been keeping yourself? We didn't see you around the holidays like we used to. . . ."

"I've been kind of busy," Jack put in, his warm tone not quite enough to cover for the quick, assessing glance Lenny darted in Grace's direction.

"Yes, I can see." And that's not all Cousin Lenny was seeing, Grace thought.

From the look on his face, it was obvious he knew the whole story, chapter and verse. Older Jewish man becomes captivated by shiksa goddess. Jack wasn't so old, and she was no goddess, but nevertheless Grace felt herself flush in the too-warm press of shoppers pushing past them.

"Purim," Jack told him. "You get Devora to make some of that heavenly *hamantaschen* of hers and I'll be over. You won't even have to twist my arm."

"Hey, bring Grace here." Lenny cast her an indulgent smile. "You ever hear that expression 'the whole megillah'? In Borough Park is where you really get it."

Grace smiled, but she felt as if she were being subtly reminded of who she was—more to the point, who she was *not*. Jack, though, didn't seem to be getting it.

"You're on," he told Lenny, clasping his cousin's arm.

Then Lenny was saying, "But, hey, why wait till then? What are you two doing tomorrow night? We're having a few people over for dinner, and you'd be more than welcome."

Feeling all at once contrary, wanting to jolt this man out of his complacent view of her, Grace spoke up before Jack could say anything. "We'd love to, Lenny . . . but I'll be performing in the circus. A trapeze act," she added impishly.

Lenny, to his credit, managed to contain the shock he had to be feeling. *Not only a shiksa—one on a trapeze.* But, as soon as he'd had a chance to take it in, he let loose a hearty laugh. "Now, *that* would be something to see."

Lenny moved up in line to pay for his fish, and then he was waving to them as he shouldered his way outside. Watching him go, Grace felt strangely deflated. He'd made an effort to be nice, but she'd sensed this before, with Jack's brothers. To them, she would always be an outsider—someone who never quite fit in.

Did Jack see her that way?

"You don't have to say it," Jack said to her when they were in a cab on their way to her place. "I know what you're thinking."

Even though his tone was light, Grace could feel herself tensing. "Oh?"

"You're wondering how a guy as young as me could have a cousin as old as Lenny, right?"

She felt herself relax a bit even as the cab rattled its way up Sixth Avenue. "Oh, Jack."

"Actually, he's only six years older than I am." His expression grew serious. "And half deaf. He wears a hearing aid; did you notice? That could be me in a few years."

"Why even joke about a thing like that?" she scolded lightly. "Anyway, you could be as old as Methuselah and I wouldn't care."

"You don't know," he said softly. She could tell he was holding back, wanting to say more but clearly reluctant to do so.

"Jack, what is it?" she urged. "Is there something bothering you?"

He sighed heavily. "Oh, I don't know. I suppose I'm all worked up over this meeting I'm having tomorrow—with Roger Young and his agent."

"Roger? I saw him at today's dress rehearsal. He was practicing some sort of act." She knew about Roger Young's infamous temper tantrums and his outrageous demands. The one time they'd been introduced, at a party celebrating Cadogan's fiftieth anniversary, she'd found him charming . . . if a bit reptilian. But there was no getting away from the fact that he was Cadogan's best-selling fiction author.

"Lion-taming, I hope," Jack growled. "Preferably with a lion that's missed dinner and isn't in a very good mood."

Concerned, Grace asked, "Jack, he's not leaving you for another house, is he?"

"I almost wish he would." Jack's face, in the strobe glare of passing headlights, suddenly looked as old as he claimed to feel. "He got . . . rough with one of our female reps. Tried to rape her, she says, and I believe her. He's a real bastard. What I'd like to do is beat the living daylights out of him . . . but it's not that simple."

"What are you going to do?" she asked, feeling both alarmed and outraged in behalf of a woman she'd never even met.

"I don't know yet. I'll have to play it by ear. You can be sure of one thing, though," he added grimly. "He won't have a chance to pull something like this again, not while I can help it."

"Oh, Jack, I'm sorry. . . ." She reached up and wove her fingers through the hair that curled down over the back of his collar, feeling, as she never failed to, a little uplift of surprise at its soft, youthful springiness. "I guess I've been so caught up in my own problems I never thought to ask how things are with you."

A corner of his mouth twisted down in a half-smile. "I've had worse days." With his eyes on her, he added, "Anyway, from here on it can only get better."

Grace shoved aside the shopping bag that was wedged on the floor between them, and wrapped her arms around Jack, bringing her mouth up to meet his. To her, that was one of the most wonderful things about Manhattan—that you could kiss a man in the back seat of a cab, you could probably take all your clothes off and make love, and the driver wouldn't even blink . . . not unless you stiffed him his tip.

Jack's kiss was warm and soft, but not too soft. His lips parted slightly, their pressure teasingly light, and now his tongue was tracing her bottom lip with sweetly maddening gentleness, right where it was most tender. With his huge hand lightly cupping her chin, he pulled her closer, his kiss deepening.

She shivered, gripped by a sudden feverish heat. No matter what Jack's shortcomings might be—and right at this moment she couldn't think of one—he was a world-class kisser. Back in high school, when she and her friends had been silly enough to keep score of such things, she'd be kissing a guy and think, *A four, maybe four and half, definitely not a contender for the heavyweight title.* But with Jack, there had never been any question. He was simply the best.

"You'll never be too old for this," she murmured into his ear.

Snuggled against him as their cab bounced from one pothole to the next, she found herself remembering their first date, nearly six months ago. It had started as a business meeting. He'd joined her and her editor, Jerry Schiller, for drinks to help them hash out some of the problems with the project she'd been slaving over for the past two years. Somehow drinks had stretched into dinner, at which point Jerry had rushed off to catch a train. Then afterwards Jack had insisted on riding home in the cab with her to make sure she'd get to her door in one piece. She, who didn't think twice about jumping on the subway after midnight, had put her foot down.

"The last guy who tried to snatch my purse," she'd told him, "I chased for four blocks and knocked down with my umbrella. Maybe I ought to see you to *your* door."

"How do I know I'll be safe?" he'd teased.

"I guarantee you won't be." She remembered wearing that silly grin of hers until the cab came to a stop.

They had settled on his apartment instead. She hadn't really meant to go to bed with him that night. But, finding that he'd had no expectations of that kind—he hadn't tidied up, and was so nervous he forgot to put a filter in the coffee maker and ended up with grounds and steaming brown water all over the countertop—she was charmed and ridiculously attracted to him, and felt herself seduced with breathtaking suddenness.

And, in the end, glad of it. Because with Jack she had recovered something she thought she'd lost forever, the wonderful feeling of waking up in the morning with a loving, lovable man curled beside you.

"What time is Chris getting home?" he asked her now, his lips grazing her ear, bringing a trickle of warm breath.

"Probably not until late—Win's taking him to a movie after dinner. Why? Did you have something in mind?"

Jack grinned wickedly, and kissed her again, his mouth tasting of the still-warm rye loaf he'd torn the end off of while in line at Balducci's. Making her hungrier than all the wonderful scents drifting up from the shopping bags at their feet.

In Jack's arms, she felt the emotional roller coaster she'd been on all day roll to a stop. She could relax now; she was safe. Later, he would wrap her up, his whole body engulfing hers, and she would not feel even the tiniest bit afraid or worried, as she often did when they made love, that by this time next year, or even next month, she'd once again be spending her nights in an empty bed.

Chapter 7

"Enough." Jack was careful to keep his tone mild, but inside he was seething.

Roger Young, hunched forward on the very edge of the deep-buttoned armchair across from Jack, merely glowered at him. The author's eyes, which appeared soulful in his publicity photo, were, in person, ringed with a liverish pigment that made them look sunken and shifty. Jack suddenly realized why photographers always shot Roger from above, leaving the lower half of his face half in shadow: the man had no chin.

"*Numbers,*" said Terrence Rait, Young's agent, a fidgety little man with a bow tie and pretentious goatee, his chair pulled aggressively a few feet ahead of his client's like a stock car gunning at the starting line. "We're talking *numbers,* the wholesalers going crazy with orders on this book, TV appearances lined up coast to coast, and you're gonna pull the plug on it?" His thin face was flushed. "I don't believe this. I fucking don't *believe* this."

Jack wasn't sure he did, either. It felt almost surreal, having this conversation with the company's biggest novelist, a guy who churned out page-turning thrillers, one a year like clockwork, and for whom it wasn't uncommon to have books simultaneously on the hardcover and paperback bestseller lists. His last book, *Operation Crimson,* had sold more copies than the rest of their whole fall list combined. Seven hundred thousand in hardcover, and they'd do twice as many in paperback.

Kurt Reinhold, when he heard about this meeting, would have his balls bronzed and made into bookends, Jack thought. Now that *he* no longer had carte blanche, Hauptman, their new German parent, could yank the plug on him in a moment. And now there wasn't much to stop them. Cadogan's gross was down 10 percent from last year, and here he was risking their cash cow. Sure, Young was under contract for one more book . . . but after this showdown, his ego would probably demand that he go with another house on his next project.

And Ben? Young was *his* author, the kid's ticket to an executive office somewhere down the line. He'd be upset. No, more, he'd be pissed as hell.

Jack could feel his heart thudding, a taste like burnt toast in his mouth. His eye fell on his favorite of the four Fuseli prints over the sofa—a heroically drawn scene from *Macbeth.*

If thou speakest false, thou shalt hang alive upon the next tree. . . .

It'll be my hide hung out to dry, he thought, but somebody has to stand up, draw the line.

If *numbers* were everything, if his life's work, all the marvelous books he'd helped give birth to, if that's all they amounted to, then he might as well throw in the towel right now. Ignoring this would make him almost as bad as Roger—a silent partner, the driver of the getaway car.

But, at the same time, Jack was hoping—no, *praying*—he could come up with some way to keep from altogether alienating this creep. Without Roger, Cadogan would be crippled, and his own future would probably take its cue from the jacket illustration on Roger's current book: a nuclear missile rising up from its silo, soon to blast the world into extinction.

Jack, feeling himself beginning to sweat under his suit,

made a conscious effort to relax his posture, and loosen the muscles in his jaw. *Stay on top of this,* he willed himself. *They've got you by the balls, but they don't have to know that.*

He was relieved to note that Roger, beneath his mask of indignation, seemed the tiniest bit nervous. Jack watched him light a cigarette, sucking in deeply and sending a stream of smoke Jack's way while his gaze slid off toward a point-of-sale display for *Operation Crimson* standing between two crammed bookshelves.

"Look here, Gold . . . who are *you* to tell me when enough is enough?" Roger leaned forward, his shoulders hunched up around his ears, making Jack think of a comedian doing a bad impression of Richard Nixon. "You wanted this bloody tour, and you're bloody well going to get it!" His Oxbridge accent was dissolving into something that sounded suspiciously Liverpudlian.

"Look, neither of us needs reminding of what's at stake in terms of potential sales here, but this . . ." Jack spoke quietly, bringing his hands up and folding them over his chest, thumbs bracketing his flowered Liberty tie—a touch of whimsy, courtesy of Grace. "Your last tour, I dealt with the complaints I got from the female reps and media escorts, about how you came on to them. I even turned a blind eye to the hookers you charged on your hotel bills. About ground the enamel off my teeth, but I figured, Hey, he's not really hurting anyone, is he?"

"Oh, stop with the Billy Graham, will you? You wouldn't be sitting here if it weren't for Roger," sneered Young's agent. Rait, quietly referred to by publishers as "The Rat." He was always trying to pull a fast one, bringing in a higher offer from someone else after a deal had already been agreed upon, manufacturing a phony bidder or two to goose up the price in an auction, sneaking manuscripts all over town regardless of the option clause. Now Rait was railing, "You did over seven hundred thou with *Operation Crimson,* close to two *million* in paper. Do you have another author who even approaches those numbers? Can you look me in the eye and say you don't owe your fucking *job* to Roger here?"

"He's very important to us," Jack said.

"Then what the *hell* are we doing here?"

"Discussing how best to handle the fact that Roger will not be completing this tour as we originally planned it." Jack held Rait's indignant gaze. He felt sweat pasting his shirt to his shoulder blades.

Meshugge, a cold voice inside him admonished. *Twenty years working your ass off to become somebody, build a company, publish books people love, and you're going to throw it all away? For what? To be holier-than-thou? For some . . .* principle?

What if he were to back off, change his tack? How much easier and smoother it would be just to go along, make believe no real harm had been done, no one had really been hurt. He was a businessman, not a moral arbiter. And Roger Young was the guy with his hand on the tiller, not Jack Gold or even their new chairman, Kurt Reinhold.

Then Jack remembered something he'd read somewhere. *You must think like a hero merely to behave like a decent human being.* But did whoever had come up with that realize that the hardest word in the English language, any language, had to be "no"?

Jack turned his gaze to Rait, watching him twist in his chair, as if he were being held there against his will. "You oughta be kissing the ground Roger walks on that he's even *willing* to do a fucking tour!" Rait snarled.

"Well, if it's such a chore, cutting it short now shouldn't

be such a hardship." But what Rait was saying was true. Celebrity authors like Roger usually had to be *begged* to do publicity tours.

"You arrogant son of a bitch, I'll . . ." Young's face contorted—no, seemed to swell—all red and swollen and shiny, like a baby's, Jack thought. A baby having a temper tantrum. Young lunged to his feet in an oddly disjointed way, his movements jerky, almost spastic. "I could have any publisher in town, just by snapping my fingers. *Who the FUCK do you think you are?*"

"Roger, I don't want to upset you any more than you already are, but do you realize it's a miracle you weren't arrested?" Jack went on in as reasonable a tone as he could muster, tensing against a sudden cramping sensation in his belly. "If Sue McCoy had decided to press charges . . ."

Rait turned to his client, cupping the air in front of him with both hands as if conducting an orchestra, quieting its crashing cymbals.

"Let's see if I've got this straight," he began. "You send Roger out with this . . . this *bimbo* who claims . . ."

"That he tried to rape her," Jack finished, for once not mincing words or bothering to hide his disgust. "This bimbo, as you put it, is a married woman with four children. She's one of our best reps. The accounts love her, we love her, and she gets high marks from our authors. But you, Roger, have put her through hell." Jack drew in a breath. "She still *might* decide to press charges, you know."

A new expression was taking shape on Young's chinless face: fear.

"No, no, you don't understand. . . . I . . . she . . ." he sputtered.

Even Rait seemed to deflate, as *that* reality sank in. "Christ, this . . . this is *suicide*. You've already sunk hundreds of thousands into this book. All those ads. *People* magazine. The book signings they're going to be lining up around the block for."

Jack felt a glimmer of triumph, and the cramping in his gut eased a little. "You don't think I've gone over the figures twenty times?" he said, allowing a note of regret to creep into his voice. "Look, sit down, and let's see if maybe we can work something out."

After a tense eternity, Jack watched the chinless wonder sink down in his chair. Jack sensed he was close to some sort of victory—but the prospect didn't excite him; it only left him feeling a bit sick with himself for having to negotiate with this prick.

"What I was thinking of as an alternative is a satellite tour," he went on softly, as if they were all completely calm and in perfect accord. "A day, two at the most, and we can have you on radio and television from coast to coast. And the print interviews, too—we can arrange for virtually all of them here in New York, if not in person, then by phone. No hanging around in airports for delayed planes, no lousy room-service meals. And by next weekend, you can be in Westport or Mustique or Antibes."

Awaiting Roger's response, Jack realized he was holding his breath. He eased the air from his lungs, slowly, to keep them from noticing.

He watched Young grind out his cigarette in the ashtray that had been a promotional giveaway for last spring's big self-help book. *Quit While You're Not Dead*, the gold wraparound lettering read. Then the novelist leaned back, folding his arms petulantly across his chest. "I never wanted a bloody pub tour in the first place. *You* were the one who asked me."

He was backing down! Jack fought to hold back a grin of relief.

Rait looked up from the paper clip he was bending as if he wished it were Jack's arm. "Listen, Jack, can you promise us that no . . . uh . . . *negative* publicity will get out?"

"I can't promise you anything," Jack said. He paused, and added, "But it wouldn't hurt for Roger to speak with the lady in question. Maybe even apologize." He cut a quick glance at Roger.

A few minutes later, as he saw Young and his agent out the door amid handshakes and conciliatory words that fooled no one, a line from *Measure for Measure* popped into Jack's head: *Which is the wiser here? Justice or Iniquity?* Either way, he thought, his heartbeat slowing to a steady march as he went over the meeting in his mind, he didn't regret a bit of it.

What he *did* regret was what he'd have to do now: tell Ben before it leaked out that there was a strong possibility Young would leave after his next book.

Ben would be livid. He smiled a lot, and appeared as easygoing as Hannah was temperamental, but underneath . . .

The divorce? Maybe, but it went back even further than that, Jack guessed, back to when he'd been struggling to build up Cadogan and was hardly ever home with Natalie and little Ben.

Then, eight years ago, Ben had come to work for him, fresh out of college and full of himself. Jack had knocked him down a peg or two by giving him a job in the mailroom . . . and Ben had *really* begun to resent his old man. All those extra hours, along with every manuscript Ben had begged from overworked editors with which to hone his editing skills and prove his worth, had been Ben's way of saying, *Damn you, I'll show you if it kills me.* Now this sleaze, Young, was going to give Ben yet another reason to carry a chip on his shoulder. . . .

Dread lay in Jack's stomach as he picked up the phone to buzz Ben's extension.

"Got a minute, Jack?"

Jack looked up to see Kurt Reinhold striding into his office. A short, wiry man with graying hair that seemed to stand on end no matter how expensive his haircut, Cadogan's new CEO reminded Jack of a cartoon of someone with his finger in a light socket—bug eyes and all. Except it was never Reinhold who got burned, he thought. Only those around him—especially the ones who got in his way.

Jack tried, as always when dealing with Reinhold, to reconcile his boss's public image with what Jack knew of his private life. The two didn't seem to mesh. Reinhold the CEO, with his in-your-face approach to management, his insistence on doing things *his* way, his habit of walking out of a meeting and leaving you hanging in mid-sentence . . . and Reinhold the family man, married thirty years, with five kids he never seemed too busy for (even with his constant jetting back and forth to London, Frankfurt, Rome, Paris), not to mention a hobby he was rumored to be passionate about: baking bread from recipes he collected on his travels.

Jack lowered the phone receiver and motioned to Reinhold to have a seat.

But the Chief merely strode over to the window and looked down on lower Fifth like a feudal lord upon his fiefdom. "I wanted to go over something with you—this business with Jerry Schiller."

"What business is that, Kurt?" asked Jack, though he sensed from the way his heart rate had begun to pick up again that it was serious.

Kurt turned around, his pale, protruding blue eyes fixing Jack with a chilly stare. "Jerry is dead wood, Jack. He's got to go."

Jack felt a sudden ache in his chest. Jesus, no, not Jerry
—he'd been Cadogan's editor-in-chief since the Ice Age. Old
Jerry, who more than once had come to Jack for a hundred
bucks or so to tide him over after loaning his own paycheck,
giving it away really, to some old-buddy author whose manuscript was never going to get accepted. Jerry, who fought
tooth and nail to keep them publishing poetry . . .

"Last year, Jerry had two of his authors—Maisie Wes-
ton and Bob Gottschalk—nominated for National Book
Awards," Jack pointed out, careful to keep his tone neutral.

"And if the two of them put together sold ten thousand
copies, I'd be surprised," Reinhold countered. "Besides
which, that Princess Di bio, that was exclusively his
screw-up."

"The board backed him up on that," Jack reminded him.

Reinhold impatiently brushed a speck of lint from the
lapel of his dark-blue cashmere suit. Jack had a sudden image of his boss with his sleeves rolled up, pounding the hell
out of a lump of bread dough.

"Jack, I know you and Jerry go way back"—he left
hanging in mid-air the allusion that Jack himself might very
well be in the same league as Jerry—"but he's pushed it too
far this time. Have you seen this?" Jack became aware now
that Reinhold was holding something—a rolled-up copy of
Publishers Weekly, as it turned out. He smacked it down on
Jack's cluttered desktop. "Without saying a word to me, he
did a piece for the 'My Say' column. A diatribe on behalf of
literary authors who supposedly get shafted by their publishers in favor of pot-boilers." Darkly, he added, "No mention of editors who bite the hand that feeds them."

"Kurt, nobody is going to pay any attention—"

"I just hope Hauptman doesn't see this—you know what
a stickler he is for company loyalty.

"If it's a question of loyalty, I couldn't name anyone here who would stick his neck out for Cadogan the way Jerry has."

"He's got to go, Jack," Reinhold told him. "And it's your job to take care of it." In a single stroke, the man had managed both to remind him that he, as publisher, occupied a mere third place in the chain of command . . . and that at the *same* time *he* was responsible for nearly everything that went wrong.

Jack felt as he had a minute ago with Young and Rait, as if he were in the midst of a bad dream. Yet there was nothing murky or dreamlike about Reinhold's unspoken message: *You could be next.*

Reinhold was still blaming him, Jack knew, for their fulfillment disasters, despite his having gone on record that the new warehouse and its systems were still not ready to ship the fall list. And when Reinhold found out about his showdown with Young . . .

Jack suppressed a shudder. No, he couldn't, *wouldn't,* let himself be bullied. "You're forgetting one thing, Kurt. Jerry is Grace's editor," Jack reminded him. "And this book of hers—it's going to be big. Look at the publicity it's already gotten. The accounts are jumping up and down. We're looking at huge orders here, and I don't think we want to jinx this by firing Jerry before we've even gone to press." He wouldn't mention to Kurt what Grace had told him, about her mother possibly suing the company to stop publication. He'd cross that bridge when—or *if*—he came to it.

Meanwhile, he'd show Reinhold that *this* old publisher (not that fifty-two was exactly antique) was not going to fade away. He'd goddamn *mobilize* the place, put everything Cadogan had behind Grace's book—a twelve-city tour, maybe even a press-conference launch on Capitol Hill. The buzz was already humming all over the country. *Honor Above All* could become *the* book everyone had to have, if not to read, at least to *own*. Look at *A Brief History of Time, The Naked Ape*. Purely from a business sense, aside from Jack's personal feelings about Grace, there could be no question, even in Reinhold's mind, of the huge potential here just waiting to be tapped. . . .

Jack brought his attention back to Reinhold. The man had not relaxed his steely gaze, but Jack could sense him relenting a bit. Still, he wasn't going to make this easy. Echoing Jack's own thoughts with uncanny precision, he asked, "What about the possible repercussions on the book's so-called murder angle? You thought about having this reviewed by outside counsel? Making sure our ass is covered?"

"Dan Haggerty's on top of it," he told his boss, hefting a malachite paperweight in the shape of a pyramid. "He's consulting with Fred Queller—best trial lawyer on the East Coast, Dan says. Far as I can see, we're okay, but if it turns out we need to take extra precautions, I'll let you know. I'll keep my eye on Jerry, too, make sure he stays out of trouble." He prayed Reinhold would let it go at that—that he wouldn't force the issue of Jerry. Later, when the embarrassment Jerry had caused him with that *Publishers Weekly* piece had faded from Reinhold's mind, he'd remind him again of what an asset Jerry was to the company.

He breathed a sigh of relief when Reinhold, as abruptly as he'd appeared, strode toward the door with the distracted air of a man who had a million agendas and never enough time.

Jack put the paperweight down, and rose heavily to his feet. He'd have to warn Jerry, tell him to keep a low profile, at least until *Honor Above All* came out. After that, if all went well, they'd both be home free.

On his way down to Jerry's office, Jack ran into Ben as he was heading out through the double doors to the art department.

"Bud Eastman's up to here with that Yugoslavian artist doing the Harrigan cover." Ben held a hand to his throat, palm down. "I got called in to help smooth things over."

"Any luck?"

"He'll make the changes Eastman wants, don't worry."

Jack raised an eyebrow. Misha was a tough cookie.

Ben grinned. "He has a show at the Pace Gallery, and I promised I'd go have a look, bring some of Mom's rich friends who collect East European art."

Jack clapped Ben's shoulder, feeling a glow of pride in his son's ability at managing tricky situations like this one. At the same time, it triggered the memory of that unpleasant incident some years ago, when his son was a freshman at Yale. Ben had been caught selling textbooks and supplies at a discount to his fellow students—stuff he'd charged to his account at the campus bookstore, assuming his father wouldn't look too closely at the bill. The worst part was that Ben had to have known he'd eventually get caught, and yet he'd run his little operation with a careless conceit that still staggered Jack whenever he thought about it. Even when he *had* been caught, Ben had been unrepentant, as if the generous allowance he considered meager had left him no choice.

It had been the one and only time in Ben's life that Jack had hit him. Not hard—a single slap across his smirking face. But apparently it had been enough to fan the glowing embers of Ben's resentment.

Was there a way to get through to his son, get him to see that life wasn't always a matter of grabbing hold of whatever you could get your hands on? His plan of having Ben work his way up from the bottom at Cadogan had misfired—instead of appreciating the value of hard work and patience, Ben had merely pegged him as a Simon Legree. But maybe it still wasn't too late. . . .

"Got a minute to step out for a cup of coffee?" Jack asked lightly.

Only Ben's father would have caught it: the slight frown, no deeper than a dimple, between Ben's thick dark brows. Then it was gone. "Sure, Dad. Just give me a sec, I'll tell Lisa."

"Meet you by the elevator."

Ben reappeared in the hallway outside the paneled mahogany doors with the name "Hauptman Group" on a discreet brass plate placed at eye level. He looked puzzled. "Lisa said Roger stopped by my office while I was in with Eastman. I didn't know he was going to be here. If there was some kind of meeting, why wasn't I told?"

Jack, who'd been hoping to forestall this until they were out of the building, braced himself as he stepped into the elevator. Why, with Ben, did everything have to be a battle?

But then a voice reminded him, *You weren't the one who fished Young out of the slush pile, who spent months of endless nights and weekends, helping him shape those elephantine, inchoate manuscripts of his into something commercial.* Only two years out of college, Ben had sold a reluctant board on offering for Young's first book. Luck, Jack had heard some of them grouse after it hit the list. Riding in with a trend, others grumbled. But it was clear Ben had an eye, a gut instinct, for what the public wanted. And the skill of a gem-cutter when it came to shaping a raw lump into something that glittered.

As they creaked down seven floors in the empty elevator, Jack briefly told Ben what had happened. "I spoke with Sue McCoy yesterday afternoon," he finished. "She came in to see me, looking like hell. The thing with Roger—it happened over a week ago, but she hadn't wanted to say anything. I give her a lot of credit for speaking out, knowing her job might be on the line . . . hell, the whole company, for that matter."

Stepping out into the marble-lined lobby, Ben looked as if he'd been kicked in the balls. His face the high, angry color of a rash, his eyes glittering like chips of broken bottle glass.

"Jesus, Dad," Ben swore. "Jesus Christ."

As if too stunned to say any more, Ben merely shook his head while they pushed their way out through the revolving door. They were met by a gust of autumn wind whirling down lower Fifth, which seemed to blow with it a honking, screeching, belching stream of cars, buses, trucks, taxis, and messengers on bikes and rollerblades. The Flatiron District, where nothing stood still. Even the sidewalk was jammed, everyone head-down intent on navigating the sidewalk in front of him. The one building in Manhattan marvelously shaped like a giant pie wedge, and no one was giving it even a glance.

Jack waited for his son to say something, but as they crossed Fifth and ducked into Andrew's Coffee Shop—good for a sandwich on the odd day when he wasn't lunching with some agent or author at the Gotham or Union Square Cafe —Ben remained silent.

Finally, seated in a booth near the back, Ben exploded. "How *could* you? Look, I'm as shocked as you are over what Roger did. But why the hell didn't you come to me first? He's my author, damnit!"

"That's *why* I didn't call you into the meeting. I didn't want your relationship with him to be affected."

"As in 'good cop, bad cop'? Roger beefs to me, and I pat him on the back and tell him I know just how he feels?"

"I wouldn't have put it exactly that way."

"You could at least have had the courtesy to let *me* decide how to play it. You had no right going behind my back like a . . . *Jesus*." He slammed his fist against the table as if he wished it were his father's face.

"I'm sorry." Jack was careful in the way he said it, so Ben would understand he *was* sorry, but only for what this would mean to Ben.

"Not as sorry as *I'll* be. Or Reinhold, when he hears about this." Ben kept his voice low as a waitress too old to be working all day on her feet filled their cups.

Despite his almost aching need to charge in, fill this bruised moment with explanations, assurances, Jack felt a dart of anger. Ben, once again, was only thinking of himself.

"It had to be done," he said simply.

He watched Ben sip his coffee, wince, put his mug down, hard enough for some of the steaming liquid to slosh over the brim. Ben took his napkin and mopped it up. In that moment, in the way he so carefully folded the sodden napkin and tucked it out of sight under his saucer, Jack caught a glimpse of Natalie.

"Speaking of Reinhold," Ben said, "he wants to fire Jerry Schiller. . . . Did you know that?" Ben stared at him, his jaw thrust forward. His pale skin, under the diner's fluorescents, held a faint violet tinge. Natalie's skin, he thought, wincing at the memory of his ex-wife's pride in what she considered to be her patrician looks, how she'd preen when some dope would tell her, "Oh, but you don't look a bit Jewish!"

Wasn't this just like Natalie, too, changing the subject just when things were heating up? Jack was annoyed, too, that the rumors had somehow gotten around the office before he could talk to Jerry himself.

"I'm aware of Kurt's reservations," Jack said carefully. "But I think I managed to convince him that firing Jerry would be a mistake."

"Why a mistake? He's dead wood, and everybody knows it."

The way Ben parroted Reinhold's own dismissive words about Jerry made something click in Jack's head. Could it have been *Ben* who'd instigated this whole thing? Maybe even going so far as to bring that *Publishers Weekly* piece to Reinhold's attention?

"You're after Jerry's job," Jack said, marveling at his own blindness in not catching on sooner. "That's what this is all about, isn't it?"

"Who wouldn't be? Anyone in my place would be a fool to turn it down," he said noncommittally.

What he was seeing in Benjamin's face now, Jack didn't like. A look that was almost . . . *proprietary,* as if editor-in-chief had already been promised to him. Jack swallowed more of the awful-tasting coffee, feeling it burn like acid.

"Have you considered the possibility," he said slowly, "that you wouldn't be up for his spot even if Reinhold *does* push Jerry out?"

"Roger Young, damnit, *he* was my ticket." A furious light leaped in Ben's eyes.

"Don't forget, Roger is still under contract for one more book," Jack reminded Ben gently.

"And after that? Unless I can pull a rabbit out of my hat, he'll be off and running. Random House, Simon and Schuster? Julie Pasternak at Bantam would *kill* for Roger."

"I had no choice, Ben," he said, shaking his head.

"Seems like I've heard *that* line before," Ben said, the bitterness in his voice unmistakable.

"If you're referring to your mother and me . . ." Jack took the plunge, not wanting *this* to be buried, like every other thing he did that Ben took umbrage at. ". . . it was nobody's fault. We grew apart, that's all."

Ben flashed him a disgusted look, but then his expression

softened, and he raised his palm in a conciliatory gesture. "Look, Dad, forget it. I'm sorry I brought it up."

Silence settled over them, brittle as the cold toast left on a plate at the uncleared table next to their booth.

Then it was Jack's turn to change the subject. "Oh, hey . . . I forgot to tell you. I've got an extra ticket to the circus tonight. Hannah can't come." Weeks ago, when he'd first invited Ben, he'd claimed to have other plans. Now Jack asked, "Sure you won't change your mind? It'll be a once-in-a-lifetime opportunity, Grace doing a death-defying act."

"I've already seen it." Ben laughed—an unpleasant snorting sound. "You don't call what's been going on with you and Grace and Hannah death-defying?" He quickly lowered his gaze. "Sorry, it was a dumb joke. Face it, Dad, Hannah is *never* going to accept her."

Jack felt the burning sensation in his stomach kick up again. Hannah's last-minute excuse was indeed pretty flimsy—calling to say she'd been invited to spend the weekend in Montauk with her friend Kath's family, acting like it was a big deal, when she was out there practically every other weekend as it was.

"That's not all that's not going to change," Ben went on. "A year from now, Grace will *still* be fifteen years younger than you."

"It was my impression you liked Grace."

"My liking her or not liking her has nothing to do with it. I just think you're getting in deeper than you should."

Jack felt as if he were hearing his own fears echoed by Ben. Every time he looked at Grace, so aglow with youth, so passionate, so *alive*—wasn't that at the back of his mind? The thought, stuck like a pebble in the bottom of a shoe: *When you're seventy, an old man, she'll still have men coming on to her.*

He started remembering his own father. How old was he

then—early seventies? Could Pop have had those same fears when he got married again? And it was awfully soon after Mom died. Had he suspected, even before he slipped the ring on Rita's finger, that one day she would be cheating on him? Not that Rita had been such a bad person—who could blame her for having normal hungers and needs? A vital woman in her early fifties stuck with a feeble old man who needed help going downstairs and who sometimes wet the bed. In a way, it had been lucky Pop died before Rita actually walked out on him.

"Maybe I am," Jack conceded, not wanting Ben to know how close he'd come to Jack's own doubts. "All I know is that I can't imagine being without her."

"Does that mean you're going to *marry* her?"

"Ben, I don't think this is something I want to dis—" He stopped, frozen by the look of contempt on his son's handsome face. He sighed. "We haven't actually talked about it, no. But that doesn't mean I'm not considering it."

Ben shrugged. "You're both crazy, you know. I mean, hey, between you, you already have two marriages, and look how *they* turned out. About the *only* thing I can say in favor of you and Grace is that you probably won't have kids. That way, you blow it again, nobody but the two of you suffers."

"You're taking a pretty grim view of all this," Jack said coolly.

"Well, if the shoe fits . . ."

Faced with his son's impassive stare, Jack grew aware of the clattering of dishes, the faint staccato hissing of the deep-frier, the friendly back-and-forth shouting between their over-the-hill waitress and a bearded man at the register. Sounds that comforted, that said the world was still going about its business, that this new yawning gulf between Jack Gold and his son would not appreciably alter the universe.

Finally, Jack asked, "More coffee?"

Ben glanced at his watch, the antique Rolex Natalie had given him when he graduated from Yale. Pink gold, almost feminine-looking, but on Ben it struck a nice note of elegance.

"Can't," he said. "I've got a meeting with Bella Chandler in ten minutes. Oh, and about tonight . . . I can't make it," Ben said. "Got a hot date."

A wry note in Ben's voice prompted Jack to ask, "Your mother?"

Ben nodded. "This fund-raiser she's chairing for the museum. You know how out of it she feels if she doesn't have an escort."

No surprise Ben didn't have a steady girlfriend, Jack thought. Not with Natalie wheedling him into squiring her everywhere. Probably one more reason the kid had it in for him. If he'd stayed married to her, Ben would be off the hook.

Jack thought about saying something—telling Ben he had to live his own life, not try to make amends to his mother for something that wasn't his fault. But Ben would have to find that out on his own. Either he'd get fed up with Natalie's demands or, better yet, fall in love.

"I'm sorry you can't make the circus," Jack told Ben.

"Yeah, me, too." Ben stared down at his hands, clenched on the table, before pushing his chair back and rising.

Are you? Jack stood up, and lightly clapped Ben on the shoulder. Almost more than anything, he wanted, at this moment, for Ben to give him that extra inch his son had been withholding for so long.

But what could he say now that hadn't already been said?

Chapter 8

Jack couldn't remember when he'd last been to a circus. Not since Ben and Hannah were kids, ages ago.

He still couldn't get over it, seeing Erica Jong in a spangled bodysuit on the back of an elephant, with a smile on her that belonged to every kid who'd ever dreamed of running away to the circus. Before that, Stephen King with his magic act, sawing a woman in half. And Norman Mailer balancing on a two-by-four set across a barrel. It was better than trained bears and lions leaping through flaming hoops —and there had been some of that, too.

But now it was Grace's turn up on the trapeze, and Jack felt something freeze inside him like the gears of a fun-house ride clanking to an abrupt halt. She looked so small up there, in a pink-and-black leotard, her hair pushed away from her face with a rhinestone-studded velvet headband. She stood alone and perfectly still, facing the trapeze artist on the plat-form opposite hers, awaiting his signal before she grabbed the bar suspended just over her head.

Applause swelled, and broke over him like distant surf. Jack was aware of it, but only dimly. All his focus was on the tiny figure poised at the top of the tall, fragile-looking steel rigging—the woman who would carry both his hopes and his fears with her when she leaped forward and flew out over the ring.

Suppose she fell? Who knew how strong those nets were?

Pride in her daring and beauty filled him. Where did she get it, this power she had to summon such emotion in him?

How had he gotten so lucky? She could have anyone, and wanted *him*, Jack Gold. Gray hair, beginning of a bald spot in back, slight prostate problem, and all.

In the back of his mind, he could hear his elderly father's querulous voice—like a warning, or a premonition—Pop pleading with his wife: *Rita, please . . . not again tonight . . . I need you.* And her cruelly lighthearted reply: *Oh, Moe, don't be an old poop! Why should I stay home just because your nitpicky doctor says you can't go out?*

Jack shifted, suddenly uncomfortable in the narrow seat that reminded him of every seat in every theatre, lecture hall, airplane, restaurant, which had been designed for a race of men smaller than he. He looked around—not your usual circus-going crowd of kids and parents cramming their faces with popcorn and cotton candy. Furs draped over the backs of seats, diamonds glinting in the half-light, starched tuxedo shirt fronts like sheets of stiff paper scattered about. Faces he recognized—publishers, editors, agents he'd lunched with, well-heeled authors, book-club people. And what appeared to be the charity-ball crowd, a few faces he vaguely knew, mostly real-estate and Wall Street types, he surmised.

There was to be a reception afterwards, at Buffy Mc-Farland's, a chairwoman of PEN for the past six years, who was always inviting him, as well as countless others, to some gathering to raise money for an imprisoned author, or to listen to a reading by a Czechoslovakian poet. Tonight's seat, along with Hannah's unused ticket, had set him back a good five hundred dollars. But worth every penny, just for the glory of seeing Grace up there, like a character out of *Green Mansions,* graceful as Rima the bird girl.

He imagined her naked, no one here but the two of them—he on the platform across from her, reaching out his arms as she swooped to meet him—and felt himself grow hard. He smiled at himself. An aging publisher in a tuxedo that had fit him better five years ago, horny as a high-school sophomore checking out the cheerleaders at a football game.

Now came the slowly building crescendo of the drum-roll, and Jack could feel his arms tensing as if to catch her. He watched Grace rise up on tiptoes, dainty and seemingly sure of herself, as she adjusted her grip on the trapeze bar. Then she gathered herself up and in one seamless movement was flying out over the ring, the lights above her catching the rhinestones on her headband in a burst of dazzling light. A collective gasp rose about him, and he saw people all around leaning forward in their seats. Then he realized he was one of them, the hard edge of his chair digging into his tailbone.

Don't fall, he prayed. *I love you.*

Though he knew she was in no real danger, he was still too afraid to keep looking, and had to squeeze his eyes shut. When he opened them, she was upside down, flying backward, suspended by her ankles in her partner's grip. Her arms spread wide as if she were embracing the whole world, a smile lighting up her whole face like a bank of kliegs.

He watched her alight on the opposite platform as smoothly as if she'd been doing this all her life. And then came another pass over the ring, and another—this time, with the swing at its highest arc, she twisted up so she was hanging from her knees. Applause, scattered at first, rose to a thunderous roar, accompanied by catcalls.

Jack felt his breath leave his lungs in a single, dizzying rush.

Clapping wildly, he rose to his feet—and was amused to see that he'd initiated a standing ovation.

When the lights came up, he lingered just inside the wooden barricade that enclosed the ring, waiting for Grace as the audience, chatting amiably among themselves, trickled off toward the exit. Briefly, he shmoozed with Grace's agent, Hank Carroll, congratulating him on a three-book contract he'd recently negotiated with Cadogan on behalf of Janice Kittredge, his best-selling mystery novelist.

"Thanks. I just hope you guys have money left for a publicity budget after settling out of court with Mrs. Truscott," Hank kidded, making Jack wish that Grace hadn't confided in him, even if he *was* her agent.

"Let's hope we can settle this *before* it goes to court," Jack said.

"Have you actually met Grace's mother?" The tall, reed-thin agent stretched his lips in a mirthless grin. "I had the pleasure myself, years ago, when Mrs. Truscott last visited New York. Remarkable woman . . . but you don't want to get in her way."

Watching Hank drift off, Jack found himself mulling over their conversation. Without meaning to, Hank had put his finger on the problem—Grace was here . . . and Cordelia Truscott was in Georgia. The key to their not being hamstrung by some bullshit injunction, Jack felt sure, lay in getting Grace to work things out with her mother. What if she were actually to invite her mother up for a visit?

After the circus, he'd suggest it to Grace, at least get her thinking about it. But he could almost hear her reaction: *Invite my mother for a visit? Are you crazy?*

Maybe I am crazy, he thought. *But it's worth a shot, and it may be the best shot we've got.*

Catching up with Grace as she wove her way through the departing crowd, in a trench coat belted about her impossibly tiny waist, he stepped forward to kiss her.

Standing so close, he could feel his own heat radiating back at him from her cool cheek. She smelled sweet, too, as if she'd just showered. Baby shampoo, and that coconut lotion that made him think of sunny beaches and piña coladas and making love under a lazy ceiling fan.

He wished they were there now, Anguilla, St. Bart, Eleuthera, some tropical hideaway, a continent away from Reinhold's ultimatums . . . from Chris and Ben and Hannah . . . from their complicated pasts.

"You were terrific," he told her. "As if you need me to tell you that. You got more of an ovation than all the rest of them put together."

"Oh, that was the easy part." She laughed. "The hard part was backstage, saying 'cheese' for all those photographers. I thought I'd never get out." She glanced around her, a sly, sheepish look on her face, like a schoolgirl with a view toward cutting her next class. "Listen, Jack, would you mind if we skipped the reception? I'm beat. What I'd really like is some Chinese takeout, curled up in bed with you."

"In that order?"

She drew in close to him. How perfectly they fit, her shoulder snug under his arm, the top of her head scooting in just under his chin. As she stood on tiptoe to kiss his ear, he felt a pang of sweet longing that was almost an ache.

"Depends how good you are with chopsticks. How about it, your place or mine? Chris is with his dad in the Hamptons, so you have me all to yourself."

"Hannah . . ." he started to say, and felt her stiffen slightly, "is spending the weekend with her friend Kath. That's why she isn't here. She sends her best." Grace looked up at him, her forehead wrinkling with unasked questions, but said nothing.

Could they pull it off? he wondered. Would they manage to get through a whole evening without their kids' somehow seeping into it? God, he hoped so. Right now, he would give almost anything for one night . . . a single, uncomplicated night of Grace all to himself.

"Jack . . . I don't know how to tell you this. . . ." Grace sat cross-legged on his double bed in the messy, half-organized bedroom she had dubbed Neo-Divorce. She was rubbing her temples the way she did when she had a headache coming on.

Jack felt something thump inside his chest, like a bird flying smack into a windowpane. *She's going to say she's tired of waiting around for me to make up my mind. That she's had enough.*

For a moment, he considered telling her about his Christmas surprise; he'd been working on it for months now. But would she take it the wrong way? See it as a proposal he still wasn't ready to make?

Damnit, why *couldn't* he simply tell her what she wanted to hear? It wasn't for lack of loving her, God knew. If anything, it was a case of *too much*—all the combined history they'd accumulated apart from one another.

"It's about the book, Jack," Grace told him. "I don't know if I can go through with it. All of it, I mean. I spoke with Win again today, and he says he tried to talk her out of it but Mother was adamant. She wants an injunction to stop publication. He says he's stalling her but he can't put her off too much longer."

In spite of himself, what Jack first felt was relief, enormous relief. It was her *book,* not *them,* that Grace wanted to talk about. But then, as the impact of what Grace was saying hit him, his mind shifted gears, became all business. If Grace left out the stuff about Ned Emory, it would still be a good read, a brilliant book in some ways, but not . . .

sensational. They'd be lucky to ship twenty-five thousand. Some respectful reviews, probably, but no media excitement, no best-seller lists, no guarantee of shoring up Cadogan's profits for the year.

Which meant it might not be just Jerry Schiller whose ass was hung out to dry.

He felt the moo-shu he'd just eaten creeping back up his throat. God knows he'd seen the thing happen enough on television, and a million stories in the papers—top executives out of work, no one wanting them or needing them. He'd felt sorry for those guys, but never, not *once*, had it occurred to him that *he* might be one of those poor slobs.

Reinhold had been gunning for him ever since he'd arrived. And Jack couldn't blame him. It was no secret that Jack had been opposed to Hauptman's acquiring Cadogan. Besides, who wanted a third-in-command who was used to being the boss? He'd had his gripes with their former parent, Sitwell Corporation, but at least they'd pretty much let him run the show.

Reinhold, on the other hand, wasn't stupid. Jack's years of experience, his connections with authors, agents, Washington insiders, coupled with his intimate knowledge of the company's veins, arteries, and internal organs—Reinhold needed those. Jack recalled the CEO's arrival last spring, Reinhold installing a state-of-the-art software program that had thrown Accounts Receivable into a virtual melt-down. Then deciding to move their warehouse from New Jersey to a larger, high-tech installation in West Virginia. Jack had tried to stop him, but, months since they'd made the switch, fulfillment was still snarled, with retailers and wholesalers both yelling bloody murder from here to Oahu.

They needed *Honor Above All*—now more than ever. If Roger Young were to walk, Grace's book might be the only thing that could maintain Cadogan as the kind of publishing company he loved . . . and save his job.

He took hold of Grace's tiny hands. Her rings, six of them, three for each hand—braided silver, turquoise, agate —pressed coolly into the fleshy pads of his palms like links in a chain.

He couldn't help thinking how she didn't belong in this room, with its massive Victorian bed and matching marble-top dresser, the bulky walnut wardrobe against the wall between the two prints he'd bothered to hang—a pair of ancient, acid-stained Blakes.

"Grace, I'm not telling you what to do, just talking off the top of my head. But has it occurred to you that the best way of dealing with this might be to confront your mother face to face? You know, you *could* invite her up for a visit."

Grace looked stunned, and then, as the prospect of it sank home, a mild panic seemed to take hold of her.

"You're not *serious.*"

"It might not solve everything, but it could be a start."

"God, it'd be like . . . well, like being a devout Catholic and having the Pope visit. I'd be on my guard every second of the day."

"Are you sure you're not exaggerating just the tiniest bit?" he asked.

"You don't know my mother." Grace was pensive for a moment, then said, "I remember, a long time ago, Mother and Sissy and I were visiting Grandma Clayborn down in Blessing. It must have been around the time Daddy was lobbying for the Civil Rights Act, because a bunch of men showed up in front of the house one night—they were carrying torches and shotguns, and yelling stuff about Daddy being a 'nigger-lover.' But Mother . . . she marched out on that porch and faced them like they were nothing more than a bunch of rowdy trick-or-treaters."

"She sounds like someone I know," Jack teased.

But Grace, hugging herself tightly, cried, "Oh, Jack, what if she's right? Is my telling the truth about Ned Emory's death worth all the anguish it's causing? Not to mention the legal hassles."

Jack took a deep breath. "Let me handle the lawyers. Just concentrate on what *you* want, apart from your mother or anyone else."

After a moment's silence, she said, "I was just thinking about Nola. Ever since we met, I've had this feeling that there's something she's not telling me. And then it dawned on me: maybe my father really *did* mean to hurt Ned Emory, maybe even kill him. God knows why—maybe he knew Ned was mistreating Margaret, and something in him just snapped. He really cared about her, you know. In some ways, Margaret was probably his closest friend. He *might* have been doing more than just protecting her."

"You don't believe that, do you?"

"Oh, Jack," she sighed. "These days I don't know *what* to believe."

Jack's gaze drifted over to the deacon's bench Natalie had decided she didn't want to keep, which had somehow become a receptacle for his clothes—shirts, socks, ties slung haphazardly over its long spindled back—until he got around to organizing his dresser drawers. He noticed, as if for the first time, the cardboard boxes stacked in the corner, yet to be unpacked after more than eight months, the framed prints propped against the baseboard. And in a flash, he saw this place clearly: as the way station of a man biding his time until he made up his mind.

But when would that be? And how could he be absolutely sure of Grace, when she, too, obviously had her own doubts?

Jack wished fiercely that he could sweep away all her

fears . . . and his. That he could somehow make everything all right. Like he'd held things together in the bloody aftermath of Hauptman's acquiring Cadogan. Always putting on a confident face, moving aggressively with their new directives, lest anyone think his leadership had been affected.

Leaning against the headboard, he put out his arms, and she was instantly pressed against him, her face resting on his chest, the top of her head brushing the underside of his jaw. Even her toes: she'd managed to tuck them up against his legs, semifrozen bits of ice thawing against his warm flesh.

He reached down and scooped up a foot, massaged it with strong circular strokes of his thumb. He loved her feet, so small they'd have fit easily into a pair of shoes Hannah had outgrown in the sixth grade. Her rose-colored nails, and the swoop of her arches—like a ballerina.

Grace squirmed in pleasure, her breasts soft and loose against him. Jack felt himself growing hard. Jesus, how could he love her this much . . . want her so badly . . . if there was all this stuff pushing them apart?

He bent his neck to kiss her, and she tilted her head up to meet him halfway, her mouth parted slightly, her arms tensing about him with wiry strength, as if he were drowning and it was she who was keeping him afloat.

She extended her leg so that his hand, cradling her foot, slid up her thigh. Silk . . . lovely silk, with tiny hairs that tickled his palm. He thought, oddly, of biting into a warm, sun-ripened peach. The sensations she coaxed from him were like small treats doled out one by one, each more tantalizing and exciting than the next.

She was an orchard of peaches, the warmth of her, the taste, as he pushed up her T-shirt and kissed first one breast, then the other. *Ah, Jesus.* She could make him into a teenager, with an appetite that had no bottom.

"Jack . . . Jack, I love you so much. . . ."

"I know . . ." he whispered as the two of them slid down until their heads were resting on the pillows, facing one another, arms and legs entwined. "No, don't turn over. Stay like that. On your side. Yes, I can . . . Oh, yes. There."

As she arched up to him, one leg slung over his hips, the other pinned against the mattress, he felt himself slide into her . . . the tightness of the angle, the syrupy warmth of her like their first time, when he'd come as fast as a kid. He strained to check himself, moving in a slow but deliberate rhythm . . . hands cupping her buttocks, guiding her deeper, closer to him, with each stroke.

He felt her breath against his neck, gentle little bursts of air that were bringing him close to the edge. Pinpricks of light danced on the undersides of his closed eyelids. But it wasn't any one physical movement, any one part of her body that was exciting him so. It was her eagerness, her energy—everything that had made him fall in love with her. Stupid to think it was in the cock, when the real power of love-making had to be in the mind and in the heart.

As if he could ever let her get away from him, Jack thought, pulled up short by a rush of feeling so strong he found himself holding her tight enough to crush her ribs, crying out her name over and over.

Later, as they lay entwined amid the tangled sheets, Jack said softly, "I meant what I said before, about asking your mother up for a visit."

"I know," she groaned. "But it wouldn't do any good. She's oil and I'm water. Whenever I talk to her on the phone, I'm invariably so frustrated that by the time I hang up I'm ready to throw something at the wall."

"Face to face might be different."

"She wouldn't come even if I did invite her."

"You never know."

"And you *do*?"

Jack didn't want to keep pushing her. But he had to. "She might. How will you know for sure unless you ask?"

She laughed—a dry, rasping noise low in her throat. "You do not know Cordelia Clayborn Truscott."

"But since I'm sleeping with her daughter, don't you think it's time we met?"

Grace was silent for so long he might have thought she'd dropped off to sleep but for the tautness in her body, like a spring-loaded hinge ready to pop. Finally, she turned her face toward his and, with the glow from the bedside lamp highlighting her cheeks, said in a voice like a tomboy accepting a dare, "All right, then, Jack Gold. I'll do it. I'll invite her. But if she *does* accept . . . well, don't say I didn't warn you."

Chapter 9

"Gabe, there's something I've been meaning to ask you. . . ."

Cordelia, kneeling at the edge of the tulip bed, placed her trowel in the wicker basket at her side. Along with an array of other gardening tools, each neatly stowed in its own canvas pocket, the basket held a handful of wooden pegs and a roll of twine with which to mark her rows.

. . . I know you didn't receive an engraved invitation weeks ago like everyone else, but will you come to Sissy's party? My only excuse for waiting until practically the last minute is that I was afraid . . . of looking foolish . . . and of risking our lovely friendship for some pie-in-the-sky fantasy. . . .

No, she couldn't say that. Gabe would be shocked and distressed to learn she had such feelings about him—feelings he couldn't possibly share. She'd sound ridiculous. Better if instead she were to invite Jared Fulton, that nice lawyer to whom her old friend Iris had introduced her at Iris's and Jim's anniversary dinner party last Saturday. Jared was in his sixties, and he loved music as much as she did—hadn't he asked her to the Philadelphia Orchestra concert in Macon for next Thursday? The least she could do was return the favor.

Besides, to invite Gabe at the last minute, wouldn't it seem an afterthought? He couldn't know that she'd had a perfectly legitimate reason for not asking him sooner. *If I had gotten up the nerve to tell Sissy about Beech cheating on her there wouldn't even be a party.*

She looked at Gabe, kneeling beside her, and felt a prickly warmth spread through her, as if she'd been out in the sun too long. Mercy! There had to be some way of ridding herself of this feeling she had around him—hot one minute and shivery the next, almost like when she'd been going through the change.

Cordelia took a deep breath, and the rich smell of the earth, damp from last night's rain, seemed to fill her whole being, calming her. She looked down at the six shallow reed baskets arranged on the grass beside her, heaped with the bulbs to be planted for next spring. Jonquils, long-cupped daffodils, snowdrops, grape hyacinth, and tulips. Oh, how she loved tulips, even their names—spotted Rembrandt, crimson-streaked Flaming Parrot, the lily-flowered Marietta, snowy Anne Frank, stout-stemmed Triumph.

She thought about how she and Gabe had spent all of yesterday troweling up the soil, working in a mixture of peat, manure, and bonemeal. The weather, except for last night's shower, had been unusually fine for December. At Blessing's altitude, this time of year could be nippy, while southern Georgia still basked. But any day now, she'd be waking up to a sugar-coating of frost over the lawn.

She rocked back on her heels, surveying the area skirting the pergola that extended off the house to the left of the back porch. Just right for bulbs—plenty of morning sun, with afternoon shade from the yew hedge that bordered the vegetable garden, now bedded down for the winter under a layer of manure and straw. By April, she'd be able to look out the kitchen and back-bedroom windows and be treated to a magic carpet of bright, nodding blooms. The orchard beyond the hedge would be blooming, too. And the branches of the dwarf-cherry and peach trees, now half bare, would be smothered in fragrant clouds of pink and white.

And where will you and I be? she wondered, once more taking in the sight of Gabe, hunkered down beside her, wearing a pair of old, paint-spotted dungarees and a dark-green Aran sweater with its sleeves pushed up over his forearms, brown and hard as a pair of thick ropes. In the sunlight that shone square against his weathered face, he sat poised, squinting at her expectantly, his eyes nearly lost in the creases around them.

How would people perceive the two of them, Cordelia wondered, Gabe on her arm, after she'd been with so powerful, so revered a man as Gene? Could he ever really be part of her life-style, the entertaining she had to do for the hospital, the university, fund-raisers? Not to mention dinner parties with old, dear friends—people Gabe didn't know except to nod hello to on the street.

Thinking about dinner parties reminded her of last night. It had been weeks since she'd first begun toying with the idea of inviting Gabe to supper, and for one reason or another she hadn't gotten around to it. First there had been Win calling her out of the blue, then meetings at the hospital that had kept her away from her garden. But yesterday, after an afternoon of working side by side with Gabe, it had seemed the most natural thing in the world to ask him to stay on.

Over supper, there had been none of the awkwardness she'd dreaded. They'd talked as easily as if they'd been in the garden planting seedlings or pruning fruit trees together—on and on, scarcely aware of what they were eating, though later she'd noted that a good portion of Netta's chicken pie and berry cobbler had somehow gotten devoured. What had they talked about? The hospital, what kind of person they should get to be the new director. The best brands of coffee at the Winn Dixie. Blessing's old court-house, which Fredda McWilliams was turning into an an-tiques mart.

Afterwards, she'd put on the stereo in the den, and they'd listened to Kiri Te Kanawa sing *Madama Butterfly,* while they played gin rummy. Quiet, friendly, nothing special, but it all kept coming back to her—little things mostly, like the ghost prints left by Gabe's Redwing boots on the deep pile of the den carpet, the friendly clutter of the dishes they'd left in the sink, and his nice smell, like the thick Hudson Bay blankets folded in the cedar chest at her father's fishing cabin out at Sinclair Lake.

Oh, but she had to stop this mooning about! All these years without Gene, she'd gotten along perfectly fine . . . and once she got over this unseemly infatuation, she would *continue* to get along perfectly fine.

Cordelia became aware of Gabe still poised beside her, waiting for her to finish what she'd started to say.

She quickly swerved to a safer topic, yet one that had also been troubling her. "It's about Grace," she told him. "She's written asking me to visit her in New York." Cordelia sighed.

"What did you tell her?"

She found herself shaking her head, admitting, "I . . . haven't decided."

"When did you get the letter?"

"A week ago."

"That's a good while."

Gabe went back to sorting through the basket of daffodil bulbs balanced on his knees, examining each one, discarding those that had already begun to sprout, his long fingers mov-ing with the swift precision that made her think of a surgeon. His head was bare for a change, a cool morning breeze ruf-fling his hair. She noticed a spark of silver here and there

among the fine brown strands, and felt a tiny nick of surprise. *Why, he's going gray!* She couldn't help feeling
pleased, as if that might lessen the ten-year gap in their ages.

She yearned, at that moment, in the rosy morning light,
with the dark, wet smell of the earth rising up around her,
to take hold of Gabe's dirt-clotted hand and press it to her
cheek.

She forced her mind back to the dilemma that had been
pulling her in opposite directions all week.

"Part of me would love to see her . . . but another part,
I'm afraid, would like nothing more than to take her over
my knee and paddle the bejesus out of her. Trouble is, I
know which part of me has the upper hand."

He winked. "Speaking of which, would you mind handing me that trowel?"

She passed it to him, and watched Gabe begin digging in
the peaty soil, uprooting one of last year's jonquils. He separated the cluster of smaller offshoots clinging to the mother
bulb, and dug a separate hole for each, using the rule of
thumb he'd taught her: make the hole twice as deep as the
bulb is wide.

"Still, it's been a whole year since I've seen Chris," Cordelia continued. "And he's not coming down with his father
this Christmas. He could be six feet tall before I see him
again."

She thought of past summers, when she would have
Chris for a week or two at a time. They'd always go to
Sinclair Lake, to the cozy, hidden-away cabin that Mother
had painstakingly kept up, and that now belonged to her.
Oh, how that boy loved to fish! Hours and hours out on
that fallen log by the stream, with his rod and extra hooks
and a jar of salmon eggs.

But after he turned ten, and Grace had begun sending

him to summer camp, she'd hardly seen her grandson. She tried to imagine what he would look like now, at thirteen—a taller, reedier version of the gangly youth he'd been this time last year—but her mind clung to the picture of him she loved best, as a round-faced little boy. So like his mother as a young girl, thoughtful and intense, asking questions like "Grandma, where do stars come from?" and "How come those roses don't smell?" She did write to him, and they spoke on the phone, but the lifeless letters he wrote back always began the same way and tore at her heart: *Dear Grandma, How are you? I am fine. . . .*

"Grace's boy." Gabe chuckled as he tossed out a handful of bulbs to mark the spots where he would dig. "Hard to believe she could have a teenaged son. I remember when Grace was that age herself—bright as a new penny. She was one of the only students who understood what it means to write what you know, and why Faulkner deserves the effort it takes to read him."

"Gabriel, you are purposely diverting this discussion."

He settled back on his haunches, fixing her with his gaze while holding his hand up against the sunlight weaving its way through the tops of the cherry trees. "Maybe I'm not the best judge of how you ought to deal with your daughter." An unaccountable sadness seemed to settle over him. "There are things about me that you don't know, Cordelia."

She felt her pulse quicken, but she tried to sound sensible when she spoke. "Gabriel, I can't imagine you telling me anything about yourself that would shock me too terribly."

Something dark glinted in Gabe's soft brown eyes, a look she'd never seen before. "You think this is all I'm about, planting tulips, mulching flower beds? A harmless crackpot who couldn't stand up to the pressures of teaching?"

"I didn't mean—"

"I have a daughter of my own, you see," he said softly . . . so softly that Cordelia at first wasn't certain she'd heard correctly.

But now his revelation was washing over her like a cold ocean wave. A daughter? But his ex-wife—why, it was common knowledge that Josephine Ross hadn't been able to bear children! Gabe himself had once told her it was one of the reasons their marriage had failed.

Misreading her shocked expression, Gabe shook his head. "It's not what you imagine—I was faithful to Josie. It happened years before I met my wife. I was seventeen, and there was a girl I was crazy about. We . . . Well, to make a long story short, she got pregnant. I would have married her, but her parents had it in mind to give the baby up for adoption . . . and in the end they got their way."

"Oh, Gabe." Cordelia brought a peaty-smelling hand to her mouth. "Do you know who adopted her? Where is she now?"

"I spent ten years looking," he told her. "I searched every hamlet within five hundred miles of Atlanta." He gave a rueful smile. "That's how I ended up settling here. And maybe that's what drew me to teaching—at the time, she'd have been around fourteen, you know. And now . . . Well, I've often wondered if, all that time I spent searching, I wasn't also running from something . . . from who I really wanted to be."

It occurred to Cordelia at that precise moment, with the sun reflecting off the sudden jewellike brightness of his eyes, that perhaps Gabe was also in some way urging *her* to find her own self—the woman she'd been before she'd moved back here to Blessing, before she'd become so respectable, so . . . *staid*.

"I . . . I'm glad you told me," was all she could think of to say.

The sadness that was making him look older and grayer abruptly broke, and he smiled, appearing once more his usual relaxed self. "I guess you see why I think it's so important, holding on to what counts."

"Grace and I have relied on greeting cards to say what we should be speaking aloud to one another . . . but I suppose it's better than nothing." She sighed. "Maybe that's why I'm having such trouble making up my mind. I'm afraid of risking what little communication my daughter and I *do* have."

"And if you *don't* go, what will you have gained?"

The same as I'll have gained by not asking you to Sissy's party, she thought. *Nothing.*

Cordelia felt suddenly conscious of the dowdy brown cardigan she'd thrown on over her gardening clothes, and the fact that she hadn't bothered with lipstick since before breakfast.

She snatched at a thistly weed, forgetting that she wasn't wearing her gloves, and felt a sharp prick.

"If you know so much, why don't *you* tell me?" Cordelia blurted, all at once irritable with him for getting under her skin like the tiny nettle she could now see sticking up from her thumb.

"I only know when I see the backside of someone running from the truth," he said, peeling the dry brown tunic from a daffodil bulb.

"And what *is* the truth?" she demanded.

"You love your daughter, and if there is even the smallest chance that you can patch things up with her, you'll be on the next plane to New York."

If there was such a thing as a mental antiseptic, she thought, Gabriel was it. All at once, she felt washed clean, faintly stinging all over. He made perfect sense, but still she felt so unsure.

She *used* to be so certain of everything, so quick to act upon those convictions, but now . . .

Cordelia rose to her feet, wincing at the stiffness in her joints. Dizziness spiraled up in her as if she were a glass being filled with some fizzy liquid. She braced herself against a column of the pergola, still hung with the raggedy remains of last summer's clematis, waiting for the dizziness to subside.

Instantly, Gabe was at her side, looking concerned. "Are you feeling all right?"

"I'm getting to be too old for all this bending and stooping," she told him with a little laugh. "Why don't we go inside? I'm sure we could both use a glass of tea. And I promised I'd help Netta put up that last batch of apple butter so she could get to the hospital in time for visiting hours." Cordelia knew Netta was worried still about her little grandson, even though he appeared past danger from meningitis.

She paused on the porch, reluctant to leave behind the sight of the hydrangeas swelling up over the railing like a great pink snow drift, and the hollyhocks along this side of the garage drooping with the spent Indian summer. She sank down onto the old glider that had stood out here for as far back as she could remember. She'd had it reupholstered twice since Mother died, most recently in cabbage-rose chintz, around the same time as she'd had this porch glassed in. Did they even make this kind of heavy-duty glider anymore? Probably not. The best things, like those old clunky cars that gave you the security of a Sherman tank, and kitchen stoves you didn't need a degree in engineering to know how to operate—where had they all gone to? Did other people miss them the way she did? Or was it just a sign of encroaching years when what you *remember* begins to outweigh what you *know?*

"This wouldn't be a good time for me to go, what with the holidays and all," she said. "There's so much here that needs doing. Organizing the benefit supper for Hilldale . . . and I'm meeting with the League of Women Voters in Macon for help in raising funds for the library. Not to mention Sissy's party this coming Saturday"—she winced inwardly at her cowardice in not inviting Gabe—"which I confess has gotten *completely* out of hand. Mercy, you'd think it was Queen Elizabeth and the Duke of Edinburgh celebrating their golden anniversary, the way she's carrying on."

"If it gives her pleasure, why not?" Gabe leaned up against a fluted porch column from which hung, on several elongated brass hooks, ceramic pots trailing the last of the pink Rose-impatiens and the cyclamen, their leaves turning yellow, and their blooms mostly gone.

"I don't know . . . All this excess, it seems tacky. She wants 'Caroline and Beech' printed in silver on every napkin, even the hand towels in the powder room."

He cast her a wry look that made her blush. "Is that what's bothering you, napkins and towels?"

Cordelia looked out at the naked, turned flower beds, and the grass alongside the old brick kitchen-garden path growing brittle with the onset of winter. Christmas was only two weeks away. Yet, from where she sat on the sunny porch, shielded from the chill, she felt almost too warm.

"Well . . . no. Sissy called this morning. She was nearly beside herself, she was so upset. She suspects Beech is having an affair."

"And you know it to be a fact." This was a statement, not a question.

"Yes." But how did *Gabe* know that she knew?

"Have you told Sissy?"

Cordelia sighed. "I kept wanting to, but what good

would it do her? She's been putting up with him for years, one way or another. This party, maybe it's all she has to show for ten years of marriage."

"Do you know the O'Neill play *The Iceman Cometh*? Some people need illusions, or they fall apart." He spoke in that slow, considering way of his that made her picture him standing before a classroom. "Everybody needs to believe in something."

"I don't want to see Sissy hurt."

"And Grace?"

"Are you telling me I should go to New York?" she asked, cocking her head a bit as she peered up at him.

"There!" he exclaimed, lifting his gaze and pointing. "Did you see that? An oriole, I think it was. I haven't seen one of those in ages."

She strained to pick out what Gabe had seen, but there was only the gold of the sun on leaves the color of ash. It wasn't until he laid his hand on her shoulder, squeezing it gently as he steered her to a different angle, that she saw it—a flash of vivid yellow and black among the branches.

She felt unexpected tears in her eyes, even while she sat there thinking how silly it was of her to be worked up over a simple thing like a touch, or the unexpected treat of an oriole, when important decisions—such as whether or not to visit Grace, or if she ought to confirm Sissy's fears about her husband—remained open and unresolved, like wounds in need of dressing.

"Come to the party," she said softly, the words flying out of her, surprising herself as much as they probably did him. "I've been *wanting* to send you a proper invitation, but I suppose it's no secret that Sissy doesn't approve of our . . ." She faltered, then straightened her shoulders and finished in a strong voice, ". . . our friendship. But this is my home, and I can ask whomever I want." Only now did she dare look

up at him. "Please, Gabe . . . It would mean a lot to me."
There, she'd said it. She'd all but admitted her feelings for
him. Well, it wouldn't be the first time she'd made a fool of
herself.

Even so, as she sat still and straight in the old glider, the
morning sunlight hot against her face, Cordelia's heart fluttered like the wings of the oriole she now saw flying out over
the weeping willows along the creek below the orchard.
Would he accept? Or would he politely refuse, not wanting
to try and fit in with Blessing society?

But it was Sissy and her shallow friends who didn't deserve the company of a man like Gabe. *Please,* she repeated
silently, not entirely sure what it was she was pleading for.

Cordelia waited, feeling oddly suspended, as if she were
holding her breath, even though she was dimly aware of air
slipping in and out of her lungs.

Finally, after what seemed like an eternity, Gabe dropped
his gaze onto her and smiled. "I'd like that, Cordelia," he
said softly, simply, releasing her heart from its frenzied flight
so she could breathe again.

T he cake Sissy had ordered had the look of a parade float,
iced in candy-heart colors and smothered with pink sugar
roses. In mint-green frosting, below a pair of silver foil nest-
ing doves, was piped: "Happy Anniversary, Caroline and
Beech."

Cordelia thought it was the ugliest thing she'd ever laid
eyes on. She felt a pang of despair. Sissy and her friends,
pretentious Junior Leaguers like Melodie Hobson and Julia
Hunnicutt, were always trying to one-up each other, no matter how vulgar the end result. Vying over who had the fan-
ciest car, landscaping, designer dress, catered extravaganza.

With people, too, position was everything. And when Gabe arrived, how they'd cluck about "crazy Mr. Ross"!

Lord, let me get through this evening, Cordelia prayed.

She turned to Netta, who stood at the far end of the dining-room table, folding napkins and arranging them in overlapping triangles by the plates and silverware. Dear Netta. Without her, this house would simply fold in on itself like the pink bakery box containing the cake that Cordelia held gingerly in her arms.

"Oh, Netta . . ." She thrust the box at her loyal housekeeper. "Would you find some sort of platter for this? The silver ought to be big enough." She gestured in the direction of the china closet, where she kept her wedding china and the antique Cristofle salvers with Great-Grandmother Clayborn's crest. The platter she'd pointed to, its pierced rim embossed with birds and grape leaves, might offset some of the tackiness of the cake.

"Looks like it could use a flatbed truck." Netta's disdain was obvious . . . but, then, with Netta she was never quite sure. Her dour middle-aged housekeeper brought to mind one of those Easter Island statues—blocky and imperturbable, with the kind of features that never seem to age, except to become somewhat blurred by the elements. The only time Cordelia had ever seen Netta cry—and even then it was only that her eyes had become very bright, like a pair of old pennies glistening in a jar—was last April, when Cordelia had given Netta and Hollis the deed to the guest cottage they'd occupied for the past twenty-five years.

"Why don't you put it over there—on the sideboard, between those two flower bowls," she told Netta, who looked stiff and uncomfortable in the alien black uniform and ruffled organdy apron—another bit of pretentiousness Sissy had insisted upon.

She felt a little insulted for Netta—a woman who'd

nursed Grace and Sissy through mumps and scarlet fever, and who could fix a broken vacuum cleaner or unclog a pipe as quick as it took to call a repairman—to have been told what to wear for an occasion such as this one. How often had she spotted Netta on her way to church on Sunday, stepping along the cottage path that wound past the main house, fitted out in a stylish suit and high heels like no one who would ever need to apologize for who she was, or how she looked?

Annoyed at herself for having given in to Sissy's demands, Cordelia offered Netta a sympathetic look, then stood back to give the dining-room table a last once-over. In the center stood a wide, shallow bowl in which a half-dozen gardenias floated amid fat, flickering candles of varying heights. At one end, her Rose Point silverware shimmered against the hand-embroidered linen tablecloth, and every plate gleamed. Should she have used her Havilland wedding china instead? No, the Limoges was just as pretty, and not quite so delicate. And, should a plate get chipped or broken, she wouldn't be heartbroken by the loss.

As if her mother were still alive, carping at her from the next room, Cordelia was reminded of the time that Mother, noting a tiny chip in one of the Havilland finger bowls, had remarked dryly, "You know, dear, hired help is replaceable; family heirlooms are not."

Watching Netta as she carefully slid the cake onto the platter, Cordelia knew that to be untrue. Despite half a lifetime of her mother's trying to mold Cordelia in her image, Cordelia vowed she would never value any *thing* more than a person.

The doorbell chimed, announcing the first guests.

Cordelia felt her heart give an unpleasant little jump, and remembered all the reasons she was *not* looking forward to this party—Sissy, in her size-sixteen brocade, drinking too much, as she always did at parties; and Beech, loud and coarse, with his hearty salesman's handshake, who would undoubtedly make some long-winded and embarrassingly flowery speech about the dear woman he was married to.

Hurrying along the narrow kitchen corridor that connected to the grander hallway by the front entrance, Cordelia wished she'd never stumbled upon Beech's dirty little secret. Worse had been that little chat she'd had with Beech following her fruitless lunch with Sissy out at Mulberry Acres, before Sissy had developed suspicions of her own.

They'd been sitting out on the sun porch, where Sissy, off showing the boys a bird's nest in the crepe-myrtle tree, couldn't overhear them.

"Beech, I know what you've been up to." Cordelia did not mince words. "And I want *you* to know I won't tolerate it. For Sissy's sake, for the boys'. This . . . affair of yours has got to stop."

"Who told you I was cheatin' on Sissy?" Beech, his wide plank of a face flushed pink, managed to affect a look of outraged innocence that wouldn't have fooled a simpleton. His piggy eyes narrowed. "Heck, me and Janet, it's just *business*. She's settin' me up with some of her neighbors out in Mulberry Acres who might be lookin' to buy a new set of wheels."

"Janet? Janet O'Malley?" Cordelia said quietly, and waited for Beech to realize he'd stuck his big foot in his even bigger mouth. She'd met Janet O'Malley only once, over at Sissy's, but Sissy was always talking about how her littlest, Beau, was such great friends with Janet's boy.

"Why, I was only . . ." He started to sputter, but she cut him off.

"In case it may have slipped your mind, *I* own the mortgage on your house." For once, she didn't bother to sweeten her tone in order to hide her disgust. "Or should I say *Sissy's* house, since it's in her name only. And I'm sure you also know that Ed Spangler is planning on opening a branch of his dealership up in Gaskin Springs. One *word* from me to Ed, and I have no doubt he would transfer you." She watched him blanch at that. "Oh, don't look so *grim*. You'd be able to drive home weekends. It's only two hundred miles, and I'm sure it'll go a lot faster when that new superhighway is finished. Of course," she'd added pointedly, "you'd most certainly be too *tired* for any sort of extracurricular activities other than spending time at home with your wife and sons."

"Now, Mother, you've got this all wrong!" Beech started to stand up, but she pinned him with a withering look that sent him collapsing back in his chair with a groan of wicker.

"One lying word out of your mouth, Beech Beecham, and I swear . . ." She didn't have to complete her threat, because now Beech was holding his big ham hands over his face.

"It didn't mean anything," came his muffled, seemingly agonized reply. "I swear on my granny's grave. It was just that one time, and it was Janet's idea from the get-go. I didn't . . ."

"I don't give a hoot in hell *whose* idea it was. I just want it over and done with. Now"—she stood up, peering out the glass at the dense green of her garden—"where can Sissy and those boys have gotten to?"

Had she scared some sense into him? Cordelia wondered as she paused to adjust a painting that was hanging a bit crooked. She hoped so . . . but with Beech you never knew. She remembered a few years ago, her pulling him up by the short hairs for forging Sissy's signature on a trust fund check in order to put a down payment on a new truck. He'd promised never to go sneaking behind his wife's back again. But

Beech was like a child, thoroughly chastised one minute and into the same old mischief the second you turned your back. Poor Sissy.

Cordelia sighed. Lord, why did she have to fret over *both* her daughters? One not smart enough to see what was going on right under her nose . . . and the other too smart for her own good.

A sour taste threaded its way up into her throat.

Despite Gabe's urging, she *still* hadn't made up her mind about visiting Grace. Even with Win now insisting she stay at his apartment, where she could be on somewhat neutral ground and still see Grace and Chris. Yes, it *was* tempting. . . .

Cordelia's gaze picked out a framed portrait of Grace among a grouping of family photos on the wall opposite the staircase. Seven years old, with braids and a gap-toothed smile as wide as the Mississippi. She felt as if something sharp were piercing her heart. Would Grace truly be glad to see her? Or would she end up pushing her away as she had when she was a baby, kicking her legs and batting her little arms to free herself from her mother's embrace?

I don't have to decide right this minute, she told herself.

Gabe thought she should go, but he didn't necessarily know what was best for her. . . .

Gabe.

She glanced at her watch. What if he didn't show up? What if, at the last minute, he'd changed his mind?

She found herself hoping he hadn't . . . but at the same time, a small, mean-spirited part of her—the part that had rubbed elbows too long with her mother's snobbishness— almost wished he would spare them both the discomfort of his presence here.

But that was silly, she told herself. *Of course* he was

coming. Otherwise he would have called. And, despite any misgivings she might have about the reception he was sure to get from Sissy and her friends, she couldn't wait to see him. And for him to see *her*.

Cordelia, passing the gilt pier mirror at the foot of the staircase, gave her hair a final pat. Next time, she'd tell Linette not to go so heavy on the spray. But her dress, at least, was just right—a lovely wine velvet she'd driven into Macon to shop for, in the designer department at Macy's. Cut on the bias, it nipped in at the waist and flared about her knees, making her feel years younger.

"Why, Cordelia, you look like you stepped out of a magazine!" her oldest friend, Iris, greeted her, handing her coat to Hollis as she stepped forward to kiss Cordelia's cheek.

"Well, will you look who's talking!" Cordelia cried. "You look pretty as a picture."

Iris was too thin, of course, but then she'd always been that way, since they were in school together. As she hugged Iris, Cordelia could feel her ribs through her crimson satin blouse, tucked into a pair of smart black velvet trousers. Cordelia remembered, when they were girls, how they used to say to each other, *If we get old . . .*

Now we are *getting old,* she thought with a ripple of amusement.

"I can't imagine why." Iris laughed breathlessly, smoothing a wisp of silver hair from her cheek. "We had an emergency at the Home, and I nearly didn't make it. Priscilla Draper fell and broke her hip. She'll be fine, but she needed a lot of hand-holding."

"Something *I* never seem to get enough of from her these days," chuckled Iris's husband, Jim, reaching for his wife's hand and giving it a squeeze. With his round face and nearly white beard, and his belly straining at the seams of a dinner jacket that had fit him better at their daughter's wedding five years ago, he had the baggy, contented look of a well-fed Saint Bernard.

Cordelia remembered to thank Jim again for his company's twenty-thousand-dollar donation to the library fund before they were parted by a wave of Sissy's friends, shedding coats, bringing a gust of frosty air and mingled perfumes. Sissy, bustling in from the parlor, darted past Cordelia and threw her arms around each new guest in a way Cordelia found cloying.

Nor did she feel easy about Sissy's high color, and the feverish glittering of her blue eyes. Clearly, Sissy had been more than sampling the champagne. Even her dress, which had looked festive on her in the store, now made her look overdone, with all those pearls heaped about her neck, and earrings bobbling like Christmas-tree ornaments.

Cordelia led the way into the parlor, where drinks were being served and trays of hors d'oeuvres passed. She was accepting a glass from a silver tray proffered by Hollis's cousin Elroy, when behind her she heard, "You look lovely tonight, Cordelia."

Gabe! How had he managed to slip in without her spotting him?

She felt herself flush, and turned to find him smiling at her, looking surprisingly elegant in a shawl-collared tuxedo that, though it appeared decades out of date, fit him perfectly. His weathered face, with its sun-reddened Indian cheekbones, set him apart from every man in this room, and yet it only seemed to make him more special.

"Can I get you some champagne?" she asked, feeling awkward and self-conscious.

"I have something even better," he told her, holding up a bottle of clear greenish liquid that bore no label. His eyes sparkled, holding her gaze, not glancing about as hers had been, to see if anyone was looking at them. "Dandelion wine; I made it myself." With a wink, he added, "Old family recipe. I brought it for Caroline, but I don't suppose she'd mind if we took a sip."

Cordelia, her heart throbbing, moved to the Dutch marquetry console that doubled as a bar. She left her untouched champagne on its marble top, and selected two cut-crystal sherry glasses from inside.

Moments later, as she sipped Gabe's wine, more to ease the tense dryness in her throat than anything else, she thought, *Could it really be this easy?* Gabe fitting in, belonging here, in this house, among her friends.

As if for the sole purpose of dispelling such a notion, Sissy sidled over. "Mr. Ross, it was so *nice* of you to come," she drawled with exaggerated politeness. "I do hope you'll find a moment to say hello to my friends. You probably remember most of them from school."

"I'll do that," Gabe said, seemingly unaware of the smirk Cordelia could see flickering at the corner of her daughter's rosebud mouth before Sissy slipped away.

Cordelia felt herself stiffen. She'd heard the things Sissy and her catty chums used to say, and were still saying, about "Mr. Ross." Just the other day, Sissy's best friend, Peg Lynch, had come up to her in the Winn Dixie and asked her, in a voice laced with incredulity, whether it was *true* what she'd heard from Sissy, that Mr. Ross was coming to her party.

"Stay away from them," Cordelia warned, laying a hand on Gabe's arm and speaking with a candidness that surprised her. "She and her silly, puffed-up friends will probably try and make you look bad."

Gabe raised an eyebrow. "Cordelia, I know exactly who I am and why I'm here. And if I choose not to be belittled, then I walk out the door the same man who walked in.

Now," he smiled, "you haven't told me what you think of the wine. Too strong?"

"It's delicious," she told him, and meant it. Cool, and not too sweet, with just a trace of welcome tartness. She'd hardly know it contained alcohol except for the tingly rush she felt . . . and her sudden, shocking desire to be away from this crowd, somewhere alone with Gabe. In that instant, she regretted her warning. Whereas Sissy's childish jabs would have rolled right off Gabe, *she,* no doubt, had made him feel conspicious. "Gabe, I apologize if I . . ."

He placed a callused finger over his lips, and shook his head. Pushing aside her anxiety, Cordelia slipped back into her role as hostess, darting forward to kiss Marjorie Killian's sunken cheek.

"Lovely party," Marjorie gushed, needlessly reaching up to smooth a wing of lacquered, frosted hair that looked as if it would survive a hurricane. "And I *adore* what you've done with your tree. Who but clever you would have thought of those sweet little glass ornaments?"

She followed Marjorie's gaze to the Christmas tree, which had stolen the show from her treasured Coromandel screen, against which it stood—a ten-foot blue spruce hung with globes of Venetian blown glass, and the precious Victorian papier-mâché cherubs she had inherited from her great-grandmother Patterson. None of those tacky strings of winking electric lights; instead, there were candles fixed to each branch with tiny brass holders, their dancing flames suffusing the room with a kind of glow that had little to do with tonight's occasion.

"Speaking of Christmas," she asked, "will you and Dan be going away this year?"

"Saint Martin," Marjorie drawled. "And you? Braving the festivities?"

Out of the corner of her eye, Cordelia caught the amused

look on Iris's face as she edged past. Though it was eons ago, who could forget the smug way Marjorie had pranced about after she and Dan got engaged? She'd saved her most pitying looks for Cordelia, no doubt believing her to be mourning the loss of her one true love.

"Actually, I've been thinking of taking a little trip myself." The words were out of Cordelia's mouth before she quite knew she was saying them. "To New York . . . to visit Grace." But before she could commit herself to something she'd later regret, she added quickly, "It's not definite yet, and in any case it wouldn't be until after the holidays, but . . . Oh, Dan . . ." She grabbed hold of Dan Killian, who was edging his way toward the bar like a barge toward a loading dock, and fixed him with her most compelling smile. "One itty-bitty thing: did you get that letter I sent you last week?" She'd written to him to refresh his memory about his long-ago promise to contribute to the library, and to remind him that their little chat in his office hadn't changed anything as far as she was concerned. "I hadn't heard from you, so . . ." She let the rest of the sentence trail off meaningfully.

Dan looked embarrassed, and glanced down at the carpet, all three of his chins sinking into his collar. "Well, you see, Dellie, with all this union fuss about a strike out at the factory . . . I, uh, I've been kind of wrapped up."

"Never mind," she told him in her most firmly polite voice. "I certainly didn't ask you here tonight to discuss business. Why don't you two help yourself to some of those lovely little salmon puffs over on that table by the piano? I'll give you a call on Monday, Dan." Careful. If she pushed too hard, Dan might back off altogether.

Distracted by a loud guffaw, she turned toward Beech, leaning up against the banister in the hallway with one beefy arm draped about the newel post. His face was red and dotted with sweat under his freshly mown crewcut as he brayed at some joke, undoubtedly off-color, that Deke Woodlawn, his sidekick down at Spangler Dodge, was telling him. In his too-tight tuxedo, Beech made her think of a schoolyard bully cajoled into wearing his Sunday best.

She saw Beech glance over at Gabe, now chatting with Iris and Jim over by the fireplace, and then lean in close to his buddy to whisper something she just knew had to be ugly. The two of them sniggered, and Cordelia looked away, her stomach knotting. Only her many years at playing hostess kept her from letting on that she minded, or even noticed.

Finally, the time came to serve supper, and Cordelia felt relieved to have something to do other than making polite conversation with people—most just curious, a few malicious—who all seemed to be dying to know why she'd invited Gabe. In the dining room, she directed Netta and the extra help in setting out the platters—roast turkey with cornbread-and-chestnut stuffing, chutney-glazed ham, giant prawns stuffed with crabmeat and deep-fried in a coconut batter, tomato-and-okra stew, tiny hot rolls arranged around a cut-glass bowl of whipped herb butter. She smiled and smiled until she thought her face would crack in two as she threaded her way through the packed room, making sure everyone had a plate and something to drink.

"Delicious!" Miriam White called to Cordelia as she nibbled on a shrimp. The old dragon had been president of the Junior League longer than St. Peter had been minding the gates of heaven, but beneath her fussy airs and that henna helmet she was a good soul. If it hadn't been for Miriam's dogged efforts, Cordelia reminded herself, the pediatric ward at Hilldale would not have gotten its CAT scan.

"*Nobody* knows how to give a party better than Cordelia Truscott, I always say," she heard a voice behind her drawl.

She turned to find Laura Littlefield, in seafoam chiffon, holding court with a circle of men. Admirers? At her age? Well, once a Dixie Queen, always a Dixie Queen.

It seemed hours and hours before the platters were cleared away and Sissy went scurrying off, swaying a bit on her satin heels, to round up Beech so they could cut the cake.

"Beech . . . oh, Bee-eech! Where have you gotten to, you naughty old thing!"

Moments later, Cordelia heard a muffled cry, followed by a thunderous crash that seemed to emanate from the back of the house. She felt the blood drain from her face.

"Excuse me," she muttered to Emily Newcomb beside her. "Netta must have dropped something in the kitchen." Pushing her way through the swinging door into the old-fashioned black-and-white-tiled kitchen, Cordelia half-hoped it *was* true, that Netta had broken one of her precious plates or a crystal glass. But she knew it had to be something far worse.

She found them in the laundry room at the back the house—Beech, Sissy, and a blond woman half in shadow, all of them frozen in a tawdry tableau. Beech was backed up against a row of shelves stacked with folded sheets and slipcovers, a furtive look stamped on his flushed face. The blonde—Janet O'Malley, she recognized now—simply looked shocked, but her smeared lipstick and half-unzipped dress told the whole ugly story. It was Sissy who was hollering—loud enough to make Cordelia grateful for the blessed thickness of old doors.

"You bastard! You fucking bastard! How dare you! *How dare you!*" Her Gerber-baby's mouth was distorted and ugly.

At her feet, twinkling in the dim glow from the hallway, lay the remains of the champagne glass she'd been drinking from. Cordelia caught the sharp smell of alcohol mixed with the more comforting scents of soap powder and fabric softener.

"Honey. Now, listen, honey . . . it's not what you think," Beech was sputtering, his speech nearly as slurred as Sissy's. "I never slept with her. I would'na even a gone this far except . . . except . . ."

" 'Cept you're a lying, cheating bag of shit!" Hectic splotches the color of the champagne punch she'd been guzzling all evening stood out on Sissy's quivering neck.

She stabbed a finger at the cowering Janet. "And *you*— I baby-sat your kids, I even baked cupcakes for your stupid Friends of Animals bake sale. Well, I hope you choke on them, you bitch!"

Cordelia, coming out of her shock, felt her limbs unlock as Sissy slumped back against the dryer and began to weep in great honking gusts. Cordelia stepped forward to gather her daughter in her arms, and looked over Sissy's heaving shoulder at Beech, fixing him with an icy stare.

"If you are entertaining one single thought of slinking out the back door, I'll thank you to get it right out of your head." She spoke softly but with an edge of steel, as if he were a teenager caught shoplifting in a store she owned. "Now. I expect you to tuck your shirttail in your trousers, and to walk out there as if nothing has happened . . . as if you're the happiest married man in the world. And I want you to tell your guests that Sissy here slipped on a wet floor and turned her ankle—nothing serious, nothing she won't be over in a day or two. Do you *think* you can manage that, Beech?"

"Now, Mother . . ." He put out a placating hand, which she froze with a look that also stopped whatever pathetic excuse he was about to lay on her. She saw the ruddy color leave his face, making the lipstick smeared over his mouth look as garish as war paint. "Okay, okay. I . . . I'll see to the guests."

"And wipe your face before you do."

He slunk out, Janet scampering in his wake.

"Oh . . . I want to die!" sobbed Sissy in the soap-smelling dimness, flinging herself into her mother's embrace.

Cordelia felt a twinge of disgust for the plump woman sniveling drunkenly in her arms . . . while, at the same time, her heart ached for her poor little girl, who had so wanted tonight to be special.

"You are not going to die. You're going to go up the back stairs and wash your face, and lie down until everyone's gone. Then you and I will have a talk, and try to decide what you're going to do."

She would also have a talk with Ed Spangler. Sissy wouldn't even have to know who was behind Beech's getting transferred. And it'd do them good to have to decide if they *wanted* to be together.

Only after she had gotten Sissy settled on the bed in her old room, amid a gaggle of ancient stuffed animals—her childhood playthings, which to this day she absolutely refused to have disturbed—did Cordelia give in to the headache that had begun hammering at her temples. In her bathroom, she splashed rosewater on her throat, and pressed cotton balls dipped in witch hazel to her aching eyelids.

Downstairs again, she put on her best smile as she moved among the guests, reassuring them that Sissy would be all right.

"Netta must have spilled something on the floor," she told Miriam White, shaking her head. "And Sissy, in those new shoes of hers—why, it was lucky she didn't sprain something, or worse." She could tell by the sympathetic yet knowing look on Miriam's face that she didn't believe that story one bit. Miriam—as well as everyone else—probably thought Sissy had had too much to drink. Well, let them think it. Better than their knowing the truth.

Then, finally, blessedly, the exodus—coats brushing up against one another at the door as kisses and promises to get together were exchanged, chirrupy goodbyes, car engines starting up, and the crunch of tires on gravel. Lydia Pinkney called out to her, "One of these days, Cordelia Truscott, I swear I am going to pry that tomato-aspic recipe loose from you!"

As the last guest was ushered out, Cordelia caught sight of Beech crossing the vestibule like a sailor aboard a listing deck, his hand shoved in his pocket, maniacally jingling his keys. She opened her mouth to warn him about driving in his condition, but, before she could get the words out, Gabe materialized out of the crowd to step in front of him.

"Why don't you let me drive you, Beech?" he said in an easy voice that suggested nothing out of the ordinary. "I'm going that way, and I can drop you off."

Beech shot him an irritated look. "No thanks, I'm okay. Besides, I have a car."

"Of course. But shouldn't you be leaving it for Caroline? She'll be needing it, soon as she's up to driving home."

"I *said* I can handle it," Beech snarled, his red face growing even redder. "Are you suggesting I can't?"

"That's not what I said."

"*Okay,* then . . ." Beech tried to push past him, but Gabe gripped his arm.

Cordelia caught the look of stunned surprise on Beech's bovine face—former star halfback of Robert E. Lee High, at least four inches taller than Gabe—when he tried to wrestle his arm away and couldn't.

A sort of dizziness took hold of her. Oddly, she felt both frightened and overflowing with admiration.

"Le'*go*," Beech muttered with a baleful glare. "I *know* you understand English . . . even if I don't get why you'd want to rake leaves for a living."

"And I know *you* understand English, Beech," replied Gabe genially, "because you earned just enough points to pass my course."

"Jesus, what's with you—you take steroids?" Beech was now clumsily attempting to laugh the whole thing off.

"Come on, Beech, let's go." Gabe spoke kindly.

Watching Beech start to sweat like a ham in the oven, then finally sag in defeat, Cordelia knew Gabe had won.

"You know, I missed last Sunday's game." Gabe spoke quickly, his arm around Beech's shoulders now. "I heard the Falcons just squeezed it out with a tremendous end run. Did you see it?"

"*See* it? Man, I was out of my mind. It was goddamn *beautiful*." Beech, who lived and breathed football, was letting himself be distracted, and be led out the door like a schoolboy. "Let me tell you how it . . ." His voice trailed off as they moved out onto the porch, with Gabe tossing Cordelia a two-fingered wave over his shoulder, mouthing, *Be right back.*

Cordelia felt her heart leap at the prospect of sharing a quiet nightcap with Gabe. Then she was distracted by the sight of Hollis, ambling toward the kitchen carrying a tray of used glasses. His hair, she saw, was white as a shorn lamb's. When had he gotten so old, and so stooped? And how, when she saw him every day, could she not have noticed this?

She felt old herself . . . and tired, so tired. Not just because of Sissy, either. What a strain it was playing hostess, she thought, always having to think of the right thing to say, to remember every name, to be informed and clever and witty. When she was married, it had been easier, because it had been *Gene* in the spotlight, people looking up to him, hanging on his every word.

Twenty pale roses—that's how many she counted in the carpet runner as, without being aware of even moving her feet, she moved down the hall and into the empty parlor.

Sinking down in the wing chair by the fireplace, Cordelia closed her eyes. She found herself remembering the day she'd first laid eyes on her husband, first heard him speak. She'd been a political-science major at George Washington University—over the "dead body" of her still vehemently alive mother, who'd insisted she go to Duke—and a damned know-it-all to boot: informing her roommate, Betty Preston, who had gotten them passes to the House gallery, that she didn't care *what* this freshman Democrat Betty was so impressed with had to say—as far as she was concerned, the way the system worked, no one man could make a difference.

She herself, just two years before, in the face of Mother's nearly hurling herself from her wheelchair onto the floor in protest, had completely neglected her classes at GWU to campaign for Adlai Stevenson. Still bitter over his defeat, she wasn't going to let herself get carried away by some other liberal idealist who, in the long run, was bound to fade into oblivion.

But on that day in 1954, as the ex-fireman from Queens, New York, stood and addressed the floor, Cordelia, despite herself, had felt her cynicism begin to melt. Tall, angular, almost scarecrowish, the sleeves of his creased suit jacket not quite covering the bony wrists of his enormous hands, he'd made her think of Jimmy Stewart in *Mr. Smith Goes to Washington*. And when he spread his arms in an impassioned gesture, opening himself wide to the attack his words would surely provoke, she found herself scooting forward onto the edge of her seat.

"There is something very wrong going on in our country right now," he began, his voice somewhat raw and unschooled, yet somehow more powerful than that of Sam Rayburn, Speaker of the House. "Deep down we all know it, but we're afraid of sticking our necks out, so we've kept quiet about it. Well, I, for one, won't keep quiet any longer. This witch-hunt being conducted by Senator Joe McCarthy supposedly in the name of patriotism is *wrong,* plain and simple. . . ."

She didn't remember the words that followed, only the ringing silence that fell over the floor and gallery when he finished. *He's committing political suicide,* she remembered thinking, and it was then, she realized, looking back—long before Betty's uncle managed to wangle her an introduction—that she'd fallen in love with Gene. He reminded her of her father, in a way. Though Daddy was an old time Georgia Democrat who'd have moved to Iceland before admitting that integration was a good thing, he'd seen it coming, and, back in the days when Negroes were relegated to merely sweeping the floors and polishing the marble of banks, he'd promoted Eldon Roantree to be a teller. Daddy, if he were alive, would have approved, in his own hidebound way, of this brave but surely doomed Eugene Truscott.

But then, not long after Gene's speech, Edward R. Murrow had come out against McCarthy on national television. And more and more voices joined theirs. She would not forget, however, that on that day no one on the House floor came forward to support the freshman Democrat from Queens, and in the silence that followed there had been the sound of only one person clapping.

That person, she remembered with a faint smile, had been she. . . .

"Cordelia?"

Her eyes flew open, and there was Gabe seated across from her in the leather club chair that had been Daddy's favorite. Smiling, looking perfectly at ease, clearly not expecting her to jump up and play hostess. No, he was not Gene, but he was kind and decent, and, as the scene with Beech had brought home to her, he was adept at handling tough situations.

Watching him scoot the ottoman over so she could put up her feet, she felt tears spring to her eyes, and realized it had been a long, long time since anyone had thought of her as needing to be coddled.

"I'm tired, Gabe," she sighed.

"I know."

"How is it *you* look fresh as a daisy, and I feel like old trampled sod?"

He laughed, and settled onto the oversized ottoman alongside her outstretched legs. " 'But in the mud and scum of things there always, always, something sings.' "

"Emerson?"

He nodded. "He's right, you know. Things that seem black at the time can sometimes turn out for the best."

"I doubt if anyone at that party had any idea just *how* black."

"I know you better than they do," he said, probably sensing her confusion. "I know when something is wrong—even when you're smiling." She felt his hand wrap itself about her ankle, as casually as if he were feeling the thickness of a branch, but she sensed that his touch meant more than that.

Cordelia shivered. "I've raised two daughters," she confided to the embers turning to ash in the marble fireplace, "and it now appears I haven't done a very good job of it."

"Appearances can be deceiving."

"Oh, Gabe . . ." She turned to look at him, feeling a new

wave of anguish. "It's not just tonight, what happened with Sissy. It's Eugene—I can't shake the feeling that, if he'd lived, things wouldn't have turned out this way."

"You're punishing yourself, and you don't deserve that."

"Then why? Why are all these awful things happening to me? Why should I have one daughter who's helpless, and another who's aiming to stab me in the back? Oh, heavens, how I'd like to turn *both* those girls over my knee!"

Fired by grief and anger and a kind of desperate exhaustion, she jumped to her feet and darted over to the walnut secretary, where she kept the articles about Eugene and every one of his speeches, compiled in several leather-bound volumes, and also every word Grace had ever had published. Snatching up the two-year-old *Time* magazine with the story about Grace's winning the Pulitzer—she knew just where it was in the stack, and could have found it blindfolded—she felt its edges crumple in her fist, and something sharp—a staple?—dig into the soft flesh at the base of her thumb. Her hand, she saw when she looked down at it, was shaking.

I was so proud of her! Cordelia thought. *And now she's going to destroy Gene, rake up something that happened so long ago. . . . Damn her!*

"Cordelia—don't!" she heard Gabe cry through the buzzing in her head, and only then did she realize that in her anger she'd actually flung the magazine into the fireplace.

With a kind of horror, she saw the embers split open with a cracking noise, sending up a shower of sparks. Watching the pages turn black, curl at the edges, and burst into flame, she felt as if her own heart were burning.

Then Gabe was beside her, his hands on her shoulders stilling her wild trembling. She felt the healing power of him steal through her . . . his magic, which made nearly dead azalea bushes bloom and grass spring up where it had been trodden to mud.

Before she knew it, his arms were around her. *How can this be?* a voice cried, before all thought, every rational cell in her brain, got swept away as he tipped her head back with the callused tip of a finger and kissed her fully, deeply on the mouth. Oh, the warmth of his lips—how could she bear it? It had been so long since she'd been kissed. Not since Eugene . . . not in *years* . . . a lifetime . . .

She felt Gabe's tongue, and the wanting that lay beyond his kiss. Her arms and legs trembled, and the dizziness she'd felt in the yard a few days ago came over her now, though this time it didn't frighten her. It was only natural, feeling this way with Gabe holding her, desiring her as she desired him. Suddenly it didn't seem strange at all, his wanting her despite her being more than middle-aged, and Gabe's being not at all the sort of man the town of Blessing would have imagined her choosing.

Now his mouth against her hair, one hand cupping the back of her head as he smoothed her hair, his fingertips lingering where her neck curved down to meet her spine. His breath, his wonderful smell, like the dandelion wine she'd tasted earlier, making her almost drunk. She clung to him, feeling a sob building in her. A queer mixture of anguish and of happiness so great it felt like a huge boulder crushing the fragile fortress she'd built around herself.

So that, when he urged softly, "Go to New York, Cordelia. Go find your daughter. I'll be waiting for you when you get back," she found herself nodding in dreamy agreement. Perhaps going to New York would be easier, after all, than making up her mind about how to go on living right here in Blessing.

Chapter 10

It was the first time they'd been up to the cabin since there was snow on the ground, and as Jack pulled the Volvo into the icy, rutted drive, Grace suddenly felt her spirits lift.

"Oh!" she cried, delighted by the sight of white everywhere, blanketing the landscape and pillowed on the branches of the trees. "When I was growing up in the city, this is how I always thought Christmas should look."

Hannah, in the front seat, shot a cool glance over her shoulder.

We don't celebrate Christmas. Grace imagined the words pasted like a cartoon bubble over Hannah's head. Well, too bad. She wasn't going to let Hannah get her down . . . not tonight, Christmas Eve, whether the Golds celebrated it or not.

Climbing out of the back seat, Grace took a last good look at the pristine snow before it got trampled by their boots. Until she met Jack, her only visits to the Berkshires had been a few summer weekends at Tanglewood—Mozart and mosquitoes; overpriced chi-chi country inns, and hay fever.

But *this,* it was magical, like something out of a fairy tale. She laughed to herself, thinking, *Yeah . . . wicked stepmother and all.*

The snow was deep. It gave under her boots with a satisfying crunch as she trudged step by labored step to where the woodpile hunkered under a thick shawl of white.

Through a scrim of leafless poplar branches, the house glimmered in the twilight, its cedar shakes weathered the silvery gray of a wolf's pelt. A light burned in the front window—Mrs. Ingram, the woman who looked after the place for Jack, must have left it on. In the front yard, holly bushes stood out in vivid splashes, their crimson berries glistening under a fine sugaring of snow.

Watching Jack gather up an armload of wood, Grace felt the stiffness in her neck from the seemingly endless drive begin to melt away. Here, at least, she'd have a chance to deal with Hannah face to face. No more being stuck in the rear of the car, staring at the back of a head that wouldn't turn when spoken to, that never once looked to see whether she and Chris were enjoying either the ride or the tape she was playing—a headache-inducing cross between reggae and rap to which Jack had seemed immune. And no more being wedged up against Chris, as mute and unresponsive as the duffel bag he'd carried on his lap the whole way.

He was probably still angry at her for pressuring him into coming. She should have known better. Despite his insistence that it *didn't* matter, Chris would miss all the Christmas festivities at Win's parents' home in Macon—the tree crammed with ornaments, the snowflake cookies Nana Bishop always made, the annual party for the neighbors with its great bowl of eggnog punch and lively singing of carols around the piano.

How could he not? All those things—she missed them, too.

"I'll get the suitcases, Dad!" she heard Hannah call out.

"Good girl." His breath hung in the frosty air like an exclamation point. "You help Grace unload while Chris and I get the fire going."

Grace clumped back to the Volvo to help, but after several trips, lugging in grocery bags, a case of wine, and extra blankets, she noticed that Hannah had taken only her own and Jack's luggage. Grace's laptop and green canvas bag—not to mention the shopping bag with Lila's leather jacket, gift-wrapped for Hannah—sat forlornly on the seat below the open hatchback like a pair of marooned hitchhikers.

A dryness settled at the back of her throat, as if from sucking in frozen air too quickly. Her feet, even in hiking boots and thick wool socks, felt numb. And here she was, in the pitch dark, while Hannah was stripping her gloves off by the fire. Grace was propelled up the icy front steps on a red tide of resentment. By the time she'd wrestled open the frozen door latch and dumped her things on the floor by the hickory coatrack, she was out of breath and had to lean back against the jamb, eyes closed, until her anger subsided.

Silent night . . . holy night . . . I won't let it get to me tonight. We're going to be together for a whole week, she reminded herself—don't ruin it by getting off on the wrong foot.

Grace found herself wishing that Ben had come along to take the sting out of her being stuck with Hannah. He was her antidote to Hannah—not only nice to her, but light-hearted and full of jokes, and great with Chris, too. But, damnit, he'd made plans to go skiing in Vail. . . .

Still, the sight of Chris and Jack crouched side by side in front of the flames now sputtering to life in the great stone fireplace reassured her some. Jack was explaining the finer points of fire-making to her son, and Chris was nodding, an interested look on his face. Okay, *vague* interest, but still . . .

Hannah was sprawled on the scruffy tartan sofa, her feet propped on the coffee table made from a ship's hatch, wiggling her toes before the fire. Out of the corner of her eye, Grace could see into the kitchen, where the groceries sat in their bags on the old wooden counter. And there was still dinner to prepare. After that, beds to be made up. *What* had she gotten herself into here?

She watched Jack straighten, grimacing slightly as his knees popped with a sound like an old hinge giving way. In his faded red flannel shirt and a pair of weathered jeans worn white at the knees, he seemed to her, oh, like a figure out of woodland folklore—Paul Bunyan or Daniel Boone. Big and bursting with vigor despite a few creaks, his silvery hair jeweled with drops of melted snow, hands smudged with ink from the newspaper he'd used to start the fire. She watched the ridged muscles in his forearms twist and knot as he hefted a cast-iron poker, jabbing at the logs. She felt like she was in high school again, mooning over gorgeous Mr. Van Harte, her misgivings about the week ahead suddenly melting away like the clots of snow from their boots, now glistening puddles by the door.

She thought about snuggling up with Jack under the down comforter in the old brass bed upstairs, of how he would wrap himself around her to warm her. Even now, as she stood, still shivering a bit in the fledgling fire's stuttering glow, she could almost feel Jack's big hands moving over her, gently rubbing her goosepimpled flesh until she began to thaw. His breath pumping warmth against her cheek, then her throat and chest as he moved lower, using his mouth to suck any last coldness from her . . .

Jack caught her gaze, and winked at her. Grace felt her face tingle with sudden heat. Then he smiled, the lines in the corners of his eyes radiating outward as in a child's drawing of the sun, and she felt something leap inside her.

He loves me. The thought came like something she'd always known or perhaps had memorized long ago.

It could be so good with Jack. If . . . if . . .

"Hey, guys, don't forget, we still have to get dinner on."

Jack addressed the room, while casting a meaningful glance at Hannah. "Chris and I'll be in to give you ladies a hand after we bring in some more logs."

Chris trailed behind Jack at a slouchy snail's pace. In his rumpled olive flak jacket and baggy jeans, with a shaggy mane that made Grace long to tie him down and run Lila's dog-clipping shears across his head, he looked like a delinquent being hauled in for some minor offense.

Grace wanted to shake some get-up-and-go into him, but her problem now wasn't Chris. Watching Hannah leisurely unfold herself from the couch, Grace felt her anxiety return.

"You know, I really love this room," Grace said, trying to break the ice. She looked away from Hannah at the faded friendship quilt that hung alongside a collection of antique trivets. On the old cherry tea table beneath it sat a blue splatterware pitcher and a hurricane lamp that, judging from its soot smudges, wasn't just for show.

"My mother decorated it," Hannah responded matter-of-factly. "It's what she does for a living, you know. She's very good at it."

"I can see," Grace said evenly. "It's not everyone who can make a country place homey without its looking like a Laura Ashley ad."

Hannah's eyes were flat and unsmiling, her arms crossed over her chest. She was wearing rumpled blue canvas overalls and a flowered shirt, Grace realized belatedly, that might actually have been from Laura Ashley.

In the kitchen, Hannah said, "I can do the pasta. We always have pasta the first night. Only Dad still calls it 'spaghetti.' Like have you noticed, when he's not thinking, he'll shake a milk carton before pouring? It's like he's still a kid, when they had glass milk bottles and the cream rose to the top."

"They had those when I was a kid, too," Grace said,

dumping lettuce and a plastic bag of anemic-looking tomatoes into the deep enamel sink to be washed. "I never thought it could be any other way."

Hannah nodded. "Sort of like with records. Nowadays, you walk into Tower Records and all you see are CDs." She sounded wistful. "Not that CDs aren't *better*. It's just . . . well, you know . . ."

"Yeah, I know . . ." Grace said agreeably, knowing it was change itself—*any* change—that Hannah was allergic to.

Hannah, rummaging in the cupboard by the stove, seemed to soften the tiniest bit. Grace could see some of the tension go out of her shoulders. Grace thought of a gunslinger dropping his hand from his holster. But all Hannah said was, "Uh, Grace . . . do you see that jar of spaghetti sauce anywhere?"

Grace braced herself. She didn't want to fight with Hannah, but Christmas Eve was special. Nervously, she cleared her throat.

"Actually, I thought we'd have something a little more . . . festive. I bought some Cornish hens, which won't take long to bake, and some of that stuffing mix my mother would faint if she saw me using. And sweet potatoes we can throw in the microwave. It's not exactly Norman Rockwell, but it beats Chef Boyardee."

A tiny frown line formed between Hannah's unplucked brows. "But we *always* have pasta the first night," she insisted.

"Well, since it's"—*Go ahead, say it. Coward, oh you coward, SAY IT*—"Christmas Eve."

"We don't celebrate Christmas."

"Chris and I do," Grace said quietly. She held Hannah's steely gaze, feeling the hammering of her pulse through her whole body. The rushing of the tap filling the sink reverberated like a waterfall in her ears. With her back to the counter, she felt cold droplets prick her forearms where the sleeves of her sweater were rolled up.

"Then why are you *here?*" Hannah asked, her eyes cold with fury.

Slowly, as if moving underwater, or in a dream, Grace turned to crank off the faucet. Hannah's words lay between them like a gauntlet cast on the worn heart-of-pine floorboards. In the silence pierced only by the hollow ticking of water as it dripped onto the lettuce leaves, she faced Hannah, then said, "I wish I could explain it in a way that you'd understand. So you'd see I'm not trying to take your mother's place . . . or yours. I'm not the enemy, Hannah. I'm not the reason your parents got divorced. I'm not the reason you're unhappy."

In the wavy glass of the old cupboard panes opposite her, Grace caught a watery reflection of herself—a small woman with tousled damp hair, her face tense, her mouth drawn tight.

"What do you know about me?" Hannah shot back, a hectic crimson blooming in her cheeks. "You don't have the slightest idea what would make me happy! If you did, you wouldn't be here."

"Well, I *am* here," Grace snapped.

"I wish you would go away . . . *far* away. I wish you'd disappear off the face of this *planet!*"

Hannah's words struck her like a bullet, searing her, making her want to double over with the pain of them. No surprise really how Hannah felt, but hearing it—actually *hearing* her say those words—oh, God, it hurt.

"I don't think that's likely to happen," she said, struggling to keep her voice low. "So you'd better make up your mind—truce, or all-out war?"

Hannah stood clutching a loaf of bread as if it were Grace's neck she was squeezing. Her eyes hot and red-rimmed, she cried, "You think you've got it all figured out, don't you? You think, just because you've fooled my father, you can fool me. Well, my mind's already made up about you, so you can save your breath . . . and you can keep your stupid Christmas to yourself."

"Hannah!"

At the sound of Jack's voice booming across the kitchen, Grace jerked around. He was standing in the doorway, an armload of kindling tight against his chest, his face hard with anger.

Hannah whirled, the bread slipping from her grasp as if it were a pass she'd fumbled. She caught it before it hit the floor, and straightened with a jerky motion, her face swollen and splotched with red, her eyes iced over with unshed tears.

"Daddy, I . . ." she started to say.

"Not in this house!" he shouted. "I won't have you talking that way to Grace under my roof, not if you—"

"Jack, please," Grace broke in, feeling panic closing in on her.

Couldn't he see how wrong this was, his charging to her defense? How absolutely guaranteed to make Hannah resent her even more? His daughter wasn't a little girl anymore, a child he could scold for breaking some rule. . . .

"—plan on being invited along yourself the next time," he finished.

Grace heard Hannah gasp.

And, in that instant, she saw the future as clearly as a sign warning motorists of dangerous curves, or an area prone to landslides. At every turn, she'd be tensing, never safe, never knowing what lay just out of sight. God, didn't he *see?*

"Hannah, listen, this whole thing has gotten out of hand. Let's sit down and talk about it." Grace was furious at Jack and at Hannah, but even more at herself, for having jumped into this with open eyes and both feet. She started to put out her hand, but Hannah shrank away. The look in her swollen eyes said, *It's all your fault. Everything. Even my father yelling at me like that.*

Then, with a sob and a creak of old floorboards, she vanished, disappearing into the next room as if swallowed up by a magician's cape, leaving a loaf of mangled bread on the counter . . . and a Christmas that was ruined before it had even dawned.

"Are you, like, gonna hide out in here the whole time?"

Hannah looked up from the sheet of binder paper she was folding into an origami giraffe—a trick that Reiko, the daughter of a Japanese publisher, had taught her the summer she turned twelve. She often did it as a way to relax.

Chris was sort of hovering in the doorway of her room, one hand still clutching the doorknob, unsure of his welcome. She felt a flash of annoyance, and wished she'd remembered to latch her door.

But then she scooted over on her bed, where she lay with her back propped against the headboard, her legs stretched out in front of her. "You can come in and sit down if you want to," she said.

Her eyes were swollen and itchy from crying, and she didn't really feel like talking to anyone. But, even though Chris was related to Grace, she couldn't help feeling sorry for him. Chris had to live with her *all* the time, except for the weekends he was with his father. She probably cornered him for hip, heart-to-heart chats about smoking pot ("We did all that in the sixties, and look how it screwed us up") and sex ("It's okay, as long as you use a condom"), and embarrassed him by walking around half naked in front of his friends. She would probably be flattered if a guy Hannah's age came on to her—which could easily happen, given how young she looked, and which made it twice as gross, her being with someone as ancient as Daddy.

"Have they gone up to bed yet?" Hannah was starving. It had to be close to ten by now, but she would have let herself pass out from hunger before admitting that in the last half-hour or so the thought of cold roasted Cornish hen had taken the place of her fantasies about Grace's being blasted into space aboard a NASA shuttle not due back for at least a hundred million years.

Wouldn't it be just like Grace to have left a Saran Wrapped plate for her in the fridge, leftover Cornish hen with all the trimmings? No, she'd have a bowl of Rice Chex instead.

"Nuh-uh. They went for a walk. He said he wanted to show her something."

"In this weather? They'll probably catch pneumonia." She knew where they'd gone—the surprise Daddy had been working on for Grace—and that only made her feel more miserable.

"I doubt it. They're dressed for Antarctica."

She noticed that Chris had crept closer, a foot or two, the toes of his dirty Reeboks parked at the edge of the braided rug between her spool bed and the pine dresser across from it. He made her think of the dog her family had once had—an Airedale named Trixie who would stand there wagging her stub of a tail like she couldn't wait for you to pet her, but as soon as you stuck out your hand she'd skitter off and hide behind the couch. She was sure that, if Chris had a tail, it'd be wagging. But she'd have bet her whole Elvis Costello collection that he didn't have many friends.

"There's a Scrabble game in the bottom dresser drawer, if you feel like playing," she said nonchalantly.

He shrugged, but, when she looked up from folding a corner of paper into a head for her giraffe, he was on his haunches, rummaging in the drawer. Strolling over to the bed with the battered Scrabble box under his arm, he might have been Don Mattingly sauntering up to bat, except for the flush creeping up the sides of his skinny neck, and the smile trying to break through the power lock on his jaw.

"Oh, hey," he said, digging into a pocket of his zippered sweatshirt. "I brought you something."

It was a bag of complimentary peanuts, the kind they handed out on airplanes. Mom, she remembered, had had a friend who worked for United, and she used to bring home shopping bags full of them. Chris must have found them stashed away in the back of the cupboard, stale probably, but it was nice of him anyway—even if he *had* forgotten she was allergic to nuts.

Thinking about her mom reminded her of how great it used to be coming up here when Mom and Dad were still together. Even Mom would get relaxed, humming while she made up the beds and joking that she hoped they didn't get snowed in again, because she'd go *nuts* listening to those scratchy old Cole Porter records of Dad's. The four of them, sitting around the kitchen table after dinner, playing hearts and Chinese checkers, and eating half-burnt popcorn that she and Ben had popped over the open fire.

Hannah felt a fresh sting of tears, and blinked them back. Dumb, stupid, pointless, going over all that old stuff. Her wishing wasn't going to bring it back. Heck, if wishing could get you anything, by now Grace would be out there orbiting Saturn.

"Thanks," she told Chris, discreetly slipping the packet of nuts under her pillow. "Sorry about dinner; did you get stuck with the dishes?"

"Your dad helped. I didn't know where anything goes." He cast a quick, almost furtive glance about the room. "You guys come up to the cabin a lot?"

"We used to, when my parents were together. If it were up to me, I'd live here all year long." Shaker Mill Pond had always felt safe to her, like those places where wild geese could nest without anyone's being allowed to shoot at them.

"What about your boyfriend—wouldn't you miss him?"

Hannah felt herself flush. Since that night she'd fled to his house after her fight with Mom, she'd been doing her best not even to *think* about Conrad. She couldn't, *wouldn't*, let herself recall every detail of the embarrassing stuff she'd done with him. The only thing she remembered clearly was Con, climbing off her afterwards, mumbling, "You okay?" And her nodding, as if it were no big deal, when the truth was she'd felt like crying . . .

"Con and I aren't like *them*," she told Chris. "We don't *have* to be together every spare minute."

Hannah blinked hard, and looked up at the wall over her bed. Hanging from pegs by their knotted laces were all the pairs of ice skates she'd outgrown since the age of six. Why did people have to grow apart, and everything have to change?

"What was it like . . . I mean, before your mom and dad split up?" she heard Chris ask.

"We used to have fun together—well, most of the time. Until Mom started her own business. After that, she was too busy to get away on weekends. At least, that was what they told us. The real reason was that they weren't getting along." She turned the Scrabble box upside down, and the wooden tiles cascaded onto the worn candlewick spread. Lining up her tiles, she saw that she'd drawn a Q, but no U. Oh well, maybe she'd draw a U or a blank her next turn. "What about you? I'll bet you miss having your dad around."

"I see him practically every weekend. Mostly, we do stuff around the city. But he has this place out in East Hampton. Not like this. More modern, I guess. He's only had it since the divorce." He grew quiet, seeming to sink into himself.

"You don't like my father very much, do you?" Hannah said when the silence had stretched too thin. It wasn't a question.

He shrugged, and became suddenly engrossed in spelling out C-A-S-T on the board. Finally, he said, "I guess that makes us even."

"I don't suppose it would do any good if we staged a hunger strike," she sighed. As if in reply, her stomach rumbled. Thinking of the Cornish hen downstairs made her realize how truly pathetic she was. How could she expect to be like Gandhi when she couldn't even go a whole night without food?

"She already thinks I'm weird. Everyone does. If I stopped eating, I'd just be racking up more couch time with my shrink."

"I don't," Hannah told him. "Think you're weird, that is."

He frowned at his letters in furious concentration, but she could feel his pleasure at her approval as surely as if he were Trixie wagging her tail. "Is E-S-O-P a word?" he asked.

"Only with an A in front, but that'd make it a proper noun, so it wouldn't count."

"Hannah?" He looked up, and as the light caught his face she saw a tiny tear, like a bead of sleep, in the corner of each eye.

"Huh?" She pretended to be busy sorting through her tiles to make R-A-G-G-E-D, which would earn her a double word score.

"Do you ever think about how much easier their lives would be without us? I mean, like, he used to care about your mom, right? And now she's history. Maybe we're next."

"It's different with kids," Hannah said, but his words were a cold finger brushing her heart.

"My dad is always saying how much he loves me . . . but when I'm with him, mostly what he talks about is my mom. Always wanting to know if she ever talks about him, and if she's going to marry this jerk—I mean, your father." He hung his head, his silky brown hair fanning away from his forehead.

It was the sight of his neck so exposed that did it. Hannah was taken aback by the wave of compassion she felt for this geeky kid who before, when she'd even noticed him, had always been more an irritant than anything else. She saw now that he was hurting like she was, maybe even more.

"Listen, I'm starved," she told him. "I could eat about six of those Cornish hens, but I'll take whatever's left. Do you think you could sneak a plate of food up to me?"

"Sure. But it's not like you're being punished or anything. I think they feel bad about what happened."

"Yeah, but I *do* have a reputation to uphold, if you know what I mean—even if it *was* partly my fault."

Chris bounced up from the bed, sending tiles skittering across the board. "I'll see what's in the fridge. I know there's lots of ice cream."

"Just as long as it doesn't have nuts. Oh, and, Chris . . . ?"

"What?" He half-turned on his way out the door, flicking his hair out of his eyes as if to get a better look at her.

"Thanks," she said softly.

"De nada."

"Just remember, you're talking to the Scrabble Queen of New York. I'm going to slaughter you when you get back."

"Up your nose."

"With a garden hose."

Flashing her a snotty grin, he was gone. A second later, she heard him clumping down the old wooden stairs with a purposeful sound that made her think that maybe, just *maybe*, she could get through this week, after all.

Throughout their silent dinner, Grace had held her anger in, but now, as they trudged along the snowy trail below the house, she let Jack have it.

"Jack, how *could* you? You've made Hannah hate me even more." Her breath blew out in ragged white streamers. "As if she doesn't already have enough ammunition against me!"

"That's for you and Hannah to work out," he said, his voice as cold as the air she could feel stinging her cheeks. "But as long as you're under *my* roof, I won't tolerate Hannah's treating you rudely."

"I see," she said. "It's not that Hannah treats me like shit. You'd just rather she did it somewhere other than in your house."

Now she stood shivering, shin-deep in snow, wishing she'd worn ear muffs and gloves. Even with her knitted hat pulled down low and her hands shoved deep in the pockets of her parka, she felt her ears and fingers growing numb.

She could hear Jack sigh—was it exasperation? "Grace, you're twisting my words. Why do you want to make this any worse than it is?"

"Worse than this?" she cried. "It's *you*, Jack. You're refusing to see what's been going on under your nose! If only you'd talked to her before this . . . made it clear to her that you and I aren't"—she swallowed—"that I'm not just some *girlfriend* who might be long gone by next Christmas."

Grace sucked in her breath. What if Jack said she was *wrong*—that he had no idea where they'd all be next year?

"Grace . . ." His voice was pitched low, and she felt something bad coming—something she needed to get away from quickly.

She walked ahead of him, the only sound now the crunching of snow under her boots—and his, as he loped to catch up with her. Now came the low reedy cry of an owl, and the distant sound of a dog barking. Bare branches arched overhead, making Grace feel as if she were in a cathedral where she was expected to walk softly and speak in a whisper, when what she wanted to do was stamp her feet and shout.

Jack was a silhouette beside her in the moonlit dark, his huge shadow tilting over the snow before him. Beneath the thickness of her down jacket, she felt him grip her arm.

"*Listen* to me," he commanded. He sounded a bit out of breath, but it couldn't have been from running. Jack was strong as a Brahma bull. "I *do* want us to be together . . . not just for now, but a year from now."

"And after that?" she challenged him.

He was silent, and it seemed then as if the cold had seeped through her heavy jacket, right down into her heart.

"I've always been honest with you, Grace," he said. "The truth is, there's a lot I'm still not sure about."

"You mean our kids?"

"Hannah and Chris . . . they're only part of it." He was shaking his head. "Grace, I'm no spring chicken."

"You're fifteen years older than I am, Jack," she reminded him, feeling almost relieved. *So that's what he's afraid of!* "You make it sound like fifty!"

"Maybe it doesn't seem like much of a difference now, but . . ." His voice trailed off, and now there was only the starchy sound of his boots punching through the snow.

"But someday you'll be seventy, and I'll be fifty-five? Is

that what's bothering you? Jack, I don't believe you! That's like me worrying over whether Hannah's *children,* when she has them, will like me."

"Easy to say when you're at the young end of the scale," he reminded her.

"I'm far from being a kid, Jack. I'm old enough to know what I'm getting into."

"You think you know. But do you? Your father died suddenly, and your mother—she's far from being an invalid, I'd say." He paused, taking a deep breath. "Grace, in twenty years, maybe sooner, you could be stuck looking after an old man. How can you make any kind of promise when you don't even know what it is you might be committing yourself to?"

"And if I don't?" she challenged. "What then? I lose everything. I'd rather have ten or twenty good years with you than spend the rest of my life regretting that we didn't take a chance."

He sighed. "I wish I could believe that."

"Jack, you've always looked after everyone. Would it be so awful to have someone looking after *you* for a change?"

"Not if it meant your feeling tied down. And you *would,* Grace, believe me. What if I weren't even able to make l———"

"Sshhh, don't talk that way." She placed a finger against his lips, but even so a shiver traced its way up her spine. Quickly, she changed the subject. "Now . . . what's this thing you wanted to show me?"

A smile crept out from under the grim mask he wore. He fished her hand out of her pocket, and squeezed it hard. "Come on . . . it's just a little farther."

"It better be good. I'm freezing my butt off."

She felt her anger fading, yet she ached inside knowing that Jack still had not asked her to marry him.

"Don't worry—if it falls off, I'll find it." He grinned, his teeth impossibly white in the shadows.

Grace felt a smile tugging at her lips, but she refused to give in to it. She couldn't forgive him for being so stubbornly practical.

"We're almost there. . . ." Jack's voice carried toward her on a plume of frosty smoke. His steps slowed as he negotiated a slippery stretch that wound down a low embankment, and he finally came to a halt at the edge of a clearing bordered by the frozen stream.

Then she saw it, where before there had been only grass and shrubs—a miniature version of Jack's cabin, all wrapped in shingles that gave off a faint scent of cedar she could smell even from here. There was a porch in front, shadowed by the pitched angle of the roof, and she could see the corner of a snow-laden deck that overlooked the creek in back. A chimney jutted up over the roofline, and she could make out the small woodpile at the foot of the stairs that led up to the door.

"Merry Christmas," Jack said softly. "Your own studio, fully equipped. Only one key to it, and it's yours. You can hole up here and write till the cows come home."

He'd built this for her! She knew from renovating her loft what a tremendous amount of work it must have been for Jack—the meetings with the architect, tracking down hard-to-reach contractors, taking time out of a busy day to look at tile samples and paint strips and door hardware.

She felt something crumble inside her . . . an almost physical sensation, as if the snow where she stood had suddenly given way, plunging her down, trapping her. At the same time, she was filled with a sense of sparkling delight that dissolved the last vestiges of her anger.

"Jack. Oh." She felt too stunned to do anything but stand there, rooted in the snow, a bitter wind whipping the fringe of her knitted scarf up against her cheek. "God, I'm so . . . I don't believe this."

"I know it's not a real Christmas, like what you're used to."

"Oh, Jack. It's better."

"Come on, I'll show you the inside." He sounded like a kid himself, as excited as Chris used to get on Christmas morning.

The interior was marvelous. Painted white, with a built-in work center of pale oak that wrapped around three-quarters of the main room. Bookshelves going all the way up to the pitched, skylit ceiling, plus a computer, phone, fax machine—everything she needed to work here indefinitely. A cast-iron Lincoln stove in the corner, set in a cove of bricks, that in addition to the gas line he'd installed would throw off enough heat, Jack explained, to keep her toasty even on the coldest days. But, best of all, sliding glass doors that opened onto the deck, where in warm weather she could sit and look out over the creek.

He showed her the tiny kitchen in back, where she could make herself a cup of tea or a bite to eat if she didn't feel like trekking all the way back to the main house. There was even a bathroom with a shower, finished in rough cedar and quarry tiles. When it was all steamed up, he said, it would smell like a rain forest.

She imagined what it would be like in the spring, sun streaming in, her papers spread everywhere, the sound of the creek rushing below.

But for now, there was only this moment, this wonderful man looking down on her with love written all over his face, holding out this incredible gift. She saw how he would fit on the deep cushiony sofa, and how the pitched roof gave him all the height he needed in this small space. She pictured him with his paperwork out on the deck, a pair of reading glasses perched on his nose, keeping her company while she sat at her computer. His quiet presence giving her a warm sense of security, like a blanket tucked over her knees.

"I love it, Jack," she told him, whispering it in his ear as she wound her arms around his neck.

"About Hannah . . ."

She shook her head to silence him. In this place, she vowed silently, whether she was by herself or with Jack, she wouldn't let anything or anyone intrude.

"I sincerely hope that sofa unfolds into a bed," she told him, smiling up into his blue eyes, feeling him draw her into the warmth of his unzipped parka. "Because, if not, I want to exchange it for one that does."

"It does," he told her, his chin resting on the top of her head, his voice like some rich, potent brandy seeping down through her, down into her bones, making them glow.

Grace watched Jack gather up cushions from the sofa and, with a single powerful jerk, unfold its mattress. She was shivering, but this time it wasn't from cold.

"Kiss me," she urged softly.

At that moment, the electricity went, plunging them into darkness. She felt Jack's lips curve into a smile as they touched hers.

"Don't tell me *this* is part of my surprise as well," she murmured.

"Only if you believe in fate."

"Absolutely."

She felt his hand pushing up under her sweater, his fingers fanning out over her belly, large and rough-skinned and unbearably gentle. Her skin tightened with gooseflesh, but not from the cold air skating along her bared midriff. It was Jack's touch . . . his wonderful sorcerer's touch. Any shred of disappointment she might have harbored, any lingering wish that this studio had been a diamond ring instead, was banished by the warmth of Jack's lips, and the great, comforting bulk of his body pressing against hers.

"I'll freeze," she protested with a laugh as he tugged her sweater over her head.

"No, you won't," he whispered. "I won't let you." In the darkness, as she wriggled out of her jeans, she was aware of him shedding his clothes. Then came the shock of his heat against her own nakedness.

She could feel his hardness, an urgent pressure against her hip. She reached down and began stroking him. She loved pleasuring him like this. She loved even the feel of him in her hand, velvet-skinned and so completely male, rising and stiffening with each thrust. Jack groaned, and she felt a shudder pass through him.

"Is my hand too cold?" she whispered teasingly.

"No . . . don't stop." His breath was coming in ragged bursts.

"Is this how you want it?" *She* wanted him inside her, but would gladly do this for Jack, knowing he would make it up to her later.

But Jack's answer was to scoop her up, holding her so that she could wrap both her legs about his middle. He carried her to the sofa, laying her gently onto her back while he lowered himself onto his knees between her legs.

"Now you," he said.

Before she could protest—tell him she wanted him inside her—there was Jack's mouth. Teasing. His tongue, light, expert, guiding her to a trembling pitch. Oh, God. How could he ever, *ever,* have believed they would not always have this?

Even as she was crying out, her hips riding the waves of pleasure now coursing through her, Grace knew there would be more. A moment later, Jack was inside her, and this time he was not holding back—she could feel him giving in to his own need, letting go.

Grace came again with a sharp little cry that for once she gave voice to, letting it swell, becoming the scream she'd held back so many times before, fearing Hannah or Chris might hear. Now it seemed to carry her to some new, uncharted place . . . and as Jack responded with a cry of his own, Grace suddenly knew where she was.

Home.

It was long past midnight when Grace and Jack finally tiptoed upstairs to bed. Passing Hannah's room, Grace saw a strip of light shining under her door. She paused, her hand on the knob, then had a better idea.

Waving Jack on ahead of her, Grace crept softly back down the stairs to retrieve the gift-wrapped box stowed among the jumble of bags she'd left by the door. Technically, it *was* Christmas morning, she told herself. Even if Hannah didn't celebrate it. And, still wrapped in the glow of Jack's lovemaking, Grace felt sure that nothing, not even Hannah, could make her feel bad.

Nevertheless, as she made her way back up to Hannah's room, Grace's heart was in her throat. She knocked softly.

"Come in," Hannah called groggily.

She found Hannah sitting up in bed, reading. Her sleepy, unfocused expression changed at once, closing as abruptly as the book she was now snapping shut. Quickly, before Hannah could ask her to leave, Grace crossed over to the bed and set the gift down on the rumpled spread covering Hannah's legs.

"Merry Hanukkah," she said, realizing even as she smiled weakly at her own joke how lame it was.

Hannah look startled, a bit sheepish. "What is it?" she asked, in the exact same tone Chris used whenever she put a plate of unfamiliar food in front of him.

This time I won't get upset, Grace told herself.

"Open it and see," she said lightly.

Hannah slowly peeled back the wrapping, as if she feared that any moment something might jump out and bite her. Or, worse, that she actually might *like* whatever Grace had gotten her.

But when the top of the box came off, and Lila's leather jacket appeared from beneath folds of tissue, not even Hannah could contain her delight.

"Oh . . . it's . . . it's . . ." she stammered, throwing it on over the T-shirt she wore in place of a nightgown. "I can't believe it. It's exactly what I would have picked out." Then, as if realizing she'd let her guard down, Hannah was blushing and once again drawing her mouth into a narrow line. In a painfully correct voice, she added, "Thank you very much. It was nice of you to get it for me."

"I sort of inherited it," Grace explained. "In another life, it belonged to Bruce Springsteen."

Now it was apparent that Hannah, as she rolled her eyes in disdain, thought Grace was pulling her leg.

"Really," Grace told her. "My friend Lila knows him— he used to come into her dog-grooming salon."

"No kidding?" She was starting to open up again, just a little bit. Her eyes gleamed. "I mean, you wouldn't make up a thing like that, would you?"

"It's true . . . but don't tell anyone. No one would believe it." Hannah didn't have to know that Lila sometimes exaggerated. "It'll be our secret."

Hannah looked a bit skeptical at the idea of there being any secrets between them, but, with the precious leather jacket draped over her shoulders, she could only nod. Somewhere outside, a windchime tinkled, and a silly thought popped into Grace's head—that bit of nonsense in *It's a Wonderful Life* about how, every time a bell chimes, it means an angel has earned his or her wings. At that moment, Hannah smiled—a natural, open smile aimed directly at her.

I'm no angel, Grace thought wryly, *but I've certainly earned this.*

"Well, I'd better be getting to bed," Grace said as an awkward silence loomed.

She was halfway to the door, feeling only a little bit let down, when Hannah called softly, "Grace?"

Grace turned, holding her quickening hope in check, in case it turned out that Hannah merely wanted her to switch off the light or lower the window shade.

"Merry Christmas," she heard Hannah say in a lovely, sweet voice, without a trace of sarcasm . . . and, before Grace could make too much of it, she added, "Would you turn off the light on your way out?"

Chapter 11

Arriving home Thursday evening the following week, Grace found two letters from Blessing in the stack of mail that awaited her. The first one, written on a thick cream note card in her mother's firm, correct hand, was short and almost painfully succinct:

Dear Grace,

Thank you for your invitation. I will be arriving January 15, and staying with Win, so there is no need for you to trouble yourself in any way. My love to Chris.

As always,
Mother

The second letter was longer, its looping scrawl instantly recognizable as Sissy's. Grace even caught a faint whiff of her sister's favorite perfume, Shalimar, from the pink stationery with flowered borders.

Dear Grace,

Thank you for the steak knives you sent for our anniversary. I have some already that Aunt Ida gave us when we got married, but not with bone handles. Too bad you couldn't make it to the party, but to be honest, I think your being there would've upset Mother, who I am very concerned about. She hasn't been herself lately, a fact which has probably escaped you.

I'll put it bluntly. Mother is seeing someone. Notice I don't mention his name, mainly on account of I can't even bear to say it much less put it down on paper. Let's just say he used to teach English at the high school, until he lost his mind or found Jesus or whatever it is that would make a grown man want to throw over everything to mow lawns for a living. I think you know who I'm referring to. She says he's just a friend, but who knows? And the other day when I stopped by to borrow her vacuum cleaner (mine's being fixed), there he was drinking coffee at the kitchen table with his shirtsleeves rolled up like he owned the place. He had Mother laughing so hard about something she had tears running down her face. I was shocked to say the least.

What I'm getting at is that I think all this stress Mother has been under on account of you-know-what, has really knocked her for a loop. Of course I do what I can to cheer her up, but even though she tries to hide it I can tell she feels pretty low (except with Mr. R., which just shows you how bad it's gotten). But I suppose it's only natural she'd be upset over her own daughter planning to publish a load of bald-faced lies about Daddy.

Grace, how could you? After all Mother and Daddy have done for you? I know you never got along all that well with her, but what did she do to deserve this? Mother has nearly worn herself into the ground raising money for Daddy's memorial library, which thanks to all those articles about your book may not get built after all. If you had any shred of *decency left, you'd stop all this and let well enough alone.*

About Mother's plan to go to New York, I worry about her traveling such a distance. Her health isn't what it used to be, but I expect some good may come of it. I know that deep down you want what's best for her, the same as I do.

Beech sends his regards. He's taken off work for a few weeks and is thinking about a career change. He'll be sorely missed down at Spangler Dodge, but there is no room for him to move up and he's much too smart to be stuck in one place. He's considering a position managing that new Sizzler opening up out by Mulberry Acres, so we'll see.

The boys are fine. Bobby's fifth-grade class went on a field trip to the cemetery, and guess what he came home with? A rubbing of Eugenia Bell Clayborn's grave, 1803–1876. She was our great-great-grandmother, in case you've forgotten.

Your sister,
Caroline

P.S. Thanks also for the boys' Christmas presents. The jogging (?) suit you sent Beau is too small, so I'm sending it back. I hope you can exchange it, but don't worry if you can't. Down here we have Little League, so I guess the jogging craze never caught on.

Grace, in a fit of annoyance, crumpled Sissy's letter and tossed it onto the floor. Her sister pretended to be so concerned about Mother, but it was really only Sissy's way of sticking it to Big Sister. Damn her!

But then, just as quickly as it had come, Grace's irritation with her sister passed. Poor Sissy didn't even qualify as a thorn in her side—more like a sticker, or a tiny splinter. Anyway, she really ought to feel sorry for Sissy, who had nothing in her life but that awful husband (*Career change, my foot—I'll bet they fired him*) and those two impossible boys.

It was Mother who was making her sweat now, despite the loft's thermostat's having been pushed down to fifty-five while she was away. Ever since Jack had talked her into inviting her mother up for a visit, Grace had been regretting her offer . . . while at the same time not really believing Mother would take her up on it. And now she was actually coming! Grace felt her stomach tighten. But it was more than just nerves, she realized—she felt so *unprepared*.

Mother, when she made up her mind about something, was nearly immovable. How could she, the errant daughter, manage to persuade Mother to drop this lawsuit she was threatening? *If only I had someone on my side other than Win—someone who could help me convince her. . . .*

Jack? He was usually wonderful at negotiating. But why should Mother listen to him? She didn't know him, and the mere fact that he was Grace's publisher would be enough to prejudice Mother against him.

But it was two weeks before she'd have to face her mother, she reminded herself. What was the point in getting all worked up about it now?

As Chris drifted off to his room, Grace went into her office to listen to the messages on her answering machine. Win had called to let her know about Mother, in case she hadn't already heard. And her agent, Hank Carroll, who'd been fielding the press in her absence, needed to talk to her about a piece *Esquire* was doing on the new rumors about Senator Truscott. . . .

Then a familiar yet unexpected voice jumped out at her.

"Grace, I think we should talk. Give me a call."

Nola. Grace's heart flipped over.

What did she want? Had Nola changed her mind about giving her an interview?

Grace picked up the phone and quickly punched in Nola's number. Busy. Damn. She waited a few minutes then tried again. Still busy. She glanced at her watch—after six. Even if that wasn't Nola on the line, she ought to be home from work by now. . . .

Grace, still in her fleece-lined corduroy car coat, impulsively grabbed the knit cap and mittens she'd left on the hall table, yelled to Chris that she was going out for a little while, and then was flying out the front door and into the elevator.

Grace mounted the steps of the once-grand, now somewhat decrepit-looking brownstone, and rang the doorbell to Nola's floor-through. Why *did* Nola call? Maybe, after reading the manuscript, Nola was having second thoughts about stonewalling her. Was she ready to talk? Or had Nola wanted simply to chew her out?

The security-barred front window of Nola's first-floor apartment was lit, but the clutch of Chinese-restaurant menus stuck in the mail slot might mean that she hadn't yet returned from work.

Even so, Grace waited, head ducked low against the cold wind that stung her cheeks and her neck, where the pulled-up collar of her coat didn't quite meet her chin. Down the street, a car alarm went off. Though she seldom paid much heed to the city's never-ending assault on her senses, Grace now wanted to clap her hands over her ears.

The intercom crackled. "Who is it?"

"It's me," Grace answered unthinkingly. Her heart began to pound.

Why hadn't she identified herself? Why would Nola even

recognize her voice? Yet Grace had an inexplicable feeling that Nola *would* know it was her.

The door swung open, and an oblong of light spilled out, exposing an imposing square-shouldered figure who stood framed in the doorway. Grace blinked, her vision blurring for a moment before adjusting to the glare, and when she looked again Nola had stepped forward and was peering out at her.

"What are *you* doing here?" Nola, wearing a tailored navy suit with gold piping, looked as if she'd just arrived home. She hadn't even slipped off the dark pumps that looked as if they'd be uncomfortable as hell, and that Grace had just noticed were unusually large.

"I got your message," she said simply.

Nola nodded, as if she didn't need to be told why Grace hadn't phoned before dropping in.

This odd connection Grace sensed between them—had Nola felt it, too? Grace thought of an article she'd written years ago, for *The New Yorker*, about the long-term effects on two men, strangers to each other, of a gruesome Mafia murder they'd witnessed. And how those two—each of whom, fearing for his life, had refused to testify at the trial —brought together for the first time after more than a decade, had fallen into one another's arms and wept, speaking of their shared fears and horrific memories as if they were long-lost brothers.

Now Nola, after what seemed like an eternity, was saying with a weary sigh, "You might as well come in. I can't afford to heat the whole neighborhood."

Once inside, Grace looked around, surprised at the contrast between the deteriorating exterior and the pleasant tastefulness of the hallway she was standing in. Sponged blue-white walls hung with primitive Haitian prints, and what looked like an African wood carving displayed on the glass top of a starkly modern wrought-iron hall table. Covering the ceramic floor tiles was a worn but colorful Tibetan rug woven in a tiger-skin motif.

Nola, who must have noted something in her expression, commented with a wry chuckle, "Nicer than you expected, huh? Call it the spoils of war. In the high-rollin' eighties, Marcus sold a lot of junk bonds. After he moved out, I was left with this"—she gestured around her, a chunky gold bracelet sliding from her milk-pale wrist down her dusky forearm—"and Marcus hangs on to all those child-support checks he never gets around to sending."

"Sounds like you got the short end." Win's support check arrived promptly the first of every month.

"Not really. I've got Tasha and Dani." For the first time, Grace saw Nola's expression soften. "They're worth everything. You know what I mean?"

Grace nodded, thinking of Chris.

A silence stretched between them, its discomfort partially broken when Nola announced in a flat voice, "The only coffee is what's left over from this morning, if you don't mind reheated."

"I'd love a cup," Grace said, peeling off her coat and following Nola into the small kitchen opposite the stairs.

Here was none of the entryway's cool chic, only friendly clutter—children's drawings stuck up on the refrigerator with magnets, beginning to curl in at the edges; boxes of cereal and a bowl of half-eaten popcorn left out on the counter; plastic placemats on the table, sticky with rings left from juice glasses.

Nola took down a couple of mugs from a row of hooks above a sink piled with dirty dishes. "I just got home, so excuse the mess. Haven't even started dinner yet. You take sugar with that?"

"Just milk.

"Hope I've got some left." Nola disappeared behind the open refrigerator door, emerging with a carton of skim milk. "We're in luck. The girls'll only drink whole. Say this stuff tastes like bathwater."

"They're right," Grace said, laughing. She was beginning to feel comfortable here, chatting with Nola in her kitchen like they were a pair of suburban housewives.

Nola stuck her head into the refrigerator again. "I think I have some fruitcake left over from Christmas. Might even be from Christmas *before* last. . . ." She chuckled.

"Did you go anywhere for Christmas?" Grace asked.

"Nope. Stayed here—my landlady, Florene, cooked this huge feast and the girls and I helped, though we probably ate more than we contributed." Soberly, she added, "Dani . . . well, she had a bit of a tough time. Marcus promised to come by, but as usual . . ." She shrugged. "It's sort of like trying to believe in Santa Claus even when you know he doesn't exist. Tasha's older—she's seen enough of Marcus to know not to expect much."

"Chris's father—he's good that way."

"Still, it's tough, isn't it?" Nola observed dryly. "Even the best of them, they're not around when it counts. We have to wear two hats at once, and most of the time we're not even having a good hair day."

Grace smiled. "Sometimes being a mother feels like jumping through flaming hoops. You make it through one, and there's another one waiting." She thought of Chris's promise to her that he wouldn't skip any more school, but this, she knew, wasn't going to solve his real problem—the reason, whatever it was, for his rebelliousness.

"Don't I know it." Nola rolled her eyes.

Just then, a pair of little girls came running into the kitchen, one of them slightly fairer than the other, with her mother's pale-green eyes and wary expression. She stopped short when she saw Grace, and mumbled a shy "Hi."

"Hi there, yourself," Grace replied, giving her warmest smile. "What's your name?"

"*My* name's Dani," the smaller girl blurted out before her sister could speak. "I'm *six*."

"This is Tasha," Nola said, her arm moving protectively to her older daughter's shoulders. "She's ten going on forty." Addressing her daughters, Nola said, "Don't tell me you're hungry already, after all that popcorn Florene made you?"

"Pizza!" crowed Dani, hopping up and down. "I want pizza!"

"We had pizza last night, and twice the week before. You eat any more of that stuff, you're gonna have pepperoni for brains."

"Who are *you?*" Tasha turned her wide eyes on Grace, addressing her with a directness that cut right through to the heart of things. What exactly *was* she to Nola? Not a friend, though she'd have liked to be. But not an enemy, either, she hoped.

"I'm . . ." she started to say.

"A lady who's got no time for nosy questions," Nola cut in, giving Tasha an affectionate swat on the behind. She handed them each an oatmeal cookie from a big jar on the counter in the shape of a pig. "Now scoot, so we can get our business taken care of."

Seemingly satisfied, the girls raced off, leaving Nola and Grace alone. Nola placed a steaming mug in front of Grace at the small, round breakfast table, then sat down across from her. She'd taken off her jacket, revealing the cool ivory silk blouse underneath. Her hair was smoothed back in a bun, but the little wisps corkscrewing down around her chin and the nape of her long neck made her seem vulnerable somehow.

Grace took a deep breath and jumped in. "You said we needed to talk."

"Is this off the record?" Nola wanted to know.

Grace met her firm gaze. "I won't lie to you. The truth is, I *do* want this book to be as factual as I can make it. And anything you can tell me about your father or mine will help."

"I hear you," Nola said, "but, before I spill my guts, I want your word that nothing other than you and what you walked in with leaves this kitchen."

Grace hesitated. Damn. She wanted so much *more,* but if it was the only way to get Nola to talk . . .

Slowly, Grace nodded. "Okay. You've got it."

"I read it," Nola told her, subtly shifting gears. "The manuscript you gave me. It was . . . honest."

"Is that why you decided to help me?"

"I haven't said anything about *helping* you, have I?" Nola's eyes narrowed.

"Then why *did* you call?"

Nola sighed and looked away, at a framed sampler on the wall below a shelf crammed with cookbooks. A picture of a house and a dog, with the alphabet carefully cross-stitched underneath. At the bottom, it read, *Emily Morris, Age 9, 1858.*

"I don't know exactly," she said softly, running her long fingers absently down her throat and catching hold of the faux-pearl choker draped over the prominent knobs of her collarbone. "I wish I did. Honestly, I don't even know where to start. . . ."

"How about by telling me why you spent months ducking my calls?" She held up her hand. "Yes, I know what you told me at lunch—that you didn't want to get dragged into any kind of spotlight. But, Nola, I can't help wondering if there aren't other things, too, that are holding you back."

Nola remained silent, her expression growing even more clenched. Then, with what seemed like a great effort of will on her part, it became flat again, like a piece of crumpled paper that's been smoothed out.

I could ask her to leave right now, Nola thought, *and she'd never know.*

How could she convey to Grace the agonizing that had brought her to the decision? How could a woman who had never had to pretend she was someone other than who she appeared to be possibly appreciate Nola's position? And, now, too, everything was complicated by her library design, which the partners at her firm had entered in the competition. If Grace or her mother were to get wind of her involvement . . .

Staring at Grace, whose heart-shaped face looked so expectant, Nola felt a tightening in her throat.

I'm not doing this for you, she wanted to tell her. *I'm doing if for ME.*

And, in a way, wasn't it for Mama, too?

The truth shall make you free. Words from the Bible, from which Mama had read to her every night before bed. Surely Mama would have understood this need of hers, this burning inside, to tell someone, especially *this* someone, after all these years. . . .

Nola took a deep breath. *Okay, girl, you asked for it. . . .*

"What I said about your book—about it being honest? It was more than just that," she began in a soft voice, her gaze directed at a point beyond Grace's shoulder. "It was so *real.* You showed how he really was. Always helping people, not thinking of himself—like the way he helped Mama and me. But there's a big piece of his story that's missing . . ."

Grace waited, her heart like a fist thumping against her rib cage.

". . . something he never told you, or anyone. . . ."

"*What?*" Grace urged in a hoarse whisper, though she suddenly had a terrible feeling she didn't want to know.

"I'm your sister."

Silence settled over them.

Gradually, Grace become aware of the giggling laughter of girls at play down the hall. She glanced over at the clock on the stove. Only fifteen minutes since she'd arrived. How could that be? She felt as if an eternity had passed, as if history books had been written about what had gone on in the world since she'd walked in.

"But your father . . ." Grace started to say.

"*Him?* The man I called 'Dad,' he wasn't my father." Nola spoke sharply, her eyes glittering with unshed tears. "Oh, he had his suspicions—he just didn't know enough to pin the blame on anyone in particular. Lucky for Eugene Truscott, or it might've been *his* life that ended that day."

"I don't believe it. It just is not possible." Grace felt a numbness spreading through her, as if Nola had opened a window to let in a freezing blast. "All these years. Someone . . . surely there had to be somebody . . . We would have *known*."

"They were very, very careful about it," Nola went on. "And remember, we're talking early sixties—no matter how liberal people thought Eugene Truscott was, it wouldn't have crossed their minds: him with a black woman."

Grace covered her face with her hands. "No . . . *no*." At the same time, she was remembering that long-ago day, Margaret calling in a frenzy, begging Daddy to come. The act of a secretary . . . or a lover?

"You see? You don't want to believe it, either." Nola's voice was hard. "But he loved her, you know. Loved *us*. It wasn't just . . . a convenient arrangement."

Love? The word hit Grace like a blow. But what about Mother—hadn't Daddy loved *her*?

It was like how she'd felt after finding Win with Nancy, the floor seeming to open beneath her, dropping her into a black, spinning chasm.

"She got pregnant while Dad was at sea." Nola's crisp voice, oddly, seemed to anchor her. "That's what started to push Dad over the edge. But thank God he didn't know the whole story."

"What about your family?" Grace asked. "Aunts, uncles, cousins—do you mean to tell me that *no one* knew?"

Nola smiled then, with a sadness that brought tears to Grace's eyes. "Mama's family all lived down around Montgomery, so it was easy in a way. It was just us. I remember, when Dad had been away for maybe six months or more, I must have been around seven—I asked Mama why Uncle Gene couldn't spend *every* night with us. She hugged me tight and told me the whole story, made me swear never to tell." She took a deep breath, and turned her anguished gaze on Grace. "That's why I got so prickly when you first started calling. With you poking around, I was scared that sooner or later you'd dig out the truth." She took a deep breath. "Then I met you . . . and the lines started getting blurred. For one thing, I kept wanting to picture you as this mercenary bitch . . . and there you were."

"Just your plain old garden-variety bitch." Grace laughed brittly. Sensation was flooding back into her limbs, making her charged, jittery.

"Yeah, something like that," Nola said with a wry smile.

"If it were my mother here instead of me, she'd be calling you a liar."

"Is that what you think I am?"

"I don't know *what* to think."

"I know it must be a shock for you. But me? It feels so

good—finally saying it out loud." Nola tipped her head back, and let out a huge breath. "God, you have no *idea*."

"But there's still so much I don't know." Grace scrambled to sort out her madly tumbling thoughts. "*Everything. From the beginning.*"

This was not going to be a talk-show reunion of long-lost sisters, Grace thought. Sally Jessy Raphael was not going to be handing out Kleenexes while they sobbed in each other's arms.

Nola leaned forward, pushing aside coffee mugs and plates, and the fruitcake they hadn't touched. She grabbed Grace's hands, her fingers hard and cool. "You believe me, don't you? I want to hear it from you before I show you—" She stopped, biting her lip.

"Show me what?"

"Just say it. That you *know* I'm not making all this up."

Grace forced herself to meet Nola's eyes, no longer the green of tide pools, but black and bottomless as the ocean itself. She felt herself shivering, almost convulsively. Even when she clenched her teeth and hugged herself she couldn't make the shivering stop.

Daddy and Margaret. How? How could a lie so monumental have remained a secret? Wouldn't Mother have known . . . or at least *suspected?* Mother had made it a point to keep herself informed about everything Daddy did; nothing escaped her, not unless it was something she didn't want to—

Grace felt something snap into place inside her, like pieces of a puzzle being joined. Mother? This was *just* the kind of thing she'd have buried . . . buried so deep that even *she* could eventually make herself believe it had never been there in the first place.

"I believe you," she told Nola in the dead cold voice of someone who has no other choice *but* to believe.

"Good." Nola sat back, and Grace glimpsed the relief behind the grim set of her features. She stood. "I'll be right back. Wait here."

Watching Nola leave the room, Grace swallowed an ironic laugh. Leave now? How could she even get up?

At the same time, a voice in her head was telling her to run . . . crawl if she had to . . . just get away as quickly as possible from this person who claimed to be her sister, and from whatever proof—*photos, a diary?*—Nola was at this very moment digging from some drawer.

Grace, recognizing the voice as her mother's, sank back in her chair.

She would stay.

She would hear it all.

An hour later, as Grace left Nola's house, she walked as if in a dream, scarcely aware of where she was going. She didn't notice the patch of ice until the sidewalk was suddenly snatched up from under her. She landed awkwardly on all fours, badly scraping one knee.

She supposed she ought to feel pain, but right now she was too numb. For several long moments, she simply stared at her knee below the hem of her long woolen skirt, watching the blood trickle down into her boot.

In her mind she was seeing Ned Emory, the white bedspread turning crimson beneath his body.

She shut her mind against the image, and pulled herself to her feet.

She had to snap out of this daze, or next she'd be walking into the path of a speeding taxi.

She thought of Jack. His arms and voice comforting her, bringing her back to earth again. After dropping her off earlier this evening, he'd said he was going over to his office to plow through the mail that had undoubtedly piled up while he was away. Maybe he was still there?

If she'd been thinking clearly, she'd have stopped at a pay phone. But in her fugue state, she found herself heading toward the Flatiron Building as if on a guided track. When she arrived, the doors to the reception area were open, but no one was behind the desk. She was about to leave when she heard an office door open down the hall. Moments later, Benjamin appeared.

As he stood gaping at her, Grace caught a glimpse of her reflection in the glass wall of the conference room, and realized what a shock she must have given him—white face, disheveled hair, bloodstained skirt, and all.

Ben quickly ushered her into the nearest office . . . which happened to be Jerry Schiller's. Seating her on the couch between helter-skelter stacks of books and manuscripts piled on the cushions, he bent to examine her knee.

"Whew. Looks deep. You probably could use a stitch or two."

"It's not that bad," she told him, pressing a balled-up Kleenex to it to stop the fresh bleeding.

"Can I get you something?" Ben asked. "Band-Aid? Or maybe a brandy, if there's any around? You look really shook up."

"Honestly, it looks worse than it feels."

"If you want to know the truth, you look like a kid who fell off her bicycle and is trying to be brave about it." Ben, raising his eyes to meet her gaze, gave her so tender a smile that she felt immediately warmed.

He got up and perched himself on a corner of Jerry's cluttered desk, his legs stretched out in front of him, narrow calfskin loafers planted on the carpet next to a stack of manuscripts. Looking at him, she imagined him the poised, accomplished young man she'd always hoped Chris would grow up to be.

It struck her again how odd it was that Ben didn't have a girlfriend. She knew from Jack that plenty of women right here in the office were interested. But no one he dated was ever brought home to meet Jack or Natalie.

"My father used to say the reason I was so scrawny was because every time I gained a pound, I'd scrape it right off," she told Ben. Suddenly it became too much of an effort, this lighthearted banter. In a bitter voice, she added, "He told me a lot of things . . . not all of them true."

As if hypnotized, she stared at the crease in Ben's pant leg. How did he get corduroy to look so crisp? And how did he manage to keep his belt looped over itself like that, as perfectly knotted as a tie?

"Grace, what's wrong?" She heard Ben speak, as if from a distance. "Forget what I said about falling off a bike—you look as if you've been hit by car."

"In some ways, that's what it feels like."

"For God's sake, what *is* it?"

Grace hesitated. "Is your dad around by any chance?" she asked.

Ben shook his head. "You just missed him. He's on his way downtown to meet with some desperate author who called a little while ago. But, hey, I'm not a bad listener.

The truth was, though she liked Ben, she didn't feel all that comfortable confiding in him. But he was here, he was sympathetic. And Jack might be unreachable for hours . . .

She heard a door slam in one of the offices down the hall, and watched the ladder of shadow and light from the building's exterior fixtures shining through the blinds behind her play across Ben's handsome face. And in that instant, while dust motes flickered through bars of rippling light, while his shadowed eyes rested on her, cool and green and somehow remote, a voice in Grace's head whispered, *You'll regret telling him.*

As if sensing her reluctance, Ben moved away from the desk, and pushed aside a stack of books to sit beside her. "Grace, whatever it is, you can trust me."

Ben was Jack's son, she told herself. And he'd always been decent to her. Anyway, she'd only promised Nola she wouldn't make any of this public.

"It's Nola," she found herself blurting. "Nola Emory, you remember her?"

"How could I forget?" Ben smiled.

"I just found out that we . . . she and I . . ." She filled her lungs, and finished in a rush of expelled breath, "We're sisters." She felt once again that sudden, spinning loss of gravity that had come over her at Nola's.

Haltingly, she told him the rest. How Nola had erased any last doubts by showing her a letter written to Margaret by her father. In Grace's mind, like an epitaph engraved on a tombstone, one line stood out: *It's killing me, Margaret, this double life. Is there a way to end it without hurting those I love?*

There were more letters, Nola had told her, but what would be the point of her reading them all? Wasn't this all the proof she needed?

Ben listened without moving or shifting his gaze. When Grace was finished, he inclined toward her, his eyes alight with more than just sympathy.

"What if you could get her to hand over those letters?" Benjamin's voice took on a quiet urgency. "Your book. My God, Grace, do you know what we'd be looking at in terms of publicity? *Sales?*"

"I wasn't thinking of my book," she replied.

Grace wished now that she hadn't told Ben. Jack would

not have reduced this to simply a matter of the bottom line.

Her head cleared suddenly, and she sat up straighter. "Ben, you won't tell anyone, will you? Not even your father, if you happen to speak to him before I do?"

"Not a soul," he promised. "But Grace, you have *got* to get those letters."

She let his words sink in. Ben might be an opportunist . . . but he also happened to be right. This wasn't just about her and Nola. What she had just learned in Nola's kitchen cast a new light on everything she had written. Everything she had ever *believed*.

"I'll talk to her again. . . ."

But she had the unsettling feeling that she and Ben were interested in the letters for different reasons.

For a moment or two, he appeared sunk in thought, his head lowered, chin held clasped in one hand. Then he raised his head abruptly.

"Have *you* told anyone besides me?"

"I came straight here."

"Good," he said, as if to himself. "That gives me time."

"For what?" Grace asked.

He smiled. "What I meant was, there's still time before we go to press. For you to make additions, or rewrite certain chapters."

"Maybe . . . but what if Nola refuses to cooperate?"

He grinned, and something behind that flash of perfect white teeth made her suddenly uneasy. But not as uneasy as his next words.

"Well, you know what they say—there's more than one way to skin a cat."

Jack held her until the trembling subsided.

"Do you want to sit down?" he asked. "Can I get you

something? I think I have a bottle of sherry in here." He turned and began rummaging on a shelf of the linen press he'd converted into both bar and catchall for things like manuscripts he hadn't yet gotten around to, ABA posters he kept meaning to have framed, promotional giveaways like the box of balloons bearing the slogan: HOW TO RISE TO THE TOP WITH BOTH FEET ON THE GROUND.

"You're the second man this evening to ply me with liquor," she told him with a shaky laugh as she sank onto the sofa. Luckily, Jack had been home when she called a short while ago. He'd offered to come right over, but she'd made him promise to stay put. She hadn't wanted Chris to hear all this . . . not yet.

"Who was the first?"

"I stopped by the office before coming here, and ran into Ben." She glanced at her watch—half past ten. How had it gotten to be so late? It felt as if she'd left Ben no more than an hour ago.

Jack poured her a glass of sherry and set it on the table by the sofa. In his apartment's good-sized living room, made even larger by an absence of all but a few pieces of furniture, she would have felt marooned had it not been for Jack.

"Now," he said, settling beside her, one arm wrapped about her shoulders. "Do you want to talk about it?"

She told him everything, including her having confided in Ben.

Jack fell back against the sofa cushion, clearly astounded by her bombshell. She was thankful that he wasn't leaping up to point out gleefully what a publicist's dream this was, the way Ben had . . . but why wasn't he saying anything?

Finally, Jack turned to her and in a grave voice said, "Are you going to be okay? Screw the book—all I care about is how you're taking all this." It was exactly what she needed.

Tears welled in her eyes. Always, all her life, it had been this way. She would twist herself into knots to keep from crying in public, but the merest hint of sympathy when she was feeling low, and she started leaking like a sieve.

"Oh, Jack . . ." She swallowed against the lump in her throat. "I'll be okay. I'm just so . . . so . . . oh, I don't know." She slumped into the crook of his arm.

"Angry?"

Grace looked at him, and realized he was right. She *was* angry, damnit. At her father, for having lied to her. At Nola, too, for waiting until now to tell her. It didn't change what had happened to Ned Emory—she knew without a doubt that his death had been an accident. But in a way, wasn't Daddy indirectly responsible? Despite Ned not knowing who Nola's real father was, he *had* been well aware of the fact that she wasn't *his*. Otherwise, would he have been driven to turn his gun on Margaret?

"How could he do this to us?" she cried.

"What makes you think he was doing it to hurt you?" Jack asked.

"Jack, don't you see? He *lied* to us. Not only that, he had a *child* with Margaret."

"A child you're afraid he might have loved more than you?"

At that moment, Grace hated Jack. But then it dawned on her that he was only trying to help her sort out her emotions. She took a deep breath.

"Maybe." Something twisted inside her, bringing a hot pain. "Oh, Jack . . . what if he did?"

"I think it's entirely possible," he began slowly, "that he loved you even *more* than he would have under ordinary circumstances. I imagine that, when he looked at you, he wasn't thinking of Nola, but of how terrible it would be if you were ever to turn your back on him."

Grace's tears spilled over, scalding her cheeks. "Yes, he loved me—that much I *am* sure of."

"What you don't know, then, is where your mother figures in all this."

Grace remembered Mother's impending visit, and clapped a hand to her mouth. "Oh, God, she'll be here in two weeks!"

"Are you going to tell her?"

Grace thought for a moment, then said, "I have to. But I have a feeling she might already know—even if it's only deep down."

"Does this mean you're planning to revise your book?" His expression gave away only a hint of the expectation he had to be feeling.

She put her hand on Jack's knee, feeling more steady than she had in the past several hours. "Yes," she told him. "Not because it'll help Cadogan—and don't get me wrong, because I *do* want what's best for you, too—but for me. I think, in some ways, I've always known there was something missing from our perfect family portrait. I didn't know what it was, but that didn't stop me from looking. Maybe that's what made me decide to write this book in the first place."

Jack smiled. "I can't help thinking of that Chinese curse: Be careful what you ask for—you might get it."

Grace stood up. "I'd better be off. I told Chris I wouldn't be gone long."

"I'll drive you, then."

"Jack, you don't have to—"

He hushed her with a kiss. "There have to be some things in life you can count on. I'm one of them."

Can I really count on you? Grace wondered. If both Win and her father—whom she had counted on and believed in the way she'd believed in the epistles taught to her in

Catechism—could let her down so profoundly, then could she trust that Jack wouldn't as well?

An hour later, as Grace was getting ready for bed, she paused in the midst of brushing her teeth, arrested by a startling thought: *Nola is more like me than Sissy is.* Shaken by the realization, she rinsed her mouth, and dropped her toothbrush onto the marble counter next to an apothecary jar filled with odds and ends—tiny jewellike seashells, old marbles, buttons, sequins, and beads—she had picked up here and there over the years.

She stared at her reflection in the mirrored medicine cabinet, absently noting the paleness of her skin and the dark circles under her eyes. One word echoed in her head: *sister.* Now that the shock was beginning to wear off, she wondered what it would be like having Nola as a sister.

Strange? Awkward? Yes, but . . .

Was it possible they could ever become friends? Would she one day be able to confide in Nola as she'd always wished she could with Sissy?

I don't know why you'd want to waste your time with someone so much older than you when you could have had Win back just by snapping your fingers. Grace could almost hear Sissy's holier-than-thou reply to a confidence she might have imparted about Jack.

Nola, on the other hand, she could imagine smiling that world-weary smile of hers, and saying something like, "Love doesn't always walk in the door with a smile on its face—sometimes you've got to take it where you can get it."

Unlike Sissy, Nola, she felt sure, wouldn't need to take pot shots at her sister in order to feel better about herself. Whatever her hang-ups or jealousies, Nola seemed the type to deal with them straightforwardly. Not only that: as a single mom, she had to be used to handling things on her own.

Like me.

As the similarity sank home, Grace watched a tiny, wry smile surface in the mirror.

She imagined, too, getting to know Nola's girls, and found herself warming to the idea. She hardly knew Sissy's boys, much less felt close to them. The one time Sissy and her family had come to visit her in New York, back when she'd been married to Win, Beau and Billy had nearly torn her place apart with all their roughhousing. And when she herself had finally scolded them, her sister had risen up in indignation, as if Grace had taken a strap to their bottoms (which, come to think of it, might not have been such a bad idea).

Dani and Tasha, on the other hand, had seemed so sweet. What would it be like to take them all the places she used to take Chris—before he'd declared a moratorium on all that "baby stuff"—the Children's Museum, the zoo, F A O Schwarz? How would Nola's daughters feel about an aunt dropping down out of the blue?

And what about Chris? How would he react to being presented with this whole new family branch? Would he pull away from Nola as he had from Jack?

So many questions. For each one that presented itself, a dozen more cropped up. Grace's mind spun. For now, all that seemed clear was that Nola's declaration, rather than being merely an epilogue to their parents' story, was just the beginning for Nola and Grace.

Chapter 12

"I'd really hate to lose this book." Ben struggled to keep from sounding like some overeager editorial assistant, but then he just couldn't hold back. "Dad, it could be big . . . really big. I thought it might just be hype, but I've heard it from two sources. Producers at Paramount and Fox are making offers. I'm telling you, all the scouts are buzzing about it."

Seated across from his father's desk, cluttered with picture frames—including a photo of him as a chubby Bar Mitzvah boy, which he hated—Ben felt as if he were on fire. His list desperately needed shoring up—in case all his wining and dining of Roger Young failed to keep Roger from walking. But, seeing Jack's contemplative expression as he sat tilted back in his thronelike Victorian swivel chair, Ben realized that his father, as usual, was going to make him sweat . . . and in the end might even say no. *Damn him.*

Ben felt himself beginning to itch all over, and knew that, if he were to peel off his jacket and roll back the cuffs of his shirt, he'd find a rash beginning on the insides of his forearms.

"Two hundred thousand is a lot to offer for a book that still needs major work," his father quietly responded.

"Somebody, and I'm pretty sure it's Random, is at one seventy, but at two I'm almost sure we could close it out. Dad, this could be *The Firm* all over again. Phil Harding not only can write, but he's with one of L.A.'s top law firms— the atmosphere's so real, you're actually *there.*"

"But what about the plot? Jerry says it has some big holes."

Ben felt like exploding, but he kept his fists, his whole body, tightly clenched. Schiller, the windy old fart, what did he know about commercial fiction?

"For God's sake, to him no one's any good unless he's William Faulkner, or maybe Saul Bellow," Ben responded in what he hoped was a reasonable tone. "We're not talking the National Book Award, Dad. With some editorial work and some decent promotion, this one could hit the *Times* list."

Ben could feel the rash on his arms and under his collar growing itchier, and remembered how his dad had had to tape socks over his hands when he was little to keep him from scratching his hives raw. He felt like that now, as if his hands were tied. Jesus. Why couldn't the old man, for once, just *once,* listen to him?

"I like your enthusiasm, Ben." His father was speaking in his I'm-the-most-reasonable-guy-in-the-world voice. "But we've got to be realistic. What I see is an author with no track record, a first novel with problems that may or may not be fixable. For twenty thousand, even fifty, we could risk taking a shot. But to make this work, we'd have to go well into six figures on marketing and publicity."

"Lou Silverstein at William Morris is hinting that we might be able to work something out. Like giving us a flow-through on foreign sales, for one thing." He didn't have to explain to his dad that, the bigger the advance, the more Hollywood would stand up and take notice.

"That could make a difference." Jack leaned farther back in his chair, clasping his hands behind his head, but his expression remained dubious.

With his silvering hair and clear blue eyes, his father could model for a life-insurance ad, Ben thought. *Put your trust in me, folks, I won't let you down.* Which was pretty much how everyone at Cadogan saw him—the editors and their assistants, the marketing-and-sales force, even the ponytail-and-earring characters in the art department. His secretary, too, lanky horse-faced old Lucy Taggert, had been in love with him for years. He remembered Dad once complimenting her on a scarf she was wearing, and damn if she hadn't kept wearing that thing every day for a month. The only one here not kissing his ass was Reinhold.

"Listen, Dad . . . I know things are kind of tight right now"—damnit, why did he have the feeling he was sixteen, asking if he could borrow the car?—"but I really believe this will work. I'll *make* it work."

You owe me this. My position in this company, my career, my whole future, was all tied up with Roger Young. And you've done your best to shoot all that to hell. Yes, he's a creep . . . but couldn't you have sent the woman on a nice trip to Hawaii instead of slapping Roger's wrist?

Now Dad was smiling indulgently, and leaning forward, planting his elbows on his desk. The morning light streaming through the vertical blinds glinted off a smiling photo of Hannah in a heavy silver frame. Ben wanted to smash it, hurl it at the wall.

Eight years ago, when Dad had offered him a job at Cadogan, Ben had figured on editorial assistant at the very least, maybe even junior editor. Forget his being the boss's son, he was a Yalie, Phi Beta Kappa, had even published in *Zirkus*. But, damnit, there was Dad, reminding him of that stupid scam he'd pulled his freshman year, rubbing his nose in it all over again, then sticking him in the *mail room* for six months. Yeah, sure, he could have walked away, gone to some other house. But he'd made up his mind: he was going to prove himself to his old man if it killed him.

And in a lot of ways, he *had* proved himself. Even for-

getting about Roger Young, hadn't it been his idea to call
their run-of-the-mill diet book *The Santa Fe Diet,* repackage
it with before and after photos of the Superrich and Formerly
Fat, then juice it onto the best-seller list?

But editor-in-chief—*that* would really mean something.
Ben could see it in his mind, just beyond his reach—Jerry
Schiller's corner office down the hall, nearly twice the size
of his own. All it would take was another little nudge in the
right direction and Reinhold would send Jerry packing. A bit
more maneuvering and it could be "Benjamin Gold" on the
brass nameplate next to what was now Jerry's door.

But with editors who'd been here longer than he angling
for the job, he'd need something extra to put him at the top
of the short list—a coup even more spectacular than his acquiring the Harding book. And hadn't Grace, the other day,
unwittingly handed him the perfect opportunity?

If it were me, *not Grace, who got hold of Truscott's
letters—and I'd make sure Reinhold* knew *it was me—I'd
be the hero when Grace's book came up a big winner.*

First, though, he'd have to find some way of prying those
letters away from Nola Emory. He recalled his first impression of her—tall, angular, beautiful in a formidable kind of
way. In a short amount of time, he'd gotten her to open up
a bit, even to laugh. And those sexy eyes—so at odds with
her cool poise. He'd pegged her at once: *She's lonely for a
man, but hell will freeze over before she'll admit it.*

The truth was, he'd actually been hoping for an opportunity to get to know her. The women he'd dated, they were
all so obvious. A dinner or two, a concert, and they'd be
dreaming of registering for wedding china at Bloomingdale's
or Tiffany's. Nola wasn't like that, he sensed. *He* would have
to do the pursuing, win her over.

The prospect excited him.

"Things *are* tight, Ben," he heard Jack say. "Reinhold is

even thinking of cutting back on the publicity budget for Grace's book."

Ben felt himself grow instantly alert. "But that doesn't make sense," he argued. "It's our lead spring title, for Chrissakes."

Jack nodded, obviously disturbed by this new twist. "Apparently he got wind that there might be some sort of legal action taken by Mrs. Truscott. Her lawyer made some noises to that effect. And now Reinhold's worried that we'll be forced to do some heavy editing before the book goes out. If there's no sensational angle . . . well, I don't have to tell you."

Ben understood completely. Without some good dirt, Grace's book would be just another footnote to history, its only distinction being that it was written by the man's daughter.

"Listen, Dad, let's get real. You and I both know what's at stake, even if Reinhold doesn't," Ben said, dropping his voice. "Did you talk to Grace last night?"

"She told me what happened with Nola." Now Jack was looking tense, his normally rugged face drawn and somehow old-looking. "But I'm afraid that, for the moment at least, our hands are tied." He held out his palm to stave off Ben's reply. "And, Ben, until we can get a handle on this, I want you to keep quiet. With Mrs. Truscott already on the warpath, we don't need the press picking up on any more undocumented stories."

Ben fought his annoyance; did his father think he was still a kid, incapable of keeping a secret? "But what if we *could* somehow get those letters? Then we'd have proof."

"That would change things, of course. But I wouldn't hold out much hope of that happening. According to Grace, Nola was pretty adamant."

"Maybe Grace just doesn't know the right way of convincing her," Ben said, smiling.

"Ben, I hope you're not going to suggest something underhanded."

Jack tipped his head in such a way that his gaze seemed to be falling on Ben from a distance, the way it had when Ben was little and Dad a good deal taller than he. How did his father always manage to make him feel like he could never measure up?

"I was just thinking that Nola might come around if there was something in it for her," Ben said mildly, knowing it would be a mistake to let his straight-arrow dad in on what he was planning. "Grace could offer her something, maybe a percent or two of her take."

"Your grandfather peddled pots and pans from a pushcart on the streets when he first came from the old country," his father said, smiling. "You remind me of him, always looking to cut a deal."

"It got him his store, didn't it?" When was Dad going to let go of this Eisenhower-era idea that you got ahead merely by the honest sweat of your brow?

"Yes, it did, at that," Jack said, laughing his great booming laugh. Ben imagined the assistants outside in their cubicles pausing from their typing to lift their heads and smile as if they were part of the joke. Lucy, just outside, would probably go into heat.

"Dad, getting back to the Harding book." Ben sensed that now was the moment to push. "Let me go to two twenty-five if I have to—give me that much. I promise you won't regret it."

His father frowned, clasping his hands in front of him, mulling it over.

"Two *hundred*," Jack said at last. "And that's it. I'm sticking my neck way out on this as it is."

"You won't regret it, Dad." Ben stood up.

"I hope not," he heard his father say, and had to grind his teeth to keep from shouting, *Damnit, why can't you ever just trust me?*

But he'd pretty much gotten what he wanted, hadn't he? Now he had to get back to his office, and make the offer. Then he'd track down Nola Emory. He'd already called her office, pretending he had some urgent blueprints for her, and had conned the receptionist into telling him that Nola would be out on site most of the day, at a building going up on East Forty-ninth.

Those Truscott letters—he *had* to get them.

Every dog has its day. Growing up, hadn't he heard that often enough? Well, this one, Ben thought, is going to be mine. . . .

Ben watched Nola Emory pick her way across the construction site—a tall woman in a billowy hunter-green coat, like a Douglas fir rising up incongruously amid slabs of precast concrete and hillocks of steel girders and cranes. She carried a roll of blueprints tucked under her arm, and was speaking to a hard-hatted foreman, gesturing emphatically. She didn't look pleased. The odd thing was that, except for her hands and arms, she remained perfectly still, not even shifting her weight from one foot to the other . . . though it was clear from the expression darkening the foreman's Pillsbury Doughboy face that she was getting her point across.

Then he pointed up at something, and abruptly Nola took a step back, not minding—or, more likely, not even noticing—that she was half-standing in a puddle of scummy water. Head thrown back, spine arched, she watched an ironworker's torch on a steel platform many stories above her send a fountain of orange sparks spraying out against the putty-gray backdrop of the Manhattan sky.

Benjamin felt his breath catch. He found himself thinking of Howard Roark in *The Fountainhead*—which he'd devoured by the buggy light of a bedside lantern the summer he was head counselor at Echo Lake. He'd loved the part where Roark, following the brilliant summation at his own trial, took his seat and yet somehow left the impression that he'd remained standing.

He imagined Nola was like that. He didn't know her, of course, but he guessed she'd be as uncompromising as Roark, and as dedicated to her vision. Though he'd been standing here a good ten minutes, sticking out like a sore thumb, she hadn't noticed him, or even glanced in his direction.

Benjamin blew out his breath, leaving a trail of vapor in the chill air. He felt apprehensive and at the same time as if he was about to embark on a thrilling adventure. She looked inaccessible . . . and delicious.

Now she was looking his way. Did she recognize him? Then a lifting of her chin, a widening of her eyes—yes, it looked as if she did. He watched her start toward him along a plank set in the rubble-strewn mud . . . and hesitate . . . then, as if resolving to deal with what might turn out to be a sticky situation, continue on.

Ben, for no really good reason, felt immensely pleased.

Her coat was not fully buttoned, and when she stopped short of him, he glimpsed her charcoal slacks and a gold sweater that hugged her curves. Her hair was pulled back in a sleek bun, and large gold hoops swung from her ears. He felt his heart leap, reminding him disturbingly of when he was Hannah's age and every gorgeous female had had that effect on him—like a bolt of lightning hitting him dead center.

"You'd think someone who'd been in construction for twenty years would know enough to grout around a tendon after it's stressed." She spoke aloud, as if to no one in particular, shaking her head in disbelief while her gaze remained fixed on the inept foreman.

Ben sensed her wariness, her curiosity, but in tossing the first serve she'd succeeded in throwing him off-balance. Score one for Nola.

"How do you know so much about construction?" Benjamin responded deftly. "I thought all architects did on a site was just make sure the design got carried out according to their plans."

This time, she looked right at him and smiled. "My ex-husband put himself through school on construction crews. I liked hanging around. You know, designing a building like this one is something like driving a car—you don't need to be a mechanic, but if you're ever stuck out in the middle of nowhere with your engine acting up, it could save you."

"Sort of like publishing," he said. "The trouble with editors is, we can tell an author what's *wrong* but we can't always come up with a way to make it right."

"Except that, with a not-so-good book, no one loses a finger or a foot . . . or their life." Nola turned and looked up at the concrete-and-steel-girder tower sketched against the sky. "Ben, right? You're Grace Truscott's stepson-to-be." Her tone was casual, but her eyes and the faint blush along the sharp line of her cheekbones told him that she remembered him.

"Not quite," he laughed. "I suppose I will be if my father ever gets around to popping the question." He thought of the day after Dad had moved out, how his mother's face—despite numerous eye tucks, lifts, tightenings—had been transformed into an old woman's. Ben felt a pull of anger, so familiar it was like a force of gravity, making him heavy, powerless.

But now Nola was meeting his gaze with a directness that made Ben forget about his father, squinting slightly, as if she were sizing him up for a business opportunity . . . or maybe just trying to figure him out.

"Did you just happen to be passing by, or was there something particular you wanted to see me about?" she asked.

Ben became fixated on a speck of ash caught on the tip of one of her eyelashes. Each time she blinked, it fluttered, seeming almost to drop away before being pulled back into the dark thicket of her lashes. He felt an insane urge to reach up and brush it away.

"This may sound dumb"—he was doing his best to sound ingenuous—"but I was hoping I could get you to join me for lunch." He glanced at his Rolex. "I don't have to be back at the office for another hour or so."

"Can't," she told him, briskly, but not—he sensed with relief—trying to brush him off. "I'll be tied up all afternoon with this. I was just going to grab a sandwich at the deli around the corner."

"Mind if I keep you company?"

"You have better things to do, I'm sure." In other words, bug off.

"Can't think of any at the moment."

She shot him a narrow look. "Give me a break."

"It's true. After the morning I've had, I'd welcome a trip to Belfast."

With a shrug, she finally said, "Okay, but the place I'm thinking of is strictly takeout. Belfast might seem like a better alternative than sitting outdoors in this weather." Her glance, as it dipped down to take in his lightweight cashmere overcoat, seemed wise to the fact that he was dressed more for show than for warmth.

Ben felt the chill, all right, but he wouldn't have traded his cashmere for the warmth of L. L. Bean, not even to impress Nola. Thank God for his grandmother's trust, he thought, grateful that he didn't have to depend on his miserly salary at Cadogan. The only downside was his mother's constantly reminding him *which* side of the family that money was coming from.

Fifteen minutes later, he was sitting on a bench in Rockefeller Plaza, freezing his ass off and wishing he'd campaigned harder for a table, comfortable chairs, a bottle of wine. Nola, he marveled, didn't seem to mind the cold at all. She was tucking into her turkey sandwich as if this were a Fourth of July picnic.

Watching her, Benjamin forgot for a moment about the cold. He found himself searching for a chink in her armor, a muss in the hair pulled tight over her head and knotted at the nape of her neck. As if such a thing might be a key to some vulnerability of hers, some small portal, like the spot on an oyster where a knife can be worked in far enough to pry it open.

He saw that she was having trouble with the lid of her hot tea, and gently took it from her. "Here, let me do that for you." His fingers, warm from the fur-lined gloves he was pulling off, found the tab on the side of the plastic lid and yanked it free.

Nola didn't thank him when he handed it back. She just sat there, her head cocked to one side, squinting at him.

"Thanks," she said. "But why do I have the feeling there's more to this than lunch al fresco?"

"I don't know what you mean."

"Yes, you do. There's a catch somewhere—I just haven't found it yet. Did Grace send you?"

"No," he answered honestly. Through his overcoat he could feel his heart beating. "Look, maybe I should have called first. . . ."

She touched his sleeve. "No, I'm sorry. It's just that . . . Lord, have you ever been woken up at midnight by a reporter calling from Los Angeles to pester you with a lot of nosy questions about your father?" Clearly, she wasn't aware that he knew who her *real* father was. "I'm just tired of all this, and crabby as hell, and there's gonna be eighty more minidisasters back at the site to go over with Fred before I'm through."

"I don't blame you for being gun-shy," he told her. "But the truth is, I wanted to see you." It *was* the reason he was here . . . part of it, anyway.

She turned to watch a group of little girls bundled in parkas and leg warmers sail out onto the skating rink on the level below. Then she was facing him once more, her smoky eyes piercing him. "Why?"

"Do I have to have a reason?"

Seeing the skepticism she wasn't even trying to hide, Ben suddenly had a wild thought. What if he forgot about the letters and just let this thing with Nola take its own course, whatever that might be?

But, no. He needed them, badly. . . .

"Am I supposed to conclude that you're interested in *me,* personally, aside from any connection I might have with Grace?" Now she sounded sharp, suspicious.

"Yeah, I know how it must look," he admitted. "Maybe this wasn't such a great idea. I'm really not sure why I'm here, except I like you. I'd like to get to know you better."

Looking away from her, at the multicolored banners whipping at the end of the flagpoles bordering one end of the rink, he felt the pressure of her hand on his arm. Even through his coat and the wool sport jacket he wore underneath it, the contact brought a tingling to his groin.

"I didn't mean to be rude," she told him, her voice softening. "Subtlety just isn't one of my talents."

"Lack of subtlety can come in handy with foremen," he teased, bringing his gaze back to meet hers. "I'm sure it's not easy with guys like that . . . your being a woman."

"I manage."

"Did you always know you were going to be an architect?" Ben asked suddenly.

"I used to love walking past other people's houses, imagining what it would be like to live in them," she told him, brushing crumbs from her lap. "When I was little, I played with Lincoln Logs instead of dolls. My mother . . ." Nola paused, like someone wading in the shallow end who suddenly finds the bottom of the pool snatched out from under her. He saw the hesitancy in her face, the worry over plunging into deeper water.

"Until I was six years old, *my* mother had me convinced that F A O Schwarz was a toy *museum*." Ben quickly guided them onto safe ground. "When I finally discovered you could actually *buy* stuff there, I went totally nuts. I made her ante up for six years in about six minutes."

"You were lucky," Nola said with a rueful chuckle. "Your parents could afford to indulge you."

"Yeah . . . except my dad was almost never around."

"Do you like kids?" Nola asked.

"Sure." Had another woman posed that question, he'd have instantly been on guard . . . but Nola wasn't feeling him out about marriage, he was certain. She was just making conversation. "How about you? Grace tells me you have a couple."

"Two girls."

"Both in school?"

"If you can call it that." He caught the bitterness in her voice.

"You don't sound too happy about it."

"You wouldn't be, either, if you had to watch your kids get knocked around, day after day, by the lousy public-school system." She crumpled her sandwich wrapper and tossed it into the paper bag by her side. "Oh, hell, don't get me started on *that,* or we'll be here all day."

Ben experienced an unfamiliar pang, a feeling of wanting somehow to make things better for her. *Careful, Ben-o,* he told himself. *Don't let yourself get carried away.*

He touched her arm. "Would you have dinner with me tonight?" He smiled. "It's the least I can do, offer you a table somewhere warm."

"Ben, I don't think that would be a good idea." Nola ducked her head so that her expression was hidden from him.

"Give me one good reason."

"Look, my life is really complicated . . . and, right now, you'd just be another complication."

"Like taking a chance on a guy you're not quite sure you trust?"

"Last time I did that, I wound up married with two babies."

"Dinner, that's all I'm offering." He held his hand up. "Scout's honor."

He could sense Nola relenting. "Well, I suppose one dinner wouldn't hurt," she told him. "But it'll have to be early. I'm warning you, keep me out past my bedtime and you'll be stuck carrying me home." She tucked the cup into the deli bag and stood up.

Ben felt pleased and uneasy both. He could sense that managing this woman was going to be a lot harder than he'd imagined. Any man who ended up carrying Nola to bed, he thought, would be getting a lot more than he bargained for.

"Nice place." Ben looked around him as he climbed the last step into her second floor living room, pursing his lips in a soundless whistle.

Nola hadn't realized how uptight she was about asking Ben back to her place for coffee after dinner, until now, feeling the tension begin to leak out of her. It *was* a nice apartment. And she'd earned it—nine years of being suffocated by Marcus.

Which is exactly what could happen, you let some other man in your life, a bitchy voice warned her.

As if it were a needle on a gauge, she felt her apprehension creeping back up into the red zone, where it had been just a moment ago, when she'd been fumbling with her keys, dropping them twice before she managed to get the front door unlocked. What could she have been thinking, asking Ben in? And even before that, taking Florene up on her offer to keep Tasha and Dani upstairs at her place for the night.

Dinner at Raoul's had been fun, for sure. But now . . . she ought to tell him to leave. This minute. Before he got any ideas. Where could this lead?

He wasn't even her type, not really—a bit too slick, too sure of himself. On the surface, that is. Underneath was a different story. In Ben, she sensed a dimension that was missing in all of Marcus's big talk and flash. Hidden depths . . . or some secret pain? She didn't know . . . and she didn't *want* to know. She'd had enough of trying to heal the wounded little boy in supposedly grown-up men.

At the same time, how long since she'd shared a bottle of wine with a man who could make her laugh? And who could draw her out of herself with his seemingly genuine interest in everything she had to say?

Shit. She cursed herself, knowing she was not going to tell him to leave. Not tonight, at any rate. She'd been listening to Florene for too long, imagining this kind of thing was as easy as falling off a log. *More like falling off a cliff,* she thought.

"It's not exactly Park Avenue," she said, moving to one of the tall French doors that overlooked Twenty-second Street. "Listen to realtors talk and they'll tell you the neighborhood's coming around. But streets like mine—it looks like they already came around and *went.* Still, a ceiling like this is enough to make it all worthwhile."

As if seeing it all through Ben's eyes, Nola took in the white walls and lofty ceiling sponged with a bluish shade of white that made it almost seem as if you were inside a huge, nearly transparent eggshell, with the sky showing through here and there. The old parquet floors stripped and varnished, with a single pale Chinese runner in front of the fireplace with its incised slate mantel.

In the center of the room, against the built-in bookshelves, sat the antique maple rocker that had seen her through the nursing of two babies. Across from it, separated by a worn Bokhara rug, was a low-slung canvas-backed deck chair in pale-green and white stripes, and a futon covered in faded green Sea Island cotton. For a change, too, Florene, had straightened up. No toys and crayons scattered around, tabletops and walls wiped clean of smudge marks left by sticky little hands.

Florene didn't need a crystal ball to know I'd be asking Ben back here after dinner.

She saw Benjamin's gaze resting on her Steinway, bought at an auction for next to nothing, then stripped and rebuilt by a friend of Marcus's—yards of ebony so brilliantly glossed she could see the cluster of rice-paper lanterns, arranged overhead in place of the old chandelier she had taken down, skimming like pale ghosts along its surface as she moved toward it.

"Do you play?" he asked. "Sorry, dumb question. Somehow I don't think of you as someone to own a thing like this just for show."

"I play," she said. "Does that surprise you?"

I scrubbed toilets, washed floors, shopped for old lady Halliday to pay for lessons, and I'll bet your rich daddy and mommy couldn't shove them down your throat.

"I don't think anything about you would surprise me," he told her.

Nola felt chagrined. Was it his fault he'd been born white and well-off? She must be getting irritable with age . . . or was it just that she'd been too long without a man?

A whole year, fourteen months really, counting the two she and Marcus had stopped making love before he moved out. And before that, what kind of love was it, lying under a man, feeling as if you're being *shrunk* somehow?

And now, why *this* man?

She thought back to their dinner, Ben asking whether she preferred Italian or French, then confessing he'd made reservations at two restaurants so she could choose. And then, at Raoul's, instead of showing off with the wine list, he'd quietly asked the sommelier's advice—though it was obvious he knew what the guy was talking about.

Was that what had impressed her? Not really. What she'd found endearing was his asking her what books she enjoyed reading, and where she liked to go on vacation ("Rome," she'd told him, "but I've only been there in my fantasies"), and how she felt about that controversial new office building going up on East Eighty-ninth.

She'd liked it when he teased her into confessing her astrological sign, then had sent her into gales of laughter with a slew of made-up Gemini attributes. Best of all was that he hadn't touched her. Not once. No meaningful glances across the table while groping for her hand. No happening-to-brush-up-against-her-leg. No fumbling kiss when they got into his car.

Maybe that was why she wanted him now.

The smartest thing for her to do, she thought, would be to make up some excuse, tell him she was fresh out of coffee . . . or that any minute the girls would be back. Or the truth, that she was bone-tired.

Right now, she could feel Ben poised expectantly beside her. But she knew that, if she sat and played the music sitting up there, Schubert's Impromptu, Opus 90 No. 3, so exquisite and sensuous, she'd be lost.

"Do *you* play?" she asked him.

"I took lessons in grade school," he told her, running a thumbnail lightly over the keyboard and sending up a rippling sound, like running water. "Right up until my mother caught me smoking pot with my teacher, Mr. Ortiz. She threatened to have him deported."

"You're kidding."

"He kept telling her he was from Cleveland. He was *born* in this country, for Chrissakes. But she wouldn't listen. My mother thinks, if your name ends with a 'z,' it must be on a green card."

He looked so artless, leaning back against the belly of the Steinway, where it curved in like a woman's waist. Wearing dungarees and a pressed blue-and-white shirt under a gray wool sport jacket that had probably cost as much as he earned in a week as an editor. Yet, as she watched him run his hand through hair even darker and curlier than her own, she caught a glimpse of that lost-boy look in his eye defying her to send him packing.

Damn.

How dare he do this to her? How dare she let him?

Then Nola found herself sinking onto the piano bench, her long fingers finding the notes, releasing them into the still, poised whiteness that surrounded her. She sensed, rather than saw, Benjamin grow very intent, his presence seeming to stretch out like a shadow, long and thin and sharp, piercing her. The music flowed through her . . . over her . . . filling the air with its sweetness.

She raised her eyes to meet his still, clear gaze, and saw that he wanted her—as much as, maybe even more than she wanted him.

Then he was behind her, his fingers smooth and cool against the nape of her neck, his thumbs moving down her spine, caressing each vertebra. She shuddered. Lord, it'd been so long . . . too long. . . .

Waiting until it made sense, or until they'd been out on a proper number of dates, none of that would have mattered. As she felt him bending to kiss her neck, the heat of him, trapped between their two bodies, sudden and nearly overwhelming, Nola knew that wanting like this—it just *was*.

The low faint humming of the piano seemed to fill the stillness until she felt herself lifted by it . . . embraced by it and by him . . . each movement, each breath, carried forth into the room like a note, round and distinct. She felt his mouth on hers, soft and trembling. She tasted him, but could not remember another taste like this—a kind of sweet sharpness at the back of her jaw, like biting into green fruit. She was floating, way up high somewhere, and no last-minute reprieve was going to rescue her now.

"Would it do any good, my telling you to go?" she murmured against him, the stubble along his jaw stinging her lips, which now felt a little bruised, swollen somehow.

"I'd only come back." He gave a low, quavery laugh, perhaps to mask his own nervousness.

Then she was leading him into the bedroom, not bothering to switch on any lights. There was only the reflected glow from the street, outlining the window grate. A path of pale light lay across the carpet, spliced with rungs of shadow.

Buttons. So many, she thought, as she fumbled with the front of his shirt, which seemed to sprout a new button for every one she managed to unfasten. At last, feeling the cold metal of his belt buckle under her fingers, she imagined she was him; she was inside his head, wanting her, impatient for her to end this awkward mating dance. And in her belly the pressure she was feeling rode down hard, igniting a sudden, frightening heat.

There's no going back now.

"Your turn," he said softly, plucking at her sweater, skimming it over her head as she lifted her arms.

He unhooked her bra easily. She closed her eyes as he began to caress her breasts, first with his hands, gently, weighing their heaviness against his palm while letting his fingers ride up over her tightening nipples. Then with his mouth.

God. Oh, God. Had Marcus ever touched her with such tenderness? Had it ever felt this good? Never . . . never . . .

"You're shivering," he said.

"I'm not cold. It's just . . ."

"I know."

"I'm not very good at this, Ben. I don't have affairs."

"You're having one now."

"I'm all wrong for you."

"I'll stop if you want me to. Is that what you want?"

"Kiss me. Please, just kiss me."

His arms curving about her now, not asking, not seeking,

just *there*. Their bodies coming together as perfectly, as neatly, as two hands joined in prayer. She guided his hand between her legs, and heard him moan, his fingers thrusting into her.

He took her against the wall, all six feet of her, his hands cupped about her buttocks, half-lifting her, one of her legs hooked about his hard shanks, her pelvis tilted up while he eased himself into her . . . and drove and drove. . . .

She heard someone cry out, and realized it was her.

The darkness turned flat and gray, and an odd humming filled her ears. Starpoints of light glimmered behind her tightly shut eyelids.

The glow in her belly seemed to fill her, radiating upward until she could feel it shooting from the tips of her fingers, the ends of her hair, like sunrays.

"Nola, Nola," he groaned her name over and over.

Shuddering with a pleasure so exquisite it bordered on pain, she arched to meet his final thrust, feeling it slam through her in a fist of heat that drove her back so hard she felt her skull crack against the wall, and tasted the sweet metallic taste of blood on the back of her tongue.

Nola thought that, if at this moment she were to die from too much all at once, her only regret would be that she couldn't do it a second time.

Ben waited until they were lying side by side on the bed and her breathing had steadied. He waited until his mind had cleared and he could remember why he was here, why he had to get hold of himself before this glow inside him turned into something else—something he didn't know how to deal with.

He touched her hair, which was soft and springy as new

grass. She smelled sweet like grass, too. He felt something move in his chest, and a lightness pour into him like sun-lit air.

Christ, it had been good with her. The best he could ever remember.

She was everything that had been missing in the endless stream of women he'd dated. Strong yet tender, cool to the touch but hot underneath. He couldn't bear it when women draped themselves all over you after it was over, pestering you with, "How was it, was it good for you? Was it really good? What about when I touched you down there, how was that?"

Nola was silent, except for her breathing.

She didn't deserve this, him. What the hell was he doing? How could he go through with his scheme now?

He felt himself growing hard again. Jesus. He had to hold himself back from kissing her, from reaching for her and making love to her all over again.

"All right, let's talk about it." He spoke softly, aiming his words at a crescent of reflected light shimmering on the ceiling. "Let's get it out in the open. No matter what I've said, you're still suspicious of me. Because of who I am. Because of Grace; maybe my father, too. If we don't talk about it, we're not going to be able to go on from here."

She let out a deep sigh. "Amen to that." He could feel her breath against his cheek. "Ben, I'll be honest with you. It's never been like that for me. Not ever. But if you're here for anything but what you see lying next to you, then it's over. Right here. Right now. As of this minute, it never happened."

"Nola, I won't lie to you. I know who you are—Grace told me." Out of the corner of his eye, he saw her dart him a startled look, but before she could say anything he stopped her by lightly squeezing her wrist. "It's not what you think. She was in shock, and I happened to be there—that's all. That's not why I came to see you today," he lied, blood pounding in his ears like a distant surf.

Nola's eyes glinted in the darkness. "She must have told you about my father's letters, too."

"Yes." No point in denying it.

"If I handed them over to you right now, would I ever see you again?"

"That's not a question," he said. "It sounds more like an indictment."

"Well?"

"You don't really think that's why I'm here, not after . . ." Ben swallowed hard, feeling suddenly like the world's biggest shit. But was it so terrible, going after what he wanted? He wasn't hurting anyone, and maybe this part—the two of them—maybe he could still hang on to that. He took a breath. "Nola, the truth is, I don't give a damn about your father's letters. But while we're on the subject, I'll tell you what *I* think."

"I'm listening."

"Hang on to them. Don't let them out of your sight." He knew she'd been expecting to hear just the opposite, and he could tell from the sharp little intake of breath beside him that he'd thrown her off-guard.

"And if I changed my mind, decided to go public?"

"The press would crucify Truscott. Is that what you want?"

"They're doing that anyway. Maybe, if people understood *why* he had to cover up the truth about Ned Emory's death, that it wasn't just a political necessity, but a *moral* one—he really *cared* about civil rights, Ben. It wasn't just talk."

Nola, he realized, was playing devil's advocate, and for an unsettling moment Ben wondered just who was setting up whom.

"Are you saying you've changed your mind about co-operating with Grace?" he asked, his heart climbing up into his throat.

"No, that's not what I'm saying." She sounded troubled.

"It's none of my business," he said cautiously, "but maybe you should talk to someone before you make up your mind."

"Like who?"

"I don't know. A lawyer maybe. There could be something in it for you."

"This has nothing to do with money!" She spoke sharply, almost angrily. Then she sighed. "I'm not saying I couldn't use some extra cash, but I'd sell everything I own before I'd take money for those letters."

"It was only a sug——"

"Hey, look, there's no point in our discussing this—it's too complicated," she cut him off.

"That's what you said about me."

She turned to look at him, her forehead furrowed. "You messing with my head, Ben? That what this Q-and-A is all about?" Her voice was soft, but its message clear: *Back off.*

He rolled over, hiking himself up on one elbow so he was looking down at her. "Do what's best for yourself, Nola. Whatever that is."

She grabbed his shoulder, the hard tips of her fingers digging into him with surprising strength. "That's what my ex-husband used to tell me. Only what he thought was best for me was usually what *he* wanted."

"I don't want anything from you."

Looking at her, at the pale line of her shoulder against the hair spilling down her back, Ben almost believed his own lie. He felt a rush of tenderness . . . accompanied by an almost drowning sense of entanglement. Christ. What was he doing? What in God's name was he doing, getting involved with this woman? He'd hoped he was putting one over on her—but what if it was the other way around? She hadn't set it purposely, but he sure as hell felt he was in some kind of trap. And maybe he'd never want to get out.

The bedspread rustled as she turned onto her side to face him.

"Then make love to me again," she said in a husky voice, running a cool long-fingered hand over his belly, raising a shiver of goosebumps in its wake. "If I'm going to be a fool . . . I might as well be fooled twice."

"I wanted to see your face when I told you," Nola said to Grace. "So I'd know whether you put Ben up to it." She gave a chopped little laugh that was more a grunt. "Right now, you look like you just swallowed something too hot."

They were seated at a table in the dining room of the Gramercy Park Hotel, where Nola had asked Grace to meet her for breakfast. Since the day before yesterday, when Grace had come to see her, they hadn't seen or spoken to each other. If Ben hadn't provided her with an excuse, would she be here now?

Admit it, Nola told herself, *weren't you curious to see how she's dealing with that bombshell you dropped on her?*

What was making her even more keyed up was that the results of the design competition for the Truscott library were days from being announced. Nola believed Ben when he said he wasn't after Mama's letters—or why would he have urged her to hang on to them? But what if Grace had sent him to spy on her? And what if he should stumble onto the fact that it had been *her* design submitted under her firm's aegis? It was a risk she couldn't take.

Last night, after Ben left, with her mind going round in circles, she'd broken down and called Grace. It was after midnight, she'd realized too late, but fortunately Grace had been up.

Now, in the cold light of day, with Grace looking like she suddenly didn't know what to do with the fork in her hand, Nola was all at once certain that Grace could not have pulled a trick like that.

"*Ben?*" Grace said, her voice barely above a whisper.

"You told him about the letters, didn't you?" Despite Grace's apparent innocence, Nola couldn't resist sticking it to her a little.

She waited, hoping she hadn't been mistaken about Grace. But Grace, rather than becoming flustered, met her gaze head-on.

"I'm afraid so. But you don't think . . ."

"I don't think anything. Yet. I'm just asking."

Grace shook her head, and set her fork down. "I wish I could help you. The truth is, I don't know Ben all that well. He's not around much when I'm with his father."

Nola toyed with her scrambled eggs, finding that she'd lost her appetite. What had she been expecting? A signed confession? It was obvious Grace was as much in the dark as she was. Not just about Ben—about a lot of things.

"The truth is," she echoed with an edgy little laugh, "you don't know me all that well, either."

"I'm still trying to get used to the idea of you being my sister."

"Kind of gets stuck going down, doesn't it?"

Grace offered her a tentative smile. "It's getting easier. I've had some time to think about it."

"And?"

"Nola, I'd like us to be friends. I'm not sure what that would mean in our case. I'm not even sure it's possible. But I'd at least like to try."

Nola felt her throat threaten to close up, and she suddenly became absorbed in arranging the napkin on her lap. Even with her head down, she could feel those guileless eyes on her, feel them waiting for her answer.

She looked up. "I guess we'd have a long hoe to row."

"No kidding." Grace cracked a smile.

"Is this where we jump up and fall into each other's arms?" Nola quipped, feeling uncomfortably like she *was* becoming Grace's friend. She sat back, folding her arms over her chest.

"Get real." But Nola could see from the overbrightness of Grace's eyes that she was on the verge of tears.

"Pass the salt," Nola said.

If this were a movie, she thought, the camera would zoom in on the salt cellar, and show our fingers brushing as she passes it to me. Heavy on the symbolism.

But in the softly lit room with its crisp white tablecloths and air of faded elegance, had anyone been curious enough to glance over at their table, he would have seen only two well-dressed women smiling at one another as if sharing some joke. No one would have guessed they were sisters.

Chapter 13

"I don't know, Jack, it just doesn't feel right somehow." Grace lowered her head and tucked her hands in her coat pockets as a chilly blast came tunneling down Eighth Street. "One minute I'm telling Ben about Nola being my sister, and the next minute he's *dating* her."

They were heading home from Theatre 80 on St. Marks Place, where they'd seen *The Lady Vanishes*. Grace adored Hitchcock, but her own life's suspense had kept her from enjoying herself. Her thoughts kept turning to Nola and Ben.

Why hadn't Ben said anything? Grace wondered. Why was he being so cagey?

"Does there have to be a reason?" Jack asked lightly. "She's an attractive woman, and he's interested—I don't see what's so strange about that."

She suddenly felt annoyed with him . . . for being so casual about all this, and for seeming so impervious to the cold wind that was chilling her through layers of mittens and stockings and boots.

"I'm not accusing Ben of anything," she said. "I'm just saying it seems a bit coincidental, that's all."

"Haven't you had enough Hitchcock for one evening?" Jack said with that certain laugh of his that she knew was meant to humor her. But then, seeing that she was serious, he added, "Okay, do you want to know what I think? Leaving Ben out of it for the moment, I think you're still pretty conflicted about Nola. Your father, too."

Jack was right, she thought. She still had not gotten over feeling angry at her father. No matter how many ways she looked at it, or how she tried to justify it, he had deceived them.

"I was just wondering," she sighed, "what he got from Margaret that my mother wasn't willing or capable of giving him."

"Maybe she needed him."

"What do you mean?"

"Just that. Your mother, from everything you've told me, is pretty self-sufficient. Maybe your father liked being needed."

Grace turned this over in her mind. "You may be right," she said slowly. She scooped her hair out of her face, but the wind only blew it back. "I'm not sure my mother ever needed anyone but herself." She held up a hand. "Don't get me wrong—in a lot of ways, that was admirable. I always knew I could count on my mother, that things would be taken care of, that she was in charge." Not just in charge of big things—like helping Daddy campaign for re-election—but making sure that drapes got dry-cleaned, the garden fertilized, school vaccination forms sent in promptly, rubber taps put on heels of new shoes to keep them from wearing, and, each Christmas, that everyone from their elderly postman to the kid who delivered their newspaper received a loaf of Netta's currant pound cake along with a crisply ironed ten-dollar bill. "Oh, Margaret was capable, too, I'm sure—around the office, that is. But, from what Nola says, she really *depended* on Daddy. She needed him in a way that my mother simply couldn't have, even if she'd tried."

Jack was silent for a beat or two; then he said, "Okay, but I doubt your mother will buy that theory. Have you decided how you're going to handle this when she gets here?"

"I don't know," Grace said, feeling no less troubled now about all this than she had in the first hours of shock that had followed Nola's revelation. "What I *do* know is that, if I tell my father's story, it has to be the *whole* story."

"And if Nola doesn't change her mind about turning over those letters?" He didn't have to remind her that Cordelia Truscott would sue the pants off Cadogan if they were to publish anything about her father and Margaret that couldn't be substantiated.

"We'll cross that bridge when we get to it," she said firmly. "Jack, we're getting off the subject. . . ."

"Oh?" He wrapped an arm about her shoulders.

"My mother has nothing to do with Ben being involved with Nola." She felt annoyed at Jack, not just for reminding her that Mother would be here in exactly five days, but for treating her as he did Hannah when she was in one of her sulks. "And, please, *don't* tell me I'm imagining things."

Jack's arm dropped back to his side. "All right, then, just what *do* you think is going on between Ben and Nola?" Despite the ear-splitting jungle beat of a ghetto blaster making its way down Eighth Street, she had nonetheless picked up a new coolness to his voice.

"Nola seemed . . . Well, she didn't go into it, but I could tell from the way she was acting that she's more than just interested in him."

Jack shrugged, pushing bare fingers through his wind-torn hair. "She wouldn't be the first. I remember, when Ben was in high school, we had to install a second phone line to handle all the calls from girls."

"Yes, okay, but why *her?* He could have his pick of any of a dozen women." Passing a pizza parlor, Grace watched through the window as a swarthy-skinned man with flour dusting his arms to his elbows expertly tossed an oval of dough into the air. "Doesn't it seem odd to you that he would have homed in on Nola? And the timing, too—it's as if finding out she was my sister triggered this sudden interest of his. The only thing I can't figure out is *why*. What would he have to gain from it?"

"Does everything have to be about *gaining* something?" Jack asked, and this time the edge to his voice was unmistakable. "Can't a thing like that just *be?*"

"You mean, the way it is with us?" The words popped out of her, laced with sarcasm.

Grace shivered, knowing she ought to drop the subject . . . right now, before this discussion veered off onto more dangerous ground. The last time she'd pushed Jack too far —on their Christmas Eve walk through the snowy woods— she'd let it drop. She couldn't, *wouldn't,* do that now, even if Jack was content for them to just go rambling on as they were, living out of two apartments but never completely at home in either one.

"I thought we were talking about Ben." He smiled and started to reach for her.

"We were. But not anymore." She pulled away from him to swipe at her nose, which was running from the cold. "Oh, Jack, you just don't *get* it, do you? Nothing stands still, especially not relationships. You're either sinking or swimming, and right now it feels like we're sinking."

"Is it any better to rush into something you're not ready for?"

Grace wanted to cry. How could someone so smart be so stubbornly obtuse? At the same time, she felt a dart of panic. Jack wasn't trying to reassure her that it would all work out somehow. But this time, anger won out over anxiety. "I want to get married, Jack. I'm too old to be stuck in some kind of dating game that doesn't seem to be going anywhere."

"Grace . . ." he began.

"Yes, I know, Jack," she sighed, "you've always been a hundred percent honest with me. But right now I'm asking you to take a chance. On me. On us. Can you do that? Or am I just wasting my time here?"

Jack stopped and spun on her, his face stamped with high color that wasn't all from the cold, his eyes glittering in the puddled glow of a streetlamp. "Is that what this is to you . . . *wasting time?*" She'd never seen him so angry, not at her.

Grace felt as if a cold iron bolt had been shot through her chest.

"Don't twist my words around," she told him, hugging herself to keep from trembling. "You know what I meant."

"Grace, I'm not twisting anything around. It's *you* who're not appreciating what's right in front of you." Jack's shoulders, in his heavy overcoat, seemed suddenly to shift downward a notch. "But let's table this, okay? Now isn't the time or the place."

"When *will* it be the right time?" she asked in a breathless rush, hating herself for sounding desperate.

"I don't know," Jack told her, leaving her no better off, and certainly no wiser, than before.

The phone was ringing when Grace walked in, but she didn't rush to answer it, even knowing that Chris wasn't home. It probably had been ringing for a while, and if she hurried to pick it up, the person on the other end would surely, at that precise moment (as such callers invariably did), hang up. She wasn't in the mood for any more cliffhangers. Let whoever it was call back.

But even after she'd peeled off her coat, the phone was still ringing. She wondered if it was Chris, calling from downstairs to ask whether he could stay over at Scully's.

Walking briskly over to her desk in its cubbyhole of book-shelves, she picked up the receiver.

"Hello?"

"Grace, hi, I was just about to give up on you," Win's smooth voice greeted her.

She felt herself grow acutely alert, every nerve tingling.

"I just walked in. Guess I forgot to leave my machine on."

"Chris isn't around?"

"He's at the Scullys'. All wrapped up in some new computer game, no doubt. Did you want to speak with him?"

"No . . . it's you I wanted. I've been trying to reach you all week."

"I know, I got your messages. Win, I'm sorry. . . . I've been really busy lately." The truth was, she *had* been avoiding him. This thing with Nola—she hadn't felt ready to let Win in on what had happened. But now that Kappa Alpha voice of his, as ebullient as during their college days, made her think of old photos, a life that, though far from perfect, had taken on a gentler patina with time.

"Too busy to meet me for a drink?"

"Win, it's awfully late. And I just got in. Is this about Mother?"

"Not exactly."

In the background she could hear the pure sweet sound of Emmylou Harris, an album they'd played endlessly when they were married. She even found herself anticipating where the record was scratched and Emmylou's voice seemed to catch on a sob.

She sighed. "All right, then. But just a quick one."

"Claire. Twenty minutes." He hung up.

Fifteen minutes later, she was sitting at one of the small tables by the window at Claire, waiting for Win to show up, and wondering what she was doing here. It wasn't as if he'd twisted her arm. She'd had enough experience with her ex-husband to know that if he'd had something up his sleeve he'd have invented a good excuse for seeing her.

So what *was* he after?

She thought of their honeymoon in Mazatlán. In her mind, she could see Win standing on a rickety wooden dock, looking down at the iridescent water into which he'd accidentally dropped his Vuarnet sunglasses while climbing out of a motor launch. Then, before she could stop him, there he was, diving in—Bermuda shorts, polo shirt, Birkenstocks, and all. A gaggle of villagers standing there, jabbering to one another in Spanish, watching him surface, oily water streaming from his plastered-down hair, gasping for air, before jackknifing down again . . . and again. By the third time, she was screaming at him to stop. *Stop.* They were just *sunglasses,* for heaven's sake. But Win kept on. Down, down. Until, finally, he was exploding upward, arm thrust high, his sunglasses clenched in his fist, while the villagers let loose a cheer—as if he'd rescued one of their children from the deep.

"You beat me."

Grace looked up into Win's blue eyes, creased with amusement, and watched him settle into the chair opposite her. She glanced at her watch and saw that it was exactly twenty minutes since he'd called.

"I'm in the neighborhood," she told him. "You must have sprouted wings to get here this fast."

"I took the subway."

"Since when do you ride the subway?" She laughed. When they were married, Win was always making a case about how dangerous it was, how she was just asking to get mugged.

He shrugged, looking surprisingly unruffled, considering the rush to get here. "If I'd told you forty-five minutes, you'd have changed your mind."

"Probably." She stifled a yawn.

"Grace, I needed to see you." He wasn't smiling now.

"It must be serious if you couldn't tell me over the phone. Something tells me it *is* about Mother. Did she put you up to this?"

He shook his head, ordering a gin and tonic from the waitress who had appeared at their table. "I spoke with her last night. She's agreed to hold off on any legal action until the two of you can sit down and talk."

Grace felt herself softening. "Win, I appreciate everything you've done. I know it isn't easy to bend Mother around to anyone else's way of thinking."

"I'm doing it for you, Grace. Just because we don't happen to be married anymore, I still *do* care, you know." In the glow of the candle sputtering in its glass in the center of their table, his eyes seemed to take on an added brilliance. Could Win actually be thinking—?

"I know you do," she told him quickly, careful to strike a tone that was no more than friendly.

"Do you?" He placed a hand over hers, his fingers pressing into hers with a heated insistence.

Grace was gripped by a weird sense of déjà vu, feeling as if they were still married somehow.

It was almost a spell Win seemed to weave. Intimacy by implication. She *knew* it in her mind, and could often predict his moves—his reaching out to brush a wisp of hair from her cheek, or smooth her collar; the way, while waiting at the door for Chris, he would begin absently shuffling through any mail she might have left out on the small hall table. But, despite knowing better, she'd sometimes find herself falling for it. Not commenting, or even hardly *noticing*, when he drifted over to the refrigerator to help himself to a cold drink. Letting him get away with lines like, "That lock on the door looks flimsy to me—why don't I call someone and have him come take a look at it?"

Was it calculated? Hard to know. With Win, getting what he wanted just came to him naturally. He went about it as effortlessly as breathing.

"Win, I don't want you to get the wrong idea about—"

"Grace, I'll be honest with you," he interrupted. "I *do* have a selfish motive in all this. I need to know if . . . Christ, I can't even say it." His voice cracked, and she caught the gleam of tears in his eyes.

The only other time she'd seen Win cry was after she'd told him she was leaving him. Then she'd almost changed her mind and backed down. Maybe he really did love her, she'd thought. Maybe she ought to give their marriage another chance.

She remembered how he'd looked then—seated in the tapestry wing chair before her, his head bowed with anguish. There had been a light shining directly on his disheveled hair, so bright it seemed as if it were coming *from* him, a golden lamp casting its glow along the polished parquet floor as she turned and began walking toward the door.

Ever since they'd split up, he'd made no secret of wanting her back. What she didn't understand was *why*. What he really wanted was a woman who would expect little else from him other than the chance to adore him. And maybe she'd been that woman when they first married . . . but he had to know she certainly wasn't now.

That didn't mean that in some ways she didn't miss him. Or maybe it was their shared history she missed—not just memories of when they were first married, or of Chris growing up. She missed dancing to songs from the sixties with someone who knew all the right moves and could even sing the words. Watching *Saturday Night Live* with someone who got all the jokes. Someone who, when she jokingly used an old slang word like "bitchin'," understood that it was a compliment, not a complaint.

Jack had never heard of the Moody Blues, and though he'd been opposed to the war in Vietnam, he'd never marched in any rally. When her generation was home watching *The Brady Bunch,* he'd been grinding away at Yale. He rarely listened to anything other than classical music and old show tunes, and thought a Stratocaster was something you mowed the lawn with. And his only definition for a lid was something that covered a pot.

Even when you were crazy in love with a guy, Grace thought, you could be with him and still sometimes feel lonely.

She drew her hand out from under Win's and in a low voice said, "Why are you doing this, Win? Why *now?*"

"Have you forgotten what day it is?" he asked.

It dawned on her suddenly, and she found herself marveling for a moment that it could have slipped her mind at all. Not even since the divorce had she failed to mark the day, if only in her mind.

"Our anniversary. Oh, Win, I really *did* forget."

"Isn't that usually the husband's screw-up?"

"Win . . ."

"I know, I know." He held his hand up. "I'm not your husband anymore. You keep saying it. I just wish I could make myself believe it."

"Look, you should have told me over the phone. If I'd known . . ."

". . . you wouldn't have come," he finished for her.

"There's no point in going over the past. What good will it do?"

But Win was smiling. "Do you remember, Grace? How

the organist's car broke down and he was twenty minutes late? You were ready to go ahead. But I just couldn't imagine you walking down the aisle without music."

"It wouldn't have been exactly quiet." She smiled. "Not with your mother crying so hard I thought she'd flood the place."

"Good thing he did show up. Your sister would have married me out from under you if we'd waited any longer."

"Sissy *did* have the worst crush on you," she acknowledged with a chuckle. "I almost felt sorry for Beech, even though she was only going with him then, the way she'd hang all over you."

"I doubt if Beech noticed. He was too busy making eyes at *my* sister."

The waitress brought their drinks, which they sipped in silence. Grace had no more than half-finished hers when she pushed her glass aside and stood up. "I'd better be going," she told Win.

"Wait." He grabbed her wrist, lightly, his fingers moist. Up close, she could see that his eyes were bloodshot.

"I'm tired, Win. And I think we've said enough."

"One more thing." His mouth twisted up in a half-smile she found oddly endearing . . . even heartbreaking. She watched him lift his glass as if in slow motion. "A toast," he said. "To our anniversary."

Grace knew she ought to walk away—no, not walk, *run* in the other direction. But she felt as if trapped in warm sand. She found herself reaching out, her arm heavy and seeming to stretch on forever before closing about her wet glass. She lifted it to her lips and, in a voice that seemed not her own, said, "To our anniversary."

"It was just one drink," she told Chris as she was pulling her coat off at the door.

When she'd phoned the Scullys' to tell Chris she was meeting Win, he'd perked up at once, promising to be here when she got back. Now, seeing his eyes bright with interest for the first time in weeks, she wished she hadn't told him. No point in getting his hopes up.

"Was it Dad's idea or yours?" Chris was actually grinning.

"His."

"I thought so."

"It was just business . . . some legal stuff we had to sort out."

"Whatever you say." His skinny arms folded over his chest, he peered at her like some wise old soothsayer reading her fortune from a crystal ball. "But if he asks you out again, don't say I didn't warn you."

"About what?" she asked, trying to look innocent.

"Dad. He hasn't given up on you two getting back together."

She grabbed a throw pillow off the couch and tossed it at him. He caught it with surprising agility and threw it back at her, laughter bubbling from him like water from a long-dry well. She pretended not to notice. If she commented or praised him, he'd retreat back into his shell, and this was too delicious a moment to squander.

She wanted to tell him, *We can't go back to the way things were.* But the look on Chris's thin, anxious face, which for the time being had lost its guardedness, kept her from saying those painful words.

"Isn't it about time for bed?" she asked, pointedly glancing at her watch. "You have school tomorrow."

He nodded, retreating back into himself. With an elaborately casual air, he said, "I thought I'd give Hannah a call first. See how she's doing."

"Oh?" Grace tried not to look too surprised. True, Chris and Hannah had seemed to get along okay up at the cabin, but when had they gotten to be good enough friends to call each other up?

"She's been kind of down lately," Chris confided, lowering his voice and looking around as if Hannah might be lurking in the background, listening. "I don't know—maybe she's breaking up with her boyfriend or something. She hasn't said anything to me, but . . ." Now Chris was giving her the narrow, critical look Grace knew all too well. "Mom, I can't believe you haven't noticed how out of it she's been acting lately."

Grace immediately felt a pang of misgiving. No, she *hadn't* noticed. Was that why Jack, too, had seemed so distant tonight? Was there something wrong with Hannah that Jack wasn't telling her about because he thought she wouldn't care?

"I'm sorry, Chris. . . . I guess I've been sort of out of it myself," she told him. "If you talk to her, give her my love."

Love? They both knew what a joke that was. The best that could be said of her relationship with Hannah was that, since their week of forced togetherness up at the cabin, they'd more or less called a wary truce.

But was that enough?

Chapter 14

"**K**ath? Are you still there?" Hannah tapped the phone's disconnect button once more to make sure she'd hadn't lost her. Call-waiting could be such a pain . . . especially when the person interrupting was Chris. She'd gotten off as quickly as she could without, she hoped, sounding rude.

Now Kath's voice, reassuringly, was coming through. "Who was that?"

"Nobody. Just my father's girlfriend's kid. Ever since he realized I don't bite, he's like this overgrown puppy who keeps wanting to jump up on me."

"You mean, like, he has a *crush* on you?" Kath sounded horrified.

"No . . . no, nothing like that," Hannah said quickly. "It's kind of a big-sister thing." Which, considering how she felt about Dad marrying Grace, wasn't a whole lot better that Chris having a crush on her. "Actually, he was just checking up on me. Seeing if I was okay."

"Why wouldn't you be okay?"

Hannah took a deep breath. Should she tell Kath? After all, Kath hadn't even noticed anything was wrong. Still, Kath was her best friend. And she was good at keeping secrets. Even as far back as the sixth grade, you could have pulled out her fingernails, one by one, and she wouldn't have finked on Lindsey Webber for taking off everything down to her underwear playing strip poker with Robbie Byrnes and Scott Turnbull. And Kath didn't even *like* Lindsey.

Hannah ducked into her pink-and-green bedroom, with its Laura Ashley–papered walls and matching bedspread, the radiophone receiver pressed to her ear, and pushed the door shut with the back of her bare heel. Mom was at work, but Ben had dropped by to pick up a chair or something that Mom was giving him for his apartment. Hannah did not want him hearing this.

"The thing is . . ." She dropped her voice. ". . . I think I might be pregnant."

Hannah felt a sob gathering in her, but she held it in. *Maybe I'm not. Maybe I'm only missing a period.*

"Oh, Hannah," Kath answered in a voice so low it was almost a groan. "Are you sure?"

Hannah felt her sinuses start to swell with the tears she was holding in. "It's been over two weeks, and I'm *never* late. I still can't believe it. I mean, like, it's not as though we just *did* it without using something."

"You and Con?" Kath sounded very far away, so faint Hannah could barely hear her, as if she were calling from Bangladesh.

"Of *course* it's Con. What do you think, that I've gone to bed with half the school?" she cried, suddenly angry at Kath—at the whole world, in fact.

"Hannah, don't get mad. You really blew me away, is all. I wasn't thinking. Listen, do you want me to come over? I'm supposed to be practicing violin, but my mom won't get on my case if I tell them you're helping me with an essay or something. They have you pegged as El Braino."

Sure, Hannah thought. She could ace Dr. Blake's humungously hard physics course, beat practically anyone at Scrabble, fashion an entire Noah's ark out of paper. But if she was so smart, how could she be dumb enough to get pregnant?

"Thanks," she told Kath, "but I'm supposed to be filling

out this college ap." The deadline for admission to Yale was Monday, only four days away, and she hadn't even started on her essay. But now the reality of her dilemma was sinking in. "God, Kath, I don't even know for sure if I'll be *going* to college." She hadn't thought it out that far ahead, but now she wondered if she, who would lay down in front of a picket line of Pro-Lifers, would have the guts to end a pregnancy.

"Have you told Con?" Kath asked, bringing her back sharply to the origin of all this.

"Not yet." Saying it aloud, she wasn't sure why not. But, then, since that night she'd gone to his house, she and Con had hardly spent any time alone. They were always in a group, hanging out at Tyler's or Jill's or Maggie's, or going out for pizza after school with the gang. Now Hannah wondered if that was because *she* had set it up that way . . . or if Con felt uncomfortable being around her. She added, "No point in telling him until I'm absolutely sure."

"Have you tried one of those, you know, home kits?" Kath asked.

"Yeah, I did." Hannah bit her lip to keep from crying. "Nothing showed up."

"Oh, well, then." The relief in Kath's voice was tremendous. "I don't get it, Hannah. If . . ."

"They don't always work," she interrupted. "That summer I was a temp in that doctor's office? There was this lady who thought she had a tumor, because she'd taken one of those tests and it came out negative. But the reason her stomach was so big, she was four months pregnant."

"God, how awful! I'd take the tumor any day. At least then my parents would feel sorry for me instead of wanting to disown me."

Suddenly Hannah realized who she'd been hiding this from. Not Con. Her parents. Especially her father. "What do you think I'm so flipped out about?" she said. "If I *am* pregnant, my *parents* will have to know. My dad . . ." She took a ragged breath. "Oh, Kath, he's always thought of me as so responsible and capable. I'd feel so stupid. A hopeless basket case."

"But he'd understand, wouldn't he?"

"Yeah, I know, he wouldn't foam at the mouth like my mom would, but he'd . . . Oh, Kath, he'd be so *nice* about it. Like when I was five and had to have my tonsils removed. The thing is, I'm not five anymore—but he'll see me that way."

Clutching the phone to her ear, Hannah burst into tears. She couldn't seem to stop herself. It really was like one of those bad movies from the fifties, where a girl gets "in trouble" (they always called it that, like she'd gotten caught cheating on a test, or shoplifting) and she'd as soon be on trial in Nuremberg for Nazi war crimes than to have to confess to her parents that she was knocked up.

Hannah trailed into the bathroom that connected her bedroom to what had once been Ben's room—even though, with him away in college before she'd even started school, she could barely remember Ben's being around. Now, listening to the faint shuffling noises coming from what had become Mom's office, Ben moving stuff around or whatever he was doing, Hannah felt a twinge of annoyance. Why was Ben always coming over? When Mom bugged him to escort her to all her functions, why didn't he just tell her to get a life?

With her free hand, Hannah reached for a tissue. The box was empty, so she tore off some toilet paper, which disintegrated even as she blew her nose into it. She pictured Kath on the other end of the phone, sprawled on the bed in her room, and wished her friend *were* here. But at the same time, she cringed at the idea of anyone, even her best friend, seeing her like this—slumped on the toilet seat in this ridiculous bathroom Mother had done in rose-colored marble tiles with brass fixtures shaped like spouting fish. With her face all blotchy and swollen, a lump of tattered toilet paper jammed up against her nose to keep it from running, she felt like a bag lady who had somehow wandered into the ladies' room at the Saint Regis.

"Listen, I'm sure it'll work out somehow. . . ." Kath sounded so miserable in her behalf that Hannah felt a fresh welling of tears threaten to spill over. "If you need anything—anything at all—I'm here."

"Thanks . . . but right now what I need most is a miracle."

"Yeah, okay, but if Con goes ballistic on you or anything, I'd be happy to kick his butt." She could hear the grin in Kath's voice.

"I'm not blaming Con," Hannah told her. "It wasn't like he put a gun to my head. Still"—she felt a tiny smile creeping through—"I appreciate the offer."

"Listen, Hannah . . . I gotta go." Her voice dropped dramatically. "The wardens are at the gate. I wouldn't want them to hear any of this."

"Sure, okay. Later?"

"Later."

After hanging up, Hannah bent over the sink to splash cold water over her face and felt a sharp cramp—not where she would have had one if it had been her period, but high up in her stomach, like a stitch from running too hard. She gasped, and clutched the cold lip of the marble counter, waiting for it to pass.

With the water running, and her breath coming in shallow bursts, the flicker of movement she glimpsed in the medicine-cabinet mirror, and the sound of the door snicking shut—the door opposite the tub that opened onto Benjamin's old bedroom—barely registered.

By Saturday, Hannah still had not gotten her period, and she was truly beginning to unravel. To take her mind off worrying, she'd plunged into writing her essay for Yale—about the kids from Inwood's P.S. 152 that she'd tutored after school last year. Then she remembered the application fee. No point in asking Mom—she'd made it plain that any school expenses were Dad's territory.

Hannah called over at Grace's, where her father usually hung out on weekends. Bingo. Chris, who picked up the phone, told her Jack was in the shower.

"Tell him I'll be right over," she said.

But when she arrived and let herself in, no Dad, and no Grace, either. There was only Chris, hunched in front of his computer screen.

"Hi." Chris greeted her without looking up.

Hannah recognized the game he was playing, Sim City, where you build this whole simulated city out of graphics and then have to figure out how to run it. What boggled her mind was how kids who could barely chew gum and walk at the same time managed to run an entire city and do a better job of it, probably, than adults. Chris looked good at it, she thought, surprised to see he *was* good at something other than his bad James Dean imitation.

"Where's my dad?" she asked, beginning to feel annoyed. "Didn't you *tell* him I was coming?" It felt creepy, being in Grace's loft without Grace around. Hannah had a sudden desire to throw away the key Grace had given her. She didn't want to feel like she in any way belonged to this place.

Chris shot her a sheepish look, and shrugged. "Sorry. Guess I forgot."

Hannah had to bite the inside of her cheek to keep from screaming at him.

"He left a few minutes ago," Chris went on. "And Mom went to buy some stuff at Balducci's. She's all freaked out about my grandmother coming to visit . . . even though Nana's staying at my dad's. She's planning this whole dinner for Wednesday night. The way she's acting, you'd think it was the Last Supper."

Chris turned to her, and in the cavelike darkness of his room his eyes seemed to carry a residue of reflected glow from the screen, his pinched face making her think of a raccoon startled by a flashlight in the midst of a midnight forage.

Hannah looked around, thinking, *God, how can anyone stand to live this way?* Gray light leaked through the partially drawn blinds to reveal an unmade bed with a chair and a dresser next to it heaped with junk—dirty clothes, piles of old comic books, empty Sprite cans, a dusty-looking bike helmet, Walkman headphones tangled amid a slew of smudgy tapes.

Normally, she wouldn't have noticed or cared, but right now everything was rubbing her the wrong way. Chris looked as if he wanted to talk, but this time she was not going to let herself get sucked into playing big sister. She started to turn away, but the bleak look on Chris's face somehow caught hold of her.

He's lonely, she thought. It struck her that Chris was kind of like herself—pushing people away while at the same time hoping they'd like him anyway.

"You get along with your grandmother?" she asked, finding a narrow edge of his bed where she could perch.

He shrugged, but his eyes softened. "Yeah. She's differ-

ent with me than with my mom. We used to do stuff together, like hang out at the cabin she's got up at this lake.
The thing is, now she acts like I'm some kind of orphan."
His gaze drifted about. "Like, when I'm visiting her, she
unpacks my suitcase and washes everything before she'll put
it away. Like she thinks my mom doesn't do the laundry or
something."

"Hey, I know what you mean. *My* grandmother still nags
me about brushing my teeth."

He dropped his head, his elbows braced against his
knees, his shoulder blades spiking up under his baggy
T-shirt. "With Nana it's no big deal, but with my mom and
dad . . ." His voice trailed off, then picked up again with
sudden vehemence. "Divorce sucks."

"Yeah, right up there with acid rain and defoliation of
the rain forests." *And being pregnant.*

When he looked up again, she was startled to see the
glimmer of tears in his eyes. "Hannah? Can I tell you
something?"

"Sure. If you want to."

"My dad wants me to live with him."

"What's new about that? It's called being drawn and
quartered. In medieval times, it was a torture practiced on
prisoners and infidels. Nowadays they call it joint custody."

"No, I mean *really*—like move in with him. Perma-
nently."

"Does your mom know?" Her voice dropped to a whisper, though no one was around but the two of them.

Chris shook his head, looking more miserable than ever.

Hannah felt slightly sick. How would it be, she wondered, if tomorrow morning over breakfast she were to announce casually to her mother that she was moving in with
Daddy?

As sudden and painful as a Band-Aid being ripped off, it dawned on her that her mother probably wouldn't care all that much. Oh, she'd haul out the box of Kleenex and get weepy, then start with the accusations, laying this huge guilt trip on her about being dumped by everyone she ever cared about, and Daddy only wanting her so he could be one up . . . but the truth was that Mom was so busy chasing after antiques and wallpapers and going to her endless benefits that, in the end, she probably wouldn't care as much as Grace would if it were Chris.

"What do *you* want?" she asked him. "I mean, if this kind of thing was completely up to us kids—which it never is."

"I don't know." Behind him, the computer emitted what sounded like the *squeep* of a cornered mouse. In the dim light, its screen glowed like a huge phosphorescent eye. "What *I* want isn't going to happen, so I guess it doesn't really matter."

"You mean, your mom and dad getting back together?"

"Sort of." He sounded embarrassed, like a kid who knows he's too old to believe in Santa Claus but does anyway.

"You want to know what I think?" Hannah was surprised to find that her own misery had receded. "I think the decision shouldn't be up to you. Not if you're not sure."

"But if tell my dad I don't want to live with him, he'll feel terrible. He'll think it's because I care more about my mom than about him."

"And your mom—what will *she* think?"

Chris didn't say anything, just stared down at the dirty tops of his Reeboks.

A hollow, uncomfortable silence settled over them. Oddly, Hannah was sorry for Grace as well. In fact, ever since that night at the cabin when Grace had given her the jacket—which she had scarcely taken off since—her feelings about Grace had seemed more confused than ever.

She found herself rising, and walking over to where Chris sat. She dropped her hand lightly onto his shoulder, gave it a clumsy pat. There was nothing she could say that would make him feel all better. But maybe he just needed to know that someone was on his side.

Someone who knew exactly how he felt.

Hannah was slipping into her leather bomber jacket when Grace walked in the door. Hannah's heart lurched; then a weird thought snuck into her head. What if she told Grace that she was scared she might be pregnant?

Grace wouldn't flip out . . . and, anyway, Grace's opinion of her had to be so low already, it couldn't get too much worse.

God, I can't believe I'm thinking this.

"Hannah—what a surprise!" Grace's chin-length hair was all windblown, her cheeks ruddy from the cold. "I wasn't expecting you."

Grace breezed past, laden with shopping bags, and Hannah felt the chill of the outdoors waft from her. Hannah's arms tightened with goosebumps as she watched Grace thunk her groceries down on the kitchen counter.

Okay, now, should she tell her? Before she lost her nerve?

Yeah, but what if she uses it against you somehow? If you had something this juicy on her, wouldn't you?

Realizing that she probably *would* do something like that only made her feel worse.

"I'm not . . . here, that is. I mean, I was just on my way

out." Hannah stumbled over her words, feeling clumsy and shy.

"Oh, well, then . . . I won't keep you." Grace didn't sound disappointed—more like maybe she was relieved or something. Hannah felt strangely let down. A few weeks ago, she'd have been happy to know that Grace was finally backing off, but now, well, she felt sort of rejected.

"Maybe I could help you unload some of that stuff first. I'm not in any big hurry." The words tumbled out before she was fully aware she'd spoken . . . and Hannah felt her head give a little jerk, as it did when perfect strangers on the subway spoke to her. Had she really offered to help Grace?

Grace looked astonished, too, Hannah could see. She stared at Hannah over the counter, twirling her key ring on one finger. It made a jangly sound that seemed to keep both of them from focusing too much on Hannah's startling offer.

"Sure," she said brightly. "I could use a hand. It's not all that much stuff, but the fortune I spent, it ought to be a truckload. I swear, the prices at Balducci's are enough to send any sane person screaming to the nearest A & P. I don't usually buy groceries there, but my mother is coming for dinner, and . . ." She grimaced. "Well, you know how it is."

Hannah listened to her rattling on, and, instead of being irritated, as usual, she felt somehow braced. Grace's chatter was like a current giving Hannah the strength to navigate the ocean of bad feelings always churning between them. She felt buoyed by it, her arms bobbing up as she lifted cans and jars and plastic sacks of dripping radicchio from shopping bags and stowed them on refrigerator and cupboard shelves.

"Looks like you're planning something really fancy." She thought of the dinner they'd had here when she'd thrown up all over the bathroom floor, and immediately wished she'd kept her mouth shut.

"You could call it that," Grace said, standing on tiptoe

to find room for a box of orzo on a crowded shelf. "Ritual human sacrifice would be more like it, though. You see, there are some things you never outgrow." She shot a glance over her shoulder. "Parents are one of them."

"Yeah, I know." Hannah managed a tight smile.

Why am I agreeing with her? Hannah wondered. Everything was getting too complicated. First getting friendly with Chris . . . and now *this*.

I'm just giving her a hand—it's not exactly universal world peace, she reminded herself quickly.

Finally, all the groceries put away, Grace scooted onto one of the bar stools facing the counter, fixing Hannah with a look of such curiosity that she felt suddenly self-conscious and . . . well, *exposed*. Hannah darted a glance toward the hallway, praying that Chris would get tired of his computer game and come wandering in here and rescue her.

From what? she asked herself. *From some dumb urge to spill my guts to someone who probably hates me? Or from finding out that Grace might actually have some useful advice?*

"Thanks for helping me. But, listen, I don't want to keep you," Grace said, giving Hannah the perfect out. "I'll tell your dad you were looking for him."

No inquiring politely about school or the Green Earth committee she was chairperson of, no little hints about all the fun stuff they might do together next summer, trips they might take. Grace, without exactly saying it, was blowing her off.

And it wasn't just today, Hannah realized. Ever since that week in the country they'd spent walking on eggshells around one another, Grace had been no more than pleasantly civil—no urging her to do anything or not do anything, no asking anything from her . . . just *there*. Hannah, thinking about it, felt pleased, and at the same time like it wasn't quite right.

"Grace?" Hannah sank down on a stool near her, feeling suddenly too weary to leave. Besides, where could she go? "Did you ever . . ." She stopped, her voice suddenly dry. "Never mind."

Hannah waited now for Grace to urge her on. But Grace didn't. She only sat there, looking at Hannah with those guileless hazel eyes, toying with a long curlicued strip of grocery receipt, winding it around and around her finger.

"You know what really gets me," she said softly, "is the coffee. There you are in Balducci's with twenty-five different kinds of coffee to choose from, and you stand there until you start to feel as if the fate of the world rests on your decision. It's really funny, because I never hesitated about buying this loft, even though it was an absolute wreck at the time. Sometimes it's easier to get bogged down on dumb little things."

If Grace had prodded, Hannah knew that she would have withdrawn into her shell. But now she couldn't hold it in any longer.

"I think I might be pregnant," she blurted, addressing a teapot by the stove, probably long grown cold, with a dishtowel twisted about its handle.

Grace was silent for so long, Hannah began to think she hadn't heard—or, worse, was *pretending* not to have heard. Then, finally, she asked, "Have you talked this over with either of your parents?"

Hannah shook her head, feeling her misery rise again. It felt so weird, confiding in Grace—like the first time she'd taken the wheel in Daddy's car, not sure she wanted to drive . . . but not wanting to stop, either.

"I'm not going to ask if someone as well educated and

intelligent as you was using any birth control. So I'll assume that whatever it was may not have worked," Grace said evenly, not lecturing, just matter-of-fact. "Am I right?"

"Conrad . . ."

"No, not your boyfriend. I meant *you*."

"Oh, well, not exactly. I mean, well, no." It had never occurred to Hannah that a condom wasn't necessarily enough protection.

"Well, then, it's simple," Grace said, suddenly brisk and businesslike as she stood and reached for the phone on the wall. "We'll just take care of it, and you won't have this worry every month."

"But what if I am pregnant?"

"If he used a condom, you're probably just late . . . but if you *are* pregnant, well, we'll just have to cross that bridge when we get to it." She grabbed a small leather-bound phone book off the counter, and started thumbing through its pages. "Look, I have a terrific gynecologist; she even takes patients on Saturday. I'll see if she can squeeze you in."

Perched on her high stool, listening to Grace as she wheedled some receptionist into giving her a last-minute appointment, Hannah felt like she'd given up more than just her secret. She'd handed over the reins of her life, too. Why couldn't she have handled this as coolly as Grace?

Half an hour later, Hannah lay on her back on an examining table in a room with soft peach walls hung with Cassatt prints of mothers and children, while a young woman in a white coat, her dark hair braided down her back, gently poked and prodded.

Hannah, not sure whether she was more scared or embarrassed, finally was allowed to sit up. Her heart was thudding as she tugged her paper gown down around her knees. She tried to say something, but her tongue seemed swollen somehow, making it difficult for her even to swallow.

The doctor saved her by saying, "I'll run a urine test— we can do it right here in the office. But I'm ninety-nine-percent sure you're not pregnant."

Hannah felt dizzy all of a sudden. If she hadn't been sitting down already, she probably would have *had* to. But now relief was filling her like some kind of helium, making her light, almost buoyant. She nodded and tried to concentrate as the woman, who looked too young to be a doctor, instructed her on using a diaphragm. Minutes later, when the results of the urine test came back negative, she floated back into the dressing room and somehow managed to stuff her weightless body into her clothes.

Walking out into the waiting room where Grace sat reading a magazine, Hannah felt herself trying to smile. But it was as if her mouth was disconnected from the rest of her, flickering on and off like a faulty light bulb.

Grace stood up. One look seemed to have told her everything she needed to know.

"You want to hear something really funny?" she said, relieving Hannah of the need to speak. "With all that talk about coffee, I just realized I didn't buy any. That little deli we passed on the corner should have some."

Hannah hardly spoke until they were in the taxi. "You won't tell Dad, will you?" she asked in a small voice, a new terror poking its way through her cloud of relieved euphoria. "I mean, there's no reason for him to know, now that everything's okay."

"No reason at all," Grace agreed pleasantly.

"Promise?"

"Absolutely."

Hannah felt almost overwhelmed with gratitude. But then a small, mean voice at the back of her mind hissed, *Watch out. Careful. Don't let yourself get sucked in. She's got something on you now, and she just might use it.*

Chapter 15

Monday, Ben left work early to pick up his BMW from the auto repair shop on Tenth and Nineteenth, but by the time he'd waited around for the asshole mechanic to finish up it was after six. He thought about going straight home, but decided on a hamburger at the Empire Diner instead, an early movie at the Tri-plex on Twenty-third. It was something to keep him occupied at least, keep him from thinking too much about Nola—an alarming habit he seemed to have developed recently.

The movie turned out to be one of those tearjerkers about some childless couple trying to adopt an unwed mother's baby. A real bore. But driving home, Ben found himself mulling over the phone conversation he'd overheard last week between his sister and her friend. Could Hannah really be pregnant? Who would have thought his smart kid sister could have slipped up like that?

He hoped Hannah's scare would turn out to be nothing. At the same time, Ben couldn't help wondering if maybe she *deserved* to be in hot water for a change. If Dad knew she was screwing around, he wouldn't think so highly of his precious little girl. . . .

Ben braked to avoid sideswiping a cab that had veered in front of him, his thoughts, as they inevitably did when his father came to mind, turning to work. No thanks to Jack Gold, he'd managed to smooth Roger Young's ruffled feathers—for the moment, at least. And the Harding book, for which he'd closed at one eighty, already had the Literary

Guild and Book-of-the-Month Club eagerly awaiting a finished manuscript. But as far as Nola's letters were concerned—zip. She wasn't offering them to him . . . and he wasn't asking.

That wasn't what was troubling him now, though—the fact that, night after night with Nola, he walked away empty-handed. The big question was why it no longer seemed to matter.

At some point over the past few weeks—he couldn't put his finger on exactly when—it had stopped being about the letters and had switched to something else—with much higher stakes. Love? Impossible—not him. But he'd never before felt this way about any woman . . . and it was scaring him.

As if to prove to himself that he could, at any time, drop her—just as he had the dozens of women before Nola—Ben picked up his car phone and punched a speed-dial button. The phone rang half a dozen times before she picked up.

"Hi," he said in a voice pitched low with intimacy.

"Hey, what's up?" She sounded a bit distracted, not all that excited to hear from him.

Ben frowned as he turned off Seventh onto Christopher.

"Nothing much," he said breezily. "Listen, about tonight . . ." He was going to tell her he wasn't coming over as he'd casually mentioned yesterday. Give her the old excuse about being wiped out from a hectic day of haggling with agents and in-house number crunchers, smoothing the ruffled feathers of authors.

But Nola was already a step ahead of him. "Oh, God, Ben, I totally forgot. Look, I'm really sorry. Dani's running a temperature, and it looks like Tasha might be coming down with the same thing. I just got them to sleep."

"No big deal, it's pretty late anyway." He spoke nonchalantly, but for some reason he felt annoyed. Who was she to give *him* the brush-off? Then he found himself saying, "Question is, who's going to tuck *you* in?"

That definitely had not been part of the script, but he nevertheless found himself holding his breath.

Nola laughed her wonderful, full laugh, sending a delicious shiver through him. "You applying for the job, mister?"

"If you're hiring."

Now, why had he said that? And why, with a briefcase full of manuscripts and the hot shower he was craving awaiting him at his place only a block away, was he turning onto Hudson, heading back uptown toward Nola's?

Ben didn't know. It was as if he were under some kind of weird spell. He wasn't seeing the avenue, clogged with traffic even at nine-thirty, or the lit-up storefronts flickering past on either side. An image of Nola filled his mind—lounging on her bed, wearing nothing but a come-hither look.

"Have you eaten?" she asked, hanging his coat on the coatrack in the hall and moving toward the kitchen. "I could fix you something, if you're not too picky."

"No thanks, I stopped for a burger on my way back from picking up the car," he told her.

"A snack, then? Florene and the girls made chocolate-chip cookies."

"I wouldn't say no to something sweet."

Getting his gist, she laughed, not resisting as he moved forward to take her in his arms. "Didn't your mama ever tell you that too much sugar is bad for you?"

"She probably did. But that never stopped me."

He started to kiss her, but for some reason she was gently

pushing him away. "No, wait. Ben, let's go upstairs and have a nice long talk, like regular people do."

"What do you want to talk about?"

"I don't know. Anything. Nothing. You've hardly told me anything about your work, for one thing. I only know who one or two of your authors are."

"Okay, I'll even give you a stack of manuscripts to read if you want," he joked, but felt oddly off-balance, as he often did with Nola. As if she were the one calling the shots, not he.

"I'm sure that won't be necessary." She laughed, leading the way up to the living room. "Drink?"

"No thanks. I'm driving home, remember?" He was unable to keep a note of irritation from his voice, remembering how Nola always insisted he be out of here before he could drop off to sleep in her big, warm bed. She couldn't take the risk, she'd told him time and again, of her girls' finding them together.

"Right, I forgot." Seemingly unperturbed, she dropped onto the sofa beside him, reaching up to run her fingers through his hair, as if he were nothing more than a child himself. Ben felt himself growing aroused, and at the same time wanting to put the brakes on, take charge of this runaway train on which he'd somehow become a passenger.

He pulled her to him, abruptly, and felt her push him away with a breathless little laugh that carried a tiny hint of annoyance.

"Hey . . . what's the big hurry?" she wanted to know. "We've got plenty of time." She crossed her arms over her chest. "Now, you were saying? About your manuscripts?"

"Most of it's pretty boring to anyone who's not in the business," he told her. "Anyway, why the sudden interest?"

"Why not?" she hedged.

He wondered where this was leading. And then it struck him.

"Is it *my* authors you want to know about . . . or Grace?"

She frowned, becoming absorbed in a loose thread on the sofa cushion. "I . . . I've been doing some thinking."

His heartbeat picked up—a slow, deep hammering that made his head throb. "What about?"

"Those letters. I've been wondering if I'm doing the right thing, keeping them to myself. Maybe I *should* turn them over to Grace."

Ben felt himself jolt upright as if he'd just sat on something sharp. What to say? *Think, think.* Striking a tone he hoped sounded no more than mildly concerned, he asked, "Do you think that's such a good idea? What I mean is . . . wouldn't you be giving her too much control?"

"Coming from me, you're gonna think this is strange . . . but I trust her."

"I'm not saying she'd try to make you look bad. . . ." Ben was starting to sweat now, his rash itching. But somehow the right words were spinning out from the heated jumble in his brain. "See, Nola, once Grace turns her book in, Cadogan will be the one pulling the strings. You know, stuff like quotes pulled out of context and stitched together to make them look more sensational."

She wrinkled her brow. "*You* work for Cadogan. Are you saying—"

"Exactly my point," he cut her off. "It just occurred to me that, if you were to give *me* those letters, I'd make sure our lawyers had access to them before anyone else. With me orchestrating the whole thing—and believe me, I'm good at that—you'd have a lot more control over how those letters get handled."

Had he sounded too eager? Nola was giving him a funny look, drawing her head back so her chin was almost tucked into the high collar of the silky ecru tunic she wore over a pair of black velour leggings.

"Hey, what is this? I thought we decided back in the beginning that you weren't gonna be a part of that whole mess."

"Sure, I know." He shrugged. "I was just trying to help out, that's all."

"Well, I'm a big girl. I don't need you."

I don't need you. Ben stared at her, not quite comprehending. He'd never had any woman say those words to him, not even offhandedly, as Nola had. What made her think she was so special?

He took in her closed expression, those hooded green eyes, and her full mouth, tucked in at the corners. She thought so, he realized, because she *was*.

Special.

Goddamn her. How the hell did she do it?

Ben, seething inside, forced a smile that felt pasted on. "Let's forget it, okay?"

Strangely, despite her thwarting him, he wanted her. More than ever.

As he took Nola into his arms, he was careful to keep his kisses soft, almost feather-light. He was burning, aching throughout, but he must not let her see it. He had to work up to this slowly.

His tongue darted in and out of her mouth, and over her full lips, which made him think of dark berries bursting with juice. Her high cheekbones, he saw when he drew back to take a breath, cast shadows down her cheeks, making her look even more exotic and mysterious. He traced the sharp line of her jaw with the edge of his teeth, and heard her make a noise deep in her throat that was more a growl than a moan.

Now Ben was cupping her breasts, feeling them warm and heavy beneath her blouse. The slippery fabric, bunching and gliding under his hands, was exciting him even more than if she'd been naked. He bent to gather a hard nipple into his mouth through the whisper-thin fabric. As he sucked, he felt the silk grow wet against his lips. She writhed slowly, deliciously, murmuring his name, whispering, *Don't stop. Oh please don't stop.*

But then, shockingly, excruciatingly, *she* was stopping. Her hands planted against his chest, pushing him away. She was out of breath, her face flushed, but not altogether forgetful of where she was, it seemed.

"Ben . . . not here. The girls, they might see us."

"I thought you said they were asleep."

She laughed, a low, raspy sound coming from some deep—and unreachable—part of her. "Obviously, you don't know kids. They're known for popping up when you least expect them. Especially after you think you've put them to bed."

"In that case . . ." He took her wrists, attempting to lift her to her feet as he rose. At that moment, he wished she were small and dainty so he could scoop her into his arms, carry her off to the bedroom. But Nola, all six feet of her, was resisting him.

"Ben . . . no. I really don't think this is such a good idea."

"Why the hell not?" He was ticked off now.

"I told you. Dani's sick. She might need me. And suppose I was with you, and we were . . ." She stopped, swallowing. "Can't it wait? Do we have to do this *every* time we're together?"

Ben felt frustrated, pissed off, and more than a little ridiculous, standing there with a hard-on straining the fly of his pants. Christ. What kind of game was she playing?

"You want it as much as I do," he said sullenly, hearing himself and wanting to cringe. Jesus, he sounded like some high-school kid.

"Yeah, but I can wait," she said. "Being a mom, you don't always get first pick."

She was shutting him out again. But what the hell—he didn't even *want* to share that part of her life. Wiping sticky hands at the breakfast table, scraping smashed crayons off the soles of his shoes, trying to look interested while some kid babbled on and on about school.

At the same time, Ben found himself resenting her for withholding even a small piece of herself from him. He longed to take her, right here, right now, on the carpet, to *force* every thought of her kids from her mind until she was screaming his name, screaming at him not to stop, her fingernails digging into his ass cheeks, clutching him as she reared up, up, to take him as far into her as she could. . . .

He turned away from her, quickly, so she wouldn't see that his hard-on wasn't going away. "Hey, it's no big deal. I really should get going anyway. I have an early breakfast with an agent, and I haven't even looked at the manuscript she sent over."

"Ben." She stood up. Her gaze, nearly level with his, was coolly unapologetic. But her mouth was curling up in a smile, and her words, when she spoke, were warm. "Can I take a raincheck? Tomorrow night? Why don't you come for dinner, so the girls can get to know you a little better."

He thought about begging off dinner and arranging, as he usually did, to take her out, or simply arrive after the kids were in bed. But something about the way she was measuring him—as if she might find him wanting—made him nod and say, "What time?"

It didn't occur to him until he was out the front door, and nearly halfway to his car, parked near the corner, that Nola hadn't said for sure whether or not she'd decided to give Truscott's letters to Grace.

Chapter 16

It was after six on Wednesday by the time Grace got home from the Forty-second Street library, where she'd spent the day combing through old magazines and newspapers for photos of her father and Margaret. She'd found only one—a blurry UPI shot of the two of them descending the steps of the Senate Office Building, Margaret a decorous step or two behind Daddy, carrying a stack of papers.

But without Daddy's letters to her, Margaret would never be more than his longtime legislative assistant. So why bother? What, Grace wondered, could she possibly gain from all her research, except maybe coming to an understanding of what it was that Margaret had been able to give her father that Mother couldn't, or wouldn't.

Let sleeping dogs lie, she could hear her mother's voice, admonishing her.

Mother.

Grace glanced at her watch. Mother's plane had gotten in earlier this afternoon. She'd be settled in at Win's by now, and in exactly two hours she'd be *here,* though, thank heaven, it was only for drinks. Bless Lila for talking her out of her original plan—think how much *more* stressful it would be sweating over dinner, her friend had pointed out. Needing no further encouragement, Grace had made reservations at Luma. But that wouldn't solve everything. And with no pots to watch or potatoes to mash, she and Mother would actually have to *talk.* How would Mother act? What would they say to each other? Oh, it was never going to work!

You didn't think you'd ever get through to Hannah, either, and look what happened with her.

Grace also remembered Sissy's letter, about their mother's being involved with their old teacher Mr. Ross. She wondered if Mother would seem any different now that she was in love, if that's what it was.

She was peeling off her coat at the door when Chris sidled over. "I told her you'd be back pretty soon," he muttered under his breath, glancing toward the living room. "She said she didn't mind waiting."

Grace felt the air leave her lungs all at once. Mother? Had she come early?

Then she saw that it wasn't her mother. Their visitor was sitting erect on the sofa, her back to them. Her smooth chignon, the square line of her shoulders—Nola? Yes. But she wasn't the type just to drop in unannounced. It had to be something pretty important.

Grace felt a jolt of adrenaline. Making her way toward Nola, she didn't dare hope that Nola had changed her mind about cooperating on the book. In fact, a small part of her, deep down, almost hoped that Nola *had* merely stopped by to say hello. And that she, Grace, would be spared having to tell her mother the painful truth about Daddy. And yet . . .

"Nola, what a surprise!" Grace greeted her. "If I'd known you were coming, I would have gotten home earlier. Have you been waiting long?"

Nola rose, smoothing the front of the fitted celadon jacket she wore over a mid-thigh chocolate-brown skirt. A pair of boots, saddle-soaped so many times they resembled old glove leather, was the only sign of a limited clothing budget.

"Not too long," she said. "And your son has been keeping me entertained. Telling me about this new computer program of his." Nola gave Chris an amused grimace. "Makes me feel like some kind of dinosaur. I never made it past word-processing. Wouldn't know RAM from ROM to save my life."

Chris flashed Nola an uncharacteristic grin. "I could show you sometime, if you want. It's not that hard."

Grace observed that Chris seemed more relaxed around Nola than he was around most people he didn't know. Maybe it was just Nola, that direct way she had about her. Every teenager, Grace thought, must have an invisible bullshit-detector, because they always seemed to know in a nanosecond when someone was just being nice out of politeness, or in an effort to make a good impression on their parents.

"I'd like that." Nola stuck out her hand, which Chris, after only a moment's hesitation, reached out and shook. "Okay, mister, you can hang it up now. Go back to your computer. You've done your duty looking after this dinosaur." She laughed, and Chris's gray-blue eyes sparkled in response.

"Better go pack your things," Grace told him as he was heading off toward his room. "Your grandmother will be expecting you." Win had asked if Chris could stay over, as a special favor to Cordelia, who was always saying she never got to see enough of her grandson.

As soon as Chris had disappeared down the hallway, Nola turned to Grace. "You're probably wondering why I dropped by without calling first."

"Turnabout is fair play," she said, remembering when she had done the same. "But, anyway, I'm glad to see you."

Nola shot her a tentative smile.

"How about a glass of wine?" Grace offered. "I have some white in the fridge."

Nola shook her head. "Mind if I sit down? I'm not keeping you from anything, am I?"

Grace knew she ought to straighten the place up for Mother's visit, make sure that she had enough ice, and that Chris hadn't drunk all the sodas she kept stored in the pantry cupboard. Instead, she gestured toward the sofa, where the deep cushions still held the imprint of Nola's body.

"Not a thing," she said.

"I can only stay a few minutes," Nola assured her. She sank down again, crossing her legs, then uncrossing them and leaning forward slightly. "Actually, to be honest, I was half-hoping you wouldn't be here." She hesitated, then bent to lift a bulky manila envelope from the briefcase Grace now noticed lying open at her feet. "Maybe this will explain why."

Nola sounded calm, but a vein pulsing in the stretched skin along her temple gave her away.

Grace felt herself go numb, unable to move or even speak. But, underneath, hope was swelling. Hope mingled with dread.

She stared at Nola's hands, her unusually long fingers with their broad, flat fingernails splayed over the back of the envelope. Where had she seen such hands before? Then it hit her. Why, of course, they were her father's hands. . . .

Nola looked up, and their eyes met. She could see that there was no need to tell Grace what was in the envelope.

It's not too late to back out, Nola told herself. *You could put them back in your briefcase and walk away. And the world would never be the wiser.*

Then she remembered how, last night, after Ben had left,

she had unearthed the shoebox from the back of her closet —the box that had lain undisturbed for nearly ten years, which she was now invading for the second time in the space of two weeks. It contained Mama's papers: copies of Nola's birth certificate, insurance documents, baby photos of nieces and nephews, the registration for an old Pontiac long since retired to the junkyard. And at the bottom, tied together with a length of yellowing string, a bunch of letters addressed to Margaret Emory in Eugene Truscott's bold, spiky hand.

Had Mama been wrong to make her promise to keep them to herself?

Sure, things were different back then. A white man and a black woman. A *married* white man, who happened to be a great senator. *She said it was because no one would understand about their kind of love, that it was special . . . and the truly special things often get twisted around, made to seem ugly.*

Except that the bottom line was that Mama had been flat-out scared—of exactly the same stuff she, Nola, would be facing when this came out. Bloodthirsty reporters that would make the ones she'd been brushing off so far seem like Halloween trick-or-treaters. Newspapers printing slimy, distorted stories. But to go on like this, with her head buried in the sand—was that the way to deal with it? Instead of feeling proud of keeping her promise, Nola felt a little ashamed. Like the hundred times she'd lied to Tasha and Dani about their daddy's being too tied up to come see them, when the truth was, Marcus just didn't give a shit.

It was Ben who had gotten her to come here—though he probably didn't know it. His devil's-advocate advice, that first night, *not* to relinquish the letters had ironically made her consider doing just that. Odd, though, how last night he'd seemed so eager to take them off her hands. . . .

But the important thing, she told herself, was that Mama's letters would not be going to some sleazy tabloid, or to a hack producer out to make a tearjerking TV movie of the week. No. She'd be entrusting them to Grace Truscott . . . her sister, yes, even though they hadn't been raised under the same roof.

Nola was seized by a memory from when she was very small—of a big man with huge, gentle hands holding her on his lap and singing to her. *Oh, Susannah, oh don't you cry for me. . . .* There was his smell, sweet and faintly medicinal, which came from the whiskey in the cut-glass decanter Mama left out on the sideboard. "Where's my green-eyed girl?" he would crow. And she would wriggle on his lap and raise her hand the way she did in school when the teacher asked a question she knew the answer to. Then, pretending not to see her, he'd look all around the room, craning his neck until cords of muscle stood raised, from his bony jaw to the knobs of his collarbone, like rivers along a relief map . . . and until she was nearly bursting . . . before finally allowing his gaze to fall on her. With a grin as swift and bright as the sun coming up over a mountain ridge, he'd say, "Hey, maybe you know her? She's about so tall"—extending his palm, flat side down so it just skimmed the top of her head—"and her name is Nola."

Nola Truscott. She nearly spoke it aloud, her *real* name.

All hesitation now seemed to have left her. Nola felt certain, as she handed her precious cargo over to Grace, that she was doing the right thing. "Here," she said. "These belong to you as much as to me."

Grace was dimly aware of clasping the envelope to her chest, but all she could feel were the tears spilling down her cheeks.

"Oh, Nola. I don't know what to . . . Thank you."

Grace, feeling as if she were in some strange dream, caught sight of the guy in the building directly across the street—she and Chris jokingly referred to him as the "Nineteenth Street Flasher"—who often walked around naked, or wearing only boxer shorts, as he was now. He was standing in full view, ironing. More than the Empire State Building or the Statue of Liberty, *this* to her was New York: strangers' lives intersecting in curiously intimate ways . . . as hers and Nola's had that long-ago day when they'd both witnessed the accidental killing of Ned Emory. She'd never met the Flasher, or even bumped into him on the street, but she knew that he was fussy about his clothes, and that he worked out with weights, and that he didn't have a wife or a girlfriend. Just as she now knew, in some deep part of her, that she and Nola, despite their shared blood rather than because of it, would be bound for life.

"It's not a gift." There was a slight edge to Nola's voice. "I expect you to do what's right. Make sure they aren't exploited."

"Don't worry," Grace told her.

"My mother . . . After he died, she got very sick. She was sick for a long time." Nola addressed a wrought-iron lamp on the table just beyond Grace's shoulder, a faraway look on her arresting face.

Grace knew all this from her research, but nonetheless she found herself saying, "Tell me about it."

"It was emphysema. At the time she was first diagnosed, I was only twelve and I didn't even know what it meant. Couldn't even spell it." Nola gave a hollow, rueful laugh. "That's when you know something's *real* bad, when you can't even spell it."

"I'm sorry."

"She lived long enough to see . . . well, to know what

Gene Truscott had become. A hero, a legend. There was that biography by the same man who wrote that book about Kennedy—his name slips my mind. And all the magazine articles and scholarly essays. She didn't miss a single one. She'd be in her bed, barely able to keep her head up, but she read every single word. Sometimes, I'd see her screwing up her face, like she didn't agree with the author. And other times, there'd be tears in her eyes . . . as if she was reliving something that had happened exactly the way it was described. I only wish she'd had the opportunity to read *your* book—when it's finished, when you've told the *real* story."

Grace's face burned where her tears had run down her cheeks. "But your promise to her . . . ?" She couldn't finish the rest.

Nola straightened, sat even taller. "I also promised always to remember what he and my mother meant to one another. And your book will do that. It won't make him any less great . . . just more human."

Grace, she thought, couldn't possibly comprehend the sacrifice she was making—the library she had designed that might not get built once these letters were made public. No way would Cordelia Truscott allow her husband's bastard daughter to share in any part of his memorial.

Nola held back from telling Grace that. The letters—they were Mama's. But the library belonged to her. And, besides, there was still a chance her design would be chosen—if Maguire remained close-mouthed about who was behind it. The fewer people who knew, the better . . .

"I never thought of him that way." Grace spoke in a soft voice. "As a man. To me, he was . . . he seemed to fill up our home even when he wasn't there."

"Maybe all that worship was *why* he wasn't there more

often," Nola said. "Even heroes need to climb down off their pedestal now and then."

Grace lowered the envelope to her lap, sensing the truth in what Nola was saying. Could she learn to forgive him, the father she'd revered, who had lied to her—but who had been, as Nola pointed out, merely human?

And Mother, when Grace showed these letters to her, as she must, would her mother forgive *her*?

"Who died?" Lila asked.

Grace could see only the top of her friend's head sticking up above the enormous floral arrangement that only a moment before had been delivered to her door. Heavens, it *did* look as if it belonged at a funeral. She opened the tiny envelope nestled amid the baby's breath, took out the card, and felt her heart sink. *So looking forward to this evening. Love, Mother.*

"You're looking at the corpse," Grace groaned.

"Remind me to send a donation to the ASPCA in your memory," Lila said, her expression perfectly deadpan. "Where do you want them?"

"On that low table . . . over there by the sofa. It'll make a great conversation piece. You can tell everyone I was rubbed out by the Mob."

"My last boyfriend, Enrico—his uncle, I think, works for the Mob."

"You never told me about him."

"Sure I did, the guy at the dry cleaner's. Gets the dog hair out of all my clothes. Finally, he asks me out. But then all he ever wants to do is hang out at my place and watch videos." Lila snorted with laughter as she fingered a blossom. "I hate to say this, but your ma has even lousier taste in flowers than I do in men."

"No, she doesn't," Grace found herself defending Mother. "You should see her garden—it's absolute heaven. I'm sure this is just a case of her not knowing the florist."

Grace was remembering the tulips in the spring, and Mother's treasure trove of roses. And the green peaches Grace always picked before they were ripe, and that invariably gave her the runs. She saw the grand old parlors and breakfast room of her mother's house, overflowing with bouquets of snapdragons and peonies and sweetpeas, roses from the cutting garden in back, bunches of fragrant thyme and basil and chamomile in Mason jars lining the kitchen sill.

Mother had nurtured and tended her memories the same way. Finding out about Margaret would be like a great frost coming along and killing them all.

Grace felt dread gathering inside her. How would she break it to Mother? Part of her wanted to keep the letters tucked away, just as Nola had done, but she realized that would be wrong. She had an obligation, not only to herself, as Eugene Truscott's biographer, but to history as well. Maybe there was some way she could make Mother understand. . . .

Grace realized, even while thinking it, how unlikely that was. Mother would be livid—not at Daddy, but at her. *She'll accuse me of doing this to get back at her.*

The last time she'd seen her mother, Grace remembered, was just after she and Win had separated, when she'd flown down to Blessing to pick up Chris after his annual visit with his grandmother. Also (*Admit it, why don't you?*) hadn't she been hoping to get some sympathy and moral support? She'd wanted Mother to see that the divorce was hurting her terribly . . . but all Mother had done, for two whole days, was pick on her. *No matter how much she disapproved, would it have been so difficult for her to put her arms around me and just hug me?*

"I don't understand—you had everything," Mother had said for the umpteenth time, as they stood at the airport security checkpoint like a pair of worn-out gladiators. She shook her head, watching Chris as he ambled through the gate. "You *have* everything a woman could want," she corrected. "How could you just throw it away?"

"You're right about one thing, anyway," Grace had told her, feeling a hot flash of hurt at her mother's indifference. "You don't understand me. You never did. I'm not even sure what I'm doing here. The only thing I *am* sure of is that I won't ever again make the mistake of expecting anything from you."

Mother had stiffened, her eyes glittering under the brim of the hat she wore. "Then don't," she said, her voice soft but its meaning unmistakable.

Don't visit. Don't bother. I don't want you. Those were the words Grace heard, roaring in her inner ear as she passed through Security, deliberately not looking back. If she had, she would have seen her mother still standing there, her slim figure as erect and uncompromising as an accusing finger.

And now, two years later, would they be merely picking up where they'd left off? Or was it possible for them to start over? To put blame and resentment aside, and let a love older than memory guide them through this new and in some ways even rockier passage?

Grace felt her stomach do a slow cartwheel of anticipation.

Well, at least she'd have Lila and Jack, who would stick up for her if she needed them to. Watching Lila cock a penciled brow as she lowered the flowers onto the table, Grace felt a rush of affection for her kooky friend.

"Anyone who loves flowers can't be all bad," Lila commented.

"Mother?" Grace sighed. "In a million ways she's *wonderful*."

"Hey, here I've been half-expecting Lady Macbeth to walk in through that door, and now I'm picturing Melanie Wilkes, who personally always made me want to puke."

"No, she's not like that, either," Grace said, trying to come up with a way of describing her mother. "I mean, she doesn't give a hoot for the local snobs, like my sister does. Still, everybody in Blessing looks up to her. I think they're a little afraid of her, too. No one would dare snub her, even though they can't abide her liberal views. She was . . . *is* . . . brave and outspoken—she's always been a big champion of people who aren't getting a fair shake."

"Sounds like someone I know."

"She's also incredibly stubborn and domineering," Grace went on, "and when something doesn't dovetail with her version of reality, she's not above twisting the truth to fit."

"Uh-oh."

Grace had told her all about Nola, so it wouldn't have taken a great leap of imagination for Lila to see that trouble lay ahead. Mother would fight tooth and nail—just as she'd fought to raise the money for Daddy's memorial library—to keep both her memories of him, and his reputation, untarnished.

Mother hadn't even arrived, Grace realized, yet already she was jumping ahead of herself. Right now she had to concentrate on getting everything ready. Wine? She opened the refrigerator, and a bottle of Chardonnay glinted up at her from the bottom rack. Beside it lay a Saran Wrapped platter—the sushi assortment she'd had sent over from Meriken.

Now she wondered if sushi might be a bit over the top for a woman who sent her roast beef back to the kitchen if there was any pink showing.

Grace shut the refrigerator door and whirled about, nearly colliding with Lila, on her way into the kitchen to fill the empty ice bucket. "Be honest with me—what do you think my chances are?"

"As in, no one gets out of here alive?" Lila gave her a half-cocked smile, tipping her head.

She was wearing a pair of silk pantaloons the color of daffodils, and a hand-painted vest over a billowy blouse that looked as if it were made out of mosquito netting. A chunk of amethyst the size of a newborn's fist hung from her neck on a black silk cord, and, in the dead of winter, the only thing between her feet and the uncarpeted floor was a pair of blue satin ballet slippers.

"Something like that," Grace acknowledged.

She imagined Mother reading those letters . . . the undeniable fact of Daddy's infidelity right before her eyes, impossible to escape. How dreadful for her! Grace wanted, at that moment, to turn back the clock, *not* to know what she now knew, and thereby to save Mother from the devastating blow in store for her.

"Maybe, on some level, she already knows," Lila conjectured.

"What's worse—living with a lie . . . or facing reality, no matter how bad?"

"That's a tough question. I mean, like, have you ever wondered about the Son of Sam's mother—what it would be like to be faced with the irrefutable evidence that your son was a serial killer? Would *you* believe it? Would you be able to admit it even to yourself?" Lila now was putting down the ice bucket and digging into a box of Wheat Thins on the counter.

"Lila . . . we're not talking about murder. My father *loved* this woman. They had a child together."

"Even so . . . it makes you wonder, doesn't it? Would

any of us really be better off facing up to every rotten truth about our lives?"

"What if I didn't tell her . . . if I gave the letters back to Nola," Grace said, knowing even as she spoke the words that she could never do such a thing.

Lila, clearly, knew it, too.

"The cat's already out of the bag as far as you're concerned." She fished another cracker from the box and popped it into her mouth. "I guess now it's just a question of what to do with kitty."

"Any suggestions?" Grace forced a smile that felt tight and uncomfortable.

"Don't look at me." Lila laughed, shaking her head so that her dangly beaded earrings tinkled and danced. "My specialty is strictly canine."

"**M**other, you really ought to try the smoked-duck salad. It's made with these baby lettuces and arugula and . . ."

"Thank you, dear, but my tastes aren't so exotic as yours," said Cordelia, looking up from her menu, politely but firmly putting a stop to Grace's gushing. "I've been away from the city too long, I'm afraid. Something plain and simple will do."

"Well, in that case, the roast chicken . . ."

"Honestly, dear, I'm *fine*. Really, I'm afraid I've been monopolizing you at the expense of your other guests." She looked around the table, beaming beneficently at Lila and Jack. Mother's way of letting her know that she was being a lousy hostess—talking too much, acting nervous, and, worse, *showing off*.

"Well, then . . ." Grace glanced about at the walls hung with tasteful prints and lit with sconces. In her opinion,

Chelsea's most interesting restaurant, and Mother was already letting her know it was somehow failing to measure up.

Grace now felt acutely aware of the fixed smile she couldn't seem to dislodge from her face. And her dimwitted babbling—it was like one of those noisy generators that flick on automatically when the power lines go down in a storm. No doubt her way of avoiding saying what she was really thinking.

"Jack, why don't you order the wine?" Handing him the wine list, again she felt foolish, a throwback, as if no woman could possibly pick a decent bottle of wine.

Jack chose a California Merlot, and turned to her mother.

"So, Cordelia, Grace tells me you haven't been back to New York since you lived here. Bet you hardly recognize the place. The Big Apple ain't what it used to be, huh?" Jack leaned toward Mother, appearing huge, his shadow seeming to blot out the candle flickering in the center of the table.

Grace felt a bit crowded by Jack, and suddenly, sickeningly, she was seeing him through her mother's eyes: too large, too loud . . . too jokily familiar with someone he'd only just met. Everything that Win was not.

Mother, though, was smiling graciously and saying, "It's noisier, for one thing. And, goodness, so . . . overwhelming. But to me the Empire State will always be its tallest building."

"Speaking of the Empire State, when I was little, I saw a man jump from the top floor," Lila put in, elbows planted on either side of her plate, her chin resting on the backs of her knobby wrists. "That was in the days before they had that Plexiglas barricade. You can't believe how long it takes someone to reach the ground from that far up. I remember at first thinking it was a pigeon, floating way up there. Until he hit. There was a lot of blood. I think that's when I decided to become a vegetarian."

Grace felt herself wince at Lila's unintended ghoulishness, then thought, *Yes, but deep down isn't that what you want? For Lila to be off-the-wall, to stir things up?* Maybe, if they could get past this polite chitchat, they might actually get around to talking about why Mother was here.

"Lila's our resident animal-rights crusader," Grace said with a laugh. "Did you know she grooms dogs for a living?"

Cordelia perked up. "Really? How interesting."

"You wouldn't believe how dog-eat-dog it can be," deadpanned Lila.

Jack let loose a hearty laugh, and Grace and her mother joined in. People at other tables glanced their way. Lila toyed with her fork, a look on her face like that of the class clown who's just one-upped the teacher.

Then Mother piped up, "Speaking of jobs . . . Grace, did I tell you that Caroline has gone back to work?"

In her bouclé-wool suit the frothy green of a mint julep, an Hermès scarf knotted artfully about her throat, Cordelia looked perfectly at ease, as if there had never been a harsh word between her and Grace. As if Sissy weren't clearly her favorite child.

"Sissy? No, I don't think so." In fact, Grace couldn't remember Sissy's *ever* having worked.

"She's volunteering three days a week at the hospital. As a nurse's aide." Cordelia broke off a tiny piece of bread and nibbled at it. "I think it's just wonderful of her, don't you?"

Grace managed a noncommittal "Mmmm."

"I'm so glad to see her doing something with herself, now that she's got more time on her hands, what with the boys in Little League . . . and with Beech . . ." She faltered a bit, and Grace thought she saw a tiny frown print itself between

Mother's perfectly plucked brows. But she quickly recovered and went on with a wry laugh, "Oh well, you know, another one of his bright ideas: going around the countryside and selling people on those prefab storage units. Keeps him on the road and out of Sis——Caroline's hair." She did a pretty good job of making it sound like the harmless meanderings of a well-to-do eccentric instead of what it was—a loser at loose ends.

"The life of a rep." Jack nodded agreeably. "It can be rough, logging all those miles. Our winter sales conference? Half the reason we hold it in Puerto Rico every year is to reward our people with a little pool time after six months of schlepping in and out of a million stores."

Grace could feel Jack's hand on her knee under the table, giving it a reassuring squeeze that said, *It's going to be okay.*

A month ago, she might have bought Jack's optimism, but since their argument the other night, she could no longer make herself believe that things generally worked out for the best. Both she and Jack were going out of their way to avoid the subject of marriage. But sometimes what's *not* being said, she thought, can convey far more than words.

Their waiter reappeared—with his wire-rim glasses and slicked-back hair, he looked more like a moonlighting investment banker than the aspiring actor he probably was—and she listened while he rattled off the specials as swiftly and expertly as if calling in orders on the floor of the Stock Exchange. She ordered the duck salad to start, and trout with grilled mushrooms, and felt miffed when Mother ignored everything on the exotic menu and requested a simple green salad, dressing on the side, and the roast chicken.

"Grace tells me your publishing house has quite a prestigious list," Mother said, turning to Jack.

Grace caught the faint irony in her tone, and stiffened. She could feel the whole length of her spine against the back of her chair, as if it were stapled there. Not that Mother would ever create a scene, not here, in front of people. She'd open a vein in her wrist with her knife before she'd do that.

"We care about what goes out with our imprint on it . . . and about what book buyers want." Jack fielded the comment smoothly. "Sometimes, it's an uneasy mix."

"But in the end, it's all about turning a profit, isn't it?"

Mother's eyes flashed; then she glanced quickly away, looking uncomfortable. She might dislike Jack for publishing *Honor Above All* . . . but she couldn't dislike the man himself. Who could?

It was Lila who rescued them.

"You should try grooming dogs for a living." She laughed, sipping her Dewar's, straight-up. "It's more than just clipping them. You've got to know about canine diseases, and worms, and . . . well, cleaning teeth and clipping nails. Not every dog will sit still for that."

Grace dabbed her mouth with her napkin so her mother wouldn't see her smile. She was expecting Mother to be put off by Lila's unsavory mention of diseases and worms, but instead Mother laughed and said lightly, "I'm not sure I would, either."

Two years ago, Mother would not have found humor in Lila's comment. Was she starting to loosen up a bit?

Grace once more remembered Sissy's letter, and wondered: *Mr. Ross?*

Their waiter poured a splash of wine in Jack's glass, and she watched while he tasted it, nodding. Jack looked handsome in his nubby gray blazer and paisley tie, but its tail was flipped back to reveal its underside, as if he'd been running to catch a taxi and hadn't noticed. She longed to smooth it back into place, yet at the same time felt the need to keep her distance.

She remembered what Chris had said to Hannah last

night, something about their going swimming in the creek up at the cabin next summer. Jack had looked the other way. Had he been envisioning, as Grace had, a summer when they might not all be together?

Right now, she could feel pressure radiating from Jack, almost hear him urging her to break the ice . . . to stop the small talk and get on with the real stuff. Easy for him to say. He'd built a career on being direct, forthright. That was one of the things that had most attracted her to him.

He's right, she thought. *If I don't confront Mother, get this out in the open, I'll hate myself and go on resenting her.*

"While we're on the subject of dogs," Mother said, "did you know Win is getting Chris a puppy? A golden retriever."

Whatever Grace had been about to say was blasted away by Mother's news. A dog? When he was little, Chris had begged for one. And, oh, the ecstatic look on his face when she'd finally, over Win's objections ("Dirty, smelly beasts") brought home big, dopey, hairy Harley. And then, after months of sneezing and runny eyes, when she'd discovered that she was allergic to dogs . . . she'd thought Chris's heart would break, and her own, too, the way he'd sobbed and clung to that collie's neck when Lila was taking Harley away.

And now Win was getting him a puppy?

What was he trying to pull?

She felt her breathing quicken, anger rising in her.

Her fingers were involuntarily shredding the paper doily that had come with her drink. She clenched her hands to regain control of them. "A dog? No, I hadn't heard."

"Chris is absolutely thrilled," Mother continued brightly. "They're picking it up at the breeder's this weekend. Chris didn't it mention it to you? How odd. Honestly, he was nearly jumping out of his skin. This is just what that boy needs, if you ask me."

Jack shot Grace a sharp look that was somehow both sympathetic and goading. In that instant, she felt her careful control snap.

"I tell you what *I* wish. I wish somebody had asked *me*." She spoke sharply, half-noticing the movement of heads at other tables turning in her direction. Enough her mother's daughter to feel chagrined, she quickly glanced down at her lap. Lowering her voice, she added, "It's like . . . like Win is sneaking behind my back all over again!"

She felt hot now. She downed the water in her glass, but it didn't quench her thirst. She felt as if she could drink every drop of water on this planet and her throat would still be dry as a bone.

Now, she thought. *She's going to start in all over again about how I blew it with Win by not forgiving him. . . .*

It was as if she and Jack and Lila were collectively holding their breath; the very air around them was suspended until further notice. Grace felt a pulse begin to twitch in one eyelid.

Mother merely lifted an eyebrow and said, "Why, dear, if I'd known you were still brooding about *that,* I certainly would not have brought up the subject."

Grace, her face burning, glanced at Jack, expecting a warm look of sympathy. Instead, she was confronted with a pair of cobalt eyes that measured her coolly.

Why are *you carrying on about Win?* his cautious gaze seemed to ask.

How dare you, Grace wanted to lash out, *when you don't even have the guts to ask me to marry you?*

Then, as if someone else were speaking, she heard herself say, "I think you know perfectly well what Win is up to with this dog, and how I'd feel about it."

"No, I'm not sure I *do* know," Mother answered, her voice pitched theatrically low, as if to warn Grace that she was on the verge of creating a scene. "But I don't doubt that, if there were anything I needed reminding of, you'd be certain to do so."

Grace saw the opening she'd been looking for, and plunged in.

"Mother, I know you're angry at me because of the book. Why not *say* it?"

"I . . . *really,* Grace, have you completely forgotten your manners?" She dropped her voice to a flinty whisper, casting an embarrassed glance at Jack and Lila.

"When did I ever do anything right, according to your standards?" Grace demanded. She felt a scalding sensation in her cheeks, as if she'd been slapped. At the same time, Grace knew that it was her mother who would be hurting when she learned the painful truth about Daddy.

"I don't believe I care for that tone," Mother said sharply.

"Mother, *please.*" Grace felt tears start in her eyes and, in the back of her throat, the sweet, acid burn of the wine she'd been sipping. "We *have* to talk about this." Start with the night Ned Emory was killed, she thought. Then you can get to the real reason Daddy risked his life to protect Margaret.

Mother's mouth opened and snapped shut. "Honestly, Grace, if *you're* not embarrassed for your guests, then I am. I can only imagine what they must be thinking, you carrying on this way."

"Don't mind me," Lila said, sounding nonchalant.

Jack said nothing, but gave Grace's hand another encouraging squeeze under the table.

Grace wanted to go on, but she couldn't. She'd do it when they were alone. All those lectures about not making scenes—they must have been like toilet-training, something she couldn't unlearn even if she wanted to.

"All right, Mother. We'll talk later," she conceded with a sinking feeling of defeat.

Throughout the rest of the meal, she listened to Jack and Lila, mostly Jack, carry on smoothly, as if nothing were remotely wrong. Jack got Mother talking about her garden, and even managed to coax a chuckle or two out of her. It wasn't until they'd finished eating—a meal she scarcely tasted—and they were stepping outside, the freezing air hitting her in the face, that Grace found her voice again.

At the corner of Eighth and Twenty-second, Grace grabbed her mother's wrist. "Let's go back to my place. Just you and me." Her heart was pounding as she shot Jack a look that he immediately picked up on.

"I believe this is my exit cue." He kissed her lightly on the mouth, and gave her mother a more dignified peck on the cheek before climbing into the cab he'd hailed. "Good night, ladies."

"Really, dear, can't it wait until tomorrow? After the flight I had, what I could *really* use is some sleep." Mother really did look all done in, Grace thought.

But she found herself insisting, "It won't take long."

Back at the loft, Grace waited only until Cordelia was seated in the living room before pulling a sheaf of Xeroxed pages from her desk drawer—the letters, which she'd copied on the machine in her office after Nola left. She felt sick to her stomach, but she had a feeling that, if she didn't do this now, she might never again get up the nerve.

"Mother, please, please, don't hate me for this." Grace pressed the copied letters into her mother's small white hands as she sat erect on the sofa, still wearing her good wool coat that smelled faintly of camphor and lilac. "No matter what you might think, I'm not doing this to be spiteful. Really, I'm not."

Cordelia looked down at the paper-clipped sheets in bewilderment, and that was when Grace realized her mother didn't have her reading glasses on, and probably wouldn't be able to make out the words.

"What is this?" she demanded imperiously. "Grace, there's no need for you to be plying me with so-called evidence. I'm not senile . . . not yet, at any rate."

"But the way you pretend that nothing could ever taint our family's reputation—you sometimes make me feel like *I'm* the one who's losing my mind."

"All right," she snapped. "It happened. Is that what you want to hear? Your father *did* struggle with Ned Emory; maybe he was even indirectly responsible for the trigger going off. But why air our family linen? It's nobody else's business."

"Mother . . ." She stopped. The sick feeling inside her seemed to be expanding, a great agonizing wave rising up from the pit of her stomach. Weakly, she finished, "That's not the whole story."

"Of course it is. Your father would never have kept anything from me. And *you* certainly haven't," Mother replied in that same curt tone.

It was suddenly, painfully clear to Grace that her mother could not have even suspected about Daddy and Margaret.

She dropped to her knees before Cordelia, taking her soft, silky-cool hands, with their gleaming pink nails, in her own. "Mother, listen, whatever Daddy did or didn't tell you . . . I know he loved us. He . . ."

"Grace, what *are* you trying to say?"

"Daddy and Margaret . . ." She stopped. "Mother, Nola Emory is their child." Grace spread her hand over the letters in Cordelia's lap. "It's all here. In Daddy's own words. Every letter he wrote Margaret."

Cordelia's face turned as white as the sheaf of papers she was now shoving from her lap, as if it were something she'd spilled that might stain. She was trembling, and suddenly Grace was afraid for her.

But Cordelia's voice, when she spoke, was strong, caustic. "You *hateful* girl!" Her eyes glittered like broken bits of glass.

"Mother, it's true. Read them." The paper-clipped pages had fallen against one of Cordelia's neat navy pumps, forming a sort of lopsided tent. Grace retrieved them, placed them once again on her mother's lap.

"Why are you doing this?" Mother's whole face seemed to sag, her voice now a ragged whisper that Grace had to strain to hear.

"I'm sorry," Grace told her. "I know what a shock it is. I still haven't gotten over it myself. But if we—"

"No. Impossible." Cordelia's mouth snapped shut like a vault closing on something of immeasurable value. "Your father . . . I would have known."

"How? You weren't with him every moment, not even every day." Tears were now running down Grace's cheeks, and she did nothing to stop them. "Oh, Mother, I'm not saying it to hurt you, but the truth is, you and Daddy lived pretty separate lives."

"And just what did you expect?" Mother cried, her voice rising, becoming shrill almost. "A family like those on television? Your father wasn't ordinary. *We* weren't ordinary."

Nola's words came back to her. "I know," Grace said. "But maybe that was the whole point—maybe he needed a place where he *could* be just ordinary. With Margaret—"

"Don't!" Mother held up both hands. "Don't you dare!"

"Oh, Mother . . ." Grace pressed her forehead into her mother's knees, feeling their unyielding hardness soothe her in some odd way—like the cool crystal doorknobs she remembered from the old house in Blessing. When Grace finally lifted her face to meet Cordelia's gaze, she saw how mightily her mother was struggling to keep from falling apart.

"I . . . don't . . . have . . . to . . . listen . . . to . . . this." Mother spoke in little bursts, through clenched teeth, her hands curling into fists.

Grace longed to put her arms around her mother, but something in the way Cordelia held herself, rigidly, without an ounce of give, warned her to stay put.

Grace watched helplessly as her mother tried to get up. But Cordelia's arms and legs buckled, and she was thrown awkwardly back into the sofa cushions, clutching hold of the papers in her lap as if to steady herself. Mother, who had always been so poised and graceful, suddenly reminded Grace of those old black-and-white eight-millimeter home movies—her movements made clumsy, herky-jerky, by the camera. Except Mother wasn't smiling as she had been in nearly every frame of those home movies. She was staring at Grace with a waxy expression, as if she were in shock.

In a clear, distinct voice, Mother said, "I believe I'll be going now. Please don't trouble yourself any further." She got up, seeming more in control, and started back toward the door, as erect as if held by a string stretching from the top of her scalp to the ceiling. The letters, which she was clutching, were now curled into a club, as if she intended to hit someone with it.

"Wait!" Grace charged after her, grabbing her arm with more force than she'd intended. Under her bulky coat, Mother's tiny bones felt almost frail.

Why were people always saying that confrontation was a good thing? Grace felt awful, as if she'd just killed someone . . . or been struck herself.

Mother turned, freezing her with a glance more disdainful than the one Grace had once seen her turn on the white mayor of Blessing, when he laughed in Mother's face for demanding that he abolish the "Whites Only" fountain in Jefferson Square. Her voice, when she spoke, was equally cold.

"I forgot to tell you . . . your daddy's library . . . a good portion of the funding we were expecting hasn't come through, and, the way it looks now, we may not get it. Of course, once you've *expanded* on your sordid little tale, there won't be any point in me even trying to raise the money."

Grace felt as if a block of stone—one heavy enough to have been used in the building of such a library—had been dropped on her, crushing her. "Oh, Mother, I'm sorry. Maybe there's something I can—"

"*You* have done quite enough." Mother yanked her arm free.

Her eyes were like the discreet diamonds flashing in her ears, hard and bright. Even as her arm was jerking upward as if she meant to strike Grace, she caught herself and lowered it stiffly to her side.

And then Grace was grabbing *her,* clutching her with both arms. Mother's flowery scent engulfed Grace, making her think of the honeysuckle she used to pluck off the orchard fence and suck on, always hoping for more than the mere trace of sweetness each blossom grudgingly delivered.

After an eternity, Grace felt her mother's head lower until her forehead was touching Grace's shoulder, lightly, cautiously, like a weary traveler pausing to let down a burden for just a beat before moving on.

The stone crushing Grace seemed to lift a bit. *Say something!* a voice inside her screamed.

But then it was too late; Mother briskly unfastened herself from Grace's embrace, marched over to the door, and let herself out. Closing—definitely not *slamming*—the door behind her.

All without a single backward glance. The tightly rolled letters still clutched in her fist.

Chapter 17

J ack swam, his long arms slicing the surface of the Mc-
Burney YMCA's pool. As he spat out a mouthful of
overly chlorinated water, he tried not to think about
last night's dinner at Luma. With her mother, Grace had
seemed so frustrated . . . which was, he also knew, how she
felt about him. *My fault,* he thought. He *wanted* to take that
last step, but something was stopping him.

As he swung into his turn and started another length,
Jack thought of his daughter. This past week or so, he'd
gotten the sense that Hannah was lightening up on Grace.
Wishful thinking? Or was it possible that one obstacle, at
least, might soon be removed from his path?

He'd tried to talk to Hannah about it, but she'd been
curiously evasive. Almost furtive. Maybe this was another of
her ploys—get Grace to relax her guard, then sock it to her.
He didn't want to believe that of Hannah. But . . .

Through the water streaming down his face, Jack caught
a glimpse of his son in the lane beside his, thrashing at the
water, not as if he were swimming, but as if he were *beating*
the hell out of it. And Ben's face, knotted with effort, nearly
purple—whatever gene, or DNA strand, made a person su-
percompetitive, he had it in spades.

Nor was Ben above manipulating people to get what he
wanted. Could Hannah, too, be capable of such Machiavel-
lian deviousness? Did her grudge against Grace go a lot
deeper than he'd imagined?

Jack swam to a stop and pushed his goggles up over his

forehead. He looked over at Ben, clutching the pool's tiled edge and struggling to catch his breath—the winner of their undeclared race, for what it was worth.

Did Hannah confide in Ben? Unlikely, but even if he knows something, it's not his first priority.

Ben proved him right. "Hey, Dad—you seen the C-print for the MacArthur cover?"

"Yes, as a matter of fact, I have." Jack had a sinking feeling. Of all the things going on at Cadogan, Ben *would* have to pick this one.

Ben grinned and scrubbed his face with one hand, water dripping between his fingers. "I've been hanging over Eastman's shoulder for weeks. He was ready to feed me to the sharks. But in the end, he ran with my idea, and I think what we came up with is pretty sensational."

"It has a certain style, no doubt about it."

"Why do I sense that you're not exactly thrilled?"

Jack noted the tight look on Ben's face. Should he have postponed this until they were back in the office? Maybe . . . but he got so swallowed up . . . and it seemed like Ben was never at his desk when Jack buzzed him.

"Listen, Ben, it *is* good . . . but too soft, too literary." Jack shook his head. "I don't think it'll fly with the chains."

"You don't think, or you *know* it won't?" Ben had to raise his voice to be heard above the swimmers thrashing on either side of them. "You talked to Walden, Dalton?"

"Del Cruzon happened to be in the office. He said the same thing. This is a gritty, hard-boiled mystery, Ben—we've got to go with something that packs a wallop."

"Behind my back!" hissed Ben. "Jesus Christ, Dad, you could have talked to me about it *first*."

Jack winced. It was Roger Young all over again. Why with Ben did he always come out the bad guy? He felt a sudden urge to snap at Ben, tell him to grow up. It was time he stopped blaming Daddy for everything that went wrong. When *he* was thirty, he'd had a wife and kid, murderous car and mortgage payments, and no trust fund. No time to feel sorry for himself, either, or pick over old bones.

"Look, Ben, this is not something you should take personally," he said evenly, without, he hoped, sounding apologetic. "I think you've done a dynamite job with everything about the book. But this cover just is not right for it. If you want, we can run it by some of the other major accounts. But I'm pretty sure we'll get the same reaction."

"Yeah, right." He could hear the sarcasm in Ben's voice. "Jack Gold always knows best. When do I ever get any credit? I smooth Roger Young's feathers, and I still feel like I'm out in left field, not getting any support." He stared at Jack, his lower lip almost quivering.

"Ben, I'm proud of you—you know that."

As if realizing he was on the verge of pushing it too far, Ben said, "Look, I'm sorry, it's been a rough morning. Maybe you're right. I'll talk to Eastman when we get back to the office. There's still time to do some noodling." He grabbed hold of the coping and hauled himself out of the pool, water sliding off him as if he were shrugging off a second skin. Then, standing at the edge, he reached down and extended his hand.

Jack, even as he was letting himself be half-hauled up to the tile deck, couldn't help feeling there was something vaguely condescending in Ben's helping him. Was he still pissed off? If he knew anything about Hannah, would he hold back purely out of spite? Yeah, he just might. Damn.

Jack waited until they'd showered, and were in the locker room getting dressed, before he asked, "You noticed anything different about Hannah lately?"

Watching his son button his shirt, Jack, for an instant, saw the freshly bathed baby he used to snap into his Dr.

Dentons. He waited for Ben to speak, but his son seemed totally absorbed in knotting his tie.

"I can't put my finger on it," Jack went on. "It's like she's hiding something. Whatever it is, it's even gotten her to cut Grace some slack. You have any idea what's going on with her?"

Ben, yanking loose the tie, dissatisfied with the knot he'd made, turned to face Jack. "Look, Dad . . . I don't know if I'm the one you should be asking."

Jack caught the guardedness in Ben's voice. And something else—something dark. Jesus. Was something actually the matter with Hannah? Was this furtiveness of hers a sign of real trouble?

Drugs? All the kids tried them these days. He winced at the idea of Hannah's popping a single pill, or smoking a joint. But even if she did, she was too smart to let herself get hooked. Wasn't she?

Or had that tennis-jock boyfriend of hers pressured her into sleeping with him? Jack remembered what it had been like for him at that age, wanting to mount anything with tits. And Ben—he'd had girls following him home from school since seventh grade. Nowadays he could sleep with just about any woman, and probably had had his share. He wouldn't know—Ben didn't confide in him. But Hannah, his baby, his little girl, with a guy just in it for the sex, she'd be miserable.

Jack wasn't about to let Ben's hedging stop him. "But you *do* know what it is that's bothering her? You've talked to her?"

"Dad . . ."

"Ben, I'm not asking you to betray any confidences here. I just want to know what you *think*."

Ben lifted his head, and in his wintergreen eyes—Natalie's eyes—Jack caught a look that he couldn't quite make out, but that nonetheless made him uneasy. He'd seen that look before—a slight narrowing of the lids, a faint glittering deep within his pupils. Did Ben hate him? Not just harboring a few gripes, the usual kid's stuff, but really *hate* him?

"The thing is, Dad . . ." Benjamin straightened up, just having tied his shoes; regarding his lean, muscular torso, Jack felt proud of his son's build, and at the same time a little chagrined at his own thickening waistline. ". . . Hannah would kill me if she knew I'd said anything."

Jack, in the midst of knotting his own tie, felt his fingers grow suddenly clumsy. So it *was* serious. Carefully, he asked, "Is it something you think I *should* know?"

"She's afraid she might be pregnant."

"Jesus. Oh, Christ."

Benjamin cut a sidelong glance at him, then said, "Look, let's get one thing straight. You didn't hear it from me."

Jack nodded, and sat down on the bench between the rows of lockers. His heart gave a dull kick before settling into a rapid rhythm. Pregnant? His Hannah, his baby?

If it *was* true, what would they do? What would *she* do?

Have to talk to her. He'd keep his promise to Ben . . . but there was no sense waiting around for Hannah to confide in him. Before the divorce, she would have come to him . . . but not these days.

Jack remembered Hannah's starting her period. Thirteen, and about as graceful as a split-rail fence, her face on fire as she whispered it to him—*him,* not Natalie. He'd wanted to hug her, but he hadn't. Instead, he'd taken her to Rexall's. He could still see her, a skinny kid with braces and no chest to speak of, hovering over by the magazine section, pretending the large and conspicuous man standing in the checkout line with the box of Kotex tucked under his arm was in no way connected to her.

Poor kid. To have confided in Benjamin, she must have been pretty desperate.

"All right," he told Ben, giving in to a sigh that weighed on him like the Rock of Ages. "I didn't hear it from you."

"You going to talk to her?" Ben looked anxious.

"I see no other choice," Jack said, feeling as if the air around him had grown too heavy to breathe.

He sat up straighter, observing a thickset man—smaller than he, but with a belly that, like his, had seen better days—wrench open a nearby locker, still gasping for breath after his swim. He felt a sour apple of dread lodge in his gut.

He thought of that line from the Kenny Rogers song, *You got to know when to hold them . . . know when to fold them.*

Now. Starting now. With Hannah. He had to stop pretending it would all turn out okay as long as they just rolled with the punches. He couldn't bear it if the two of them ended up like Grace and her mother.

W hen Jack called to ask Hannah if she'd have dinner with him, she'd told him she was swamped with homework. Not wanting to seem too anxious, he'd arranged to take her out the following night. Now they sat at a wobbly-legged table in the back room of Hannah's favorite grungy pizza parlor, Arturo's, on West Houston, where the pizza was slid from coal-heated brick ovens on long-handled wooden paddles, and the waiters and waitresses took turns performing at the microphone.

But Hannah, who usually could put away half of an enormous pizza dripping with mozzarella, ate only one slice, and then sat picking at a second while Jack gobbled up more than he knew was good for him. More than Hannah, policewoman of his cholesterol count, would have let him get away with, had she not been so wrapped up in herself.

He remembered, when she was little, how they'd dance around the living room to Patti Page's "Tennessee Waltz," with her small feet planted on his shoes, as she giggled and clung to his trousers to keep from losing her balance. Looking down at the crooked part in her hair, at her flowered nightie billowing about her spindly ankles, he'd felt both so vulnerable and so protective.

He wanted to protect her now. But she was acting as if she barely knew him.

It wasn't until the waiter was clearing away their plates that Jack ventured, "How's it going with you and Conrad? Seems like I haven't heard his name pop up on the old hit parade lately." He smiled, hoping his anxiety didn't show.

Hannah's gaze fixed on him for the first time that evening. "I don't know," she said with what seemed an elaborate pretense at nonchalance, "I guess I haven't seen that much of him lately, except at school."

Jack waited. "You mean you two are no longer an item?"

She rolled her eyes. "Daddy, you're so old-fashioned. *Nobody* talks like that anymore. Anyway, I'm not sure we ever were, as you put it, an 'item.' " She dabbed at her chin with a napkin she'd folded into a neat square.

"Oh?"

"He's not really my type. His big dream is to be a lawyer someday and make a ton of money."

"You can still be head over heels about someone who's not your type."

"You mean like you and Grace?" She said it jokingly, a rueful smile lurking at the corners of her down-turned mouth, but he caught the barb.

"Sort of," he answered guardedly.

"Daddy, this is the nineties. Kids my age don't even *date* anymore. My friends and I, we just hang out, that's all. It's sort of like you're in this club, and if you like somebody and he likes you, well, that's cool . . . but it's not necessarily this big deal."

Unless you happen to be sleeping together.

Jack pictured himself as Fred Flintstone, cudgel in hand, swinging it at Conrad, whom he'd met only once, but imagined to be the kind of heartless jock who'd have bragged about his conquest in the locker room. No, that had to be another of his anachronisms. Nowadays it was all about safe sex, making sure you were "protected." But what about when someone got hurt—who, or what, was supposed to protect you from that?

"Hannah, I may belong to another generation . . ." he began cautiously, covering her hand with his. ". . . but one thing I *do* know—when you get involved with someone, however casual it might seem, you can't help having feelings, certain expectations."

She rolled her eyes. "Daddy, you don't have to tell me. I'm *not* in kindergarten."

I know . . . because, if you were, I wouldn't let you out of the house dressed like that. Levi's so worn they looked as if they'd been through a paper shredder, slouchy black lambswool sweater with holes big enough for him to put his thumb through. But at least her hair was washed and neatly combed—dark silk draped in overlapping sheaves over her back and shoulders. He remembered when he used to braid it for her every morning before school, in two long plaits, sometimes having to do it more than once, until he got the part straight enough to satisfy her.

"I just don't want to see you get hurt, that's all," he told her.

Hannah sat silently picking at a strand of dried mozzarella stuck to the table. Arturo's had gotten crowded and noisy, and now he could hear someone at the microphone in the next room launching into a lively bluegrass number.

"Daddy, what are you getting at exactly?" she asked, squinting at him as if peering through a rifle sight.

"In other words, 'Chill, Dad'?"

She grinned. "Where did you hear that?"

"I get around."

"I'm impressed."

"So you're not . . ." *Pregnant.* The word hovered on his lips. ". . . worried about anything in particular?"

She shrugged. "What gives you that idea?"

"I don't know. . . . You haven't been yourself lately. And as your friendly neighborhood warden, I can't help being concerned."

Hannah's eyes narrowed. "Have you been talking to Grace?"

"About you? What makes you think that?"

"I don't know. I just wondered."

"Is there something Grace knows that's happening with you that I don't?"

Hannah just stared at him, her eyebrows drawing closer together, until they were meeting over the bridge of her nose. "Oh, I get it. *She* made you promise not to say anything."

"Hannah, it wasn't Grace—" He stopped himself before he could blurt out the truth. Ben.

"Oh, Daddy, I can *always* tell when you're covering up. You're so obvious. Why don't you just come out and *say* it? You know about my stupid pregnancy scare, *because Grace told you.*"

Even with her voice lowered, he felt the blast of her fury.

"I don't have to talk to Grace to see that you're young and beautiful and just as interested in boys as I'm sure they are in you. One thing that hasn't changed since I was your age—teenagers' hormones still come in the large economy size."

She didn't even smile at his attempt to be lighthearted. She just stared at him, her eyes with their inky lashes seeming to grow darker, larger, giving her face a tender, bruised look.

"Oh, God! I don't believe it! I don't *believe* I fell for it!" She startled him by jumping up, slashes of color making her cheekbones stand out. "She was only *pretending* to be my friend, just so she could run to you and rat on me."

It wasn't supposed to turn out this way, he thought numbly. "Hannah, it wasn't Grace who . . ."

"If it wasn't her, then *who?* I know it's Grace, because she hates me. Don't you get it? Can't you *see* how she hates me?" She was weeping now, her lashes spiky with tears. Hannah, who hadn't let him see her cry since that day he'd moved out, when she'd sobbed and begged him not to go. His fastidious little girl, now wiping her nose on her sleeve like it hadn't occurred to her to use a handkerchief or even a napkin.

Jack's heart ached for her. But, Jesus, he couldn't just sit here and let Grace take the rap. It was unfair, both to Grace and to Hannah. On the other hand, if getting Grace off the hook meant breaking his promise to Ben, what would that be saying to Ben? Their relationship was already so precarious. . . .

"Grace doesn't hate you," Jack said, choosing his words carefully. "Believe me, she had nothing to do with this."

Hannah took a huge, shuddery breath, and the look she fixed on him cut him to the bone. As if in some terrible way he had betrayed her.

"Hannah." He tried to take both her hands in his, then felt them sliding from his grasp.

"Oh, Daddy," she said, a heartbreaking catch in her voice, like when he was walking out his and Natalie's door for the last time and she'd said goodbye.

"Here's how we do it. . . ." Tim Fitchner sketched an imaginary display in the air with his pencil. "A riser with a photo of Grace and a bigger one of her father, and, right between the two of them, a small inset of Nola Emory. And we can do the same thing in a smaller version for the counter displays. And then posters for the stores that don't want displays . . ."

Watching Cadogan's excitable marketing director wave his pencil and pump his arms like Kurt Masur conducting the Philharmonic, Jack remembered Grace calling him a few evenings ago, an hour or so before Cordelia was due to arrive for drinks.

"Jack, I have them—Daddy's letters. . . ." She'd sounded out of breath, as if she'd been running.

"Nola?" he'd asked.

"She just left. I don't know what made her change her mind, but she . . . she wants me to use them. Now we can publish the *real* story about my father. Oh, Jack, do you know what this will mean?"

He did . . . not only for Grace, but for himself.

Over the past few days, with Grace hard at work rewriting and adding new inserts to her book, he had set the machinery in motion here at Cadogan. And today's meeting was showing him that he wasn't the only one with high expectations for *Honor Above All.*

Reinhold, adieu, maybe now you'll get off my back, he thought.

The only downside, as he saw it, was that by the time they published they'd have lost some of the momentum being generated by the publicity over Nola's story. Jack still couldn't believe how quickly it had gotten out. Someone at Cadogan—the same big-mouth who'd leaked the Ned Emory story? But it could have been anyone—an editor at one of the book clubs, or Grace's agent putting the bug in Hollywood's ear. Something as big as this . . . almost impossible to keep a lid on it.

Jack did some quick mental calculations. Could they move up publication by a month or so? Up the print run to three hundred thousand? And if they were lucky, with at least a 70 percent sell-through, the bottom line would look good enough to satisfy even Reinhold.

But there was still the advertising-and-promotion budget to settle. Everyone was keyed up. Nell Sorensen, in publicity, had been deluged with calls since the squib in the *Daily News* yesterday. Everyone in the world seemed to want to interview Grace and Nola. They'd probably be getting more orders than it would make sense to fill. And they still needed the final okay on the budget from Reinhold. The three hundred Jack wanted to spend on promotion alone would be as much or more than they'd be putting out for all the rest of their spring list put together.

But Reinhold, as usual, was late.

Jack glanced at his watch. He was supposed to meet Grace any minute—they were having lunch in the neighborhood. She might even be waiting in his office. If Reinhold didn't get here soon . . .

"We can get dumps on a lot of the lease lines." Marty Weintraub's grating voice brought him back to the meeting. He looked over at Marty, who was rubbing his jaw, already shadowed with stubble at twelve in the afternoon. "God knows what the chains will charge us to join their promotions, but if we can get the superstores to feature it up front, we're looking at twice, ten times, the visibility."

"How do you see the breakdown?" Jack asked. "Between advertising and what we lay out for point-of-sale?"

Jack saw in the Brooklyn-born-and-raised Marty a cruder version of himself: Thread broker turned book rep, who in nine years had risen up to become director of sales. Tireless, creative, terrific with people . . . but Jack couldn't help wincing at the diamond signet on his pinkie.

"I know you fellows are concerned about how much we're going to have to spend, but the biggest exposure we're going to get," Nell Sorensen spoke up, "won't cost a red cent. I just got off the phone with *People,* and they're interested in doing a story. Possibly even a cover."

Marty nearly jumped out of his seat. "Will the Emory woman agree to be interviewed?"

"How should I know?" She shot Marty an annoyed, harried look. "I just found out about this whole new angle myself—I haven't even had a chance to phone her."

"What about ads?" Jack asked.

What ensued was an endless debate about the effectiveness of radio versus print ads. Jack fought the itch to glance at his watch again.

Instead, he announced, "Folks, have your final proposals on my desk by tomorrow morning. And, Tim, I'd like to see numbers on half- and three-quarter-page versus full-page layouts." He stretched his legs out under the vast rosewood conference table—the only piece of furniture on the entire floor that allowed him this luxury. "I'll need to go over them with Kurt before we nail down the final budget."

But who knew when he'd be able to catch Reinhold? The guy was always flying in from London or Munich or Helsinki, wherever Hauptman had offices. Probably thought it was safer. Make Jack the sitting duck. Let him get blamed for anything and everything that went wrong here.

"Sorry, gang. My meeting ran over."

As if on cue, Reinhold strode in, his perpetually wind-blown hair even more scrambled than usual, his tie slightly awry. He dropped into the chair across from Jack, hiking one foot up on the opposite knee. His double-breasted jacket fell open, revealing red suspenders underneath.

Jack tried to ignore the looks exchanged around the table.

"We were discussing the ad-promo budget," Nell offered. She began assembling her papers as if to pass them over to him, though an identical report, neatly bound in its plastic cover, lay on the table before him.

"I've gone over the figures," Reinhold said. "And, frankly, I think you're over the top on this one. It's a promising book, no doubt. But three hundred thousand? What about our other projects—Boone MacArthur, for example? The way I see it, we'd be robbing Peter to pay Paul."

Jack felt himself stiffening. He wondered if Reinhold had been talking to Ben, then quickly dismissed the idea. It wasn't much of a secret that Reinhold would be happy to have Jack gone. *He'd never admit it, but I make him nervous.* Reinhold wanted to be the one in charge, yet when a decision needed making, people at Cadogan all still looked to Jack.

Nonetheless, he couldn't let Reinhold know he was worried. Sidestep now, and work on him later? Might succeed, though he'd lose face.

Then something occurred to Jack that made him smile.

"Kurt, have you actually *read* this book?" he asked softly.

Silence fell over the room. Reinhold was giving him the old poker player's bluff, but Jack could see him squirming.

"If I read every manuscript we publish, I wouldn't have time to run this company." He gave a forced chuckle.

"True," Jack said amiably. "But let me tell you, when

you *do* get the time, it'll knock your socks off. Grace Truscott could make the life of Millard Fillmore a page-turner."
He held up a hand. "Oh, I know you're probably thinking
I'm prejudiced, but, my personal feelings about the author
aside"—Jack waited for the chuckles to subside, and con-
gratulated himself on having defused any grenades on that
score that Reinhold might have lobbed his way—"let me tell
you, it's superb reading. Not just because of the sensational
stuff, either. Among other things, it sheds all kinds of new
light on Kennedy and Johnson. History buffs are going to
have a field day."

Heads all around the table were nodding in agreement.

"Absolutely the most gripping biography I've ever read,"
Nell piped up.

"Great stuff. Really hot," put in Marty, letting his wrist
go limp and waggling his hairy hand.

"I'm sure you're right." Reinhold pushed himself to his
feet. "But you'll have to excuse me—I'm expecting an over-
seas call. We'll take it up later?" He looked pointedly at Jack
before striding out.

The meeting was adjourned.

Back in his office, Jack felt rewarded by the sight of
Grace, seated in the wing chair opposite his desk, flipping
through Cadogan's spring catalogue, which featured *Honor
Above All* on its cover—the famous photo of Eugene Truscott at Martin Luther King's funeral, a cautionary hand held
aloft, as if to ward off the camera's eye, the shine of tears
visible even with his head partly bowed.

Grace was wearing a fitted red wool jacket with black
velvet lapels over simple black pants and leather boots. With
her cheeks pink and her short dark hair windblown, she
looked as if she'd just ridden in from a hunt and hadn't had
time to change. Jack felt his heart expand. God, she was so
beautiful.

Kissing her lightly on the cheek as she rose, he fought the urge to catch her hard in his arms, hold her tight against what he could feel coming next. Because the look on her face told him she wasn't going to like what he'd planned to tell her over lunch—about Hannah. In fact, from her stony expression he suspected that she already knew.

"I heard from Hannah last night after you called," Grace said, as if she'd read his mind. "She was pretty upset."

"I can imagine." Damnit, why had he waited to tell Grace?

"She seems to think I spilled the beans." Her voice was low and dangerous, making him think of thunderclouds. "For God's sake, Jack, what did you say to her? How did *you* even find out?" Her words brought the icy downpour.

"Ben told me. But I promised him I wouldn't let Hannah know where I'd heard it."

"So you just let her guess, right? And, bingo, my number came up." She faced him squarely, five feet four inches of barely restrained fury. "It just so happens, Jack Gold, that she *did* confide in me. For the very first time, she opened the door—just a crack, but enough to let me get a toe inside. Enough to let me see what it could be like if . . . if . . ." She swallowed hard. "And that's why you didn't hear it from me. Because *I* keep my promises."

"So do I." Jack wanted to take her in his arms, cover her with kisses, beg her forgiveness . . . but he didn't quite know how.

"Grace," Jack said gently, "I told Hannah it wasn't you I heard it from. This will blow over. She'll get over it in no time." He felt like a liar even as he spoke, knowing it almost certainly wasn't true.

"How can you say that? Like it's some kind of virus—a twenty-four-hour flu." She smacked the catalogue down on his desk with a sharp cracking sound, sending papers scattering to the floor. "Do you really believe that? God, Jack, you're either a whole lot more naïve than I thought . . . or you're purposely lying just to try and smooth things over between us. Either way, I can't believe you'd do it—that you'd . . . you'd just sacrifice me this way! Or aren't I important enough for it to matter?"

"My son happens to be important, too."

Hearing the pompousness in his tone, Jack cringed. But she was pushing him into a corner, giving him no choice except to defend himself.

"Explain it to Ben, then! Tell him what happened, and see if he'll talk to Hannah himself. I think he likes me. Thank heavens one of your children does. And I think he'd want to help."

"Grace, for God's sake, Hannah is sixteen, and five minutes from now, I guarantee you, she'll be thinking about nothing but that tennis ace with the terrific backhand and the brain of a lentil."

"Jack, just listen to yourself. Either you are ducking this, or you don't know Hannah half as well as you think you do." She gave him a hard look.

"Grace, this isn't the time—"

"*Now* you sound like my mother."

"Whoa . . . wait a minute now, just back off, lady. Play fair." He felt himself growing angry.

"Jack, do you really still think all this is about being fair? Is it *fair* that I'm being blamed for your leaving Natalie? Is it fair that I have to tiptoe around your family like I'm some kind of pariah?"

"No, it isn't, but don't you think you're blowing this whole thing out of proportion?" He recognized the same tone he used with Hannah when trying to calm her . . . and knew with a sinking feeling that Grace probably had, too.

"Actually, I don't."

"Damnit, Grace, can't you just *drop* it?"

"Maybe you'd like me to just forget the whole thing."

"What are you talking about?"

"Oh, Jack." She said it just the way Hannah, last night, had said, *Oh, Daddy,* and now he felt the same tightening along the back of his neck, the same sour-apple clutch in his gut.

Give it a rest, Jack. Don't push her.

Grace was so mad, she wanted to punch him.

She had trusted Jack, and he had betrayed her. Obviously, blood *was* thicker than water.

She'd believed in the two of them . . . that, in spite of their differences, they could make a go of it. But could all the loving gestures in the world make up for Jack's not sticking up for her when it counted?

Do something, a cold voice inside her commanded. *Tell him it's over.*

Suddenly she saw the whole thing clearly. Jack's not asking her to marry him—all this time, she'd simply been waiting for him eventually to get around to it. But why did it have to be up to Jack?

Why couldn't *she* be the one to decide? To say to Jack that any man who wasn't jumping at the chance to marry her didn't deserve her?

"Marry me, Grace."

Grace shook her head, staring at Jack, wondering if she'd only imagined hearing him say those words. But the look on his face told her. Yes—oh, God—he actually *had* asked her to marry him.

Funny how there was none of the rush of excitement she'd imagined she would feel, only a dull emptiness.

"Why, Jack?" she choked. "Why *now?*"

Instead of this being the happiest moment of her life, as it should have been, Grace felt as if she were a starving dog who'd been tossed a bone.

"Why don't we talk about it over lunch?" Jack put an arm around her shoulders, disturbed by the tension he could feel in her, humming like a high-voltage power line.

Asshole. You sure do know how to pick your moments. But how could he have, when he even hadn't known he was going to say those words? They had simply jumped out of him. Why? Not hard to figure. They'd been on the tip of his tongue for weeks. And how stupid he'd been, letting his head—his penchant for weighing every little thing and totting it all up—get in the way of his heart.

"Forget lunch," she told him. "I'm not hungry."

"Dinner, then? I'll fix us something at my place."

"I don't know." She paced over to the window, and stood there for a moment, looking down at lower Fifth. Then she said in a firm voice, "No. I can't see you, Jack. Not tonight."

She turned to look at him—a long, measuring look that sent a cold ache to the center of his chest; a look that made it clear she was having serious doubts, not just about his sincerity, but about the whole rest of their lives.

Chapter 18

"Mom?"

Grace started at Chris's voice over the phone. He sounded so faint and almost . . . lost. She'd been up half the night before, brooding about Jack, and indulging herself, too—crying into her pillow as she hadn't since the divorce. A moment ago, she could hardly keep her eyes open. But now, huddled at the breakfast table in her robe, she felt strangely alert.

"Hi, sweetie. Having a nice visit with Nana?" She made her voice light, hoping that she was only imagining there was something wrong.

"We went to the museum yesterday after school," he volunteered glumly. "It was fun, but Nana wanted to see practically every exhibit."

"Did she wear you out?"

"Sort of."

"I remember once, when I was around your age," Grace said, "Grandma made me go to a party at some embassy. By the time it was over, I was pooped . . . but she was as perky as ever. After we got back home, she stayed up half the night writing little notes to people she'd met, who she hoped would contribute to your grandfather's campaign fund."

"Sounds like Nana." Chris managed a weak chuckle. Then he took a deep breath and said, "Look, Mom, I'd better go or I'll be late for school. The reason I called is, I was wondering if it'd be okay with you if I stayed at Dad's a while longer."

"You mean while Nana's there? I thought that was the plan."

"Yeah, sure . . . but after she leaves, I was thinking maybe . . . well, uh, that it might be easier for everybody if I just . . . you know, sort of hung with Dad."

"For how long?"

"I don't know. . . . A while."

Grace felt herself trembling. What was Chris saying? That he wanted to *live* with Win?

"Chris, why don't we talk about this later—after I've had a chance to speak with your dad?" She was amazed at how calm she was managing to sound despite the rapid, sick pounding of her heart.

"Yeah, okay . . ." Chris sounded wary.

"Is your dad there?" she asked, fighting the dizziness that seemed to spiral up from the pit of her empty stomach.

Then Win was coming onto the line, his voice soothing as the worn flannel robe she was wrapped in. "Grace, believe me, I know what you must be thinking. I was caught off-guard by all this myself. When Chris told me that he wanted . . ." He stopped, lowering his voice as if he didn't want Chris—or maybe Cordelia—to overhear. "Listen, I don't think we should be talking about this over the phone. Could we get together later on? Why don't I stop by your place after work?"

Grace found herself agreeing, even as she wondered if this might be some new trick of Win's to get her back. Then, with a sickening jolt, it occurred to her—could *Mother* have put this idea into Chris's head?

Was Mother capable of something so underhanded?

Underhanded, no. But if she truly believed it was in Chris's best interest . . .

And what, exactly, *was* in Chris's best interest? Grace wondered. Was she being selfish, holding on to him when he so clearly preferred being with his father?

Maybe . . . but Chris needed her, too. He just didn't know how much.

Grace stayed home most of the day, letting her machine answer the phone when it rang. Twice, it was Jack, sounding so unhappy she'd nearly given in and picked up. But mostly it was reporters. Someone from *Harper's Bazaar,* desperate for an interview. Bob Tillotson, from *A.M. America,* wanting do a spot on Nola and her. A woman from National Public Radio, who left both her office and home numbers, urging Grace to call her back tonight, no matter how late.

She thought about calling Nola, to see how she was handling this media onslaught, but then thought better of it. She pictured Nola, cool and imperious, with her smile that could turn frosty in a blink. Though she'd probably never had occasion to do so, Nola would instinctively know how to field even the toughest questions a reporter might throw at her.

As expertly as Mother would . . . once the press got wind of her being in New York.

By late afternoon, the phone had stopped ringing. Grace, knowing she ought to be at her desk madly finishing the last rewrite, couldn't seem to rouse herself from the sofa, where she lay curled, listening to the soft gurgling of the radiators, and the occasional rumble of a subway passing underneath her building. She was waiting for Win . . . but it wasn't her ex-husband she wanted to see walk through her door.

Jack. She couldn't bear thinking about him . . . but at the same time she couldn't seem to stop.

At last, with the light fading, Grace blinked as if waking from a long nap—how many hours had she been sitting here?—and hauled herself off the sofa to get dressed.

Minutes later, just out of the shower, she looked about

her bedroom, where evening shadows, deepened by the gloom of the rain that had just begun to fall, angled through the skylight, casting her iron bed in a faint bruised glow. In the corner, by the window, was a low round glass table holding a vase with the spray of pussy willows she'd picked up yesterday at the greenmarket—a sign that spring finally was on its way.

A beautiful room, simple, almost Zenlike. Just a few pagan touches—the richly colored mohair shawl thrown over the bed, the intricately embroidered Susani hanging on the wall above. Yet, pleasing as it all was, it made her think of those eggs she and Sissy used to blow out and paint for Easter, lovely on the outside, hollow on the inside.

No one sharing it with her. Not Jack. Not even her son.

My little boy. Was he really gone for good? She found herself listening for the muffled pounding of Chris's stereo. But there was only the soft patter of rain against the skylight.

She thought of how she'd occasionally resented Chris, his sullen moodiness, and the times he was being really irritating, when she could have cheerfully thrown him out a window. But didn't every mother get fed up from time to time? Probably Chris had felt that way about her, too.

Apparently more often than she'd realized.

Why else would he rather live with Win?

She felt a tightness in her chest that was sending out tiny darts of pain. *How could he love Win more than me?* But it wasn't hard to imagine, not with Win—Win, who seemed impervious to bad moods, who had a way of making them disappear.

Damn you, Win.

He would be here any minute now. Furiously, she toweled her hair dry, jammed her legs into jeans, and yanked on a baggy sweater.

Moments later, Grace was opening her front door to let

her ex-husband in, realizing as she did so that she had swung it open too wide, as if for a larger man—a man, say, about Jack's size. Her heart contracted.

"Hello, Win," she said.

"Hi," Win replied, seeming to hesitate, as if not sure of his welcome. As he stepped inside, he grinned, cocking his ear at the familiar Miles Davis tune drifting from her stereo, lazy and undulating as cigarette smoke in a roadside bar.

She took his coat, draping it over her arm. "Is it still raining?" Dumb. She could feel the coat's dampness through the sleeve of her sweater.

"It won't last," he told her.

"That's not what I heard. They're predicting three inches."

Win shrugged. "Call me an optimist."

Yes, she thought. That was Win. But what if she were to remind him that even the sunniest outlook wasn't always enough to keep a person sane when raising a child, especially a *teenager,* full-time?

Easy, she told herself. A drink first, maybe two. Then you can turn on the charm, try to convince Win that assuming full custody of Chris would not be in his own best interest. All that extra responsibility tying him down, getting in the way of his work, his social life.

For Chris's sake, she'd *beg* if she had to. And if that didn't work? She couldn't bear even thinking about it. Because, if Win was determined to take this to court, she'd have no choice but to back down. It wasn't just that Win's powerful connections and legal expertise would give him a good chance of winning—she simply would never subject her son to such an ordeal.

But, looking at her ex-husband now, she wondered that she, or anyone, could think him capable of fighting dirty. In his navy suit and pale-blue Oxford shirt, with the striped

Dunhill tie she'd given him the Christmas before they'd split up, he looked like a handsome, clean-cut senior-class president posing for his graduation photo. Despite everything, she felt oddly reassured by him—the way certain doctors, by their mere tone of voice, can seem to transform an imagined tumor into a benign cyst, or an especially personable saleswoman could send her out of a store with a dress or a pair of shoes she didn't need and couldn't afford.

Grace gestured toward the sitting area; Win waited for her before seating himself in the Morris chair. When he folded his hands in his lap, one atop the other—like a Flemish nobleman in a painting by Van Dyck—she smiled at the formality of the gesture. It felt so strange, their sitting together like this, as if it were some kind of pantomime that any minute would send them into peals of laughter. She had a weird sense of their leading parallel lives, as if, while they sat here enacting this old-fashioned drawing-room drama, their real selves, which had never ceased being married, were loafing around in stockinged feet, sipping wine, and giggling over the funny things that had happened that day.

"How's Chris?" she asked, making sure not to sound too anxious. "Does he need anything?"

"He's fine. Did he tell you about his new Macintosh?"

"No, he didn't," she told him, straining to keep her voice even. First a dog, and now a new *computer?*

"I guess you two had more important things to talk about." Win sounded sheepish.

He's feeling guilty, she thought. She could tell from the way his knees were jiggling. Also, he was looking everywhere but at her. Good. Maybe she could play on it.

"To Chris, nothing could be more important than a computer. If he ever got shipwrecked and washed ashore on an island with no food or water, the thing he'd miss most would be Nintendo."

She watched Win smile his class-president smile, no doubt relieved that she wasn't giving him hell.

"Last night, he was teaching your mother a game called Tetris. Ever play it?"

"I don't have much time for games," she said, more sharply than she'd intended.

But Win didn't seem to notice. "Maybe not these days, but remember when we were first married and we couldn't afford the rental fee for the TV cable?" he recalled with a smile. "All we had was that deck of cards. After I taught you to play two-handed bridge, I swear, you wouldn't let up until you'd beaten the pants off me."

"And you, of course, were too much of a gentleman to let me keep on losing."

"I had no choice! You'd have kept playing until you either won or wore me into the ground."

"That bad, huh?" She gave a rueful laugh.

"Not all the time."

His mouth relaxed, but the smile remained in his eyes, creasing their corners. He shifted a bit, leaving his face half in shadow. She found herself thinking of the hall light they'd started leaving on all night after Chris was born, how Win's face on the pillow beside hers had seemed dissected into two halves, light and dark, like a harlequin mask.

But she couldn't, not for the life of her, remember what it had felt like when he'd kissed her . . . or any of the things he must have whispered to her when they were making love.

Whereas Jack, while softly caressing her face, her neck, her breasts, her belly, and between her legs . . . and murmuring to her how beautiful she was, how much he wanted to be inside her . . . could almost make her come. *Oh, God, Jack . . .*

But she mustn't think about Jack now.

"Win . . . I don't want to lose my son." She heard the crack in her voice, and willed herself not to cry.

"You're not losing him," Win told her. "He loves you as much as ever."

"Easy for you to say."

"Maybe what he needs right now is just a change of atmosphere." He paused, as if gathering himself up to launch into a courtroom argument. "From what Chris tells me, things have been sort of tense around here lately."

"Look, Win, all this stuff with the book, and now with my mother here . . . you know, it hasn't exactly been a picnic."

"I wasn't talking about Cordelia."

She could feel heat rising in her cheeks. "What are you getting at?"

He shrugged. "I'm not here to judge you, Grace. Believe me, that's the last thing I want to do. My main concern here is Chris's welfare. He's obviously not happy. He's not up to his old tricks, but even so . . ."

He didn't have to elaborate. She knew he was thinking of that awful time Chris had been caught shoplifting. She'd told him about Chris's cutting school, too.

"I know he hasn't been happy," Grace admitted. "But since when do teenagers need a reason to be moody?"

"I'm not blaming you, Grace," Win repeated.

"Then don't do it, Win—don't take him from me!" She jumped to her feet, feeling as if she were trying to hold her balance aboard a rushing train, the floor seeming to tilt and sway beneath her.

"I . . ." He stopped, as if he'd thought better of whatever he was going to say. Finally, surrendering, he spread his hands and looked up at her, his handsome, clean-cut face full of longing and confusion. "The last thing I want is to hurt you, Grace. Maybe the thing to do is to let Chris stay with me, just for the time being. Until your mother leaves."

"When will that be?"

"I don't know. I don't think she does, either. She's been running around visiting as many of your father's old New York friends and cronies as she can find, trying to drum up contributions for the library. Also, a lot will depend on whether or not she goes ahead with this lawsuit of hers."

"But . . . she *can't*. The letters . . ." The whole room was spinning now, seeming to rock her from side to side.

"*You* say they were written by your father," he explained, patiently, as if to a child. "But have you had them verified by a handwriting expert? And if so, are you prepared to have his or her testimony refuted in court by an expert witness of your mother's?"

"Win, I *know* my father's handwriting. There's no question the letters are genuine."

He held up a hand. "Look, let's not get off-track here. Cordelia might stay another week, maybe two. But a lot could change in that time, as far as Chris is concerned. I promise I won't push him into any kind of final decision. Then, when the smoke has cleared, we'll talk it over with his therapist—the three of us. We'll decide together what's best."

Grace felt relief wash through her. It wasn't quite what she'd hoped for . . . but better than what she'd feared. Standing before Win, feeling unsteady, she suddenly realized she'd barely eaten all day, and hadn't slept more than a few hours the night before. Now she felt herself sinking to her knees onto the carpet, slowly, gracefully even, as if she were kneeling to pray.

She became aware that Win was staring at her, longing in his face. And wouldn't it be the most natural thing in the world simply to hold out her hand for him to pull her to her feet?

She felt the air around them grow charged.

Then Win was moving toward her, falling on his knees beside her, cradling her in his arms. And how odd now that, instead of being alarmed, she felt a strange, floating relief. He wasn't clinging, as he had when she'd told him it was over between them, but holding her sweetly, almost tentatively, as if claiming her for a dance. Tears stung her eyes.

"Oh, Win . . ." She brought her forehead to rest against his shoulder. He smelled faintly of the outdoors and of English Leather—a scent as familiar to her as her own.

His arms tightened about her, almost convulsively. "I play it over and over in my mind. . . ." His voice was tight, too, almost choked. "I keep trying to come up with a new ending. Only I can't. It always ends up the same . . . and I . . . I can't turn it around. I'd give anything if I could."

She'd heard this before, but back then she'd been a woman made of glass, his apologies distant-seeming and hollow, sliding off her like raindrops from the windshield of a speeding car. Now his words pierced her.

"I forgave you a long time ago," she said, looking up and meeting his blue eyes, which were full of sorrow.

"Not soon enough." She caught the faint bitterness in his tone, which dissolved into remorse with his next words. "But you had good reason, God knows."

"Look, Win, what's the point in going over all that again?"

"Because . . ." He swallowed hard. "Because I thought that, in spite of everything that happened, what we had was pretty damn good."

"Some of it *was* good."

"I put on a tie in the morning, and I still walk away wondering if it's the right one," he went on. "You used to choose my ties, remember? And coffee. I never seem to get it right. A heaping tablespoon for every cup, but then it's too strong. I buy it from this deli near my office, but I hate drinking it from a Styrofoam cup."

"Coffee I can do," Grace said. "You're forgetting how I always used to burn the English muffins."

"I never much liked English muffins anyway. And who said it was your job to feed me?"

"Win . . . don't."

"Grace, please. I love you. I never stopped."

This is getting too intense, Grace thought, feeling a twinge of panic. But hadn't Win been heading toward it for a while? And, in a way, hadn't she been *letting* him?

"Win, we're not married any—"

He stopped her with a kiss, his mouth gentle against hers, as if delicately seeking an answer to some question. *Wrong, all wrong,* she told herself. But at the same time, Win kissing her felt weirdly right, as comfortable and comforting as a wedding band worn smooth—as if Jack were the interloper, and Win the one she belonged with.

Drawing back, he murmured against her hair, "Let me stay the night."

"What about Chris?" She spoke without thinking, realizing as soon as the words were out of her mouth that she hadn't told him no. *Stop this!* she should have shouted. *Go home!*

"He's with your mother. He won't think anything. Sometimes I stay over at the office when I'm really swamped."

"Win, this is crazy."

He kissed her again, harder this time, using his tongue. His slender hands cradling her head gently while his thumbs stroked her temples, crooning her name, over and over, *Grace, Grace, oh, Grace.* She felt herself beginning to respond, with a spreading warmth that was more than an echo of what they'd once shared.

If Win, at that moment, had again said, "I love you," or

if he'd pressured her in any way, she'd have had to step back
and take an honest look at what she was getting into. She
would have had to insist he go.

But he only stood there, waiting, his arms about her, his
breath warm against her hair. She could feel his heart beating, hard and fast, like someone tapping insistently at a
window.

Grace sighed, and as she drew away brought her finger
to rest against his lower lip, full and chiseled, just like their
son's. She traced her finger down his chin and throat, stopping at the perfect square knot of his tie.

Feeling as if she were floating—as if this were happening
to someone else, or in a dream she was having—she loosened
the knot and drew one end of the tie through the loop, the
heavy silk sliding like butter through her fingers.

God help me, she thought.

Yet it seemed completely natural, after she had led Win
to her bedroom, to slip out of her clothes in front of him.
He'd known her naked body in other forms—the flat-
tummied, small-chested bride she'd been, and pregnant with
Chris, her belly huge, her breasts swollen. He'd seen her
stretch marks fade from vivid purple to faint silvery lines.
And, yes, he'd witnessed the inevitable pull of gravity as
well—the drooping of her breasts, the slight sagging of her
behind.

Only Win seemed unchanged. Still as fit as he'd been in
college, with the long, muscular grace she associated with
swimmers and dancers. When he was naked, she could see
where the faded glow of his summer tan deepened slightly
just above his collarbone, and below his elbows, where the
sleeves of his tennis shirt must end. As he stepped forward
to draw her into his arms, it was as if a piece of puzzle were
falling into place. She could feel him, hard against her, growing harder. A soft moan escaped him.

"Grace, oh, baby, you feel good. So good."

Grace squeezed her eyes shut, wishing he wouldn't speak. Wishing somehow that this were all a dream she could wake from the next morning with no regrets.

Then Win was stroking her, touching her in all the ways he knew she liked to be touched. She sat on the edge of the bed, while Win knelt on the mattress behind her, massaging the lingering tenseness from her shoulders, his thumbs digging in with just the right amount of pressure. His hands so expert, so smooth, so knowing.

And now, while he reached around to caress her breasts, his mouth, too, was finding the most tender spots on the back of her neck, moving down her spine with tiny flicks of his tongue. He stopped at her waist, wrapping his arms about her and pulling her gently onto her back. Where his thumbs had played over her nipples, now his tongue was making them prickle with a sensation that made her think of when she used to nurse Chris, the delicious warm feeling of her milk letting down.

It seemed the easiest thing in the world, then, to open her legs and guide Win into her. Easier than anything she'd tried or accomplished in the weeks, months, years since the last time she and Win had lain together like this. She felt his breath quickening against the side of her neck, and her own body responding to his deep, sweet, perfectly timed thrusts.

The exquisite tension building in her was an old song, one she'd played many times. She knew exactly when to pause, when to quicken, how to stretch out each note to prolong her pleasure and his. When she came, moments before he did, it was more intense than she could ever remember its being with Win, seeming to rip up through her middle like the scream that was wrenched from her throat.

Not until her trembling had subsided, as she lay in his arms struggling to catch her breath, did it occur to Grace that part of what had made it so intense was that she'd held back from coming longer than she usually could. Not just to prolong her pleasure—she'd been afraid, too.

Afraid of what might happen if she gave herself over completely to Win.

Chapter 19

Nola looked out her front window, and felt herself snap wide awake. Reporters! She counted at least half a dozen—many accompanied by technicians armed with minicams—gathered on the sidewalk outside, talking among themselves, sipping from steaming paper cups. One of them, a stubby man in a trench coat, looked up, squinting as he tried to make out the tall shadowy figure peering out from behind semisheer drapes.

Almighty God, seven in the morning, she hadn't even brushed her teeth, and already they were circling in for the kill. Grace or Ben or someone at that publishing company must have spilled the beans about Mama and Gene.

Wasn't this what she'd been hiding from? What Ben had warned her about? Sharks circling, ready to make mincemeat out of her before Grace's book was even published.

The phone calls she'd gotten over the past few months, from newspeople after any dirt they could dig up on the accidental killing of Ned Emory—those had been nothing compared with what *this* was going to be like.

You asked for it, a cool voice reminded her.

"Mama?" Tasha, still in her PJs, padded over to the window, yawning. "Who are all those people?"

"Nobody we know," Nola told her, pulling her warm little body close, breathing in her just-out-of-bed smell.

"But what are they *waiting* for?" Tasha persisted.

My hide, thought Nola.

"They want to talk to your old mama," she said, trying

to make it sound like it was no big deal. "Do you believe it? Now, if only I could get you and your sister to pay me that much attention."

Tasha's eyes widened, and her thumb hovered near her mouth, obviously dying to get plugged in. "Is it 'cause of Ben?"

Nola felt a plunging sensation inside her, as if she were in an elevator that had just shot up six stories. *From the mouths of babes.* Tasha, thinking anything this big and possibly scary had to come from the new complication in her mother's life: Ben Gold.

"It certainly is not," Nola told her.

"Mama?"

"Yes, sugar?"

"Is Ben gonna be our new daddy?" She said it in exactly the same tone with which she asked, when the pediatrician was about to give her a shot, "Is this gonna hurt?"

Nola felt her throat tighten. Poor Tasha, so pinched and worried, like a little old lady on the verge of losing her pension. She was only voicing what Nola knew in her heart—had known almost from the start. Was it only three weeks since their first date? Like a roller-coaster ride that lasts only a few minutes but seems an age, the fever pitch of her affair with Ben had distorted her sense of time. But no matter how much fun a roller coaster was, she recalled, you were always glad when it came to a stop.

"No, baby," she said gently, "Ben is not going to be your daddy. And this"—she gestured toward the scene outside the window—"is nothing for you to worry about, either." All Tasha and Dani knew about their grandfather was that he'd died a long time before they were born. She hadn't told them *who* he was, not yet. She would *have* to now, sooner than she'd intended, sometime today. But not like this. "Hey, where's Dani? She up yet?"

"I *told* her she'd be late for school, but she won't get out of bed." Tasha, doing her prissy-schoolmarm imitation, lips puckered, chin up, made Nola want to laugh out loud. But Tasha, who had no idea how she sometimes came across, would no doubt be offended.

"Well, guess what?" Nola put on a bright smile. "Dani can sleep in. And you can watch TV if you like. No school today."

Tasha's eyes narrowed, sensing something that might be too good to be true. "How come my teacher didn't tell us?"

"Because your teacher isn't the one who decides what's best for you." She lightly swatted Tasha's behind. "Now, go on, get dressed, while I make breakfast."

Forty-five minutes later, with the girls fed and dressed, and Florene esconced with them in front of the TV, Nola prepared herself to enter the fray. She was dressed in a long black wool skirt and fitted, military-style red jacket at least five years out of date. Letting herself out the front door, she saw that the cluster of reporters had grown. Now there had to be at least a dozen. And all of them surging toward her, shoving cameras and mikes in her face, yammering and yipping at her.

"*Ms. Emory . . . are you claiming that Senator Truscott was your father?*"

"*Are you aware that the Senator's widow denies your allegation?*"

"*Why did you wait so long to go public with this?*"

"*Is it true you've made a deal with Cadogan for a share of the book's profits?*"

Nola found herself whirling about, nearly knocking over a stocky, lantern-jawed woman clutching a mini–tape recorder. "I have nothing to say," she spoke out, raising her voice to be heard above the clamoring. "Except, yes, Senator Truscott was my father. And, no, I have *not* made any sort

of deal. Now, if you'll excuse me . . . I have to get to work."
She tried to push through, but the reporters wouldn't
give way.

*"Does the Senator have any other illegitimate children
that you know of?"*

"Have you contacted his family?"

*"Do you feel you're entitled to a share of your father's
inheritance?"*

Nola shook her head, no, no, no. Shouldering her way
past a salt-and-pepper-haired man she recognized from
Channel 4, the one who always looked like he was audition-
ing to be a member of the British royal family, she noticed
that he was chewing gum as if it were a cud.

*"Is it true your firm has been selected to design the Eu-
gene Truscott Library?"*

The question seemed to leap out at her, innocent-
sounding, but sizzling through her like a bolt of lightning.
Nola felt her limbs jerk and twitch, her face suffuse with
sudden heat. Where had *that* come from? The results of the
competition had not yet been announced. Was he merely
goading her into saying something she shouldn't?

"You'd have to ask my boss; that's not a project I'm
involved with," she replied tersely, flinching as a flashbulb
went off.

Lies. Why did she have to go on lying?

But Nola knew why. Because, if she didn't hold on to
this one last secret, then her library would never get built.
Cordelia Truscott and the rest of the selection committee
would rule out her design quicker than it would take to slam
a door.

"Ms. Emory . . ."

"Just one question . . ."

"Do you have any idea . . ."

She was keenly aware of them, their hungry voices, their

smell of damp wool and warm coffee swirling around her, as she hurried away. But she didn't dare stop and turn around, didn't dare even let them see her face. Because they might see in her expression that she was not the paragon of truth she pretended to be.

"I saw you on the six o'clock news. You were wonderful. You didn't let them beat you down—you were really on top."

Ben, lying beside Nola on her big bed, smoothed a warm palm up the inside of her thigh, stopping to rub his thumb gently over the faint groove her panties had left when he'd impatiently pulled them off her a short while ago.

Nola shivered. They'd just finished making love, and he was still turning her on. *Girl, get a grip on yourself.*

"You like it when I'm on top?" she teased.

Ben laughed. His hand pushed up even higher, toying with the springy hair between her legs, still damp from their lovemaking. But she found herself scooting away from him.

No more leaping in feet-first. She had to start using her *head.*

This morning, the wary look on Tasha's face when she'd asked about Ben had hardened Nola's resolve. This couldn't go on, Ben and her. No matter how delicious he was in bed.

But it was like making up your mind to go on a diet . . . and suddenly feeling you had to eat every sinful thing in the world before then. Right now she wanted him more than ever.

Nola sighed. "Truth? I wasn't as on top of it as you think," she told him. "In fact, I was pretty rattled."

"The main thing is, it'll sell a shitload of books. It's just too bad about the timing. Even if we rush publication, we lose some of the momentum." He paused, wearing that brooding look he'd been getting a lot lately. Serious, gloomy almost. Was he having second thoughts about them, too?

"Ben, what's wrong?"

Get *him* to say it, she thought. That way, she wouldn't end up the bad guy.

"Nothing," he said, rolling onto his back.

Nola sat up and looked down at him. "Don't give me that. You've been like this for the past couple of weeks. Happy as a clam one minute, and the next acting like somebody the ayatollah put a death threat on. What's going on?"

But she knew, didn't she? Ben, underneath his charm and cool demeanor, was scared. Playing daddy to an instant family—*Just add man and stir*—was clearly not his scene. She thought of last week, Ben taking them all to that movie, and halfway through Dani whining that she was tired and wanted to go home. Ben had looked so annoyed—as if he were just barely restraining himself from snapping at Dani —that Nola had wanted to snap at *him*: Man, if you can't stand the heat, then get the hell out of the kitchen.

The girls—they've picked up on it, too. Or maybe they've known all along what it took me this long to figure out—that you don't seem to give a shit about them. Unless it's just kids in general you don't like.

Either way, she couldn't risk having Ben turn out to be another Marcus, who only called when the spirit moved him— about as often as he remembered his own daughters' birthdays.

"I was just thinking," Ben spoke, addressing the ceiling.

"Of what?"

"Of how much easier all this would have been if you'd listened to me in the first place."

"You mean if I'd gotten rid of the letters? Flushed them down the toilet? Thrown them onto a bonfire? Ben, they're important. And not just to me."

"What about *me?*" He spoke quietly, but his voice had a nasty edge to it. "Where do I figure into your grand scheme of things?"

"I don't know, Ben," she said quietly. "Why don't *you* tell me?"

What if I did tell her the truth? Ben thought. *That I'm not the nice guy I pretend to be?*

But that wouldn't be the whole truth, he knew. More than Nola's relinquishing those letters to Grace—which had pissed him off at the time, but which had now faded a bit —what was bugging the shit out of him was the idea that he might actually be in love with her. And if he didn't get it off his chest, he was going to explode.

"Christ, Nola, *don't you get it?*" His eyes glittered in the half-darkness. "That's how this whole thing started. Us, you and me. I was *using* you. I was hoping you'd turn those letters over to me, so I could play the hero with Cadogan. . . ."

Ben's heart was thudding. What was he saying? What had he *done?* At the same time, he half-hoped she'd use this as an excuse to dump him. Because God knew *he* didn't have the guts to end it. He was in deep . . . and getting deeper every day.

"But then a funny thing happened on the way to the forum," Ben went on, all at once unable to bear her thinking badly of him. "I started to . . . care." He couldn't bring himself to use the word "love"—it just wasn't in his vocabulary. "Jesus, it's the last thing I wanted. A wife, kids, ready-made family. Father Knows Shit. Not for me. *Damnit.*" He punched his fist into the pillow beside him.

Nola felt a coldness creep through her. She shivered, and drew the sheets and blankets about her, knowing that they wouldn't make her warm. She knew she should feel angry at him for using her, trying to trick her, but for some reason what she felt now was . . . sorry.

For him, Ben, the lost little boy she'd been drawn to from the very start. What she wanted to do was hold him, comfort him. Maybe she *had* loved him . . . for a little while.

But now it was over. Really over. Ben's confession was merely the last stop on a train going nowhere she wanted to be.

"Maybe you're *in* love with me . . . but that's not the same as loving." She spoke as gently as she could. "Mostly what we do when we're together is . . . *this*." She swept her arm over the rumpled bedcovers.

"Are you saying that's all it ever was for you? Sex?" His voice rose, becoming petulant.

A warning bell went off inside her. Marcus, too, when they argued, would twist everything she said.

"Don't you see?" Nola felt a great weariness overtake her. "I've got two little girls. They're upstairs with Florene right now, where they've been spending far too much time lately. Ben, I have a family to look after. Work I haven't been doing because I've been too busy with you. I can't put either my job or my girls on hold for you."

"Who asked you to? I could move in with you—or we could get a place together." Ben couldn't believe the words that were tumbling out of him. Where were they coming from?

Part of him wanted to snatch them back . . . and start working on forgetting that he'd ever met Nola. She was too much her own woman, too much in control. And right now, damnit, that control seemed to be over *him*.

"Ben, stop this," Nola said sharply. "You don't mean it."

"I've never been more serious about anything." The desperation in his voice was almost frightening to her.

"I'm getting dressed now," she said, moving to the edge of the mattress. "And then I think it'd be a good idea if you went home."

She started to get up, but he grabbed hold of her arm, pulling her—almost *yanking* her—onto her back.

"Ben, what are you . . ."

Staring down at her, his face hard and twisted, he demanded, "What are you saying, Nola?"

"I'm saying that it's time for you to go home."

"And then what?"

"Then we'll talk about this in a day or two, when we've both had a chance to think about it."

"Damnit, Nola, I spill my guts, and all you can say is, We'll talk about it?"

"Ben. You're reading all kinds of things into this that aren't there. And anyway, the plain fact is, you hardly know me. We've known each other—what?—a whole three weeks?"

"So what? I'm not saying we should get married. And wouldn't it be easier if we were living together?"

"In some ways, maybe. But—"

"Just give me an answer—yes or no. Is that so hard, Nola?"

"Yes, it *is* hard."

"Why? *Why* does it have to be?"

"Because you're pushing me and I don't like that."

Panic seemed to split his face into two, one half a thwarted child stunned with disappointment, the other a bully demanding his way.

Suddenly his full weight was on her, pressing down, his mouth smashing against hers until she could hardly breathe.

"Ben . . . no, *no*, not like this," she gasped.

Nola couldn't believe what was happening. Ben holding

her down, forcing her legs apart with his knee. It was almost as if he were . . . *raping* her. . . .

Can't be. He wouldn't do that to me.

But his fingers were now being shoved up inside her, and she wanted to pummel him, scratch him, *hurt* him.

"Stop it!" she cried, twisting beneath him, scrabbling to get some leverage against his chest to push him off her.

But he was too strong for her . . . and rough, so rough. Almost as if he'd become someone else, a stranger shoving her legs apart as he thrust himself into her. She could feel his fingernails, the sharp little corners where he'd clipped them, raking at her skin. She tried to help him, just to stop the pain . . . but he pushed her hand away and growled, "Goddamnit, goddamnit, Nola," while he bucked against her, driving her spine into the mattress, sweat from his face dripping onto her clenched eyelids.

"*Get . . . off . . . me.*"

Nola had been feeling shocked, scared . . . but now she was livid, a white-hot torrent of anger. How *dare* he!

She heard him cry out, and, with a final quivering heave she felt all the way down to her tailbone, he slackened his terrifying grip. Then, in a single fluid motion, he was rolling off her and off the edge of the mattress. She watched the pale triangle of his back dip and surface among the shadows as he rooted in the semidarkness for his pants, and pulled them on.

Nola, shivering, her teeth clenched to keep them from chattering, crawled to the edge of the bed and clambered to her feet, scooping up one of the black patent-leather pumps that lay toppled on the floor. She stood with her legs wide apart—they were quivering so hard it was the only way she could keep her balance. But when Ben turned to face her, his expression not only unrepentant but actually *aggrieved*, as if *he* were the injured party, she felt suddenly galvanized by fury.

"What the *hell* was that all about?"

"I thought you liked it rough."

Even as he said it, Ben felt like a gangster in a B movie, mouthing lines that had nothing to do with him. Christ, had he really done that to her? Was he any better than that shit Roger Young?

Now he'd destroyed any chance he'd had of reaching her. *Why* had he done it?

You're scared, Ben-o, that's why. What if she had taken you up on your offer? Then you'd be stuck. . . .

"That was *rape*," she spat. "Jesus God Almighty, these days they teach *college* girls about what just happened here so they won't ever let it happen to them."

"Oh, come on, Nola, you're not exactly a kid."

Nola hurled her shoe at him, missing him by inches. She heard a thud as the lamp on the nightstand hit the floor, and then the awful sound of the old glass cracking. Seeing her treasured Handel lying in jagged shards on the floor, she felt a wrenching in her gut, as if inside her something had been broken as well.

"You *bastard!*" She grabbed her blouse, which was draped over the end of the bed, and tugged it on, her fingers twitching and sliding over the silky fabric as she struggled to push the buttons through the buttonholes. "I can't *believe* I let myself get sucked into this. I've spent half my life trying to get away from men like you."

"That's why I get stuck paying for the sins of your ex-husband?"

Nola pictured the red handle of an emergency brake, which she was now forcing down. "Get out," she said between gritted teeth.

"Nola, wait, I didn't mean . . ." He extended a hand, as if in apology.

"Get *out*." She walked around the bed and picked up the old lamp base, which felt cold and heavy in her hand. She wanted to cry, but she was too furious—at herself, mostly, for having allowed herself to become infatuated with this man. "I'm giving you thirty seconds to get dressed and get your ass out that door. Or I'm calling the cops."

He lifted his tormented face to her, his mouth twisted, making him look like a gargoyle. "And have me arrested? Go ahead, Nola. Think what a great story it'd make."

She shuddered, thinking of the times she'd reveled in his hands on her body, of her opening herself to him, greedy.

"Time's up," she told him. She felt oddly depleted. The anger had gone, leaving only a bone-deep weariness. Even after what he'd done, the things he'd said, there was a part of her that felt sorry for Ben.

"Don't worry, I'm out of here," Ben told her. "There's just one thing. . . ." His jacket over his shoulder, he turned, his eyes glittering with unshed tears. "I know you probably won't believe this, but I really meant what I said before. That stuff about us living together. And about . . ." He stopped.

"You loving me?" she finished, even though she couldn't recall his ever actually saying those words. In a voice rich with irony, she added, "Yeah, I know."

The call came two days later, while she was mulling over Ronnie Chang's rough sketches for the Schulman house. An acre of prime East Hampton beachfront for which he'd drawn what looked to be little more than a collection of cubes, like a Mondrian abstract. Ronnie liked to think of himself as the next I. M. Pei, but this wasn't the Louvre pyramid or the Hancock Tower. People were going to have to *live* in the place. . . .

"Nola, could I see you in my office?"

Maguire's voice on her intercom propelled her off her high stool. And then she was weaving her way between the work stations in which her colleagues sat hunched over their drafting boards.

In his office—a cheerful zigzag of postmodernist chairs, tables, bookcases—her boss greeted her warmly, but there was a look of guarded enthusiasm on his thin, anxious face.

"I just got word," he told her. "The Truscott committee has chosen your"—he caught himself—"*our* design. . . ."

Nola felt a rush of happiness like a great wind blowing through her . . . blowing her clean, making her shine. Had she heard right?

Maguire's next words turned her to ice.

"But there's a snag. They have a funding problem. So . . . until they can come up with another million or so, we're on hold."

"What do they mean? How long will it take?"

She realized she was shaking. Since the night before last, that ugly scene with Ben, she'd been strung out, jittery, jumping every time someone called her name.

"Until all this publicity dies down, for one thing." The smile he'd been wearing when she walked in now dropped from his face. "After that, who knows? Once the committee gets wind of you working here . . ." His voice trailed off.

Was she being fired? Was that why he'd called her in here?

Nola wrapped her arms about her chest, as if she might somehow contain her shivering, and the mad thumping of her heart.

"But don't they already know?" She remembered that reporter the other day, trying to trip her up.

"If they do, nobody has said anything to me about it."

"Then what you're saying is, it's only a matter of time."

"Nola, we're not talking about the sleepy directors of some insurance company. You're up against Cordelia Truscott. Can you imagine her reaction when she finds out you're even remotely associated with this project?"

Nola wanted to argue, but she knew he was right. She couldn't fault him for overreacting, either. Even when he'd learned that she was Eugene Truscott's daughter—she'd told him the day before it came out in the newspapers—his reply had been an oddly wry but supportive, "I won't say I should have known . . . but in some ways I'm not surprised. You have that mark on you, Nola. You'll go far. Partly because you're not afraid to be different."

Different. Was that why most of her life she'd felt as if she were swimming against the tide? Why she often looked at things upside down instead of right side up?

It was that kind of upside-down thinking that caused something inside her to click now. Cordelia Truscott. Suppose she didn't just find out? What if somebody actually *told* her—not just that Nola Emory worked at Maguire, Chang & Foster, but that *she* was the one who'd come up with the winning design?

And what if I were that somebody?

Crazy? Maybe. But wouldn't it be better to act now, take a gamble, no matter how stacked against her the odds were? Because there *was* a chance, however slim, that she could convince Cordelia Truscott that only she, his flesh and blood, could make the Senator's library what it ought to be. Like a suit of clothes tailored to his exact measurements, her design would embody every principle he'd stood for, every battle he'd fought, every ideal he'd aspired to.

"You're right, Ken." Along with her pulse, Nola's mind was racing. "She has to know it's my design."

She watched Ken's jaw drop. "I didn't mean—"

Nola stopped him with a sudden sweeping gesture. "If I met with her, face to face . . . made her see that I'm the only one who could do this right . . . Oh, Ken, am I dreaming? Isn't there a chance she might come around?"

"Nola, I know what this means to you," he said. "But in this business we rarely get what we want. It's a terrific opportunity, sure. And the library most likely *will* get built . . . somewhere down the line. It just may not be your design. I know, it's frustrating, but that's life, huh?"

He walked over and, for the first time ever, put an arm about her shoulders. But even though her body—with every nerve still rubbed raw from Ben's assault—automatically tensed, she knew it was just Ken, in his own bumbling way, being kind. Letting her know in a nice way that, if she were crazy enough to approach Mrs. Truscott, the library would go from being a lame duck to a dead one.

But did that mean she ought to forget it, write the whole thing off? After all the weeks and months of slaving here till midnight; of her dreaming and longing to somehow be one with her father? No, she couldn't bear to. She wouldn't!

"Life is also when you do something dumb because you have nothing to lose," Nola told him; then she turned and walked out.

Back at her work station, she picked up her phone and punched in Grace's number. Grace answered with the first ring.

"Hey," Nola said. "It's me."

"Hey there, yourself. How are you holding up?"

An odd camaraderie seemed to have sprung up between them. They were like two soldiers crouching in the same foxhole, Nola thought.

"Okay," Nola lied. "You?"

"I'll survive. But, listen, if there's anything I can do to help . . ."

"Don't ask why," Nola rushed in, "but I need to get hold of your mother. Mind giving me her number?"

She heard a sharp intake of breath on the other end of the line, but Grace, bless her, wasn't prying. "Mother is here in New York," she told Nola. "She's staying with my ex-husband." She recited the phone number and address.

Nola said a hurried goodbye, and pressed the disconnect button. As she dialed the number Grace had given her, she could feel her breath coming in shallow bursts. What if Cordelia hung up on her? Listening to the hollow ringing on the other end, Nola was on the verge of hanging up herself.

Then a sweet, almost singsong voice came on the line. A voice she recognized instantly as belonging to the petite, always impeccably dressed woman who used to stop at Mama's desk to say hello on her way into her husband's office.

"Hello?" she was saying now.

And Nola—becoming once again a little girl with her coloring book and crayons, crouched out of sight behind her mother's desk—was suddenly tongue-tied.

"Who *is* this?" Cordelia was starting to sound impatient, suspicious.

Nola took a breath.

"It's Nola. Nola Emory," she plunged in. "I was hoping we could meet. Just to talk. Please. It's important."

There was a pause during which Nola could feel herself sitting taller, becoming her grown-up self again.

Then Cordelia was saying softly, but with unmistakable firmness, "I don't believe there's anything we need to talk about, Miss Emory. As far as I'm concerned, you've already made your position perfectly clear."

"There's more. Things you don't know. Please."

"Is it money you're after? Is that what this is all about?"

She sounded agitated, as if she might be on the verge of losing her temper.

"No!" Nola snapped, horrified. "I don't want anything from you. I never even wanted *this* . . . this whole situation." She dropped her voice, struggling to regain control of herself.

"Then what *do* you want?"

"Just to meet with you. Talk. Ten minutes. That's all. I can be there in"—she glanced at her watch—"half an hour."

"No. Not here. My grandson—"

"The park, then. The playground at Sixty-seventh."

No answer. But she wasn't hanging up, either.

"I don't see why I should give you the time of day," Cordelia said in the same curt tone. "We have nothing in common."

"Why don't you decide on that *after* you've heard me out?"

A long silence seemed to wrap about Nola, as if the walls of her work station were pressing in on her, making it impossible to breathe.

"I'll be there," Cordelia finally said.

Nola's lungs opened up. She felt a dizzying glow warming her all through, as well an odd untethered feeling, as if she'd been cut loose from the earth's gravity. Maybe this was what it was like to be crazy. Or maybe it was the other way around—she'd been a little crazy all her life, and now she was finally becoming sane.

Chapter 20

A full minute after she'd hung up the phone, Cordelia sat staring at the receiver as if it were a poisonous snake that had bitten her. Had she really agreed to meet this woman? Oh, what *could* she have been thinking?

She tried to recall the somber little girl she occasionally used to glimpse playing at her mother's feet. But the image that kept overlapping was of the tall, imposing woman she'd seen last night on TV. The woman who'd looked straight into the camera and said, *Yes, Senator Truscott was my father.*

Cordelia had wanted to blot out that image and those words, even as she now sought to silence the small voice of reason deep inside her that was asking, *Why would she lie?*

Win? Where was Win? He'd know what to do. The night before last, hadn't he handled those reporters who, unable to reach her in Blessing, had called here, hoping to speak with her lawyer? Win had made sure they stayed away, answering their awful questions about Gene as smoothly as if from a memorized script.

But Win was at his office . . . and Nola wasn't a reporter. She had to resolve this on her own. Just as she had always attempted to do with every problem, no matter how sticky.

Seated on the sleeper sofa in Win's extra room, Cordelia observed for the first time since she'd arrived that, for a man's study, Win's had an oddly fussy appearance. Marbleized green bookshelves with squatty little pottery figures set strategically here and there among the bright-jacketed best-sellers, and a thick leather-bound edition of the Social Register. A truly hideous African mask on the wall over the sofa—some decorator's idea of what represented masculinity, no doubt. She could see no imprint recognizable as Win's. But could that be because she didn't know him as well as she'd imagined?

A knock at the door startled her, and her heart jumped. "Come in," she called.

It was Chris, in his baggy jeans and too-big sweatshirt, like a waif out of a silent movie. Cordelia longed to drag him into her arms and smother him with kisses. But he was too old for that; she'd only embarrass him. These days, Chris allowed such affection only from the dog trotting in on his heels, a half-grown golden retriever with big feet that seemed to trip over each other as he bounced and frisked at Chris's side.

"Are you okay, Nana?" Chris asked, stopping to peer at her. "You look kind of . . . I don't know, sick or something."

Does it show that much? Cordelia wondered. She had to pull herself together. She mustn't let Chris think anything was wrong.

"Not a bit," she told him with a brightness she had difficulty mustering, even with her many years of practice. "You know, dear, as much as I love New York, perhaps I am overdoing it a little. All the museums and galleries and department stores—I simply can't keep up the way I could when I was younger." Not to mention her making the rounds to all of her and Eugene's old friends and colleagues, trying to muster their support for the library.

"Sure, Nana." Chris rolled his eyes. "I'll bet you could run in the marathon and come out ahead of everyone else."

"That," she told him, keeping her expression dryly deadpan, "is entirely possible."

Cordelia felt gratified by the smile she could see lurking at the corners of his mouth. But Chris was still troubled about something. She'd been aware of it since she arrived, but had hoped it was merely a case of hormones running amok.

"Nana . . . can I ask you something?" Chris knelt on the rug in front of the sofa to pet his dog, his hair falling in front of his face. "Do you like my mom?"

"What a question!" Cordelia, even so, felt herself wincing at his needing to ask it. "Goodness, she's my daughter."

"Then why are you staying *here?*"

"Well . . . it's rather complicated, dear. Your mother and I . . . we've had our differences. But that doesn't mean we don't love one another."

"So you can love someone and still not want to live with them?"

Cordelia realized that Chris was no longer talking about her and Grace. "Why, yes, I suppose so," she said softly, careful to tread lightly, as if over newly seeded lawn. "It would depend on the circumstances."

He looked up, and she caught the shine of tears in his eyes. "My dad wants me to live with him . . . but I don't know. I miss my mom. I feel really bad about telling her I'd rather stay here."

"Oh dear." Cordelia, feeling her spine begin to sag, forced herself to sit up straighter. "Chris, have you told your father how you feel?"

"Sort of . . . well, actually, yes." One skinny arm snaked about his dog's neck, and he pressed his cheek into the feathery golden ruff. "Dad, he . . . uh, never mind."

"What did your dad say?"

"He didn't mean it. He wouldn't *really* do it."

"Chris, whatever it was, it's obviously bothering you, so

why not get it off your chest?" She spoke gently, not wanting to frighten him away.

"He said he'd understand, but . . ." Chris's voice, with his face pressed against the dog's neck, emerged faint and muffled. Finally, lifting his head, he finished in an agonized rush, ". . . that if I went back to Mom, Cody would probably be too much trouble for him to keep all by himself."

Cordelia felt appalled. Win had said that? How terrible! Poor Chris, no wonder he was so upset.

She began to see Win in a different light—not as the thoughtful son-in-law who always remembered to send her cards on her birthday and Mother's Day, and who'd fit in so perfectly at family gatherings . . . but as someone who'd casually, maybe even callously, instigated that affair.

"But your mother? Won't she miss you terribly?" Cordelia was astonished to find herself filled with compassion for the daughter at whom she'd been so angry.

"I was sort of hoping . . ." Chris caught his lower lip in his teeth.

"Chris, what is it?"

"Something my dad . . ." He stopped. "I don't know if I'm supposed to tell."

"Mercy, I've had enough confidences heaped on me in the past few months to last me my entire life." She managed a wan smile. "I suppose one more won't hurt."

There was a long silence, during which Chris busied himself scrubbing behind Cody's ears and, when the overgrown puppy rolled over onto its back, its belly, too. Then he said in a small voice, "Do you remember the night when Dad stayed over at the office? Well, that's not where he was. He told me he was at Mom's. He spent the night with *her*."

Cordelia felt a little shocked, not so much at what Chris was telling her, but at Win for being so indiscreet. A year ago, just a month ago, she'd have been hopeful—yes, even gleeful—over such a sign that Grace and Win might be reconciling. Now she felt neither excited nor disapproving . . . merely flat. Was it her imminent appointment with Nola Emory, pressing down on her, leaving little room in her heart for anything else?

"And you're hoping they'll get back together?" she asked gently. "That would solve everything as far as you're concerned, wouldn't it?"

"I *was* sort of hoping that would happen," he admitted. "But with Jack and everything . . . I don't know. Nana, what should I do?"

She was on the verge of telling him that *she* would speak with Win, possibly Grace as well, but she stopped herself. Hadn't she done enough meddling? Wasn't it time she stepped out of her children's lives, and let them make their own mistakes?

"You should talk to your parents," she told him. "Tell them *both* how you feel."

"I *want* to be with my dad," he told her, his expression deeply troubled. "But I want to be with my mom, too."

"Well, then, that's what you must say. And let *them* decide what's best. It's too much of a burden on young shoulders to have to take on parents' problems as well."

Chris nodded, but his expression remained clouded. As he shambled out of the room, his dog in tow, Cordelia realized she ought to listen to her own advice. Be honest, she'd told Chris. Tell the truth.

And had she been honest with herself? Had she avoided even glancing at those letters because she was certain they were all lies . . . or because, deep down, she feared they might be true? But maybe it wouldn't be so bad, what was in them. Maybe she would live through it after all.

Cordelia got up and reached with a trembling hand for

the sheaf of papers that had sat atop the credenza ever since she'd arrived home from Grace's that night. She'd been in such a state then, but now she was a little calmer. And with a few minutes yet before she was due to meet Nola, she must see what she was up against, look the enemy in the eye, so to speak. Isn't that what Gene himself would have done? And Gabe, too—he was never one to flinch from conflict.

She found her reading glasses and slipped them on, sinking into a deep-buttoned chair. As she shuffled through the pages, the words jittering and blurring before her eyes, one paragraph seemed to leap out at her.

> *My Dearest Margaret,*
>
> *I've thought long and hard about what you said the other day when you were seeing me off at the airport. And I still want more than anything for us to be together, out in the open. But at the same time, I have to admit you're probably right. I can only imagine what it must have cost you to say it. I care about Cordelia too. But I've always seen her as strong, not really needing me, or anyone. It took you to make me see how deeply wounded she would be, and how so many others would be hurt as well, if the truth about you and me were to come out. . . .*

Cordelia dropped the piece of paper as if she'd been scalded. And now tears were welling, hot, burning her eyes and inside the bridge of her nose. She was shaking her head, a hand clapped over her mouth, as if by denying them she could make those words go away.

It couldn't be. Gene. Margaret. He never. He wouldn't have. So many years. All that time, not loving *her*. She would have known. *She would have known.*

The letters had to be fake. Yes, that was it. Of course.

Win had suggested it to her the other day, but she hadn't really known what to think. Now she felt sure.

Gene could never have written these.

He'd loved her, not Margaret.

Hadn't he?

But then she was remembering that awful day when Gene had called her from Margaret's house, sounding not at all like himself—shaken, distraught, hysterical almost.

"Cordelia, I've killed a man. I was trying to . . . He had a gun. I had to stop . . . God help me . . . it was an accident."

And while her own heart had raced with panic, she'd calmed him, saying, "Of course. Of *course* it was an accident. Now. Tell me *exactly* what happened." After she'd gotten the whole story out of him, which left her weak with shock, she'd had to sink down on the nearest chair to keep from collapsing. Then pulling herself together, she'd found herself speaking with remarkable calm. "Listen to me carefully. You didn't arrive at Margaret's until just a few minutes ago. It's very important, Gene, that you tell it right when the authorities get there. Margaret phoned to tell you she'd found her husband dead, a suicide, and you drove right over. Now. Call your friend at the FBI, Pat Mulhaney; he'll help you. I'm sure I don't have to tell you the police must be kept out of this."

"I . . . Cordelia, I can't go on like this. . . . You have to know . . ."

But she'd stopped him, searing the words before they could leave his mouth, as if cauterizing a wound.

"I know everything I need to know," she'd said. "You were only doing what any courageous person would have. Why let people distort it, make it into something it isn't? You let Mulhaney take care of it, Gene, and it'll be as if it never happened."

As if it never happened.

Was that what the past had become for her, a thing she'd rewritten to suit herself? Even her own memories—were they reinvented as well? When she thought of Gene, was she merely remembering a love that had been polished so many times that its original shape was scarcely distinguishable?

Cordelia, as she rose from her chair, felt like the world's oldest human being. Every bone and muscle protested the effort it took just to walk the dozen steps to the door, open it, step through. How she was going to make it to the elevator, through the lobby, and then across the street to the park, she couldn't begin to imagine.

But somehow, by some miracle—or maybe it was the curse of being Cordelia Truscott—she was doing it. Putting one foot in front of her, then the other. Galvanizing her will and forcing her body to move as she would have a reluctant child dragging its feet.

She would keep her appointment with Nola Emory if it killed her.

Cordelia glanced around her at the cigarette butts, crumpled paper napkins, aluminum pop-tops littering the ground beneath the park bench on which she sat, waiting for Nola. Years ago, had the park been this filthy? Back then she'd thought Manhattan a fairyland, exciting, sparkling, delicious. Going home to Blessing after Gene died, at first it had seemed like squeezing into a pair of old shoes she'd long since outgrown. Her ailing mother, the ancient elms with their beards of Spanish moss, her school chums now middle-aged ladies with teased hair and pink frosted nails, even the humidity, all like some huge sweaty hand pressing down on her, compressing her into something too small.

But there had been compensations. Her old friend Iris. And Stanton Hughes, with whom Cordelia had shared a microscope in biology—he'd offered her a seat on Latham University's prestigious board, of which he was chairman. And soon after Mother died, when she'd learned from Iris about the black "granny" midwives who were being hounded out of business by the AMA, how she'd leaped on that! Working every day, even on weekends, sending letters, making calls, scouting for teachers, doctors, nurses, anyone willing to donate time to the certification program she'd gotten the local health authorities to agree on.

And there was her garden.

Back home, she thought, the first of the narcissi would soon be pushing up through the rich, black soil—green spears that looked sturdy enough but soon would bow beneath the weight of their blossoms. Gabe would be preparing the seed beds in the greenhouse, and spraying the fruit trees with dormant oil to keep away the scale.

She felt a sharp ache of longing. She wanted to be back in Blessing, with Gabe, away from all this, from Grace and Nola Emory and even Win, who lately had been pushing her to let him file for an injunction to stop publication.

She'd gone along in the beginning—*urged* him—sensing that Win wanted what she did, to put an end to this ugliness. But getting involved with complaints that would be publicly aired, affidavits, depositions, sordid courtrooms—wouldn't that make it all still more unbearable?

Even if she sat on her hands and did absolutely nothing, her life was *never* going to return to normal. It was as if the people who'd mocked Columbus had been right all along, and she'd just sailed off the edge of the world.

Cordelia shivered in her gray cashmere coat, watching a young woman jog past, a girl in sweat pants and a nylon parka who made her feel suddenly far older than fifty-nine —an old lady in the park, her precious memories all that was left.

And now even those had been threatened.

She thought back to that tense time when Eugene had been lobbying relentlessly for his civil-rights bill—cornering his congressional colleagues in their offices and homes, at parties, even on the street, badgering them to support his bill. And all the hate mail, vicious phone calls, old friends snubbing her. Visiting her family in Georgia, and being hounded by the Klan. But she would have gone through it all again, every awful, frightening minute, if that could have spared her the ordeal of meeting Nola Emory.

The library—that's what she had to think of now. Wasn't that what had kept her at Win's long after she felt she'd overstayed her welcome? Let's see, it had been almost two weeks now. Tramping all over the city, putting on her best clothes and visiting with every old fan of Gene's who would agree to see her. Some, of course, wouldn't give her the time of day; but Hammond Wentworth, who clearly hadn't forgotten all Gene had done for him back when Ham was heading the parks department, came through with a hundred thousand.

But none of the rejections she'd met could come close to the agony of reading that letter. Forged or not, its words echoed in her mind like the relentless pounding of the jackhammer being wielded by a construction worker on the street not far from where she sat.

"Mrs. Truscott?"

Cordelia started, and looked up into a pair of green eyes that seemed to be studying her carefully, dispassionately, the way a doctor might examine someone for signs of illness. As if all that mattered was a correct diagnosis, not how the patient felt.

But, no, she saw, after a moment, that the woman standing before her, dressed in a simple black coat with a bright-red scarf tucked about her neck, was simply holding a tight rein on her emotions. The hand she offered was trembling slightly.

She looks like him.

Why hadn't she noticed the resemblance when she'd seen Nola on television?

She realized it wasn't so much a duplication of Gene's features as something about her self-possession, the erect way she held herself, despite the anxiety she had to be feeling. *Just like Gene . . .*

"May I sit down?" she heard Nola Emory asking, but she sounded far away, like one of the mothers she could hear in the distance calling out to their children.

Cordelia moved over an inch or so to make more room.

"Ten minutes," she said with what she hoped was a firm, businesslike tone. Her heart felt huge, swollen.

"It won't take long. I just want to talk to you."

"Whatever *for?*"

She watched the blood leave Nola's face. "The library. I'm here about the library."

Cordelia's heart lurched. This woman, Margaret's daughter—what could she know about Eugene's library? What could she want with it?

Cordelia thought of the design she'd picked out of all those portfolios—with virtually no hesitation—knowing the committee would go along. And, though taking their sweet time in doing so, they finally had. She could see it in her mind, half a dozen drawings mounted on thick cardboard. The soaring lines and windowed expanses, the majestic shape of the thing. As if the architects had taken her formless fantasy and, through some kind of telepathy, made it real.

"The library is none of your concern," she told Nola crisply.

"I'm afraid you're wrong about that." As Nola turned slightly to watch a bicyclist whirr past, Cordelia could see a pulse fluttering in the graceful column of her neck. "You see, it's mine—I designed it."

Now she was looking straight at Cordelia with those unwavering eyes, and Cordelia felt the shock of her words as if she had been struck by a taxi.

"*You?* Are you saying that . . ."

"I'm with Maguire, Chang & Foster. When I heard about the competition . . ." Nola shrugged, but her tension was evident in the tightness of her shoulders. "You see, it was—*is*—important to me that it be wonderful. Right for *him*, not just the people who'll be using it. Not one of those pretentious masoleum-looking things. He . . ." She straightened. "My father would have hated that."

That word, *father,* pierced Cordelia.

"*Don't,*" she cried, her eyes filling with tears, the bare trees and winding stone pathways all blending into a gray soup. "You have no right."

"Look at me," Nola commanded. "For God's sake, Mrs. Truscott, *look at me.*"

It was the richness of Nola's voice, the power in it, that finally made her look. What she saw made her want to shrink away, cringe as if from a too-bright light. She saw . . .

Gene, rising to speak to the Senate floor, the fire in his eyes, the fervent conviction radiating from every inch of his long, loose-limbed body.

"I'm his daughter," Nola said, but her voice was soft, not fiery or righteous. "You *know* it, even if you can't or won't admit it. Are you so afraid of the truth? Will hiding from it—as I did for too long—really be good for you in the long run?" Color rose in Nola's cheeks now, and her eyes glittered.

Cordelia wanted to run . . . far away . . . someplace where Nola's words couldn't reach her. But some force kept her rooted to the bench.

"What makes you think you could possibly know what's good for me?" Cordelia snapped. "You haven't the faintest idea of who or what I am."

"I know that he loved you." Nola dropped her voice, now like some kind of soothing balm against a stinging wound.

"If you really *were* his—and I'm not saying I believe that—then how would it be possible for him to have loved me?" Cordelia recoiled from her own words. How could she be revealing herself to this woman she didn't even know, bare doubts she'd scarcely been able to admit to herself?

"Nothing is ever that simple," Nola said.

"I don't—" Cordelia, on the verge of arguing that, no, Gene would *not* have betrayed her, instead found herself unable to go on.

She was feeling once again the pain of that letter, how for an instant it had been as if she were hearing Gene's voice speaking those dreadful words. . . .

It's true, spoke a voice from some deep place inside her. *She is his child.*

"He loved me," she echoed softly. "I *do* know that. Even if . . . if he might have wavered. That could have been partly my fault, I suppose. I was the one who didn't want to move to Washington. In another two years, I kept saying, he might not get re-elected. And then, when he became a senator . . ." She stared at a black woman pushing a baby stroller in which a white, golden-haired infant sat, feeling her lips knit themselves into a cold smile. "Well, by then we were used to the arrangement. It suited us, in a way. . . .

"Oh, I suppose there were moments when things seemed . . . not quite right. Times I phoned him late at night and he wasn't there. But then I'd put it right out of my head."

Cordelia buried her face in her hands, feeling all the fear, worry, hurt that she'd kept locked inside herself come forth in a boiling rush. But she wouldn't, *couldn't,* let herself cry, not now, not in front of Nola Emory. She strained to withstand the shivering that was gripping her. If only Gabe were here, holding her, steadying her.

She felt a light pressure against her shoulder, and caught the musky scent of Nola's perfume as she leaned close. "I'm sorry," she said. "I know this isn't easy for you."

Cordelia shook her head.

"It's not easy for me, either," Nola went on. "For weeks I refused to take Grace's calls. I never wanted any part of this. But when she shoved it right in front of my face, I realized I couldn't go through a whole life of telling lies."

Cordelia raised her eyes. What she thought she saw in Nola's was compassion, and it stunned her.

"What do you want from me?" Cordelia's voice emerged as a croak.

"The same thing *you* want," Nola told her. "For his library to get built the right way—the way he would have wanted."

"If you and Grace have your way, it may *not* get built," she snapped. "Remember Cape Kennedy being changed back to Cape Canaveral after that woman in Florida started saying those things about JFK? People were so outraged. With Gene, all this publicity . . . Well, I don't have to tell you. Using your design—it would be like adding insult to injury."

Nola was quiet for a long moment; then she said, "What if no one knew . . . that it was me, my design?"

"There would be no way of keeping it a secret, not if you're with the firm."

"And if I weren't?"

"What are you suggesting?"

Nola at first didn't know how to answer. Then she found herself saying, "I could take a leave of absence. For a few months, until the rest of your funding comes through." She thought about Dani and Tasha, the money she'd saved for private school, and felt a wrench of misgiving that was almost a physical pain. She'd need to dip into that nest egg. But in the end, wouldn't it be for them, too? It was their heritage she'd be making them proud of with this library. . . .

"I can't let you do that," Cordelia was saying. "I won't be responsible for your being out of a job."

"Who's asking you to be responsible? It was my idea. *I'll* deal with the consequences. All I need from you is your promise that, *when* you get the funding, you'll go with my design."

She waited, not realizing she'd been holding her breath until Cordelia's next words released the air from her lungs.

"You want promises? Well, I can't give them to you." Cordelia's eyes flashed. "This . . . this whole situation, it's like some kind of . . . ghastly nightmare. I don't know you . . . and I don't *want* to know you."

"You don't have to," Nola pressed. "Just know that, on this one thing, if nothing else, we're on the same side. We both want this library."

"You can't imagine . . ." Cordelia started to say.

"Yes, I can. It's *you* who can't begin to imagine what this means to me. All my life, I've been pretending to be someone I'm not . . . but this library, it says whose daughter I really am. Even if the public doesn't know, *I'll* know."

After a long pause, Cordelia said, "All right, then . . . I'll think about it."

"Will you let me know before you go back to Blessing?" Nola fished in her handbag, and pressed her business card —on which she'd also printed her home number—into Cordelia's hand.

"I'm leaving next week . . . but I will let you know by then." Cordelia slipped the card into her coat pocket and crossed her arms over her chest, one of her butter-soft suede gloves pulling back to reveal the slim gold watch on her wrist. Her voice lowering, becoming wistful almost, she added, "He *did* love me, you know."

Whatever bitterness Nola had been harboring was, at this moment, eclipsed by her genuine sympathy for the woman beside her.

"I know," Nola said.

When Sissy called—as she had done nearly every evening since Cordelia had arrived—Cordelia was in no mood to talk to her or anyone. Despite her long bath, the cold cloth pressed to her forehead, and three Extra-Strength Tylenols, her head felt as if Gene Kelly had been tap-dancing on it.

She'd barely said "hello" when Sissy's voice broke with a great, burbly gasp.

"Mother, he's gone. . . . Beech . . . he says he wants a d-divorce." Between gulps and sniffles, Sissy managed to spit it out. "He's muh-moved in with that . . . that slut. I'll just b-bet she's slept with every man in B-Blessing. Oh, M-Mother . . . it's so *humiliating.* . . ."

Cordelia had to restrain herself to keep from quietly hanging up. Sissy was like a five-year-old to whom it has yet to occur that other people have troubles, too. Before unloading all her miseries, would Sissy ever think to ask how *she* might be feeling?

"Not nearly as humiliating as spending the rest of your life married to a jackass." Cordelia, tightening the belt on her terry robe, sank onto the sofa bed in Win's den.

She pictured Beech and his blond girlfriend in the laundry room. . . . Then she was seeing Gene and Margaret, making love, or just talking quietly in the evening, Margaret in her bathrobe pouring him a shot of the Old Turkey he liked a nip of before bedtime. She screwed her eyes shut for a moment, willing those images away.

There was a short silence on Sissy's end, filled with long-distance buzzes and clicks—as if a swarm of gnats was whining in her ears. Then Sissy's voice came through, a terrible wail that felt as if it might shatter Cordelia's eardrum.

"Moooootthher! How can you say that? He's the father of your grandchildren!"

"More's the pity. You know perfectly well I never thought much of him. Why, the very first time you brought him home with you, I could see he would never amount to a hill of beans. And that loud mouth of his! If Beech Beecham is descended from Robert E. Lee, then I'm the Queen of England."

"Are you calling Beech a liar?"

"Well, if he wasn't lying to you all those times he was courting the clap over at Mulberry Acres, then I don't know what you call it."

"I just don't *believe* what I'm hearing. Here I am, crying my eyes out, and you are acting like my husband's leaving is the best thing that ever happened to me! Don't you even care?" Sissy's voice took on a mournfully aggrieved tone, and in a terrible flash of insight, one she did not want to have, Cordelia could see all this from Beech's point of view —how Sissy's whining must have worn him down, the way blowflies can drive a cow insane.

Cordelia heaved a deep sigh. "Now, Sissy, of course I care. . . ."

"You don't! You said yourself you never liked Beech! Why, I'll bet you'll go tell Grace, and the two of you will laugh your heads off!" She was off and running now, and when she got like this there was no stopping her.

"Sissy, you don't know what you're talking about." Cordelia's head felt like it was going to split in two.

"If I can't expect a little sympathy from my own moth——"

"Stop it!" Cordelia snapped. *"Stop it this minute!"*

A shocked silence filled her ear, and the static on the line seemed to swell like a vast swarm of insects. The African mask on the wall, with its strings of hemp hanging down like dirty hair, seemed to be scowling down at her, accusing her somehow. And yet she didn't feel guilty. She felt . . . good. She should have spoken her mind to Sissy years ago.

Then Sissy broke into a new torrent of weeping, and Cordelia was reminded of how much Sissy depended on her. What had always been for Cordelia an act of love now seemed a back-breaking burden.

"I only wanted your h-help," she wailed. "Oh, Mother, I d-don't know what to doooooo."

Cordelia realized that, for the first time since she had given birth—on one of the hottest days in Manhattan's recorded history—to a nine-and-a-half-pound baby she'd named Caroline after her mother's mother, she no longer wanted the responsibility of looking after her younger daughter.

"Well, you'll just have to figure it out for yourself," she told Sissy, not unkindly. She hadn't, after all, stopped loving her.

"You mean . . ."

"That's right. It's time you made up your own mind about what you're going to do."

"But how will I . . . ?"

"Oh, you'll survive, Sissy. *That* much you can count on."

It's living that takes work—like tending a garden, Cordelia thought, seeing Gabe in her mind, kneeling in the flower bed by the gazebo, his battered khaki hat tilted over his brow, his bare hands working the earth, digging to form holes for the flowers he would plant there.

"Well, thank *you*—for nothing!"

Cordelia heard a click in her ear as Sissy hung up.

Immediately, Cordelia began to feel guilty. She'd been too harsh. Her meeting with Nola Emory had left her short-tempered. Maybe she ought to, if not take back what she'd said, then at least soften the blow. Yes, Sissy needed to stand on her own feet, but Cordelia would reassure her that her mother would always be there for her, love her, no matter what.

She picked up the phone, but before she could even start to dial, a man's voice boomed out at her, startling her. Then came Chris's, softer, more tentative.

"Uh, Jack, is my mom there?" Chris was talking over the bedroom extension. "I called home, but she didn't answer. I thought she might be with you."

"To be honest, Chris, I haven't seen her in a couple of days." Jack sounded tense and unhappy. "Anything I can help you with? Is everything okay?"

"Yeah, sure." Chris sounded anything but okay. "You probably heard . . . I'm going to be staying with my dad from now on."

There was a brief, awkward pause; then Jack said, "No, I didn't know. But I'm sure your mom will miss having you around. You know you mean everything to her."

Suddenly Cordelia was seeing Jack in her mind, the zest with which he'd torn into his meal at the restaurant, like one of those old-fashioned locomotives into which coal had to be shoveled at an alarming rate as it raced along the tracks. Not conventionally handsome, but, then, except for Win, she had always mistrusted men who were endowed with more than functionally good looks—the type who secretly admired their reflections while pretending to gaze at window displays. Jack Gold, in passing a store, would wonder how much it rented for, and to whom, and if there might be an opportunity in it for him somehow.

Yet, even during that tense dinner, she'd sensed his kindness, his generosity. She'd seen the tender solicitude he'd shown Grace, the way he'd smiled at her friend Lila, accepting her as if she'd been one of his publishing buddies. And now he was trying his best to smooth things over with Chris.

"I *know* my mom cares about me," she heard Chris say. "I don't need *you* to tell me."

"Hey, don't bite my head off—I only want what's best for you."

"Yeah, well, maybe the best thing'd be getting to live with *both* my parents."

"Chris, that's not going to happen." Jack's voice was even.

"What makes you so sure?" Chris's voice rose, cracking on a high, girlish note. "I'll bet you didn't know my dad spent the night with my mom. What do you think of *that?*"

Oh, Chris. Cordelia had to bite her lip to keep from speaking up.

After a long silence, Jack finally spoke. "If it's true, I think that's something for your mother and me to discuss." He sounded shaken to the core, but he was handling Chris extremely well. Cordelia's admiration rose a notch.

"You don't believe me?"

"That's not what I said."

"Well, then, go ask her! Go ask Mom! There's just one thing I wish all of you so-called grownups would do, and that's leave me out of it! I'm sick of people acting like they want me around when it's obvious they don't give a shit. *All I want is to be left alone!*"

Cordelia carefully lowered the receiver, then sat there,

too stunned to move. She knew she had to do something. Those awful things the boy had said to Jack! Heavens, she'd have to warn Grace.

She could feel the cold bead of resentment she'd been nurturing against her older daughter start to melt.

Cordelia dressed quickly. Buckling a belt around the pale-gold sweater dress she'd worn this afternoon, she noticed it was the wrong color. But who cared? She wedged her feet into the first pair of shoes she came across in the closet.

Making her way down the hallway to her grandson's bedroom, one hand on the wall to keep herself steady, she realized something was different. *It's so quiet.*

Usually Chris had his tape player going full-blast, that awful music that sounded like a bunch of rioting thugs on the street. But the odd noise coming from his room now was . . . She couldn't place it at first, then she realized. . . .

Silence.

Cordelia knocked on his door. No answer. She knocked again, harder this time, each blow sending pain from her knuckles up into her head. Still no answer.

Finally, she opened the door and cautiously peered into the darkened room, with its jumble of unmade bed, discarded clothing, strewn computer discs. But no sign of Chris. And no dog, either. *He must have taken Cody for a walk.* He had to have slipped out just after he got off the phone. There was only the faint hum from the glowing screen of his computer. She drew closer, and saw that he'd typed something there . . . and that it wasn't, as she'd first thought, the start of a homework assignment.

Dear Dad,
    I can't live with you. I don't blame you if you end up hating me for this. I just can't take being in the

middle. Don't look for me. I'll call you sometime just to let you know I'm okay.

Chris

P.S. Cody is with me. Don't worry.

Everything that had been blurred now jumped out at Cordelia with vivid, knife-edged clarity. She hurried out into the living room, its white plush carpet spongy beneath her feet, seeming to slow her as she made her way over to the phone on the table next to the deep cordovan sofa.

A young boy all alone in this city—anything could happen to him.

She was halfway through Grace's number when she thought better of it. She ought to call the police first. Then go over to Grace's, tell her face to face, reassure her.

Even with her control slipping out from under her like a patch of icy sidewalk, Cordelia clung to the conviction that, yes, everything *would* turn out all right. Hadn't she always made sure that things ran smoothly, that no one got hurt? And if lately her life seemed to have gone haywire, then she would just have to see that it got set back on course. For, if you couldn't believe in yourself, in your power to do good, to solve problems, what else was there?

Chapter 21

"It's Chris. He . . . It appears he's run away."

Grace studied her mother's face for signs of panic. As Mother went on about Chris—something about a note left on his computer—she found herself not so much listening as allowing herself to be lulled by her mother's carefully modulated tone. True, she looked a bit more flushed than usual, but that could have been from being hurtled over here, and half scared to death by one of New York's kamikaze cabbies. Mother would have politely thanked him for his unnecessary speed . . . and stiffed him his tip.

"You must have misunderstood," Grace said. Otherwise, wouldn't Mother seem more upset?

"I can read as well as you, thank you very much." Then all at once Cordelia's face seemed to sag, revealing the tiny lines scoring its smooth, powdered mask. Now Grace *was* beginning to feel alarmed. "Grace . . . I didn't want to upset you by letting myself get into a dither over this . . . but I have every reason to believe that Chris is serious about not coming home—to you *or* Win. Dear, are you going to ask me in," she asked wearily, "or must I stand out here all night?"

Grace realized with a start that her mother—in her coat, with a pretty flowered scarf knotted under her chin—was still standing in the hallway outside her door. As she entered, Mother's presence somehow took over, leaving Grace, as she dutifully took her coat, feeling as if it was Cordelia who lived here, and she the visitor.

In the living room area, she watched her mother lower herself carefully into the deep chair across from the sofa, her arms extended stiffly on either side of her to ease her descent. She looked tired—more than that, actually *ill*. Not that she'd admit it.

No. Autocratic and stubborn, she'd suffer the worst headache rather than let on to a soul. Admitting to being sick, in her book, showed a lack of character.

"Some coffee or tea?" Grace asked. "To be honest, you look as if you could use a shot of brandy."

She felt something fluttering in her chest, like the moths and butterflies she had, as a child, held cupped in her hands, their wings frantically beating in an effort to escape. She must not go to pieces. She must act normal, play the perfect hostess, or this thing inside her *would* break loose.

"Thank you, no. Grace, dear, sit down. Please. You *must* listen. I'm not imagining this. I haven't lost my marbles, and I'm not the type to rattle easily, as you know." She took a deep breath. "My grandson is out there somewhere . . . and he might be in trouble." She gestured toward the bank of tall windows, dark except for the room's partial reflections swimming ghostlike in the glass.

My fault, Grace thought.

That's what you're thinking, isn't it, Mother? All my fault. Divorcing Win. Leaving Chris with a broken home, a broken heart. If only I'd been a better mother, a better wife, then Chris would right now be toasting marshmallows with his Boy Scout troop instead of roaming around the park with his dog while we all worry ourselves sick.

She felt a dark rose of anger blooming in her chest, its thorns sharp, pricking her. She had to concentrate to hear her mother's soft voice as she went on.

"Grace, I overheard him on the phone with Jack. He said he'd been trying to reach you . . . that he called here and there was no answer. It couldn't have been more than an hour ago."

"I was out of milk," Grace remembered. "I ran down to the corner store."

"He was upset. Jack tried to get Chris to open up, talk to him. But Chris got angry . . . said some things which he shouldn't have."

"What things?"

"He told Jack about you and Win . . . that Win had spent the night with you."

Grace slumped down onto the sofa. There was a queer, flat buzzing in her ears, like from a phone receiver that's been left off the hook.

Jack knows. . . . Oh, God . . . he knows he knows he knows. Her mind whirled. She thought about Jack, how she'd been avoiding him and missing him at the same time. Wanting to return his calls, but not sure what to say. And now would he ever forgive her? How could he?

Chris. To have lashed out at Jack like that, he had to have been more than merely upset. Confrontation wasn't Chris's style. And how had he even known? Could Win really have been such an idiot as to have told him?

"All right, yes, it's true." Grace felt sixteen again, caught necking in the back seat of Clay MacPherson's Olds Cutlass: her face on fire, her whole body seeming to fold in on itself.

But Mother—wasn't this just what she'd hoped for? Wouldn't she secretly be pleased?

Cordelia surprised her by saying, "Grace, there's something you ought to know about Win. . . ." She stopped, frowning, appearing to reconsider.

"Win and I aren't . . . I mean, just because he spent the night doesn't mean we're getting back together."

Chris was the one she ought to be explaining this to—

but where was he? The fluttery thing in her chest was breaking free, swelling, becoming huge, until she could hardly
breathe. What if he *wasn't* in the park, or at a friend's? What
if he was roaming the streets, heading for God knows where?

As if she'd read her mind, Mother was telling her, "His
note said he'd be all right, and not to worry." She sat up
straighter, squaring her shoulders, as if by good posture
alone she might somehow shield them both. "The good news
is, he can't have gotten very far."

"How do you know?" Grace, as she pushed her hands
through her hair, noticed that her palms were wet.

"I heard him on the phone not ten minutes before I discovered he'd gone."

In Grace's mind, Chris was four again—a little boy in
Oshkosh overalls who hadn't yet lost all his baby fat, wandering around out there, alone, frightened, prey to the muggers, perverts, crazies who haunted the streets of New York.

She forced herself to her feet. Only a short distance from
here to the phone on her desk, but it felt like a continent.

"The police," she said, as if there were another person
inside her, riding shotgun, coolly instructing her. "I'll call
the police—isn't that what people do?"

She had never in her life summoned the police, not even
when she'd had good reason—like the time she'd used
Chris's old cap gun to scare off a burglar up on her roof
trying to break in through her bathroom skylight.

"I've already taken care of that, dear." Cordelia sighed,
smoothing the lap of her already perfectly smooth dress.
"They can't help us. Not until he's been missing at least
forty-eight hours. The officer I spoke to suggested we sit tight
and wait for him to come to his senses and return home.
Most of them do, he said."

"Did you apologize for bothering him, and thank him

for his trouble?" She hadn't meant to say that—the sarcasm had just slipped out.

Cordelia didn't move, not even to flinch. She merely stared at Grace with a calmness that might have seemed eerie had Grace not noticed how tightly her lips were clamped together.

Now she was rising, the effort seeming almost too much, causing her arms and legs to quiver. Dull patches of color stood out in her cheeks. Grace felt ashamed for snapping at her, when it was obvious Mother was only trying to help.

"Mother, I . . ."

"I suggest we start with Chris's friends," Cordelia said briskly. "Do you have a notepad and a pencil? I can start calling while you make a list of their numbers."

"I have a school directory," Grace told her. "I could try his classmates. He doesn't have many friends, but maybe . . ."

"No maybes," Cordelia cut her off, once again in perfect control. "Heavens, I can't think why I went off my head, getting so worked up over nothing—of *course* he's at some friend's house. No grandson of mine would be addle-headed enough to wander the streets in this nasty cold when he had someplace warm and safe to go to."

"Remember how you were always out looking for *me* long after dark?" Grace recalled. "Sometimes, I'd hear you calling me and I'd hide so you wouldn't see me."

"Just to be contrary." Cordelia sniffed. "Now, what about that directory?"

"How far could they get, a boy and a dog?" Grace fought to keep her hands from trembling as she searched on the bookshelf near the entrance to her office for the St. Andrew's directory.

"Farther than you might imagine," Cordelia replied in a soft voice heavy with sorrow. It wasn't just Chris she was talking about, Grace realized.

Grace, her eyes welling, thought of all the missed opportunities for closeness that stretched between her and Mother like mile markers along a lonely stretch of highway. She prayed that she and Chris wouldn't end up like this—two people linked by a bond closer than any other, but strangers to each other.

"You can start with the A's." Brusquely, so Cordelia wouldn't see how choked up she was, Grace handed her mother the school directory. "I'm going downstairs to ask Chris's friend Scully if he knows anything. Then I'm going to call Jack."

Jack.

Please, God, let him understand, she prayed, even while she knew in her heart that such a thing was beyond understanding.

Let it not be too late.

More than an hour later, after exhausting every number in the school directory and getting nowhere, Grace collapsed onto the sofa, feeling utterly drained. She knew that she ought to call Win at his office, that she couldn't keep putting it off. But after going to bed with him . . . God, how could she face him? She felt both foolish and angry, mostly at herself, but at Win, too. How could he have raised Chris's hopes by telling him? What kind of father would have done that to his son?

Even so, she found herself saying, "I should call Win."

"Yes, of course," Cordelia agreed.

Grace stared at her, trying to read her expression. Was Mother hoping this crisis would accomplish what Win's charms had failed to? That her and Win's shared worry over Chris would somehow reunite them?

"I know what you're thinking," she told her mother, unable to hold back any longer. "If I hadn't left Win in the first place, none of this would have happened."

"I suppose you're right," Cordelia said, "but if you hadn't left Win, you wouldn't have gotten to know Jack."

"I thought you didn't like Jack."

"What on earth gave you that idea?"

"But you and Win are so . . ."

"I know what I must seem like to you," she broke in. "A pigheaded woman, set in her ways, not willing to bend or change. Not willing to accept that a marriage I thought was perfect could be anything but." Her hands, loosely laced in her lap, suddenly knotted, the diamond wedding band she had not taken off after her husband died flashing against a whitened knuckle. "But lately I've been forced into seeing a lot of things."

"Daddy." Grace nodded in understanding.

Cordelia bowed her head briefly, bringing her tightly laced fingers to her forehead. "I wonder if you can know what it's like, to love someone so much that the thought of being without him, or of him not loving you back as deeply as you love him, is almost like death."

Grace thought of Jack and hoped he loved her even half as much as that. Enough, at least, to forgive her.

"After you and your sister were born . . ." Mother dropped her hands and lifted her head, her silver hair fanning across her cheeks. "It was as if . . . the four of us, we formed some kind of magic circle, and nothing bad could ever get through to hurt us." She took a deep, shaky breath. "I didn't count on the hurt coming from *inside* our circle."

"He didn't do it to hurt you," Grace said.

"Maybe not. But whether he meant to or not doesn't make it any easier to bear."

Grace saw anger in the pinched line of Mother's mouth, and in the queer flatness of her gaze. Good. She wasn't keeping it locked inside.

"I know you're angry at me, too," Grace said, keeping

her voice soft. "And I don't blame you for thinking I wrote this book partly to get back at you. I didn't, of course, but that's not the point, is it? You and I—the problem we have with each other goes way back."

Grace's throat closed up—like when she was little, after something bad at school, wanting desperately to ask her mother for comfort but unable to say the words.

"You were such a willful girl," Mother stepped in, not without gentleness. "Always crossing me, questioning every bit of advice, every ultimatum. I suppose I thought you needed a strong hand to guide you." Her mouth, oddly naked-looking without the rose-colored lipstick she almost always wore, turned up in a rueful smile. "For all the good it did either of us."

"A strong hand wasn't what I needed," Grace answered. "All I ever wanted was for you to listen to me. Like I want you to listen to me now."

"Some things are just too hard to hear."

"Even the truth?"

"*Especially* the truth." Cordelia looked away, her face contorted with pain. After a moment, she added, "I spoke with Nola Emory."

Grace stared at her. "When?"

"Today. We met in the park."

"Oh, Mother . . . " She suddenly was overwhelmed with compassion.

"Things are seldom as terrible as you imagine they'll be," Cordelia said in a strained voice that seemed to deny her words.

Grace managed to get up and walk over to her mother. She placed a hand on Cordelia's shoulder, feeling the sharpness of her bones, like one of the delicate but sturdy pieces of antique furniture that filled the old house in Blessing.

"But don't you see?" she said. "In the end, he chose *us*."

The words hung in the air, seeming to echo in the cavernous space.

"Yes, he chose us," Mother replied, staring at the bookcase in front of her. "But that doesn't change what's happening now, does it? All this scandal—I can't imagine what it'll be like back in Blessing. And his library—so many pledges will disappear because of this."

Grace cleared her throat. Since her last run-in with her mother, an idea had been taking shape in her mind. Now she realized that she must have known for some time what she was going to do. As Eugene Truscott's daughter, she had no other choice—not if she wanted to feel good about herself.

"How much do you need?" she asked.

"At least a million, in addition to what we've already raised."

"I can't promise that much . . . but I'll do what I can."

Cordelia stared at her, not comprehending. "Grace, what are you saying?"

"The money you need. I'm donating the proceeds from my book to Daddy's library. My agent is negotiating deals in a number of foreign countries, and several producers in Hollywood are interested. There should be at least five hundred thousand to start—maybe more, once the book is published."

"But . . . why?"

"Because it seems right somehow, my book helping make his library possible. And because I want to."

Cordelia's eyes filled. Then Grace saw they were tears of anger, not gratitude. "How can you? This book—it's an affront to everything he ever stood for."

"It's *because* of Daddy that I wrote it. *Honor Above All*—there's no irony in that. Yes, he was honorable . . . in every way but one. If he could have brought himself to tell us . . ." She sighed. "He couldn't. But now *I* can be his voice." Grace felt the old fight in her springing up like trampled grass. "And it's because of Daddy that you're building the library. We both loved him. We just have different ways of showing it."

Cordelia was silent for so long that Grace began to feel annoyed. Was Mother going to refuse her? After all her words of conciliation, was she going to use *this* as another wedge to keep them apart?

But when Mother did begin to speak, her voice was calm, even a bit rueful. "You know, it just occurred to me that a week ago, even yesterday, I would have said no. But things are different now, aren't they? And I suppose you're right, I haven't always listened to you. Your wanting to help with this library—even if all it means is that the two of us will be working toward the same goal—that's enough."

"Then you accept?"

"Do I have a choice? If I said no, you'd find some other way of making sure it got into the right hands." She smiled as she said it, as if acknowledging that they weren't so different after all.

"I don't suppose stubbornness is in the genes," Grace offered with a small laugh.

Cordelia rose then, easily, gracefully, holding out her arms. And suddenly Grace found it not at all difficult to move forward, into the warm, perfumed embrace that all her life she had felt was not hers to claim. Mother's arms felt light as leaves . . . not demanding anything from her, just *there*. Grace found her head dropping onto her mother's wisp of a shoulder, with its delicate knobbed bones, feeling as if she had come to a place that was, if not exactly home, then the next best thing.

If only Chris would let me hold him like this.

She imagined him cold, hungry, wandering the streets.

She began to tremble, and felt her mother gently draw her closer. But Mother was not attempting to console her with platitudes. She merely held her, as if she understood that to speak might have broken the spell that had brought them together, after so long and so many, many miles of misunderstandings and misguided actions.

Grace suddenly understood what had been so precious to her mother that she would lie—even to herself—to keep it. Because Grace wanted the very same thing—the magic circle of her family, complete and unharmed, the family that she could see gathered in her mind as clearly as a photo on a Christmas card: Chris, Jack, and, yes, Ben and Hannah, too.

Chapter 22

Jack listened to Grace's message on his answering machine, then punched the rewind button and played it again. It wasn't that he'd missed part of it—no, what he wanted, *needed,* was simply to hear her again.

Her voice, its peculiar sweet lilt, calmed him. He needed to keep on hearing it, because it might be the only piece of her left for him to hang on to.

"Why, Grace? *Why?*"

But now her words were penetrating.

Jack, please call me. I know you're probably upset with me . . . but something really awful has happened. It's Chris. He's run away. Oh, God, I don't think I can get through this without you. . . .

In a minute, he was out the door and in a taxi, heading downtown.

As he stared out the window at Park Avenue crawling past, his anger flared. He wanted to hit someone, smash something. *Damn that kid. And her, too.* And that bastard Win! Christ, even if he thought there was a chance of his getting back together with Grace, what right did he have letting his son in on their sexual escapade?

By the time the cab dropped him off at Nineteenth and Seventh, Jack felt in control again, barely, but his anger remained—a small, glittering diamond that flashed inside him like cold fire. When he discovered the elevator wasn't working, it was what propelled him up six flights on foot . . . and what hardened him against the anguish he felt when

Grace answered his knock, looking like a lost child herself in raggedy jeans with the tail of her wrinkled chambray shirt trailing down to her knees.

"Jack." She spoke his name almost like an apology, or maybe a plea—that he put his feelings on ice for the time being?

Then, looking past her, he saw the muted-plaid blazer tossed over the back of the sofa, and the slight, athletically built man just beyond, standing over by the bookcase with his tie loosened and a drink in his hand.

"Win." Jack nodded curtly, but his blood had begun pounding again. He wanted to tear into Winston Bishop III and kick the living shit out of him. The guy's smug smile made him think of Grace in bed with Win . . . opening her mouth to his. . . .

He clenched his fists. *Stop this . . . got to stop.*

Then he noticed Grace's mother, seated with her back to Win. She looked distraught, anxious, which was more than Jack could say for her former son-in-law, who was now walking over to the coffee table and setting his drink down, remembering first to wipe the bottom of his glass on his shirtsleeve so it wouldn't leave a ring. As if this were *his* home.

Jack forced his hands, which felt frozen and knotted, to unclench. *Back off, Gold—not now.*

"We've called everyone I can think of," Grace told him, taking his coat before he could hang it up himself. Damnit, he *knew* where the closet was. *Give me that at least,* he thought.

"What about the police?" he asked, trying to focus on her through the white rim of fire that seemed to be encircling his skull.

She shook her head. "I raised hell with the desk sergeant at our precinct. They agreed to keep an eye out, but that was only after I called headquarters and yelled my head off. Officially, he's not missing until the day after tomorrow." She crossed her arms over her chest, hugging herself tightly. Tears stood in her eyes, making them bright. "Jack, I'm going crazy here. I don't know what else to do. Where to go."

"You look like hell," he told her. "First thing you have to do is sit down and take a breather."

Her face was gaunt with worry, her hair lank and separated into greasy strands where she'd been raking it with her fingers. She was barefoot, too, her toes almost blue with cold. Jack had a crazy urge to take her in his lap, and warm her feet with his hands.

"Jack, I'm fine," she protested, like Hannah used to at bedtime, denying she was even the slightest bit tired, when her eyes were so droopy she could hardly keep them open. "When this is over, I'll sleep for a week, but right now I have enough caffeine in me to swim the English Channel. I couldn't rest if I tried. And if *I* look like hell, you take second prize." She gave him a tender look, reaching a hand toward him that stopped short of his jacket lapel before drifting back to her side.

Jack shuddered, closing his eyes and taking a breath.

She's touched that you came, and she feels sorry for you, that's all. You're no kid—you should've known better. A young woman like her, entirely different background—did you really believe it would work?

"Grace . . ." Jack gripped her. He wasn't quite sure what he wanted to tell her, but, whatever it was, he didn't want it to be within earshot of Cordelia and Win. "I could use some of that coffee. Any left?"

She nodded, looking up at him, the flesh around her eyes almost bruised-looking with weariness and worry. "I'll get it."

"No, you take it easy. I haven't forgotten my way around

here . . . not yet, anyway." He heard the note of bitterness in his voice, and observed that it had hit home. *Cheap shot,* he chided himself.

Jack felt Win's eyes on him as he moved about the kitchen, reaching into the cupboard over the sink for a mug, easily finding the one he always drank from—dark blue, with KILLER INSTINCT scrawled on it in blood red—a promotional giveaway from the ABA in Washington a few years back.

There was half a cup left, so he made a fresh pot while finishing off the dregs. It was something to do . . . and he couldn't deny the pleasure he took in Win's glowering watchfulness.

"What about video arcades?" Jack wondered aloud. "That kid lives and breathes Nintendo. Remember all the times, Grace, when you had to go and drag him home from that arcade in Penn Station? And there must be a dozen arcades in Times Square alone—a longshot maybe, but we should check them out."

"If you knew Chris at all, you'd know he wouldn't leave a dog tied up outside a video arcade in Times Square." Win strolled over to where Jack stood, at the end of the kitchen counter. His voice was smooth, and he moved with an easy, unhurried grace. But there was no mistaking the hostility in his tone.

"You're right, I wasn't thinking." Jack said mildly, forcing himself not to rise to the bait. "But, okay, now that you mention it, what *about* the dog? My guess is he'd risk getting caught before depriving that dog in any way. That means feeding it, and keeping it warm. What about the youth shelters—do they take kids with pets?"

"Oh, I wouldn't think so," piped Cordelia. "Fleas and lice, you know."

"I know!" Grace suddenly became animated. "I'll call Lila. She's a walking encyclopedia on dogs. I'll bet *she'd* know if there was any place near here where Chris could have gone with Cody."

As she dialed, Win walked over and slipped a proprietary arm around Grace's waist. And Grace, maybe too distracted, or maybe *liking* it, wasn't shaking him off or drawing away. As she hung up, after leaving a lengthy message on Lila's machine, she even dropped her head briefly onto his shoulder.

Jack felt his control slipping, despite his promise to himself. But with that man fucking *flaunting* his coziness with Grace—damnit, it was too much.

He'd bet a week's pay it had been Win's pressuring that drove Chris into moving in with him in the first place. In fact, seeing Win's vaguely sheepish expression—that of some fraternity jock sobering up after a night of hard drinking, and wondering how that dent got in the front fender of his sports car—he was almost sure of it.

Jack waited until Win was walking back to retrieve his drink.

"You know something you're not telling us." Jack stepped in front of him, facing him squarely, noting that Win was several inches shorter than he. Now, standing so close to him, he could almost *smell* it, the sour stink of a man who's covering his ass.

"What the hell are you talking about?" Win snarled.

"You're covering up," Jack went on. "You *know* why Chris ran away. I can see it in your eyes."

"Get off it, Gold." Win tried to brush past him, but his tan cheeks had colored a deep sienna.

"I appreciate the fact that Chris is your son, and you must be worried about him," Jack said, speaking as evenly as he could. "But if you can think of any reason he might have wanted to light out for God knows where, I think Grace should know about it, don't you?"

He pressed a hand on Win's shoulder, which Win angrily ducked, twisting away with the fluid grace of a downhill skier.

"Who the hell are *you* to tell *me* what to do?" he spat.

This close, Jack could see from Win's high color, and his bloodshot eyes, that the drink on the coffee table probably hadn't been his first. He guessed, too, that Win was *glad* for this opportunity to pick a fight they'd both been spoiling for since Jack first walked in.

Christ, wouldn't it be good to smash right into that Confederate nose?

Instead, he responded, "I'm someone who doesn't want to see the boy get hurt over something you said or did that you're too much of a coward to own up to."

"Really! Absolutely nothing will be gained by your going at each other like this!"

Behind him, Cordelia's voice rose on an indignant, somewhat imperious note. But Jack hardly heard her, because Win was lunging at him, hands splayed open as they slammed into Jack's chest, shoving him hard—as if he wanted to throw a punch but was too much a gentleman to go that far.

"You *bastard,*" Win shouted.

"Win, no!" Grace's sharp cry pierced the muffled roaring in Jack's ears as he staggered backward to catch his balance.

Ignoring her, Win sneered, "This isn't about Chris. You don't give a *shit* about my son. You're just using him as an excuse to show Grace what a big hero you are. Well, I'll tell you before Grace gets around to it—you don't have a leg to stand on. So why don't you just go home? This is *my* family.

There's nothing here for you, nothing that's any of your concern."

"*Win!* How dare you?" Grace's voice broke with outrage.

"When Grace herself tells me I'm not welcome here, that's when I'll hear it," Jack said. "And if you think this is just about Grace and me, you're way off base. I *do* care about Chris . . . enough to risk looking like a damn fool if I'm wrong. *Am* I wrong?"

Win's balled-up knuckles looped up so suddenly that Jack was caught off-guard. He had just enough presence of mind to feint to one side, causing the blow to catch the edge of his jaw, a glancing cuff that stung more than it hurt.

Hot rage flooded through him, and Jack swung—a blow that surged from the blue-white center of his fury. He felt the shock of his fist connecting with bone, and saw a blur of blue-striped fabric that was Win's shirttail flying out from under his belt as he hurtled backward, arms pinwheeling in mid-air.

Then his vision cleared, and there was Win sprawled on the carpet at Cordelia's feet, his feet tangled amid the sinuous wrought-iron legs of the coffee table, one elbow shakily supporting his weight while his forearm rested on the toes of his former mother-in-law's shoes. Cordelia sat gaping down at him, as if she wasn't quite sure whether to help him up . . . or pull away in disgust.

"Damn you! Both of you!" Grace shrieked.

Jack's anger cooled abruptly. He felt himself dully, almost creakily, swiveling in her direction. But before he had turned all the way around, he could see her out of the corner of his eye—standing erect and fierce.

He started to move toward her, but then he heard an odd, gurgling sound that made him turn back toward Win.

The man was trying to get up, one knee under him and the other bent with his foot planted on the floor, half-facing Cordelia in a position that made Jack think somehow of a Victorian swain begging his beloved's hand in marriage. Blood was threading down from one nostril of his aquiline nose—*Even that he does beautifully, like a Hollywood stunt man,* Jack thought. But something was wrong with this valentine. . . .

Win was crying. *Real* tears were coursing down his cheeks in shiny rivulets.

"Win, really, you *must* tell them what got Chris so—" Cordelia's imploring was cut off by Grace's rushing over, crouching before Win.

"For God's sake, if you know something . . . please, please, tell me! Even if it is something you're ashamed of. I deserve to know. I *have* to know. Chris's *life* might be at stake. I know you love him as much as I do. I know you don't want anything to happen to him."

Win's head dropped. Tears dripped off his chin, pink with the blood smeared over it. His voice, when it came, was low and guttural.

"He . . . he wanted to go home. So I told him about us, the other night. I figured it was only a matter of time before we were a family again, all under the same roof. And my having Chris—well, it would help you make up your mind that much faster. Chris wanted to believe it, but he was scared, too . . . of getting his hopes up and being disappointed. I guess I just . . . I lost it." His head sank even lower. "I told him, if he went back to you, I didn't know if I'd be able to take care of the dog on my own. I didn't mean it—I swear to God I would never have gotten rid of Cody. I was . . . desperate. He had to have known I wouldn't have done a thing like that. . . ."

Cold anger—not the instinctive rage of a moment ago—

filled Jack. He wanted to grab Win by the throat and shake him. But that wouldn't bring Chris back.

While Grace stumbled to her feet, Jack strode over to where Win was still crouched, his forehead resting on his one bent knee. He grabbed hold of Win's elbow, and pulled him to his feet, roughly, but not unkindly.

"Let's go," he said tersely. "We have a lot of territory to cover."

"Wha——?" Win blinked at him in teary-eyed confusion.

"He can't have gone too far, not with the dog. So we can rule out Greyhound or Amtrak. And I doubt he'd get very far on foot, or hitchhiking. I suggest we follow up on those phone calls to his friends with a visit—one of them might be covering for him. We'll check back in a little while, see if Lila has any other ideas."

Out of the corner of his eye, he saw Cordelia get up and move toward the kitchen. A moment later, she was back with napkins and some ice for Win's bloody nose, which she tended to briskly and efficiently. When Win was cleaned up, she gave him a little nudge in Jack's direction, as if to say, *Go on, now, be a good boy.*

Jack could feel Grace's stricken gaze following them as he steered Win toward the vestibule and dug their coats from the closet. He was almost out the door when he heard her call his name, a cry so faint it seemed to be coming from a great distance. Jack turned to see Grace gliding over the rug, her bare feet making small whispering sounds against the its silky nap, her eyes full of anguish.

"Jack." She stretched a hand toward him as she had done before, but this time she didn't let it fall to her side. She held it there, aloft, as if she were directing someone who was lost, pointing the way toward safety. But all she said was, "Take the umbrella. It's going to rain."

He heard the deep throb of loss in her voice, as if she were warning him, not of a rainstorm, but of something far worse.

Jack didn't have to ask what it was, because he already knew. He could find Chris; he could bring home the moon in his pocket . . . and still it wouldn't change anything. This grim fantasy he'd had since the beginning, of waiting for the other shoe to drop, fearing that in a year or two she would leave his bed for that of a younger, handsomer, more vigorous man—it was now a cold reality.

He felt unbearably sad as he watched Grace step forward and reach into the closet for the umbrella, and hold it out to him.

Jack shook his head. "Better not. I'd only forget to return it."

What he didn't say, and what she clearly dared not ask, was that after tonight, after Chris was found, he wouldn't be back.

Chapter 23

H annah stared at her brother. "I don't believe you."

"It's true. . . . I was the one who let the cat out of the bag," Ben told her. "Go ask Dad. *He'll* tell you. He was just covering my ass, because I made him promise."

Was this an apology? she wondered. But when had Ben ever owned up to his shit? Like the time he put that dent in Dad's car, and said some idiot must have run into him when he was parked.

"How did you even find out?" she asked.

"Look, I wasn't spying on you or anything. I heard you on the phone with your friend. You weren't exactly whispering."

Hannah, who'd been making herself dinner—strawberry jam on toasted freezer waffles, apple slices, and some leftover Chinese noodles from the night before—set down the knife she'd been using. Ben had come by to pick up Mom for one of her thousands of engagements, but even in a formal jacket and tie he looked a little messed up, like he'd taken the subway instead of riding over here in his car. Come to think of it, he'd been like this, a bit rumpled-looking and out of sorts, the past few times she'd seen him.

"I don't get it," she said, growing angry. "Why are you telling me this now?"

Keep him talking, she told herself, *stay pissed at him.* That way she wouldn't have to face the sick feeling, welling up inside her, that *she* was the bad guy—for blaming Grace, and for turning Grace against Dad.

Ben shrugged and looked away, pushing at a crumb on the cutting board with one elegantly tapered finger. "Maybe I've had enough of getting jerked around by other people. I know what it feels like . . . and I don't want to do that to you."

"You're too late," she told him. "I already blew up at Grace."

"What's new about that?"

He had to be talking about Christmas Eve—her throwing a fit with Grace. Dad must have told him.

"Well, in this particular case, she didn't deserve it. And, for your information, it just so happens that I'm *not* pregnant." She lowered her voice so Mom, getting dressed in her room down the hall, wouldn't overhear.

"If you're not careful from now on, you will be." He didn't say it meanly. It was just Ben, as usual, thinking the worst.

Hannah screwed the lid on the jam jar, and began brushing crumbs off the counter before Mom could see what a mess she'd made. And so Ben wouldn't see the tears in her eyes.

"No, I won't," she told him, clearing her throat. "Con and I . . . Well, I can't say it's over, because I'm not sure it was anything much to begin with." She felt stupid, telling all this to Ben, who would have been the last person she confided in if he hadn't been standing right in front of her. What did she expect Ben to say? How could he know what it felt like, wanting so bad just to be held that you'd sleep with someone even if you knew that person didn't really love you?

But Ben surprised her with the sympathy she heard in his voice when he said, "You'll get over it."

"There's nothing to get over," she told him. It was this emptiness inside her she wasn't so sure she'd recover from. Maybe, if she had truly loved Con, and he had felt the same way about her, then she'd at least feel brokenhearted. Instead, she was left with this feeling that something momentous had slipped by when she hadn't been paying attention.

"You missed a spot." Ben pointed at a smudge on the snow-white Formica.

"Thanks," she told him, swiping at it with her sponge harder than necessary.

"Look, Hannah, if it means anything, I'm sorry." He straightened one of the copper pots hanging in a shining row over the Wolf range. "I know what it's like to break up—even when it's something you never really thought would last to begin with."

He was rescued from revealing any more by Mom, sweeping in on a cloud of chiffon and Chanel No. 5. "*There* you are." Her high heels clicked over the Mexican-tiled floor to where Ben stood. Rocking forward onto the balls of her feet, Natalie tipped her face up to be kissed. "We'd better hurry, or we'll be too late for cocktails. I don't want to miss seeing Louisa—she's having her place in East Hampton redone, you know."

She turned to Hannah, a tiny frown appearing between her expertly arched brows as her gaze swept the counter Hannah had just finished wiping. "We shouldn't be too late . . . and, sweetie, *do* remember how much I hate coming home to a mess."

Hannah waited until they'd been gone ten minutes or so; then she grabbed her mother's car keys from the cloisonné dish by the phone. She'd gotten her driver's license last fall, but had never driven the Mercedes before—Mom was too worried she'd put a dent in it. All of a sudden, Hannah didn't *care* what her mother would say or do . . . even if it meant being grounded until she was eighteen.

She scrawled a note on the pad by the telephone, and stuck it up on the stainless-steel refrigerator with a magnet shaped like a dragonfly.

Gone to Berkshires. Don't worry, will take good care of car.

Several hours later, Hannah lay on her bed in her father's country house, staring at the shadows on the ceiling.

What, she wondered, could she have imagined she'd accomplish by sneaking off, coming all the way up here? The drive had been fairly easy, only one real traffic jam, but when Mom found out her Mercedes was missing, she really would shit a brick.

And for what? It wasn't cozy or comforting up here, the way she'd thought it would be. In her underpants and flannel pajama top, she was shivering in her unheated bedroom on the top floor of this empty cabin, while everyone else was miles and miles away, probably living it up and not even noticing that she'd split.

A tear slid down her temple, tickling along her hairline. She felt like such a jerk . . . wanting to go on hating Grace, and at the same time hating herself for not even giving Grace the benefit of the doubt before shooting her big mouth off.

Why couldn't she get it right for once? Why couldn't things just *work out?*

Hannah became aware of a steady ticking noise, and realized it was the icicles dripping onto the sill outside her window. Somewhere off in the distance, a dog barked, and she heard a truck door slam, followed by an engine roaring to life. Two floors below, in the cellar, the old boiler kicked in, and the heat register by her bed began its asthmatic rattling.

She clung to the familiarity of these sounds, so she wouldn't have to think too hard, or let in the feeling that was tapping against her rib cage. She thought of the family therapist Mom and Dad had dragged her and Ben to when they were breaking up—what Hannah remembered most about those sessions was that stupid wave machine in the waiting room, a continuous stream of white noise so you couldn't hear the voices in Dr. Dickenstein's office. Right now, she wanted a machine like that to drown out the voices clamoring inside her head.

No wonder Daddy would rather be with Grace; just look at you, sulking all alone in the dark.

Hannah pictured a clean square of origami paper, and now she was folding it in half, once, twice. She could almost feel the folded paper sliding along the pad of her thumb as she pressed it to a pleat, neat, precise, the way life never was. Why couldn't she get along with the people she loved, and who she knew, deep down, loved her?

Shivering now, she climbed under the covers, and pressed her face into the softness of the cotton pillowcase. The creaks and rumblings of the old cabin made her heart beat a little faster. Suppose some burglar, one of those escaped convicts or mental patients she was always reading about in the paper, were to break in? She imagined that she could actually bury herself in the mattress, so that, should anyone happen to look in on her, all he would see would be the slightly rumpled chenille spread under which she lay submerged.

But suppose, in the middle of the night, the furnace cut out. She'd freeze! As she drifted asleep, she imagined herself, come morning, a solid block of ice, her wide-open eyes fixed on the ceiling.

Daddy would be sad for a while, but in the end they'd

all realize—Mom, Ben, and especially Grace—how much better off they were without her . . .

Klonk!

Hannah, jerked from a sound sleep, bolted upright. Her fingers automatically spider-walked over to her old teddy bear, scrunched between the bed frame and the wall. She clutched Boo-Bear against her wildly pounding heart.

Klonk-thunk.

There it was again. A raccoon? Sometimes they got into the garbage cans if Daddy or Ben forgot to put the lids on tight. Once, she'd heard a raccoon on the roof, right overhead, and it had sounded like road work was going on up there. But this was different—it was . . .

Inside. Coming from *inside,* downstairs.

Hannah felt her heart vault into her throat. Her armpits were suddenly swamped. "Please, God," she tried to whisper. But her voice had dried up, and all that came out was a hoarse croak.

Then she heard a new sound, an odd skittering noise like . . . like . . .

She thought of Roo, an English spaniel they'd had until she was fourteen, and how, after he got old and sick, he used to wander around at night, his toenails making that same clicking noise on the old floorboards in the kitchen.

Yes, that was it. A dog. She could hear it whining softly, the way Roo used to when he was in a strange place.

What kind of a nut would break in with a *dog?* Suppose the Purina Strangler got tired of hunting dog biscuits and came upstairs after her? No matter how scared she was, she wasn't going to lie around waiting for that to happen.

Hannah slipped out of bed as quietly as she could, and crept out into the hallway, her legs nearly buckling with every step. Descending the stairs, she hugged the wall, where every footfall wouldn't creak. At the bottom, she cautiously rounded the newel post and peered through the darkness of the living room to where an odd glow was illuminating the kitchen.

He was standing silhouetted in the open refrigerator's light, a thin boy in a dirty orange parka, his white face stamped with red patches of cold, his sneakers caked with dried mud. Beside him crouched an equally scruffy-looking golden retriever, its nose up in the air, sniffing at the wealth of smells that were wafting from the refrigerator.

The boy must have heard her, because he looked up sharply, wearing an expression that wavered between shock and embarrassment.

"Hi, Chris," she said, trying to sound nonchalant.

"What are you d-doing here?" he stammered.

"I could ask you the same question."

"I thought nobody'd be here. I . . . I was hungry. The back door was unlocked."

She stared at him, wondering how Dad, or even Grace, would have handled this. Chris had to be in some kind of trouble . . . and she'd bet anything that right now Grace was tearing her hair out looking for him. But Hannah had a feeling that grilling Chris would be the wrong way to go.

"Anything look good in there?" Hannah asked, suddenly aware that she was wearing only her flannel pajama top, which came halfway to her knees. But Chris was, well, almost family. She strolled over and peered into the fridge.

Chris shrugged, but she could see his shoulders slump with relief. "Not much," he said. "Some old bread, and a carton of eggs. Some cheese, but I think it might be moldy."

"How about I make us an omelette? You can cut the mold off the cheese, and toast the bread." She leaned down to scratch the dog behind his ear and was rewarded with the thumping of his tail against the kitchen floor. "What's his name?"

"Cody."

"Nice dog."

"He's okay." But there was no mistaking the utter devotion in Chris's eyes.

She was putting out eggs, Tabasco sauce, wire whisk, a bowl with a chipped rim that Ben and she had used for pitch-the-penny, when she felt a light touch against her elbow. She turned, and there was Chris looking at her like a cornered spy in a James Bond movie who's just realized that his life is in the hands of his captor.

"You won't tell, will you, Hannah?"

"Cross my heart, hope to die, stick a needle in my eye."

"You mean it?" He caught his lower lip between his teeth.

"Is there a three-letter word that starts with 'y' and ends with 's'?" What she didn't say was that, with a little urging on her part, she was pretty sure she could get *him* to call home.

Chris started toward her, and for a panicky second Hannah thought he was going to hug her . . . but then she saw he was just reaching for the cheese on the counter behind her.

"Check the cupboard under the sink; there might be a can of dog food in there somewhere," she told him, her back to him while she rummaged around in the spice cabinet for some paprika. "Can opener's in the drawer by the stove. And don't you dare open it anywhere near me, or I'll puke."

"Hannah?" She turned to find him standing at the sink holding a rust-speckled can of Alpo in one hand and a can opener in the other. He looked so pitiful, she really *did* want to hug him.

"What?"

"Thanks for not being a jerk."

"It's not easy, but sometimes I can manage it."

"If my mom found out I'd hitchhiked up here . . ." His voice trailed off.

"Yeah, I know. Mine will skin me alive for taking her car. In the meantime, why don't we both just shut up and eat?"

She waited until after they'd devoured their omelette before saying what was on her mind. "Look, I know it's none of my business, but *shouldn't* you give your mom or dad a call? I'll bet they're pretty worried."

"They'll get over it." A hard look made Chris look suddenly older than thirteen.

"I know how you feel," she sighed.

"You do?"

"Sometimes, around my mom and dad, it's like being in the middle of a war zone. It's mostly my mom—she's always after me for dirt on *your* mom. Maybe that's partly why I gave Grace such a hard time: if she wasn't in Daddy's life, maybe Mom would stop bugging me. Not that she cares about *me,*" she added bitterly.

"I'm sick of being in the middle," Chris told her. Wearing a woeful look, with dots of jelly smeared in both corners of his mouth, he looked about four. "Why can't they just . . . *stop?*"

"Because they're stuck in it, too. They don't always know how to handle it, either." Hannah, surprised at her unexpected insight, quickly added, "It wouldn't hurt just to call. You don't even have to say where you're calling from."

"I don't know. . . ."

Hannah backed off at once. "Suit yourself."

Chris remained silent for a time, shoving a crust of toast around and around his plate to scour up the last bit of omelette.

Finally, in a small voice, he said, "I guess you're right." With a deep sigh, he rose heavily from the ladder-back chair across from where she sat. A minute later, she could hear him speaking over the phone in the next room. "Mom? It's okay, Mom, I'm all right—don't cry. I'm with Hannah, I'm *fine*." He sounded as if he were on the verge of crying himself. "Can we talk about it later? I'm kind of tired right now. . . ." The rest was muffled by a rattling burst from the heating vent.

Hannah was washing up the dirty dishes when she heard Chris, behind her, say, "I told her I was going to spend the night here. Is that okay?"

"Sure," she said lightly, keeping her back turned so he wouldn't see that she was holding her breath, hoping he'd agree to what she was going to say next. "We'll drive back first thing in the morning."

Chris didn't argue.

"It'll sure beat hitchhiking," he said.

Even after stopping for breakfast in Great Barrington, they were back in the city by ten-thirty—but that was late enough for Hannah to escape the immediate wrath of her own mother, who would have long since left for work. Hannah carefully maneuvered past a double-parked van and pulled the Mercedes into a tight spot in front of Grace's building. Switching off the engine, she sighed with relief. No dents, not even a scratch. The only thing Mom would have a fit over was Cody's hair and muddy pawprints all over the back seat.

Beside her, Chris looked apprehensive. "Mom will be mad," he said.

"No, she won't," Grace told him. "The worst she'll do is hug you to death and cry all over you."

In the elevator, going up, Chris turned to her with a

shaky smile and said, "You don't have to do this, you know." But he looked grateful to have her with him.

Hannah didn't tell him she had her own reasons for not just dropping him off at the curb. The person Grace would be mad at, she thought, was *her*. Maybe after she explained . . .

But Hannah could see, the moment they got out of the elevator and Grace's front door was flung open, that she wasn't going to get that chance. Grace appeared, the look of relief on her face so huge it blotted out everything else. With a small cry, she dashed forward and flung her arms around Chris, crushing him to her.

And the amazing thing was that Chris, instead of doing his usual Incredible Shrinking Man act, was hugging her back. With Cody dancing in circles around them, barking with excitement, they looked like one of those Hallmark commercials Hannah usually found sickening. This time, though, she couldn't suppress a smile.

Hovering in the doorway, Hannah could see an older woman who she guessed was Chris's grandmother. She looked tired, too, but her silver hair was neatly brushed and she had on fresh lipstick. When Grace finally let go of Chris, his grandmother stepped forward to give him a brisk, fierce hug.

"You gave your mother and me such a fright," she scolded, but the relief and affection in her voice were unmistakable. "If you weren't so big, I'd take you over my knee and paddle you."

Chris merely looked bewildered. "How come you're here, Nana?"

"Nana was keeping me company," Grace supplied. "Until you called, I wasn't doing too well."

"Someday, when you have children of your own, you'll understand," Chris's grandmother told him with a sigh.

Suddenly, as if Grace had just then she'd noticed her standing there, she turned her brimming eyes to Hannah and said, "Would you like to come in?" She didn't sound mad or upset . . . only grateful.

"No thanks," Hannah muttered. "I should be getting back." Thinking of her own homecoming—which would be nothing like Chris's—she felt a pang. Maybe she'd stop at her father's office on the way. But first she asked, "Is Dad around?"

"No, he's not." The sad way she said it caused Hannah's heart to lurch. It was as if . . . as if *he wasn't ever going to be around.*

It was what Hannah had been hoping for, at times even scheming toward, but now, for some reason, she couldn't remember what it was she'd so disliked about Grace. Or why she'd thought her dad would be so much better off without her.

Chapter 24

Two days later, when Jack finally called, Grace was so glad to hear his voice that she stubbornly ignored its grave tone. He wanted to see her, to talk things over. *It's going to work out,* she told herself, even while she was filled with dread. When he offered to drive Mother to the airport that afternoon, which would give them a chance to talk on the way back, she was quick to accept.

The ride to Newark, however, was tense. While Mother chattered on about Chris, her plans for her garden, the people she had to call about the library, Grace couldn't keep her eyes off Jack. For, even as he smiled and responded to Mother, his eyes were sad and his jaw tight. She felt sad, too, and scared . . . but, in the best Clayborn tradition, Grace kept a bright look on her face while smoothly discussing the details of the trust she was setting up to handle the money for Daddy's library.

Finally, Jack was turning onto the departures ramp, and double-parking at the Delta curb. He unloaded Cordelia's suitcases onto a porter's handtruck, then sweetly, if a bit formally, bent to kiss her cheek. "I'll stay with the car while Grace takes you inside," he told her. Not, *I'm sure I'll see you again soon.*

It was Mother, with a warmth Grace found surprising, who said, "Jack, it's been a pleasure. When Grace and Chris come for a visit, I hope I'll be seeing you as well. You're welcome in my home anytime."

Jack nodded, smiling. Grace could see his Adam's apple

working, but he managed not to let it show in his voice. "Thank you, Cordelia," he told her with a courtliness that was almost Southern. "The pleasure, I assure you, has been all mine."

Inside the bustling terminal, Grace walked Cordelia as far as the security gate, then turned to hug her. Mother, in a pale-pink suit and ivory blouse, smelled of gardenias. Her eyes seemed overbright. Tears—or was Grace only imagining it?

"Goodbye, dear," Cordelia murmured.

"Have a safe trip. Give my love to Sissy."

Grace felt stiff, awkward, as if, despite their rapprochement of sorts, an ocean of unspoken things remained between them. She felt anxious, too, to get back to Jack.

"I'd better hurry," Mother said, glancing at her watch.

"You have more than an hour before your plane," Grace reminded her.

"Yes, I know . . . but I have a phone call to make. It's rather important, and I promised I would call before I left."

Cordelia lowered her gaze, busying herself by withdrawing her ticket from her handbag. Would Grace guess who it was she was in such a hurry to call? she wondered. Perhaps Nola would eventually tell her.

But Nola couldn't know of the agonizing that had led to Cordelia's decision. Or of the late-night call to Gabe, asking his advice. It was Gabe who once again had boiled it all down to the essence of what mattered.

"Suppose you decided against using Nola's design . . . would you be just as happy with another firm's?" he'd asked.

"No . . . no, of course not. None of the other entries even came *close* to what I'd envisioned," she'd been quick to tell him.

"Well, then, doesn't that answer your question? What's

it all been for, Cordelia, all your efforts, if you don't end up with exactly what you want?"

He was right . . . but still she'd hesitated. Even knowing that, with the money she'd be getting from Grace, her library, Gene's library, *would* get built. . . .

I ought to feel angry at Gene, I know. How odd it must seem—even to Grace, who worshipped her father—that I'm so willing to forgive him. There will be those who will think me noble and large-minded because of it . . . and only I will know the truth. . . .

Gabe. *He* was the reason she could be so forgiving toward Gene. A year ago, it might have been different. But Gabe—he was offering her a second chance, and if she didn't learn from the mistakes she'd made with Gene, then what good was any of it?

Grace noted the almost rapturous look on Mother's face, and thought, *It's him—Mr. Ross—that's who she has to call. . . . Probably he's meeting her at the airport in Macon.*

"Well, then . . . I won't keep you," Grace told her.

Mother started to walk ahead, but turned for one last look and said, "Don't let him get away, Grace. Don't you let that man slip between your fingers."

Grace had a swimming sense of déjà vu. Was it Win she meant? She felt the years between now and the last time she and her mother had stood together like this, in an airport, dissolve like the low mist she could see through the bank of windows on either side of her.

But, no, Mother could not have meant Win. Since the other night with Chris, Mother had been noticeably cool toward her former son-in-law. For the past two nights, she'd stayed with Grace.

She's talking about Jack, Grace realized. Mother hadn't changed—she was still trying to run her life, but this time Grace was listening.

"I should be giving you the same advice," Grace said, smiling. "Tell Mr. Ross I said hello."

"You can tell him yourself when you see him," Cordelia said crisply. Her expression softened as she added, "And it's time you stopped calling him 'Mr. Ross.' You're not sixteen anymore. It's *Gabe*."

Leave it to Mother, Grace thought, amused. Managing to turn a touchy subject around as deftly as a seasoned politician. As she waved goodbye, she couldn't help envying the very quality in her mother that she'd once found so frustrating. She only hoped some of it had rubbed off on her— would she be able to turn things around with Jack?

But on the drive home, she and Jack seemed to talk about everything except themselves. They spoke about *Honor Above All,* with bound books due in another month or so, the huge orders they'd gotten from the chains. And her tour, in the throes of being organized by the publicity department. Yesterday, Jack told her, a producer from *Oprah* had thrown Nell Sorensen into an ecstatic frenzy, and the publicist was in the midst of negotiating a date, along with a slew of other Chicago appearances—book signings, radio and TV, even a benefit for a children's charity.

They were approaching the Holland Tunnel when Jack asked, "What about Chris—will he be staying with Win while you're on tour?"

Careful, Grace thought.

"I suppose so," she said, taking a long, shallow breath. "I know what you must think, but Win isn't a bad father. He wasn't a terrible husband, either. Just . . . awfully self-centered."

"How does Chris feel about all this?"

"The three of us sat down last night and talked. I think we sorted things out. I know that Win may have had other ideas . . . but I made it clear both to him and to Chris that we're not ever going to be a family again."

"I'll bet that didn't go over so well with Win." She heard the bitterness in his voice.

"Oh, I don't think it came as a huge surprise, not after the way he used Chris." She kept her eyes on the road, unable to believe she was speaking so calmly with her heart racing ninety miles a minute. "Jack, I want you to know . . . that night with Win . . . it . . ." She'd been on the verge of saying it meant nothing, but that wasn't entirely true. "It wasn't what you think."

Now came the tunnel, swallowing them, filling her ears with the humming of tires. Grace, as she often did, imagined the curved tile walls cracking, rivulets of water from the river above leaking in, slowly at first, then gathering to a thunderous downpour as the entire structure gave way. She shuddered.

Jack's voice, when it came, seemed to hang suspended in the semidarkness. "This isn't just about Win." Beside her, his silhouette flared and receded in the glare of oncoming headlights. "I was hurt, yes, but I'm not blaming you. I know you were upset with me over Hannah . . . and you had every right to be."

He didn't sound angry—only unhappy.

"Where does that leave us?" she asked.

"Sadder . . . but maybe a bit wiser, too." He shook his head. "Grace, I can't help thinking something like this would have happened sooner or later, that it was only a matter of time. Whether it was Win . . . or someone else."

"Someone younger, you mean?" Grace felt as if her seatbelt had grown too tight, and was cutting into her chest. "Jack, don't you get it? *That's* why we're falling apart—not because of Win, or even Hannah. Because you won't see that

I love you for what you are . . . and *part* of what you are is fifteen years older than me."

"There's a lot you don't understand, either," Jack said, his voice rising with emotion. "You expect so much—the moon—and you want it gift-wrapped and delivered overnight express. Of course Hannah is going to resent anyone new in my life! But you take everything she says as a personal rejection."

"How can you *not* take it personally when someone is screaming that they hate you!"

"She's just a kid, Grace."

"Well, I'm not a saint, Jack. I can only take so much."

They were emerging from the tunnel now, the bright winter sunlight stinging her eyes even as she shielded them. Jack took the ramp that circled around onto Hudson, the Volvo bumping over the cobblestones that hadn't yet been paved over in this section of boarded-up warehouses.

His voice, when he finally spoke, was choked. "What's the use, Grace? We can't go on like this. We're only making each other miserable. Is that what you want—for us, and for our kids?"

"Oh, Jack . . ." She covered her face. "I wish this *were* about Win. Then I could ask you to forgive me."

"This isn't about forgiving," he said. "Do you really think that's why you left Win in the first place? Because you couldn't forgive him for cheating on you?"

"I might have forgiven him," she said, "but what I couldn't change was how I felt about him after I found out about Nancy. If you can't trust who you're with, then it all falls apart."

Suddenly, in saying it herself, she understood what Jack had been trying to tell her. Win wasn't the cause of Jack and her coming apart—he was merely the result. They had been heading in this direction for quite some time . . . and now they'd finally come to a stop at a place from which there seemed no turning back. Grace felt a great sorrow smash through her, leaving her weak and trembly.

"Grace, we both need some time . . ." he began, and stopped, his throat working.

Jack remained silent all the way up Eighth Avenue. Then he was turning onto her street, braking expertly to avoid hitting a delivery boy on a bicycle who cut across his lane. Only when he came to a stop in front of her building and unbuckled his seatbelt so he could face her did she see the deep lines etched in his cheeks, which hadn't been there three days ago. She wanted to reach out, run her fingers along those grooves, tell him all the reasons for their staying together, all the things they *did* have in common—his laughing at her jokes and her laughing at his . . . their mutual obsession with visiting every bookstore they happened upon . . . the hours one could spend absorbed in a book or manuscript without the other's feeling left out . . . the pleasure they took in finding little out-of-the-way gems of restaurants. . . .

But not now. Now they needed time to heal.

"Goodbye, Jack," she told him, feeling as if she ought to be stepping on a plane like her mother, to be borne away somewhere far. How could she bear it otherwise? Knowing he was so close—close enough to run into at the office, or at some publishing party, or even at the opera or the ballet.

Even so, she clung to the belief that somehow . . . if they gave themselves some time apart . . . maybe they could find their way back to what had drawn them together in the first place.

Nola was at her desk when the phone rang. She picked it up, expecting it to be Ronnie Chang, barking at her because the plumbing mechanicals he'd asked for weren't quite finished. But a woman's voice floated out at her, firmly correct, softened by a Southern accent.

"I'd like to speak with Nola Emory, if I may."

"Speaking," Nola said, cupping her hand over the receiver, and lowering her voice.

"It's Mrs. Truscott," spoke that formal, lilting voice. "Do you have a moment? Can you talk?"

"Go ahead," Nola told her, praying Randy didn't poke his head over her partition.

"I've thought about what you said, and I . . ." The rest was drowned by a loud droning that sounded like a plane taking off.

"What did you say?" Nola clutched the receiver tightly, her knuckles straining.

"What I said was . . ." Cordelia's voice was coming through again. ". . . I've decided to go ahead with your design. And the wonderful news is, it seems that we'll have the additional funds we need. An unexpected source has come through." She paused. "But there must be no misunderstanding between us. Do you absolutely agree to keep this confidential?"

Nola was on the verge of reminding her that it had been *her* idea in the first place, but she bit her tongue. Anyway, she was too excited to care. Her mind was already racing ahead, imagining the library already built, casting its shadow across the grassy expanse on which it stood.

"I want this as much as you do," Nola told her. "Don't worry, I'm not going to screw it up."

"Well, then . . ." She cleared her throat.

"Thank you," Nola breathed.

"Oh, they've just announced my flight. . . . I have to run."

Nola hung up, feeling dazed. Her mind whirled, like when she'd been staring at a blueprint too long. Was this for real? Had Cordelia Truscott actually agreed to go with her design? And she even had the money for it!

A thing so hugely important—a thing that had been eating at her for weeks, months—and with one brief phone call it was settled. Even with her heart racing, Nola found herself smiling at the irony of it.

Even more ironic was hearing it *now*, after she'd already made up her mind, Cordelia or no, actually to *quit* her job. Crazy? Without a doubt . . . but if she didn't get the decision off her chest, she would go nuts. Nola slipped off her stool, and made her way through the maze of partitioned cubicles. A minute later, she stood outside the open door to Ken Maguire's office.

"Come in," he called distractedly, looking up from a set of blueprints on his desk, held down at each corner by a glass brick.

"I just heard from Cordelia Truscott," she told him. "She's given us the go-ahead. And they're ready for us to start putting together working drawings for construction bids." She kept her voice low, in case anyone happened to be in the corridor. But her excitement was nonetheless coming through, invading her like a strange virus that left her jittery and fluctuating between flashes of hot and cold.

"That's terrific! I honestly didn't think even you could finesse it, Nola. My hat's off."

He stepped around his desk and crossed the carpeted expanse to the door, which he closed. There was nothing exceptional about this sharp-faced man in a corduroy blazer except that he was the fairest boss she'd ever known. She hoped that fairness would work in her favor now.

"Ken, we need to talk."

He smiled, holding up his hands, anticipating her. "All right . . . all right. I know what you're going to say, and no question you're due a raise. Listen, I'll have to speak with

Chang and Foster. On my own, I'm not authorized to . . ."

"I'm not asking for a raise," she told him.

He stopped, a startled expression on his face. "What *do* you want?"

"A severance bonus. Just enough for seed money—rent on a small office of my own, telephone, supplies."

He whistled, taking a step back so that he was leaning against a walnut credenza piled with rolled-up blueprints. "You want to go into business for yourself? Nola, do you have any idea . . ."

"It's not going to be easy, I know," she finished for him. "But, Ken, I have to do this. My designing the Truscott library, it got me to realize that I'm just treading water here." She picked up a glass brick off her desk, weighing it, feeling its cool surface against her palm. "Oh, it's not that you haven't been good to me. But maybe I'm more like my father than I knew—I need something more . . . and I'm not afraid of taking risks."

"We'd hate to lose you, Nola. Look, there's an associateship coming up in a few months; if you're interested, I could put you in for it."

"Thanks, Ken, but, as crazy as it may sound, I'm not going to take you up on that offer."

He shook his head. "These are tough times. Do you know how many *big* firms are falling by the wayside? How can you expect to make it on your own?"

"Maybe because I'm *not* a Goliath," she said softly. "Just one of the little guys, with a slingshot and pocketful of ideas."

Damn if she'd spend the rest of her life just *dreaming* about a better life for herself and her girls.

The Truscott library, it might have seemed like a pipe dream when Cordelia first conceived it, but against every odd the woman had pulled it off.

If she can do it, so can I.

It would hurt, watching from afar while others took the credit for her design . . . but after this, she wouldn't be in anyone's shadow ever again.

Ken, whom she'd expected to be put out, maybe even angry, startled her with a laugh that was both rueful and admiring. "If anyone can do it, Nola, my bet's on you."

"I'll need that bonus we talked about."

"How much?"

She took a deep breath. Maybe if she said it forcefully, without lowering her eyes or in any way looking as if she didn't deserve it, he might not realize what an enormous sum she was asking for.

"Twenty-five," she blurted.

Ken, to his credit, merely lifted an eyebrow. Maybe it wasn't so much after all, not to a firm of this size. Or maybe he was just amused that she'd had the balls to make such an outrageous request.

"Ten," he told her. "That's all I'd be able to squeeze out of Chang and Foster without them kicking up a fuss." Before her sinking heart could reach bottom, he added, "The rest I'll front you. Call it a loan, an investment, a silent partnership, anything you like. I'm not worried I won't get it back. In fact, I'll be expecting a good return."

"Thanks, Ken," she managed to get past lips that had gone numb with gratitude. "You won't be sorry."

They wouldn't really be in competition, either. Any jobs she landed, initially at least, probably wouldn't be big enough for a firm the size of Maguire, Chang & Foster to begrudge her.

"Hey, I'm sorry already. But only that you're leaving." He put out his hand. "Good luck, Nola."

Nola felt as if she were gliding back to her work station on greased runners. But as soon as she'd settled back at her drafting table, she saw the Post-it stuck to the mechanical drawing she'd been working on—a message from Ben. It wasn't the first message he'd left. Her spirits plummeted.

She was tempted. Part of her wanted to forget last week's ugly scene. She sat back, rubbing her temples. But Ben wasn't for her. And she wasn't responsible for him. Anyway, she had more important things to worry about now. . . .

Nola crumpled the message, and tossed it into the wastebasket at her feet. She would miss him in a way—especially at night, when she lay awake, an ache between her legs that wouldn't quit.

A hard man is good to find, she could hear Florene quip.

Nola grinned. Maybe so . . . but she'd do one better. For now, at least, she'd explore what it was like living with Nola Truscott—the woman whose name she had every intention of engraving on the brass plate that was going on the door of her new office.

Grace Truscott to Endow Father's Memorial Library

Grace Truscott, author of the recently published *Honor Above All*, the controversial biography of her late father, Senator Eugene Truscott, yesterday announced that all royalty income due to her from the sale of her book will be donated to the library to be built in her father's memory.

"This book is my memorial to my father," Ms. Truscott said, "and I think it's only natural that one should flow into the other."

Ms. Truscott declined to comment on the "secret" life led by the Senator and his longtime assistant, Margaret Emory, with whom he had an illegitimate daughter, Nola Emory, 36, though it was the publicity surrounding this now well-documented relationship that many industry insiders claim as the main reason for the instant success of *Honor Above All*, which rose to the number one spot on the best-seller list within a week of publication.

The library, to be situated on the campus of Latham University, near Blessing, Georgia, is slated to begin construction in August. Blessing is the hometown of the Senator's widow, Cordelia Clayborn Truscott, who sits on the Latham board, and has been raising funds for the library over the past several years.

"I'm delighted that my husband's memorial will finally see the light of day," said Mrs. Truscott. "During his lifetime, he was dedicated to the education and enlightenment of our nation's youth, and we believe this library will be a reflection of that commitment."

The Truscott Memorial Library Committee, headed by Mrs. Truscott, recently sponsored an architectural design competition. The winning design was submitted by the architectural firm of Maguire, Chang & Foster, of New York City.

"It's fitting that Grace should play a role in this library," said Mrs. Truscott of her daughter's announcement. "My husband accomplished much in his lifetime, but he considered his greatest achievement to be his children."

Chapter 25

"Grace, are you sitting down?" Jerry Schiller's voice boomed out at her from the phone.

"Not exactly," she told him.

She lay on her king-sized bed, on the side closest to the bureau, where Jack used to sleep, and where every morning for the past three and a half months—except the two weeks she'd been away on tour—she had woken to sheets tangled by nothing more than her own restless dreams.

"It's on *every* list." Jerry sounded excited enough for both of them, and Jerry almost *never* got excited. "Number one again next week in the *Times,* number two in the *Washington Post,* and Ingram and both chains. Walden alone is reordering another twenty-five thousand. . . . Grace, are you there?"

I should be over the moon, Grace thought.

But what she felt now was . . . flat. A leaky tire that no amount of air seemed able to fill up.

"I'm here," she said, pulling herself together for her editor's sake. "I thought you didn't get excited about mere commerce, Jerry," she teased him, her chapped lips cracking open in one spot as she smiled.

She tasted blood, salty-sweet. *I ought to get out of bed,* she thought. *Call somebody, celebrate.* But she didn't feel like moving. Usually she was up at the crack of dawn! But lately she'd been sleeping in every morning until eleven or so, as if she had the world's longest hangover.

She heard Jerry's raspy chuckle, which made her think

of Lionel Barrymore's nasty Mr. Potter in *It's a Wonderful Life*. Her elderly editor even looked like Lionel Barrymore, only Jerry was sweet, kind, a bit of a fussbudget.

"*Your* book, my dear Grace, is not mere commerce." He paused, then said, "Oops, I'm being paged. I'll call you later. With more good news, I trust. . . ."

As she hung up, thinking of *Honor Above All*'s success, Grace felt a moment's elation. It *was* wonderful . . . better than she'd ever dreamed. And she felt proud of herself—for not giving up, for writing the book *she* had wanted to write. In every city she'd hit on her tour, she'd been besieged with reporters, requests for additional TV appearances, photographers asking her to smile for one more shot. And at every signing, hundreds lining up . . .

All right, the book is going strong. But what about ME?

Grace sat up, and started to get out of bed. But her head was spinning, as if she really did have a hangover. She had to stop staying up half the night. It wasn't fair to Chris, making him eat breakfast all alone.

Chris. She felt her spirits rise. These days, he seemed more at ease with himself, and with her. And just in the last month or so, seeing him arrive home from school with an occasional friend in tow, she was so happy for him that she didn't mind their vacuuming out the refrigerator with their bottomless appetites.

Yes, Chris was definitely happier. But what about her? Was she ever going to get over Jack?

First you have to stop pretending there's still a chance.

It *was* over, she told herself, hoping that this time she'd believe it. They hadn't seen one another, except at business meetings, and the publication party Cadogan threw for her, for almost four months.

The trouble was, she still loved him. She *missed* him—

his voice calling to her from the next room, his wet tooth-brush next to hers over the bathroom sink, his arms holding her in the night. . . .

Right now, this minute, if Jack were here in bed with her, he'd be hooking one long leg about hers, drawing her close to him, her head nestled in the crook of his arm while he played with her hair, ruffling it and combing it with his fingers until her scalp, her whole body, tingled.

God, if only he *were* here.

Suddenly she was remembering the time they'd stopped at the Carnegie Deli after seeing *Me and My Girl*. They'd been seated at one end of a long table filled with boisterous out-of-towners. It was late, she was tired, all she'd wanted was a cup of tea and to share an order of *rugelah* with Jack. She'd excused herself to the ladies' room, then returned to find Jack translating the menu to the people at the adjacent table, a rapt audience of Rotarians from Minnesota.

Gefilte fish? Well, it's sort of a cold fish dumpling. A little bland but, with a dab of horseradish, really delicious. But, a night like this, you'll want something hot. Try the mushroom-barley soup. . . .

That was Jack. Even late at night, when he was tired, and surrounded by the come-and-go anonymity of New York, he would take time to be nice to a bunch of strangers in a restaurant. . . .

"Mom! Are you up?" Through the fog of self-pity and longing she'd wrapped herself in, Grace heard her son banging on her bedroom door.

She rolled out of bed, and tugged on her terry robe.

"It's open!" she called.

He kept banging.

When she opened the door, she saw *why* he'd been knocking. He was balancing a breakfast tray, containing a plate with fried eggs that looked more like hard-boiled, a piece of slightly blackened toast, a glass of orange juice flecked with bits of pulp.

Her heart turned over, as if in slow motion, one of those *ABC Wide World of Sports* "thrill-of-victory" moments, a diver tumbling over and over in mid-air. She wanted to hug him until he yelped.

"*Definitely* DOA," Chris said, looking down at the tray in disgust. "But I figured, if you were sick, you probably wouldn't notice."

"Hey, buster, what's this about me being sick?" She caught a glimpse of herself in the full-length mirror on the back of her closet door, and thought, *My God, I do look sick*. Puffy-eyed, greasy-haired, pale.

A corner of Chris's mouth twitched. "Either that or you're just lazy. And I *know* that can't be it."

"Speaking of which, why aren't you in school?"

"Staff-development day."

Today was . . . what? It had to be Friday. She'd lost all sense of time.

"In that case, what do you say we hit the town?" She took the tray from him, planting a kiss on his cheek, not caring whether he would try to pull away from her or not. "Hey, my book's still on the list and, come to think of it, we never celebrated. Hamburgers at the Hard Rock . . . or how about bicycling around the park and a sundae at Rumplemeyer's? I hear the Met has this great exhibition of—"

Chris was shaking his head, looking sheepish. "Mom, I can't. Me and some of the guys, we're going out."

"Oh, anywhere in particular?" Her heart did a little flip.

He shrugged. "I don't know yet. The Village, maybe."

Honestly, what could be more normal than a bunch of teenagers without a clue in the world as to what to do with themselves? And now Chris was making friends at school;

he was "one of the guys." Wasn't that reason enough for celebration?

She wasn't certain what had made the change in Chris . . . whether it was just that he was growing up, or if things finally coming to a head with Win and her had taken some of the pressure off him. And kids, they were so self-centered—even though it broke *her* heart, Chris was probably thrilled that Jack was out of her life. Whatever the reason, she couldn't help feeling grateful for getting her son back—even if it meant his spreading his wings and eventually leaving the nest.

"Well, then, another time," she said lightly, carrying the breakfast tray over to the bed, and scooting back against the little hill she'd made of her pillows and mohair spread. "I'd better eat this before it gets cold."

"It's already cold. But it wouldn't have tasted any better hot." Chris shot her a smart-alecky grin.

"Chip off the old block," she told him. "Face it, we're just not cut out for kitchen duty."

"I'll bet Darryl Strawberry couldn't make Jell-O."

For no reason at all, that struck her as hilarious, and she began to giggle. Then Chris was laughing, too, and she saw that the sun, which was shining straight down through her skylight, had formed shimmering pools of reflection on the grease-coated eggs Chris had made for her.

She remembered something her mother had once said: *Raising children, it's like being blind and deaf and having to conduct a symphony.*

Grace thought she knew what her mother meant, but right now she felt as if she were hearing that music. Swelling, ebbing, lyrical, and sweet.

If only Jack were with her, hearing it, too.

She thought about inviting him to lunch, to toast the book's success, which she owed as much to his canny marketing as to the book itself. But, no, chatting about business over a plate of pasta and listening to his hearty congratulations would only make her feel worse.

So this is how it ends, she thought.

Two people who love each other, but who can't live together. Not a symphony after all, but one of those cowboy love songs where hearts are always breaking and people forever disappointing one another.

She ate her eggs and toast, not tasting them, thinking of the day—what was left of it, anyway—that stretched ahead of her like an endless parade without the ticker tape or the cheers . . . and with only herself to march in it.

Chapter 26

Hannah looked at the poster for next week's GET With It rally (*GET* for Green Earth Teens) that she'd been working on practically the whole day. *SAVE OUR PLANET*, it read in twelve-inch script that she'd drawn to look sort of raggedy, as if half eaten away by acid rain and pollution. Between the letters, like a sort of collage, she'd glued origami animals representing endangered species. It was turning out pretty well, she thought. So why didn't she feel any sense of accomplishment?

She stared at the Magic Markers spread over the rugged old kitchen table in the cabin. Almost dinnertime, she realized, glancing at the grease-spotted clock above the ancient stove. Her stomach felt funny, sort of on the verge of a cramp. But she wasn't hungry.

"About done?" Jack had wandered in from the living room, where he'd been building a fire, and now stood looking over her shoulder.

Weekends, when the two of them got up here, first thing he did was make a fire. Then it seemed like he'd spend pretty much all day Saturday and Sunday tending it, poking at embers, rearranging logs, to make them burn brighter, as if the fire could never get him quite warm enough.

The day was more than half over, and Daddy hadn't been outdoors except to bring in more logs from the woodpile.

"Just one more elephant to go." Hannah let her head fall back so it was resting against her father's stomach as he leaned in close to get a better look. "Does that look like an elephant?" She held up her origami creation.

"I thought elephants had tails."

"This one's a mutant. Probably as a result of the destruction of its natural habitat." She was hoping to get a laugh out of him.

But Dad remained silent.

Come to think of it, she couldn't remember the last time he'd let loose with one of his rip-roaring belly laughs. It wasn't like he went around moping, but as if he were mulling over some sticky problem without being able to come up with a solution. She thought of that stupid hamster she'd had as a kid that used to wake her up in the middle of the night going around and around on that wheel of his.

He wasn't talking about it, but Hannah was certain she knew what was bugging him.

Grace.

Why couldn't he tell her? At least just to get it off his chest. Was it because he blamed her, at least partly, for their breaking up?

But what if somehow Dad and Grace got back together?

Aren't you sort of hoping *they will?* a voice inside her asked.

She hated the whole idea—it was repulsive—but deep down, just the tiniest bit, didn't she actually miss Grace?

With her head against Daddy's belly, she could hear it rumbling. Was he hungry? It wasn't yet dinnertime, but he'd eaten only half his sandwich at lunch. And he'd been losing weight. His pants were so baggy, they'd be falling off if his belt weren't holding them up.

What if Daddy got sick, *really* sick, from this? Men his age could have heart attacks.

"I'll start dinner in a minute," she told him, hoping her

concern wasn't showing. "Spaghetti and meatballs, just the way you like them."

"No hurry. Soon as I get the fire going good, I'll give you a hand." He ruffled her hair, and then was lumbering aimlessly about the old pine-floored kitchen, straightening a cookbook that was sticking out unevenly from its shelf, rubbing a smudge of grease with his thumb from the bottom of a copper skillet hanging over the stove.

"Daddy . . ." She wanted to tell him that today was too warm for a fire. But then she thought better of it. "Do you ever wish things had turned out differently?"

"What things?" He was distractedly leafing through a manual for the new coffee maker he'd just bought.

"You *know* what I mean." Hannah fixed him with what she hoped was a commanding look. "You and Grace."

Jack gave a deep sigh. "What made you think of her all of a sudden?"

"Daddy, look at you, you're a wreck! I'm worried about you."

He smiled as if he was touched by her concern, or thought it amusing, one of those cute things kids say that fathers like to repeat to their friends.

"Relax, kiddo, I can take care of myself," he told her. "You've got enough on your plate without taking on my problems."

"So, there *is* a problem!"

"You're getting to sound like a lawyer. Should I start putting away for law school?"

"Daddy, you're just sidestepping the issue. I *know* you miss her. You're like Patrick Swayze in *Ghost*, mooning after Demi Moore without being able to touch her."

He laughed, tossing the manual down on the counter. "Listen, why don't *I* get dinner started and let you finish your poster?"

"In other words, this is none of my beeswax, right?"

"Did we forget to buy pasta?" Now he was rummaging in the cupboard above the toaster.

"Wrong shelf; check the one below. Daddy, you didn't answer me."

"Found it." He waved the package of spaghetti over his head. Hannah couldn't help noticing how shiny his eyes were, and the tiny muscle leaping in his jaw. Then he was standing at the sink with his back to her, cranking on the water, loud as Niagara Falls as it gushed into the big pasta pot . . . almost loud enough to mask the sound of a grown man struggling not to cry.

Hannah felt like crying herself. She felt so sorry for him. And so ashamed of herself.

"Miss Truscott, I'm such a fan of yours! . . . And, oh, would you make that out to Amelia? Happy Birthday to Amelia from Christine . . . and from *you*, of course."

Grace dutifully scribbled the inscription on the title page of her book—one of more than a hundred she'd auto-graphed over the past two hours—ending with "Best Wishes, Grace Truscott." She smiled as she handed it back to the Chanel-suited matron in front of her table. The line at one point had stretched all the way back to the register, but now, thank heavens, it had dwindled to only a dozen or so. She glanced at the antique pendulum clock on the wall of the bookstore. Two-twenty. Only ten or so more minutes to go.

She couldn't wait.

The cramp that had started in her hand now had spread up into her forearm. Her neck hurt from craning up at peo-ple from the dignified but too-low wing chair in which she sat. And the floral arrangement on the Queen Anne–style writing desk in front of her, with its profusion of phlox and stephanotis, was making her eyes itch.

But how she felt was not the point. She had to be *on*—careful to smile, say thank you, ask for correct spellings of names, look as if she recognized that man she didn't know from Adam who'd said, "Remember me? We met at that writers' conference in Phoenix, two years ago. You gave me such wonderful advice about finding an agent. . . ."

Grace could recall when she'd loved doing signings, even when only a handful of people showed up and two of them were her publicist and her editor. It was not so long ago when she'd have felt honored beyond belief to be signing books at stores that were overheated or cramped, where they gave her a pen that leaked ink all over her fingers, and where they had a filthy broom-closet of a bathroom.

But right now she was tired and thirsty and wanted to go home.

She straightened her jacket, a man's checked sport coat, which she wore over a gold silk tunic and slim black slacks (her Catskills-comic look, Lila called it). Would it be okay for tonight as well, Lila's party? No, not dressy enough.

At once, she was reminded of the blind date Lila had lined up for her for this evening, which she'd agreed to in a moment of weakness. It was only a party, Lila had reassured her, just the bunch she liked to hang out with getting to-gether at her place, no pressure, nothing heavy.

Okay, fine; so, then, why did the prospect of washing her hair when she got home seem vastly more appealing than going off to meet some man she didn't even know?

"Would you make that out to Hannah? Hannah Gold."

Grace's head shot up.

At the head of the line, holding out a copy of *Honor Above All*, and looking smartly casual in jeans, and a tapestry vest worn unbuttoned over a denim campshirt, stood Hannah.

So pretty, Grace thought. Hannah's long dark hair was woven into a French braid, nicely framing her face. And those cheekbones—what most women wouldn't give for those!

"Hi, Hannah." She made herself sound casual, as if Hannah's dropping by was an everyday occurrence.

Had Jack sent her? What did she want?

Since the morning that Hannah had brought Chris home, nearly four months ago, Grace hadn't laid eyes on her. Now the only sign of there being a problem was the tiny line marching up Hannah's forehead between her two dark, unplucked brows.

"I read in the paper that you were going to be here," Hannah said as Grace signed her book and handed it back. "Congratulations—I hear it's selling really well."

"I can't complain."

"I could've gotten a copy from Dad . . . but I wanted to see you, and this was the only way I could think of."

"Well, here I am."

"Grace, listen—can we talk?" Hannah dropped her voice, darting a glance at the store's silver-haired proprietress, who stood at her elbow greeting an old customer. "I mean, I can wait until you're done here, if you don't mind me hanging around."

"Okay. I should be done in just a few minutes." She was careful to scour all expectation from her voice.

But as Grace signed the last few books, all she could think of was how much Hannah reminded her of Jack, in the way she was now running her fingertips across the spines of books lining the bookshelf at the front of the store, exactly the way Jack always did when in a bookstore or a library, as if greeting old friends.

It seemed an eternity by the time she was finished and stood chatting with the owner. She remembered to thank the clerks, who'd been so attentive, bringing her Perrier and gently hurrying along the customers who wanted to hang around and shmooze. Finally, she was looking around for Hannah, who was nowhere to be found.

Grace, her gaze sweeping past the rows of mahogany bookshelves, felt strangely let down. And then she caught sight of Hannah, leaning up against a brass-fitted rolling library ladder, reading from a slim volume.

She looked up as Grace wandered over. "I loved this one. My dad published it—it's about this poet in China who gets imprisoned for being anticommunist. It's sort of an allegory." She put the book back, and together they walked outside.

It was mild, too warm even for the sport jacket Grace was wearing. They strolled down Madison Avenue, past chic overpriced boutiques displaying clothes for women who had little else to do but shop. As they were passing a café with tables set out on the sidewalk, Grace said, "It's like the daffodils coming up—you know summer's just around the corner when you see tables on the sidewalk. Are you hungry? I'm starved. You have no idea how much of an appetite you can work up just signing books."

"I guess I could eat something," Hannah mumbled.

Don't do me any favors, Grace felt like snapping. But Hannah, she realized, was, in her own way at least, trying to be nice.

"How's everything?" Grace asked when they were seated. How long, she wondered, before Hannah would mention Jack?

"Okay." Hannah drummed her fingers against the checked tablecloth while she squinted down at a menu she wasn't really reading. "Ben's an asshole, but that's nothing new. He finally told me what happened, that he was the one who finked on me to Daddy about my pregnancy scare. Listen, Grace, I'm sorry if I acted . . . stupid. No, that's not the right word. I was a bitch. I was just looking for an excuse to blame you."

"I won't say it didn't hurt."

"I really *am* sorry."

"I understand."

"You're not mad at me?" Hannah glanced up quickly, then back down again.

"I *was*."

"But not now?"

"I was more angry at the situation than at you. It's not easy playing 'stepmom.' By the time you think you've got the rules figured out, you realize you had it all wrong and have to try and start all over. Sort of like 'Go directly to jail, do not collect two hundred dollars.' "

Hannah smiled—a slow, rueful smile. "Grace, can I ask you something personal?"

"Shoot."

"Are you back with Chris's father?"

"God, no." Grace felt her cheeks burning. Hadn't Jack told her? Or was the subject of Grace off-limits these days?

Hannah shrugged. "Sorry, didn't mean to pry." She became absorbed in peeling the paper off the straw that had come with the iced tea their waiter had just set in front of her. "How's Chris doing? Does he still have that dopey dog?"

Grace nodded. "Chris visits him every other day or so, and on the weekends. His father hired someone to walk Cody when he's not around."

"Sounds like a pretty good compromise."

"It's a toss-up between his dog and his computer, but I'd say Cody has the definite edge."

"I always wanted a dog," Hannah said, "but my mother was afraid it would shed. Do you think Chris would mind if I visited sometime?"

Was she hearing right? "I'm sure he'd love it. Why don't you ask him?"

Hannah nailed her with a hard stare. "I didn't think you'd want me around. I mean, I was really awful."

Grace's heart ached. God, if only she and Hannah could have talked like this *before*.

"How's your father?" Grace said impulsively, hating herself for it the moment the words were out.

"Terrible," Hannah said, folding the paper from her straw into neat accordion squares. "He's miserable all the time, and he's always bitching at everybody over the littlest things. You want to know what I think? I think he misses you, but he won't admit it. And he calls *me* stubborn."

Grace absorbed this wonderful new revelation as if it were a drug she'd just been injected with. All at once she felt giddy—lightheaded, almost—a state of grace was what the nuns in Catechism used to call it. Or maybe, in her case, it was just Grace in a state.

"I miss him, too." Grace sighed. "But maybe it's for the best. We're just so different. And we both have so many other responsibilities. . . ."

"Like me and Chris, right?" Hannah gave a wry smirk. "You know, Grace, I never thought I'd be the one saying this, but I think you and Dad are blowing it. Why should you care so much what Chris and I think of you two? Not," she added, "that I have all that much against you—not these days, anyway."

"What changed your mind?" Grace asked, though she couldn't help feeling she was setting herself up for a fall.

"I don't know. All I know is, he wasn't like this when you were around."

"Well, he ought to be happy about how well the book is selling." *Nice try, Truscott—can't you do any better than that?*

Hannah wasn't falling for it, either. She was giving Grace her best how-lame-can-some-people-be? look. "*You* know what I mean," she said. "Of course he's happy about all that other stuff . . . but you've seen enough corny movies, I'm sure, to know this isn't how it's supposed to end. Jeez, who would pay seven-fifty for *this*?"

Grace started to laugh, and then, with her partially shredded napkin, she was dabbing at her eyes. A peculiar happiness stole through her, not enough to make up for losing Jack, certainly . . . but enough to let her enjoy this particular moment, the warmth of the sun on her shoulders, the delicious coolness of her iced-tea glass against her palm . . . and the company of this funny, frank young woman seated across from her.

"You made it! I was beginning to think you'd copped out on me. Either that, or you met some irresistible hunk on the way over." Lila had to shout to be heard above the din.

"Sorry I'm so late. I had to pick my dress up from the cleaner's, and then Chris showed up and I remembered I hadn't thawed out anything for dinner." Grace had to flatten herself against the vestibule wall to squeeze past the closely packed bodies.

Lila looked even more outrageous than usual. Her spiky platinum hair sprinkled with glitter, and a comet's tail of glitter brushed below each brow. Over her gold lamé leggings, a crushed burgundy velvet top that looked like something Sir Walter Raleigh might have worn . . . and on her feet a pair of red satin Chinese slippers embroidered with dragons. Huge earrings dangled from her ears. The sight of her was like a tonic, Grace thought.

"Anyway, it's a good thing you're not taken, because there's a certain someone here who's *dying* to meet you. . . ." Lila was chattering away, heading into the crush.

Grace felt short of breath, like when she was about to give a speech at a writers' conference. But this time what she had to brace herself against was the possibility that she might actually *like* the guy. If Lila was so high on him, he'd be interesting at the very least. An artist probably. Most likely the lean and intense kind—long on charm, short on cash.

What am I even doing here? I don't want to meet this person. I don't feel like making small talk or pretending I'm interested in someone who'll probably bore me stiff. I want to be home in bed, watching an old tearjerker on TV and crying my eyes out. . . .

But, hey, they say you're supposed to *force* yourself out of the house whether you feel like it or not. Getting back into circulation, she thought, had to be like recuperating from a stroke. You needed to learn all over again how to move your lips, speak correctly, move about like a normal person. It'd been so long since she'd been out with any man but Jack. . . .

Jack.

She stood frozen, looking out over the tiny, packed living room of Lila's East Village walk-up. Screw this. She was going home. Lila would understand. She would tell her the truth, that she needed to . . .

What?

. . . grieve.

Yes, that was it. She *needed* to let herself fall apart—and not just a little bit, but all the way—or how would she ever be able to start putting herself back together?

But before she could take flight, Lila was tugging on her

arm, dragging her into the throng. She felt someone step on her toe, and a wet glass brush against her back, where the low-cut black dress she now regretted choosing left it bare.

Another thing that was wet and cold nudged at her hand, and she looked down to see Lila's gray-muzzled old Lab, Pookey, grinning up at her.

"Hey, Pook, you having a good time?" Grace patted his sleek head.

"You must be Grace."

A warm hand rescued hers from being licked by Pookey's insatiable tongue, and Grace looked up into a pair of friendly brown eyes. He was older than she'd expected, around forty, his short beard tweedy with gray, and his brown hair receding a bit. He looked more Italian than Irish. And not *too* good-looking. Like Al Pacino on a bad day . . . or Danny Aiello on a *good* day.

"How did you know it was me?" she asked.

"Easy. A fellow dog-lover."

Lila stepped in with a laugh, saying, "Here I am, at the tail end, as usual. Grace, this is Kevin. Kevin Feeley."

Grace fought the urge to smile. Even so, she couldn't help thinking, *Feeley? You must be good with your hands.*

Then, feeling embarrassed, awkward, she found herself staring down at the hand that somehow had yet to detach itself from hers. A good hand, wide and thick, but not too blunt. Long fingers. Like Jack's.

Grace drew away, and felt her face growing warm.

"What do you want to drink? No, don't tell me. Club soda with a slice of lemon, right? Bo-ring." She could hear Lila speaking, but the voice sounded faint, as if her friend were at the other end of the room. Out of the corner of her eye, Grace watched Lila, glittering like a tinsel star, edge past her, moving in the direction of the bar.

When she looked back at Kevin Feeley, he was down on

his haunches, scrubbing Pookey's ears while Pookey licked his face. An artist? Probably not. He looked more like a rancher in a Gainesburger commercial, Grace thought. Faded Levi's, scuffed leather boots, a pressed cotton shirt.

"Looks like Lila's got competition," she said. "Pookey seems really attached to you."

"She is. I'm her doctor." He tipped a smile up at her.

"Her *what?*"

"I'm a veterinarian. Didn't Lila tell you?"

"I'm sure she must have, but I probably got it mixed up." But Grace knew Lila all too well. Lila's cockeyed strategy had probably been to get her thinking her blind date was going to be some kind of deadbeat wannabe-sculptor . . . then spring this nice, down-to-earth guy on her.

"I'm allergic." Grace said the first dumb thing that popped into her mind.

"To vets?" His smiled widened.

Now she was really blushing. "I meant dogs. That's why I don't have one. Besides making my eyes water and my nose run, they give me hives." She found herself absently scratching her elbow, and forced herself to stop. "Sometimes even Lila gives me a rash. All that dog hair—everything she wears is covered in it. Her closet ought to be registered with the American Kennel Club."

Kevin laughed. He had a good laugh, she thought—deep and rich without being falsely hearty. "I hope I don't have the same effect on you. Would you like to try dancing with me?"

Grace glanced around. "Here? It's a little crowded, don't you think?"

"We could try the fire escape. It won't be much good for dancing, but it'll be cooler at least."

Grace shrugged, which he clearly interpreted as a yes, because now she was being gently but firmly steered over to the open front window. Climbing up over the sill, she saw that other couples had had the same idea. Lila's friend Vyrle, whose hair was even shorter and wilder than Lila's, huddled with a Hispanic man Grace didn't recognize. And over by the ladder, wasn't that Doug, Grace's head groomer, in a clinch with his boyfriend?

"It's reassuring, isn't it? I think we're the most conventional-looking couple here," Kevin murmured against her hair.

"Why reassuring?"

"I'm used to being the square peg," he told her. "Coming home from the clinic at the end of the day, smelling like something you wouldn't let in your back door, I sometimes wonder if I wouldn't be better off with a desk job."

"What's stopping you?"

"Guess I must be addicted to it. Either that or I'm just plain crazy." He chuckled.

She found herself nodding. "I know what you mean. Writing seems that way to me sometimes. Lately, though, I can't complain."

"Lila told me all about you. But she didn't have to— who *doesn't* know about your book?"

As he chattered on about the good reviews he'd read of *Honor Above All*, she found her thoughts turning to Jack. God, she missed him. He'd have his arm around her now, and would be pulling her in close, making her glow.

"Lila was right."

She became aware that Kevin had spoken. "About what?" Grace struggled to bring him into focus.

"She said you were my type." He gave a self-conscious little smile.

Grace didn't say anything. There was nothing she *could* say. Because, if he'd looked into her face at that moment, this nice, nice man, he'd have seen the tears in her eyes, and he'd wonder why. Oh, this was bad, far worse than what she'd anticipated—one more aspiring artist or actor she could write off in a minute. But here was a man a woman could fall in love with. And that's what hurt—knowing that she couldn't. That it would be a long, long time before she could feel the kind of love she'd known with Jack.

She thought of what Hannah had said this afternoon: *You and Dad are blowing it.*

Well, it wouldn't be the first time. And if tonight was any indication, it wouldn't be the last.

"Do you mind if we go back inside?" she asked. *I'm dying . . . I'm dying out here, wanting you to be Jack. And knowing you never can be,* she wanted to tell him, but all she said was, "I'm a little chilly. And, anyway, I really can't stay. . . ."

Chapter 27

Frankfurt, Germany
October 1992

66 endelssohn Strasse, *dreiundvierzig*," Jack told the driver.

As his taxi pulled away from the airport curb, Jack wondered, as he did every October upon arriving in Frankfurt, about how odd it was that back home he had to ride around in rackety seat-sprung Yellow Cabs, and in Germany, which had *lost* the Big One, the cabbies all drove sleek, immaculate Mercedes.

As he sped along the autobahn, his thoughts turned to tonight's party—Hank Carroll had one every year to fête an author whose book was being published in a lot of languages. And at this one, Hank's centerpiece would be Grace Truscott.

Grace. Jack felt his stomach knot. All that caviar and champagne they'd been shoving at him in first class, which he should have declined.

No, it wasn't all that rich food. It was *her*.

After nine and a half months the need to see her, touch her, was as undiminished, goddamnit, as the eternal flame burning on her father's grave in Arlington Cemetery. He had to stop feeling this way. What was the point?

Jack forced himself to push Grace from his mind. Clothilde Grandy—she was his real business here this year. The septuagenarian had pulled out all the stops with her *roman à clef* about her years as a cabaret singer *cum* Resistance operative in the dissolute atmosphere of Nazi-occupied Paris. And that was *before* she eloped to America with Patton's top aide. The Bertelsmann offer was low, but who could expect the Germans to be keen on a Nazi story? In Italy, though, Rizzoli was still bidding against Mondadori. And now that he'd gotten Clothilde to agree to return to France and do publicity, Hachette and Les Presses de la Cité would probably kill each other for the book, which was going to make for some great fun.

Except, right now, after his long night flight, what he wanted was to get to his *Pension* and climb into bed. He wondered if Frau Strutz had picked up a few more words of English yet . . . or if she'd gotten a little more mellow about the under-sink hot-water heater that her American guests usually forgot to shut off. He considered—as he did every year—the possibility of booking into one of the deluxe hotels, the Intercontinental or the Park. But the Spartan accommodations at Pension Strutz were more than compensated for by its closeness to the fairgrounds, and the price, sixty dollars a night, instead of four hundred.

Besides, despite her carping, he'd probably miss the old lady. And who else would do his laundry overnight, and at no charge? Twenty years, one week every October, he'd been coming to Frau Strutz—longer than he'd been married to Natalie.

Funny, Jack thought, how lately he was always thinking about numbers in terms of weeks, months, years. And now he found himself adding up the time that he'd been apart from Grace. Nine months, two weeks, to be exact.

Hell, I ought to be patting myself on the back. With *Honor Above All* showing sales of over four hundred thousand, hadn't he pulled Cadogan out of deep water and salvaged his own position in the bargain?

But as a lover? A man?

Jack felt a wrenching in his gut, a heat spreading through him.

Knowing he was going to see her, *be* with her—in exactly ten and a half hours—wasn't helping. Tonight he'd need more than a cummerbund and mother-of-pearl studs to keep himself fastened in place.

He'd need a goddamn anesthetic.

Jack gazed out the window at the rectangular high-rises jutting up beyond the flat green farmland skimming past. He wondered about this city before the war. He'd been told how charming it had been back then, before half of it had been bombed to rubble. Well, there were still the cobbled streets of old Sachsenhausen, but that was for tourists mostly—a kind of Disney World for those who like munching on pig's knuckles and guzzling ale in quaint beer halls. On the whole, the Frankfurt he knew was mostly towering glass façades, an unlovely monument to German commerce and human resilience . . . as well as a reminder that what's lost and gone cannot be brought back.

As if he needed reminding. Seeing Grace wherever he turned. On *Oprah,* in *Newsweek* and *People,* at her publishing party, and in D.C. at the ABA. And last week's marketing dog-and-pony show for the forthcoming paperback, with only ten feet of polished red mahogany tabletop separating them . . .

What had happened to his worrying that he was too old for her? A voice at the back of his mind kept nagging: *Is it really too late? What if she feels the same as you?*

You know she doesn't, he told himself, not anymore. Anyway, you were the one who ended it.

The taxi now was cruising along Friedrich-Ebert Anlage. Jack could see the *Messe* on his right—a sprawl of modern white-stone-and-glass buildings, which would soon be teeming with publishers, agents, editors, from more than fifty countries around the world. Book lovers in their roles as businesspeople rushing about to find buyers in Finnish and French, or to acquire rights for their companies, get a jump on the new "hot" books—like Clothilde Grandy's, he hoped. Strung overhead across the avenue were banners trumpeting various books, authors, and publishers, as well as one in German simply welcoming the conventioneers.

Stopping in bumper-to-bumper traffic, he found himself thinking of Benjamin. How much had Ben had to fork over to wangle himself a room at the Parkhotel? The kid had been livid when Jack told him Cadogan wasn't footing the bill. If Pension Strutz was good enough for *him,* Jack had tried to explain, then it was good enough for the troops. For a min-ute, Ben had looked as if he was going to lose it . . . but then he'd backed down, and had agreed to pay for it himself. God knew who he was trying to impress.

He rubbed a hand over his face. Sleep, that's all he needed. A few hours, and he'd be okay, back on track.

His taxi had turned down a residential street, and now it was pulling into the driveway of a slightly rundown stucco, brick-trimmed mansion partially shaded by trees—a late-nineteenth-century building, fortunate to have escaped the Allied bombs, since then chopped up into flats.

After climbing to the third floor, he buzzed and was let in. Frau Strutz, a tall, broad-hipped matron, her gray hair worn in a blunt bob, greeted him with the same military correctness with which she had been welcoming him for the past twenty years. She showed him to his room, with its bay window overlooking the front lawn and sidewalk beyond—large, Spartan, furnished with a double bed, sink, and For-mica armoire. But the bed—ah!—it was covered with a cloud-soft goosedown duvet, and sheets so clean and white and starched-looking they appeared to crackle.

Where was Grace staying? Jack wondered as he peeled

off his rumpled clothes. He'd forgotten to ask Nell Soren-sen, or, more likely, had purposely avoided making it his business.

Like he'd avoided asking around to see if she was dating anyone. He tried to imagine her with another man, drinking coffee at the breakfast table with him each morning—Grace all rumpled and smelling sweetly of the fabric softener she used too much of so the sheets wouldn't wrinkle if she didn't have time to fold them.

But the only thing that was real to him was the inter-minable evenings and weekends when he couldn't see her or touch her. He missed watching her emerge from the shower, wrapped in his robe, its hem trailing across the bedroom carpet. He missed her laugh, they way she lapsed into hic-coughs when he really got her going. He even missed the way she'd nibble off his plate in restaurants. . . .

Enough.

Jack pictured a massive steel door clanging shut. Final, immutable. And that's how he had to be if he was ever going to put Grace behind him.

He drifted asleep in Frau Strutz's brick-hard bed under the crisp duvet, wondering what Grace would be wearing when he saw her, if she'd smell of the Opium he'd bought her on his way home from last year's Frankfurt . . . and whether she'd remember that tomorrow would be nine months, two weeks, and three days since he'd last made love to her.

The Carroll Agency's party was always at the same place —an art gallery in Sossenheim, twenty minutes or so from the heart of Frankfurt. But well worth the drive, Jack thought as he was climbing out of his taxi. Far from the huge, overly ornate hotel banquet rooms where most *Buch-*

messe parties were held, the Luxembourg was a series of rooms, one leading through wide archways into the next—clean, white, bare except for the startlingly modern paintings on the walls and the occasional modernist sculpture.

Jack, handing his coat to the attendant at the door, glanced to his left, where a buffet had been laid out—not the usual heavy German fare, but oysters and clams on a bed of shaved ice, endive leaves arranged like petals on a rose, each with a tiny dollop of sour cream and caviar, some sort of chopped meat rolled up in phyllo leaves, a platter of poached *haricots verts* and wild mushrooms. All of it looking good enough to make him wish he had an appetite.

But his lingering jet lag fled at the sight of Grace. She was standing at the head of a receiving line made up of Hank, Gina Ransome, who handled Carroll's foreign rights, and Douglas Kruger, who was in charge of scouting for foreign publishers. She looked . . . spectacular. She wore a filmy ankle-length sheath in a brilliant pattern of greens and blues, her shoulders bare, a diamond pendant about her slim throat. Diamond studs in her ears. Her hair swept back from her forehead with a black velvet headband.

Jack felt a bubble of insane hope rising in him.

He realized he was shaking someone's hand, a Swedish publisher he'd had lunch with only a month ago, but whose name now slipped his mind.

Then, thank goodness, it came to him.

"Good to see you, Sven, you're looking well. Did you ever settle that problem you were having with your scout?" Somehow the correct words were rolling off his tongue.

The gaunt, bearded Swede nodded, vigorously pumping Jack's hand in both of his. "Ya, I fired him. What is the reason I pay a thousand dollars a month, I tell him, if I hear of these books before you have told me?"

Plump, motherly Francesca Zenterro now was swooping

down on Jack, kissing him on both cheeks. "I shall withhold all future payments to Cadogan until you promise you are taking better care of yourself. Look at you! So thin! Have you been working too hard?" She peered up at him, her brow wrinkled with concern.

"Jet lag," he reassured her with a laugh, though it was true he had lost weight. His tuxedo was almost baggy.

But Francesca, who had the face of Sophia Loren and the body of Roseanne Arnold, darted a glance at Grace and clucked knowingly. "Yes, I know," she said. "Some people, it takes a long time to catch up. Take care of yourself, Jack."

"Nice lady, lousy publisher," Kurt Reinhold muttered in his ear as Francesca was squeezing past them. "She killed Young's last book in Italy. Bad cover, zero publicity. Let's see if we can get someone else for the next one."

Jack bristled, but said nothing. What was there to say? Reinhold simply couldn't stand it that Jack had robbed him of a good reason for firing his ass.

But would that have been so terrible? Lately he was starting to wonder if he might not be better off just retiring to his cabin in the woods. . . .

Jack's gaze fell on Benjamin, elegant in a shawl-collared tux and muted paisley cummerbund. His son, deep in conversation with old Hauptman himself, appeared to be holding the interest of the garrulous gnome, who was peering fixedly up at Ben with those pale-blue eyes that had always made Jack think of a peregrine's. A good sign? Jack hoped so.

He found himself drifting over toward the receiving line, toward Grace. He'd been dreading this. But at the same time, nothing could have kept him from her. Touching her. Speaking with her, even if it was only pleasantries.

Then she was greeting him, her small hand engulfed by his, smiling a smile that he wanted to believe was wistful.

But most likely she was jet-lagged, too, and it was simply one of exhaustion.

"Hello, Jack."

He kissed her cheek lightly, but even that was almost more than he could bear. She *was* wearing his perfume. "I should have said hello before this," he told her. "Forgive me."

Her gaze seemed to challenge him. "Oh, come on, Jack."

Jack thought: *I want to kiss you.*

"Can I get you a drink?" he asked.

"I'd love one . . . anything. I'm parched."

"You look wonderful," he told her. "New dress?"

"New-old. I bought it at an antiques fair. When I went into the bathroom to try it on, guess who was there? Brooke Shields. And you know something? She seemed just as anxious about how she looked as I was. After that, I stopped worrying." She laughed. "It cost a small fortune, but I thought I'd treat myself."

"You deserve it. Grace, I can't tell you how pleased we are. You've done a terrific job . . . and you deserve every bit of your success."

He thought he saw a shadow of something—anger? disappointment?—pass over her face, but then it was gone. She had to be thinking how full of it he was—bullshitting away like a goddamn emcee of a Miss America pageant. What she didn't know was how close he was to losing control. . . .

"Thanks," she said. "I was lucky. We both were."

"Spoken with your mother lately?"

She shrugged, and the light caught her diamond pendant. He stared at the little bird-shaped hollow at the base of her throat, and thought about touching it, lightly pressing his finger to her warm flesh, where he could see a pulse jumping.

"I wish I could say all this stuff about how my father

had brought us together. Let's just say we're working on it. Mother is . . . oh, I don't know, softer. Not so judgmental. I think it might have something to do with this man she's been seeing, but it might just be that she's mellowing. Like telling Sissy she could *not* move back in simply because she's getting divorced. If someone had told me even a year ago that Mother would be keeping Sissy at arm's length, I wouldn't have believed it."

" 'There are more things in heaven and earth, Horatio . . .' "

She cocked her head at him, her smile definitely wistful now. "You've ruined me forever for Shakespeare, you know. I can't see a play or hear someone quoting *Hamlet* without thinking of you."

Jack felt a pain twist up through his chest. But all he could do was stand there wearing what felt like the stupidest of grins. Happiness, he thought, was like trying to ride a Brahma bull—you had to hang on to it until your arms and legs were about to be pulled from their sockets and your heart was bursting. But all those months ago, with Grace, he'd taken the easy way out: he'd let go because his *head* had told him to.

"People tend to take Shakespeare way too seriously, anyway," he said. "Hold on, I'll get you that drink."

He turned away abruptly. What he felt like doing was grabbing her hand, pulling her away from all this, out into the chilly October night, where he could wrap his arms around her. So what was stopping him?

Time, he thought. Too much time had elapsed. There was an awkwardness between them now. And why let himself get hurt all over again?

Yet somehow he was functioning. He brought Grace her drink—soda with a twist of lemon. But now she was surrounded by a bevy of Koreans, and could only nod to him in thanks.

Suddenly Jack found himself whispering in her ear, "Meet me outside in fifteen minutes. There's a little courtyard in back."

He walked away quickly, before she could tell him yes or no. Jesus, what would he say to her? At the same time, he was feeling better than he had all evening.

Maybe . . . just maybe . . .

Back at the bar, he killed time by shmoozing with Herr Hessel, who managed the gallery. But just as he was about to go, Bernhard Hauptman collared him, holding out his hand. Jack managed to look interested while the old man launched into some tale about when his company—now with book clubs and publishing houses in fifteen countries—had gotten its start publishing Westerns written by a German who'd never set foot on American soil, and who thought that buffalo, as recently as the fifties, still roamed the plains.

"We were all of us so full of enthusiasm in those days," the old man went on in his oddly slurred, Manchester-accented English, derived from his British wife. "Too busy to check every detail. Perhaps it was a bad thing . . . but I miss that energy." His sharp eyes fixed on Jack. "Your son has that kind of dynamism. He's very sure of himself."

"He works hard," Jack agreed. But the cold light in Hauptman's watery blue eyes hadn't escaped him. Had Ben been singing his own praises to the old man? Jesus, didn't he know that Hauptman, like Jack himself, was of the old school—work your way up from the bottom, respect your superiors, show some smarts, but be humble where it counted?

"Benjamin has told me of his desire to be the youngest

editor-in-chief in the history of Cadogan. Rather ambitious, don't you think?"

Jack tried not to react. "It's not impossible," he said.

"But have you not recommended him for this position? He left me the impression you had."

He was being set up, that much was obvious. A trap that, if he walked into it, would make Ben look bad. But, damnit, he wasn't going to lie. This time, Ben *had* gone too far.

"You've met Jerry Schiller, haven't you?" Jack hedged. "He's been with the company as long as I have. Right now, I can't imagine anyone else who could do a more effective job as editor-in-chief."

"That's not what Ben tells me."

"What exactly did he say?" Jack asked, no longer attempting to hide his dismay.

"He intimated that perhaps you yourself are not acting in the best interests of Cadogan."

"It sounds like you two had quite a conversation."

"Quite." The old man now was leaning forward, about to impart a secret that Jack wasn't sure he wanted to hear. "Do you know the old fable, Herr Gold, about the man who nurses a viper, only to get bitten? I, too, once had a son such as yours. No, he is not dead—I only speak of him in the past tense. As far as I am concerned, he is no longer my son."

Jack remembered now the rumors a few years back— something about Hauptman's son conspiring to oust his father. Apparently the old boy had been wilier than the young man had counted on.

"Ben may go overboard at times," Jack said, "but he's not out to get anyone, least of all his own father." Remembering his own conversations with Ben, Jack wasn't so sure, but he wasn't admitting that to Hauptman.

"You are his father," Hauptman replied. "You will be the last to see it coming. Believe me, I know. That is why I have saved you from the task of seeing that he is let go. . . . Kurt, I believe, is speaking to him right now."

Jack couldn't breathe for a moment, as if the wind had been knocked out of him. Before he could protest, or even comment, Hauptman turned on his heel and was gone, swallowed up by the crowd.

Christ. He had to find Ben, warn him. At the same time, Jack wanted nothing more than to let Ben get what he had coming.

Navigating his way through the people thronging the main gallery, he scanned the room, trying to spot his son. But no sign of Ben, not even in the WC or the cloakroom. Could Reinhold have taken him outside, where it was quieter?

Jack found the narrow corridor in back with a door at the end that opened onto a tiny brick courtyard. He pushed his way outside, then stopped.

In the center of the quadrangle, a shadowy figure lounged against a sculpture made of wildly juxtaposed Plexiglas cubes held together with what looked like PVC pipe.

"Checking up on me, Dad?"

Ben. He'd been drinking. And from the ghastly whiteness of his face, it was obvious he'd gotten the word from on high, via Reinhold, who was nowhere in sight.

Jack sucked in a breath, and leaned against the doorpost, looking up at the clouds strung like dingy laundry between the flat roofs on either side. A handful of stars shone through, but so faintly he could hardly see them.

"I was looking for you. Seems you've made quite an impression on Herr Hauptman."

"You bet. Only guess what? Turns out he's a lot like

you, he's got a thing against young upstarts who crowd in on the old-boy network." Ben's voice was flat—as if he hadn't yet fully absorbed Reinhold's blow.

"I hate to say it, Ben, but this is one you brought on yourself."

Ben grinned, a flash of white that jumped out from the shadows engulfing his face. "You're so damned predictable, Dad. I always know what you're gonna say. But this time, I don't have to swallow it. Because, as of tonight, *I don't work for you anymore!*"

Jack, feeling a little sick to his stomach, watched his elegant son languidly unfold himself from his seat on that ugly modern sculpture. Ben was losing some of his ashen, shocked look—but in its place was a high, fevered color Jack didn't like.

Ben stepped forward, staggering a bit and grabbing hold of a twisted length of PVC pipe. Jack realized he was more than just pleasantly lit. Kid was flat-out drunk.

"We'll talk about it when you're sober." Jack heard the stern note in his voice, and wished, for once, that he were less civilized—he'd like to pull Ben up by the scruff of his neck and shake some sense into him.

But now Benjamin was swinging around to face him, his arm linked to the crooked pipe as if in some cartoonish parody of a do-si-do, his eyes glittering in the narrow band of light now falling across it. "Get off it, will you, Dad? I'm not your whipping boy anymore."

"Ben, you've already caused enough damage for one night. Don't say anything else you're going to regret."

"The way I look at it, this conversation is way overdue." Ben's voice dropped to a low rasp.

"Maybe, Ben, maybe. But not now." Jack felt as if he'd stepped outside of himself, and was seeing himself through another, more critical pair of eyes—a man who had screwed up as a father, let his children down in some obscure way, and was now paying the price. "You're drunk . . . and you're starting to piss me off. Like I said, we'll talk tomorrow." He started back inside, but Benjamin lunged forward and grabbed hold of his sleeve, jerking him so hard that Jack nearly lost his balance.

"Not tomorrow—*now*." Benjamin's handsome face in the grainy light was a twisted mask.

"Ben, you're acting like a spoiled three-year-old. Now, grow up. I don't need this, and neither do you."

Jack, feeling both sorrow and disgust welling up in him, gazed at his son, swaying on his feet as he straddled the courtyard's old frost-heaved bricks like a punch-drunk boxer who doesn't know when to quit.

"What *I* need," Ben said, "is a father who gives a shit, instead of one who treats me like I'm just the new kid in the mailroom. Come to think of it, that's how I've *always* felt, even when I was a kid—more like your goddamn employee than your son."

"Go back to your hotel, Ben, sleep it off."

He started to turn away, but Ben's swollen eyes narrowed as he caught sight of something, or someone, beyond Jack's shoulder. Jack saw her then, framed in the wedge of pale light slanting from the kitchen doorway.

"Grace," he said softly.

She glanced warily from him to Ben.

He started to walk toward her, but was frozen by a sudden noise behind him. It was Ben—sobbing in harsh, ugly gulps. *His son.* And, in spite of himself, he felt torn.

Jack yearned to go with Grace, to leave Ben to wallow in his misery. But even as he willed himself to move forward, he found his feet remaining firmly planted on the uneven bricks. And now, as if it were the courtyard itself that was slowly rotating, he found himself turning . . . turning back toward the son his head urged him to ignore but his heart could not.

"Jack . . ." he heard her call, but her voice seemed to be coming from a distance, just another voice from the party inside.

Grace stared at Jack in disbelief. She'd heard enough of Ben's nasty accusations to know that Jack didn't need *any* excuse to walk away. Yet he was hesitating. He'd asked her to meet him, gotten her hopes up, and now . . .

Nothing's changed. When push comes to shove, he'll always put his kid's demands—however childish or unwarranted—before me.

Even so, she felt herself lingering, almost afraid to breathe, for fear of crushing what little was left of her hope.

"*Jack,*" she beckoned once again, more urgently this time.

"I can't," he groaned. "Not now."

Jack turned his head to explain, to ask her if he could meet her later at her hotel, but she was gone, vanished like a moth from the lighted doorway.

His gaze was drawn back to his weeping son. Ben moaned, covering his face with his hands, and sinking to his knees.

"Dad, I'm . . . s-sorry." Ben's voice was hollow and muffled, like someone at the bottom of a deep well crying for help. "Please . . . oh, God, please don't hate me. I need you. I need you to . . ."

Jack thought: *I could still go after her. It's probably not too late.*

He hesitated a moment longer, then leaned down and grasped Ben's shoulder, pulling him gently to his feet. In the dingy gray moonlight, his son's face, as it turned up to meet his gaze, was a raw wound.

"Okay, okay . . ." He spoke roughly, his voice seizing in his throat as he crushed his son in his arms. "I'm here, Ben. I'm here."

Chapter 28

Grace, as she took her seat, noted that the first-class compartment was only about a third full. What a relief. If the whole plane was like this, maybe she'd even be able to relax once they were in the air. It probably went against every law of aerodynamics, but to her it was simple—fewer passengers meant less ballast to weight the plane down during takeoff. After that, the only thing capable of holding aloft tons of steel and engine and cargo, she felt sure, was . . . magic.

The same magic that right now was keeping her from falling apart.

I'll be okay, she told herself. *And in an hour or so, I'll be in Paris . . . far enough away from Jack.* Four days of wallowing in Old World luxury at the Lancaster, just off the Champs-Elysées, and she'd get Jack out of her head once and for all.

Yeah, sure—like Ingrid forgot about Bogie in Casablanca.

But it had been *over* for nine months. This new longing was just temporary. Like one of those acid flashbacks she'd heard about from ex-hippies who'd done LSD in the sixties.

She forced herself to count her blessings. Chris, her baby, her son, was really coming into his own. Now that he was president of his computer club, with more than just Petie Scully downstairs to hang out with—kids in and out of the loft at all hours, stomping about in their high-tops like a basketball team in training, leaving their jackets, bookbags,

Walkmans tossed over her furniture—he probably hadn't even noticed that she hadn't called this morning.

And Nola, she had to remember to send her a postcard from Paris. Grace thought about the night before she'd left for Frankfurt, Nola at her loft with Tasha and Dani, helping Chris build a complicated-looking model of a medieval fortress out of popsicle sticks. Then Chris smearing Elmer's glue over his fingers and, when it had dried, sending the girls into squeals of delighted horror with his macabre trick of peeling it off as if it were skin. It still made her smile.

And soon she'd be in Paris, being wined and dined by Hachette, getting interviewed by *Le Figaro* and *Paris Match*. Treating herself each morning to a *grande crème* and a basket of warm brioches and croissants in the Lancaster's intimate, jewellike breakfast room.

"You *will* have a good time in Paris, a *great* time," she hissed to herself between clenched teeth.

Grace looked up, and caught one of the flight attendants eyeing her.

But the stewardess, a blond version of Marlo Thomas in *That Girl,* merely asked, "Ma'am, can I get you something to drink—an orange juice, some champagne?"

Oh, wasn't first class wonderful! They stuffed you with so much food and booze that, even if the plane *did* happen to go down in flames, you probably wouldn't notice.

"Champagne, please," Grace said. Normally she didn't drink on airplanes, but if she didn't do something to numb herself against this perfectly ridiculous and unwarranted misery she couldn't seem to shake, she could see herself bursting into tears somewhere over Luxembourg.

What would Lila do in my place? She'd get up and find an airphone and dial Jack's hotel. Then she'd tell Jack precisely what she thought of him. That any man stupid enough to let her slip through his fingers not once but *twice* deserved to spend the rest of his life deprived of her. She'd . . . Oh, but this was absurd. Lila wasn't the one sitting here. And the thought of having to deal with the unfamiliar German telephone codes, only to end up struggling in her virtually nonexistent German to communicate with whoever answered, felt like far more than she could handle.

She drank her champagne in two long gulps. But it hardly helped.

She thought of the summer before last, her clumsily tripping on a subway grate and breaking her toe. And Jack, up in the country with Hannah, despite Grace's protests, driving all the way back to New York, in the middle of the night, in the pouring rain.

But where was he when she really *needed him?*

"You're a fool, Jack Gold," she muttered. This time the glance that Marlo-the-stewardess shot her was downright suspicious. Grace merely signaled with her empty glass that she was ready for a refill.

But he *had* tried phoning her at her hotel. This morning she'd had a message from the front desk, saying *urgent.* She'd almost caved in and called him . . . but something stopped her. Why start things up again with Jack just when she'd finally begun to adjust to life without him?

Adjust? Is that what you call this?

Grace saw she was clutching the arm rests, and made herself drop her hands to her lap. But her mounting sense of doom wasn't subsiding. She felt like thumbing the call button, summoning help, but for what? And who, really, could comfort her?

Now the engines were roaring to life, and she heard the stewardess, over the PA system, instruct the passengers to fasten their seatbelts.

Grace looked down and saw that hers was already tightly fastened, but she couldn't remember having buckled it.

Come to think of it, she couldn't remember why she had ever thought it would be a good idea to fly to Paris in the first place.

The plane had just begun to pull away from the gate when the throbbing of the engines suddenly died.

Damn, she thought. *Now I'll be stuck here for the next two hours while mechanics tinker with a loose wire in the wing flaps or something.*

Grace glanced out her window, and saw an orange maintenance vehicle speeding toward them across the tarmac. God, it must be some kind of emergency. A bomb threat? Germany was full of terrorists.

She felt a jolt of adrenaline, and sat up straighter, ignoring the cold seatbelt buckle biting into her middle. There, see, she did care—she wasn't ready to cash in her chips. Maybe there was some hope.

She glanced around at the other passengers, who appeared not the least bit concerned. What did they think, that paying three times more for first class automatically protected you from disaster? That, if anything bad happened, only those peons back in coach would suffer?

Only the skinny blond stewardess looked ruffled. No, more as if she were . . . annoyed. Well, at least she wasn't panicking. Usually, they only got annoyed when it was . . .

"Excuse me, but is this seat taken?"

. . . some VIP running behind schedule with enough clout to get the plane to pull back at the very last second.

Grace looked up, startled, but it was a moment before the face that had appeared above her swam into view. Even so, she would have known that voice anywhere.

"Jack!" She clapped a hand over her mouth, then dropped it to her lap and whispered, "You scared the hell out of me. What are you doing here?"

"Same as you. Flying to Paris."

He looked as if he'd run all the way from the *Messe,* his curly graying hair more rumpled than usual and his forehead shiny with sweat. She felt giddy from all the champagne . . . or was it just seeing Jack? Suddenly she didn't care if he'd hijacked the damn plane, she was just so glad he was here.

"But how did you know . . . ?" She stopped before she could make a fool of herself. Was it just a coincidence that they both happened to be going to Paris at the same time?

"I did my homework." He winked.

"But, Jack, how on *earth* did you manage it?"

"Friends in high places. Plus, I can be incredibly pushy." He grinned as he folded his long frame into the seat beside her. "I called your hotel, and they told me you'd checked out. I think it was the concierge who'd noticed from your luggage that you were flying Lufthansa. And by the time I'd gotten Frau Strutz's son-in-law at Lufthansa to comb through the passenger lists on all of today's flights to Paris, I'd almost run out of time to grab this one."

The engines started up again, and the jet picked up speed as they taxied onto the runway. The blond stewardess was smiling her *That Girl* smile as she took Jack's coat, as if trying to figure out whether she'd seen his face on TV or in the newspapers.

"How did you know I was going to Paris?" Grace finished what she'd started to ask a minute ago.

"Just a hunch." He tapped his temple.

"A pretty big one, if you ask me."

"Actually, it was Lila," he confessed. "I called her last night, when I couldn't get through to you. She told me you were going to Paris."

"So you just assumed I wouldn't mind if you tagged along?" She found herself glaring at Jack, anger rising in her.

"*Do* you?" His eyes were no longer blue, they were gray, the color of battleships and barbed wire.

"Stop this, Jack," she said.

Jack kept his eyes on her, burning into her, like those of a lawyer cross-examining a difficult witness.

"You still haven't answered my question."

"I don't have to. If it mattered so much to you, why didn't you follow me last night?" Her anger was growing, and it felt good, canceling out the falsely glinting happiness of a moment ago.

"Grace," he said hoarsely. Just that, her name.

Damnit, if he didn't stop this, she *was* going to cry after all.

"Can't we just let it go?" she asked softly. "Like we've been doing?"

"No," Jack said. "Not unless it's over."

"It *is* over."

"Who says?"

"You did, remember? And I went along." She briefly closed her eyes, struggling for control. "Jack, I think we've both said more than enough. I think it's time to just bury it, go on with our lives." She was saying the words, yes, and they sounded fine, good, brave. But did she mean them?

He twisted himself toward her and grabbed her firmly by the shoulders, and she felt something cascade through her like champagne bubbles—a thousand tiny sparks pricking her insides.

Oh, God, it felt so good to have him holding her. His hands seemed to say that this time, even if she tried, he wasn't letting her slip away.

Yet she found herself struggling to break free.

"Don't," he stopped her, his voice ragged and shaking with emotion, "don't do this. Tell me I'm full of shit, that we'll never learn to trust each other. I'll even buy it if you tell me you can't handle being a stepmother to my kids. But don't say you don't love me—I won't believe it."

"I'm afraid," she whispered.

He gave a thin, crooked smile, and said tenderly, "You, the Fearless Young Woman on the Flying Trapeze?"

"Nothing's changed. Not really."

"Is that what's stopping you? That we were never a perfect match?"

"Oh, Jack. It wouldn't be easy."

"What is?"

"I let you down. You let *me* down."

"And we'll do it again, no doubt."

"Your kids . . ."

"Back to that again, are we?" He smiled.

"Did Hannah tell you she'd come by to see me?"

He shook his head. "No, but I'm not surprised. She asks about you all the time. She's gotten to be a real pest."

"Chris the other day told me that, if you and I ever decided to make up, then Hannah would be his sister, and that would be pretty cool."

"What do you think?" he asked lightly, the way people do when something matters so terribly that to let it show would be unbearable. She was aware of his hands gripping her tighter, and his eyes searching hers for an answer.

But what was the answer? Did she know?

"Jack, are you asking me to marry you?"

She waited, her heart high in her throat. Her body like foam, light, insubstantial, as if it might blow away. *Why isn't he saying anything?*

And then Jack *was* saying something . . . not with words, but with his hands, his whole body. Folding her once more in his arms. Murmuring against her hair, "Yes, damnit . . .

if you'll have me." He drew back, his eyes crinkling. "In fact, I took a chance and booked us the bridal suite at the Bristol."

"You mean we get the honeymoon before the wedding? Somehow, with us, that doesn't surprise me." Grace was grinning, weeping, all at the same time. And now she didn't care one bit who was watching.

"For a man who makes his living from words, I'm not always very good at expressing myself," he told her in a low voice, the voice of a man wonderful as a book you wish would never end. "But one thing I do know how to say. . . . I love you. Grace, I love you so much I'll go out of my mind if I have to spend the rest of my life missing you."

Grace thought that, if the plane were to take a sudden nosedive, she probably wouldn't even notice—she was too far over the moon.

Then she was reaching into her oversized purse, scrabbling blindly amid the little fleamarket jumbled inside—wallet, passport, sunglasses, old business cards, keys, mini-recorder, three Uniball pens, and a snapshot of Jack that she'd forgotten, or more likely purposely neglected, to throw out.

"Grace . . . are you okay?" Jack asked.

The blond stewardess was staring openly now, as if she thought this weeping woman might actually be groping for a gun. Grace looked up to see that the overhead "Fasten Seatbelt" sign was off.

"I'm okay," she told him, clutching her Visa card and the tattered address book she'd been hunting for. "I'll be right back."

New strength flowed into her as she squeezed past Jack and made her way to the airphone at the front of the cabin. *See,* she told herself as she inserted her Visa and began to dial, *it wasn't so hard after all.* But maybe that was because it was the Lancaster she was calling—to cancel her single room overlooking the courtyard.

Afterwards, she felt calmer. She held Jack's hand while Frankfurt's high-rises dwindled to little cubes, and the surrounding green countryside gave way to the neatly stitched patchwork of the Champagne countryside. She wasn't worried anymore about crashing. And if there was enough magic to keep this enormous plane in the air, she thought, then there had to be enough left over for a hundred-and-ten-pound female about to launch herself once again over the precipice.

Cordelia Clayborn Truscott
and the Trustees
of Latham University
cordially invite you to attend
the dedication of the
Eugene Truscott Memorial Library
on
Sunday, June 26, 1994
at
2:00 p.m.
Reception to follow

Chapter 29

From her study on the second floor, Cordelia had a clear view of Gabe on his wooden ladder securing her Crimson Glories to the trellis that arched like a bridal bower over the orchard gate.

He wasn't wearing his khaki hat, and the early-summer sunshine thrusting through the branches of an overhanging tulip tree lay like a friendly arm across the yoke of his blue work shirt. He worked at a steady, unhurried pace, ends of twine and deadheaded blossoms gathering in a little pile at the foot of his ladder.

She saw him snip a long runner curling down like the bottom half of a question mark, and felt as if she were being cut as well.

After Eugene died she had felt utterly empty, a seashell washed ashore. But if she were to lose Gabe, the worst punishment would be knowing that it was her own doing.

Yet what else could she do? Marry him?

Cordelia, seated at her dainty desk with its inlay of tiny birds and sprigs of apple blossom, looked down at the small ivory RSVP card on the blotter in front of her. Eight days, she thought. The library for which she'd badgered half the continent for money, wrangled with steelworkers, stonemasons, plumbers, building inspectors, and over the past eighteen months watched rise from its concrete foundation to become a marvel of stone and glittering glass façades—it was to be dedicated in little more than a week!

But, as excited as she knew she ought to be feeling, what

tugged at her now was the picture in her mind of Gabe's face last night when he'd asked her to be his wife. The faintly ironic light in his tea-brown eyes, the slight crinkling about the corners of his mouth, as if he'd known what her answer would be.

I would be happy with him . . .

. . . for a few years, maybe five or even ten. Then what? She'd be an old lady in her seventies, and Gabe still vital, a man barely past his prime. And Gabe would be trapped, maybe even reduced to wheeling her about, cutting up her food into tiny bits, lifting her into bed at night.

Bed.

The great four-poster in her room, where she and Gabe had lain in the sleepy afternoons that followed mornings of gathering, raking, planting, shearing . . . the bed where he had patiently coaxed her body, like a garden long dormant, into blooming once again.

A slow heat rose in Cordelia. She was remembering Gabe undressing her for the first time, how self-conscious she'd felt at first. Apologizing for her wrinkles, the sagging flesh that would never again be firm, no matter how many sit-ups or leg raises she might force herself to do at the Lucille Roberts salon to which Sissy had dragged her on several occasions. And how Gabe, dear Gabe, had shushed her with a kiss. Not just one kiss, but many—tiny kisses sprinkled all over her face and neck and shoulders and breasts like sweet rain.

"I wish I could be young again . . . for you . . . for this," she'd whispered.

"You're more beautiful now than you've ever been," he'd assured her, smiling as he smoothed her silver hair from her temple with his callused palm. "I wouldn't trade a single wrinkle."

And, oh, how her body had surprised her! Long past

childbearing though it was, no longer the fertile place where a man could plant his seed and watch it grow. But capable still of such richness of feeling, and the courage to go new places, try new things.

But now, seated alone in her study, she wondered how long it would last, the passion, the reveling in one another's bodies. As if a cool breeze had kicked up suddenly and was blowing in through the open window, she shivered. When she was no longer just a bit past middle-aged, but truly aged and feeble, would Gabe still love her?

And what of all the busybodies around town—their looks, wagging tongues, snide remarks? Not that she cared one fig! But Gabe, how would he feel? How many times can a man turn the other cheek?

And Sissy! Cordelia could already hear her carrying on as if she personally had been struck by some awful calamity. And, yes, Cordelia thought, Sissy *would* have to put up with the sniggers and with people whispering that she now had, in addition to two fatherless boys, a mother who was losing her marbles.

Yet Grace, the daughter she'd always felt hadn't understood her one whit, would probably be her staunchest—possibly her *only*—support, were she to marry Gabe. *She* approved of him. She understood that such a marriage would have nothing to do with money to be gained or marbles lost. *She'd understand, too, if I decided not to marry Gabe.* It was Grace who'd written, in a letter she'd sent last year around this time, that marriage for her was more than a partnership of two people. Counting in kids, sisters, brothers, parents, it was like a corporation.

Grace. Cordelia felt the patch of sunshine that was creeping up the faded primrose wallpaper cast its warm glow over her. She found herself awash, too, in memories of Grace's wedding the Christmas before last. She'd flown up for the occasion, knowing only that it was going to be small, but not having been told what else to expect . . . and, oh, how lovely it had been! Even the synagogue Grace and Jack had chosen for the ceremony, a glorious old Lower East Side landmark in the process of being restored, drafty, a bit decrepit, but the perfect setting for her forever-bucking-the-tide older daughter. Even Grace's dress was nothing like what one would have expected—at least not on this continent—a simple, ankle-length sheath of brilliant turquoise with an overlay of whisper-sheer silk, the material for which, Grace later confided, had been purchased in an Indian sari shop on Lexington Avenue.

There had been no bridesmaids, no best man. Just Grace and Jack's children, gathered about them like the bouquet of out-of-season roses Grace clutched. Cordelia smiled, recalling how uncomfortable Chris had seemed in his suit and tie—and yet not entirely displeased by the whole affair. Jack's daughter, Hannah, in a dark-green velvet dress, with all that marvelous hair piled atop her head, had made Cordelia think of a girl straight out of an E. M. Forster novel. And that son of Jack's—he'd looked handsome enough to be the groom himself, except for the fact that he wasn't smiling. Hadn't Grace told her that Ben was the troubled one of Jack's two children? Something about Ben seeing a therapist, and Jack accompanying him fairly often to his appointments. Yet it had been clear from the tender way Jack had clasped his children about him at the end of the ceremony—after kissing Grace—that he loved them both dearly.

At the small reception afterwards in Grace's loft, the handful of guests had gathered to watch Grace and Jack dance the first dance. And then Jack, as the jazz duo launched into "Tennessee Waltz," had scooped Hannah into his arms. Seeing them together, father and daughter—Hannah, at one point, laughingly kicking off her patent leather pumps and delicately planting her stockinged feet atop Jack's as he whirled her across the floor—had brought tears to Cordelia's eyes. If only Gene could have lived to see this! Grace, so entranced with her new husband, embraced by his family. It would have made him happy, too, to see Nola, looking as if she belonged there, chatting comfortably with Grace's friends and moving about the loft with the ease of a frequent visitor. Though Cordelia, still not quite sure how to act around Nola, had kept her distance, she had often found her gaze drawn to the sight of Nola and Grace, standing together, quietly talking or laughing over some shared joke. *Like sisters,* Cordelia had thought, with a twinge of pain, regretting that Sissy, her nose out of joint, had declined Grace's invitation.

Cordelia, caught up in the whirlwind of the library's construction, had not seen Grace since her visit to New York. Now, with the dedication ceremony little more than a week away, Grace, with her family, would be coming to stay— her first visit to Blessing in nearly four years.

She'd had Netta get Grace's old room ready and make up the fold-out bed in the rumpus room for Chris. Hannah could sleep in Sissy's room, which would probably rankle Sissy, who still nurtured a slight grudge over having been "turned out into the cold," as she called her mother's refusal to let her move back in. Oh well. Cordelia gave in to a tiny smile, thinking that it was high time Sissy realized the entire universe did not revolve around her.

Besides, Sissy would get over it. Look how she'd progressed since her divorce—taking that paying job as a teacher's assistant at the elementary school, and now running a remedial-reading program for its poor, mostly black students. Eugene, she thought, would have been proud. And Sissy had lost at least ten pounds. It was a start.

Cordelia, glancing out the window again, saw that Gabe

and the ladder were gone; only a neatly contained pile of clippings on the grass marked his having been there. It struck her then that she hadn't yet received Gabe's RSVP. Had he actually told her whether he was coming . . . or had she merely assumed he was?

But after she'd told him she couldn't marry him, would he still want to come?

A lump formed in her throat, and she seemed to be hearing a rustling noise in her ears that made her think of the little sachet bags full of dried lilac and rose petals tucked in each of her dresser drawers . . . only this one was made up of whispers. Voices whispering all the reasons why she *should* go ahead and marry Gabe . . .

He loves you. You love him.

Think of Gene, how short a time you had together. There are no guarantees, not ever. Live for the moment. That's all you or anyone really has. Think of what you'd be losing. . . .

Stop being sensible—follow your heart for a change.

Then, once again, she was seeing the stares and cold shoulders she and Gabe would have to endure at Shady Hill, where her family had belonged forever. She thought of Lucinda Parmenter dropping by the other day to pick up the begonias Cordelia was donating to the Garden Club's annual sale, and how the old biddy had nearly fainted at the sight of Gabe, at eight in the evening, seated at her kitchen table in his shirtsleeves drinking a beer.

"A word to the wise," she'd whispered to Cordelia on her way out. "I know you've always gone your own way, my dear. But remember that not everyone will be as broadminded as I am about your . . . friend."

No, it would never work. It was time she started giving herself a good sharp dose of reality.

Cordelia pushed her chair back on the worn Aubusson carpet, and stood so abruptly that a swarm of tiny fireflies flitted at the corners of her field of vision. She remembered that she had skipped breakfast, and thought, *I must eat something.* Perhaps Netta still had some of last night's chicken in the icebox, and those tasty ham biscuits. Oh, and there was that lovely tart she'd made from the rhubarb springing up everywhere in the grassy borders around her kitchen garden.

A picnic, that was it. She'd break it to him then.

Downstairs, she packed a hamper, and went off in search of Gabe.

She found him in back, by the toolshed, cleaning and oiling his shears and pruning saw while arguing good-naturedly with Hollis about the benefits of manure over chemical lawn fertilizers. The tips of his ears were sun-burned, she saw, and the beaked bridge of his nose. Who would have thought it would be so blazingly hot this early in the summer? In her light cotton blouse and gabardine slacks she felt much too warm all of a sudden.

"I packed us a lunch," she said, holding up the hamper. "Let's eat out in the gazebo, where it's cooler."

Gabe looked up from wiping his saw blade with a chamois rag to cast her a brief, questioning glance. But then there was only his slow, sweet, and somehow knowing smile, and the thoughtful way in which he nodded. She watched as he washed his hands under the garden hose with a sliver of soap he kept on the little stone ledge above the faucet. With droplets of water still sparkling on his reddened knuckles, he took the hamper from her, and they started down the gravel path that wandered past the newly planted vegetable garden with its rows of seedlings, past the strawberry patch and a low fence against which grew clusters of nodding hollyhocks and foxglove and delphinium.

Stopping at the white lattice gazebo, Cordelia felt a sharp pang at the thought of what she had to tell him.

Oh, if only he didn't make it so hard! She saw that he'd cleaned the dust and dead leaves off the gazebo's benches, and swept the spiderwebs from its latticework. As if he'd known she'd want to come here today.

She felt her heart fill with anguish. She was destined to go on loving a man who could never wholly be a part of her world . . . a man both intelligent and kind, who thought of little things, like spreading one of the checked napkins she'd brought over the wooden bench for her to sit on.

"You did a nice job." She pointed up at the weeping willow he'd pruned earlier this spring, noting how he'd managed to tame it without sacrificing any of its natural sweep.

Gabe nodded, and took the drumstick she offered him. "I patched it so it wouldn't bleed." She saw how the sun slanting through the lattice had cast a net of brilliant diamonds over the scuffed toes of his work boots.

Cordelia felt nearly sick with what she knew she must say. Had he already guessed? He *must* have, she thought. His words, seeming to mean more than what he was actually saying, were cutting into her, reminding her that, even if she couldn't marry him, there was no going back to the way things had been before.

"I remember when we moved back here, the girls and I, after Gene . . . well, when Mother needed looking after. Grace was almost fourteen, and hadn't yet discovered boys. She used to spend all her time down there scooping up tadpoles and God knows what else. I swear, she had a permanent ring around her ankles from wading in that filthy water."

"You must feel nervous about her coming back after all this time."

Funny. Anyone else would have assumed she'd be looking *forward* to Grace's visit, or maybe even *dreading* it, but Gabe knew her too well.

"Why, yes." She smiled at him, noticing the pale squint lines at the corners of his eyes. "I *am* a bit. It's true she invited me to her wedding, but I don't think she's altogether forgiven me for being her mother."

"And you don't know that you've quite forgiven her for not being the daughter you wanted?"

"Perhaps. But I'm learning that not everything ought to bend to my way of thinking. Heavens, look at Sissy! She's always gone along with me—except for marrying that dreadful Beech—and look where it's gotten her."

"She'll come around. What you're doing for her now is the greatest gift any parent can give her grown child."

Gift? Sissy had done nothing but whine and complain! Why, half the folks in Blessing were probably saying she'd pulled the rug right out from under Sissy's feet.

"Gabe, I don't know what you're talking about," she said, somewhat peeved. "I've done absolutely *nothing* for that child since Beech moved out except listen to her carry on."

"Yes, but you're letting her find out on her own what she needs to do. You're letting her grow up."

Cordelia hadn't thought of it that way, but all at once she felt as if she'd been granted some kind of reprieve, and along with it a whole new perspective.

"Well, maybe I've done a little growing up myself," she admitted. "A little odd for a woman my age . . . but I'm finding out that things I would never have believed could happen have a way of happening anyway."

"You mean Nola?"

"Partly, yes. All that dreadful publicity when Grace's book came out. But now . . . it's like some kind of miracle, seeing the library she designed all built, big as life. Almost as if it were Eugene himself who . . ." She stopped.

Gabe simply nodded, letting her know she didn't need to finish the sentence. He understood.

"She sent me a note along with her RSVP," Cordelia told him. "She'll be at the dedication, but she asked if she could stop by sometime beforehand. I invited her for tea."

Gabe raised an eyebrow, but said nothing. She was pleased to see that she was capable of surprising him.

The truth was that her invitation had surprised Cordelia, too. She still had such mixed feelings about Nola Emory! Mostly, she wished that the young woman would simply turn out to be a bad dream, that one day Cordelia would wake up and Nola would no longer exist.

Then why had she invited her? Good manners? No. More than anyone else, Nola Emory had a right to be there on the day Eugene's—and her—library was dedicated.

Gabe looked up at the branches curving over them and remarked, "God's cathedral. We cut and prune, but, in the end, we can never really lay claim to any of it, can we?"

"You and Gene would have been great friends," she told him. She'd always known it, of course, but she seldom spoke of Eugene to Gabe, especially not in any way that might sound as if she were comparing them.

"I'm sure we would have," Gabe replied mildly.

Cordelia fell silent, watching a cardinal stitch its way among the branches searching for twigs for its nest. She felt completely at ease, yet at the same time pressingly aware of what she had to say. "Did I tell you? The Governor will be coming," she said brightly, wanting desperately to postpone the inevitable. "He's promised us some sort of speech, though I swear, if he says one word about that new highway he's trying to railroad through here, I will personally see to it that he is tarred and feathered and run out of town on a rail."

Gabe chuckled, wiping his chin with his napkin. "I know you, Cordelia. The most you'll do is seat him next to that woman who heads the Green Belt Berets."

"Wilmadene Klempner? Mercy, she's enough to make him *wish* he'd been tarred and feathered instead." She smiled as she nibbled at a cold ham biscuit. "But that's not a bad idea. . . . I wonder if I ought to invite her? It'd be worth it, almost, just to see the look on Lottie Parker's face."

"Just like the look she'd give you if you were to show up with me on your arm?" There was a subtle challenge behind the lightness of Gabe's tone, and Cordelia felt herself grow very still. The sun weaving through the latticework seemed suddenly to imprison her, a cage made of light and shadow.

"Gabe . . ."

He put a hand over hers, gentle and at the same time urgent. "I know what you're going to say, Cordelia. I see it in your face. All I'm asking is that you give it some more thought, don't give me your answer right this minute. I can wait." He smiled, and she was nearly shattered by the glimmering of half-formed tears in his eyes. "Patience is the art of hoping, a wise man once said."

Cordelia felt that she herself might die if she hurt him, but then the words were spilling out of her: "Gabe, I love you, but I don't think I can marry you."

"There's a difference between thinking something and knowing it absolutely."

"I'd only make you unhappy."

"Are you sure it's my happiness you're concerned with, Cordelia?" A slight chill stole into his voice.

"I'm not young anymore. And you . . ."

"I don't see growing old as a handicap," he said. "For either one of us." He smiled. " 'Grow old along with me! The best is yet to be.' "

"Oh, Gabe, quoting Browning won't help when you're looking after a doddering old lady. You *know* what I mean."

"Yes, I think I do." Carefully, he wrapped his chicken bone in a paper napkin and replaced it in the basket. When he looked at her, his face was full of sorrow.

She placed a hand on his arm, wishing with all her heart that its weathered strength, those sturdy bones standing out in relief on the back of his wrist, the faint tracing of sun-bleached hair along his forearm, all could be hers forever and ever to be comforted by.

At that moment, Gabe pulled her into his arms, and kissed her. His mouth tender, seeking. Enveloping her with his smell—that of green things and new beginnings. She wanted more than anything for his kiss to go on and on, for his arms never to let go of her.

But, in the darkest chamber of her heart, she couldn't keep from wondering if their love, like a fragile flower protected by tall hedges, would survive if exposed to the harsh elements.

You're a fool, Cordelia Truscott, whispered the voice she now recognized as that of the young and idealistic ingenue whom Eugene, on a trip home to Blessing to announce their engagement, had once made love to in this very same gazebo, under a moon made for fools.

Gabe, drawing back and pressing a finger lightly to her mouth, shook his head, as if to silence whatever she'd been about to say. Right now, she wasn't sure what that was, because her heart was thundering so in her ears that it had shaken all her thoughts loose, and made her wonder if maybe she *was* losing her marbles.

"Wait," he said. "A few days, a few weeks. Will you give us that much?"

It was the "us" that decided her. How could she say no to a man who understood that—if she said goodbye—she would be hurting herself as much as, maybe even more than, him?

Nola had had to change planes in Charlotte, with a twenty-minute layover that had stretched to an hour and a half. On the flight to Macon, she'd picked up a copy of *U.S.A. Today,* which featured a half-page photo of the newly completed Truscott Library. As she scanned the article below it, a paragraph about Maguire, Chang & Foster had jumped out at her.

I should have been the one getting credit, she thought now as she followed the airport exit signs in her rented Blazer. *It's my name that should have been in that article, and on the brass plaque beside the entrance.*

But then she reminded herself that, if her name had been there, the library would never have gotten built. And it was still *her* design, even if only a few people knew it.

Anyway, it had all worked out. Her ten-thousand-dollar severance bonus, plus the fifteen Ken Maguire had invested, had set her up nicely in a small office at Thirty-ninth and Eighth.

Now, after more than two years, it was still hand-to-mouth. But things were picking up. Just in the last month, she'd landed a commission for a drive-through bank in Greenwich, and two apartment renovations. And she'd also been joined by her old rival, Randy Craig, who'd gotten them a strip mall in Ridgefield, and an elegant shingle-style vacation home out in East Hampton.

So why was she *here* instead of back home in New York, buried in vellum and eraser shavings, where she belonged?

I have to see it, just once. Even if I'm the only one at that damn ceremony besides Cordelia Truscott who knows. . . .

Now, as she sped east along Interstate 16, Nola felt sure she was on a fool's mission. What had she been hoping to find when she got to Cordelia's? A red-carpet welcome?

The woman, after all, had kept her end of the bargain. Never breathing a word, and at the same time watching over the library—according to Ken Maguire—like a mother lioness while it was under construction, making sure no corners were cut, no aspect of the original design sacrificed for the sake of economy or simplification.

So what more could she expect?

The dotting of the "i"? The crossing of the "t"?

She'd told Cordelia she ought to be arriving around five, and already she was late, with more than an hour's drive ahead of her. By the time she got there, Cordelia would be ready for supper, not tea. Should she stop somewhere and call?

Nola decided to keep on driving. Either Cordelia would want to see her anyway, or her lateness would provide a convenient excuse to back out.

A slide show of cow pastures and Burger Kings whisked by, one forgettable image blurring into the next. What stuck out in Nola's mind was how hot it was. Even with the air-conditioner on MAX, she was burning up. She'd forgotten how unbearable the South could get in summer—hot enough to grill hamburgers on the hood of your car. Kudzu weather, a friend of hers used to call it, because at night, when it was quiet, you'd swear you could hear the kudzu growing.

Nola reached Blessing shortly before sunset, when the shadows that had been hiding out from the heat had begun to creep out from under houses and parked cars and the huge old copper beeches lining Ambrose Avenue.

She turned down Main Street, braking to let an old spotted hound amble across the intersection. Even though she no longer needed them for the glare, Nola had left her sunglasses on. She didn't want to have to look too closely at all the changes that had taken place since she'd been down here last. How long had that been? The year she graduated from U. Mass., she recalled. She'd been visiting her friend Alice Blackburn in Atlanta, and on a whim had taken a bus to Blessing to see the house where her father's widow lived.

Now, almost twenty years later, she saw that the pleasantly nondescript nineteenth-century brick commercial buildings had been torn down and replaced with smart-looking shops and low-rise office buildings. Even the neoclassical courthouse, though still standing, had been split up into shops, geraniums spilling over its upper veranda, and large painted wooden signs hanging between the paired columns with names like "Mad Platters Record Shoppe," "A Stitch in Time," and "Late Great Antiques."

Several of the large old houses had "No Vacancy" signs in front. The bed-and-breakfast business, it appeared, was booming in Blessing. Nola's gaze took in some kids cruising by in a white convertible, smartly dressed ladies clutching shopping bags with store logos on them, and men in business suits climbing into their Lexuses and BMWs. Only a few black faces, here and there.

Tracing the route she'd marked off on her map, Nola turned off Main Street onto Coolidge, then took the first fork. As she wound her way up Fox Run Hill, with its grand old white elephants and golf-link-sized lawns shaded by sixty-foot trees, she thought how eerie it was that the passage of time appeared to have had almost *no* effect on this neighborhood—almost as if a bell jar had been placed over it. Gracious Greek Revivals, their Doric columns gleaming like pale sentinels in the twilight. A handsome mansard-roofed Second Empire dozing benignly beneath a pair of spreading oaks, while a fleet of automatic sprinklers cast a jeweled net over the green baize lawn.

She spotted a stone house that resembled a fortress, with a prominent "No Trespassing" sign strung across the entrance to the drive between a pair of cast-iron jockeys. *One concession to the nineties,* Nola thought. Back in the old days, the jockeys' faces would have been black. Now they were painted white.

The Truscott house was the last one on the left, at the crest of the hill, a really fine example of Queen Anne with a huge wraparound porch and a fishscale-shingled turret ringed with windows from which the reflected sun now glowed like precious rubies. Exactly as she remembered it.

What would it be like inside? she wondered.

Nola, her throat so dry she could have swallowed a spoonful of dust and not have noticed, parked the Blazer at the curb and climbed out into the soupy heat. She was immediately drenched with sweat, and as she made her way up the circular drive, she had the distinct impression of swimming—no, not swimming, more like dogpaddling—down a mossy, leaf-strewn stream. She could hear the faint tinkling of a piano—Chopin's Nocturne in F Major, it sounded like.

Crossing the porch, as long and as deep as a country lane, its twilit shade heavy with the sweetness of the honeysuckle climbing up over the spindled railing. Now the doorbell—the old white porcelain kind. She pushed on it, heard its trilling deep within, and thought: *I don't belong here.* She should have called from the airport when her plane got in so late, made her apologies then.

The porch light snapped on, and a heavyset black woman appeared at the door wearing a flowered dress and thick-soled shoes. She peered suspiciously at Nola, but before she could shoo her away, a pinkish blur flickered in the wavy glass of the sidelight, and a light voice called, "Why, it's Nola Emory. I'd about given up on you."

"My plane was delayed," she apologized. "Am I too late?"

"No, of course not. Come in. I'll have Netta put some hot water on for tea. Unless you'd rather have a glass of sherry? Or perhaps some of my . . . Gabriel's homemade dandelion wine?"

Oh so civilized. As if she were a cherished guest, a beloved friend dropping in for a long-overdue visit.

Mrs. Truscott even looked the perfect hostess, wearing a pastel-print dress with a softly ruffled neckline, her hair glowing like polished heirloom silver. Her nails painted a pretty coral pink. A pair of cobalt eyes that studied her intently without seeming to stare.

"Dandelion wine? That would be nice," Nola found herself saying as she was ushered inside.

"Why don't we step into the parlor? It's a bit cooler in there. I'm afraid this old air-conditioning of mine is on its last legs. But I just hate the thought of them coming in here and ripping things apart. It's amazing, don't you think, what one can put up with when one has to."

Cordelia, walking ahead of her, prattled on without seeming to address anyone in particular, as if she were a docent leading a museum tour.

"Amazing," Nola echoed.

She looked about her at the ornate marble fireplace carved with rosettes and the gilded mirror above it, at the heavy mauve drapes and the oil paintings of ancestors on the walls. A Steinway. Did she play, too?

Nola sank onto a wide, claw-footed ottoman, its old bottle-green velvet worn smooth as glass. "You get a picture in your head of how something is going to look, and mostly you're disappointed," she said, gazing up at the Waterford chandelier twinkling overhead like a far-off galaxy glimpsed through a telescope. "But this . . . it's just as I imagined it."

She brought her gaze back to Cordelia, now seated on the edge of a rather large and imposing Eastlake sofa, her legs crossed demurely at the ankles. "It's lovely."

"I'm glad you've come." Cordelia spoke softly, almost dreamily, though her eyes remained fixed on Nola with a sharpness that was making her nervous. "The library . . . it's as beautiful as we both knew it would be."

Nola felt herself warming, as if under a gentle sun, before she remembered that she'd been mostly shut out of her daddy's life . . . and now she was going to be robbed of the credit she was due as well.

My choice, she reminded herself as the cold began once again rising in her like bitter sap. *I can't hold that against Cordelia.*

She was, and always would be, her father's bastard daughter. Oh, damn, why *had* she come? What had she expected? Surely not the warm friendship that had come to her from Grace.

Maybe, in the end, all she'd wanted was an answer to the question that had haunted her all her life: *Why, Daddy? Why* this *woman, and not Mama?*

Nola's thoughts were interrupted by Netta bearing a heavy, embossed silver tray with two slender cordial glasses as delicate as spun sugar, and a green bottle bearing no label.

"I'll pour, Netta," Cordelia told her. "You go on, now —I can take care of dinner, too. I want you to go put a nice cold pack on that shoulder of yours. Gabe says it's the best thing for bursitis. He's got some sort of herbal potion he wants you to try. He's bringing it by tomorrow."

Netta rolled her eyes, but she was smiling.

"Fancy that," the old housekeeper said, as if she were used to this Gabe person, whoever he was, playing medicine man.

When they were alone again, Cordelia poured some of

the pale amber-colored wine into each glass. "He makes it himself, you know. Not just dandelion. Raspberry, elderberry, apple, pear. You should see his basement—over the years, it's become a regular wine cellar."

Nola sipped her wine. Delicious. Like something out of a fairy tale, ambrosial, magical, making her suddenly lighter, as if her whole body had lifted, and was hovering over the ottoman.

"I almost feel like I'm in *Arsenic and Old Lace*," she said, her voice seeming to come from far away. "You know, where these dotty old ladies lure their victims into the parlor with a poisoned glass of elderberry wine, then bury them in the cellar."

Cordelia laughed, a soft silvery tinkle. "It's not poisoned, I assure you."

"I know." Nola, sobering, stared at her. "I guess, to you, I'm already kind of dead and buried. I mean, now that the publicity from Grace's book is pretty much over with, and the library built, you won't have to worry anymore that I'm going to disrupt your life."

The words, honest and plain, seemed to come flying out of nowhere, like wasps from a nest accidentally disturbed.

Cordelia's mouth tightened. "I don't see any point in—"

"Please, can't we at least be honest with each other?" She kept her tone even, but Cordelia could not have missed the tension that had risen suddenly between them. "All this talk about the library, my precious design . . . but I *know* you've got to resent the hell out of me. Why else would you have gone on keeping my name from ever being even remotely connected with it?"

"If I remember correctly, it was *you* who suggested we keep it a secret," Cordelia replied tartly.

"That was back when it mattered—when my saying something might have stopped it from getting built."

"Are you saying you're planning to go back on our bargain now?" Cordelia sounded alarmed.

"No." Nola herself grew slack, her sudden burst of anger dissolving. "You kept your end . . . so I'll keep mine. I didn't come here to stir up trouble, believe me."

"You haven't done so badly, from what I hear." Cordelia's eyes seemed to grow sharper, and even more blue, like sapphires against a background of velvet. "Your new business is going well?"

"Well enough so I can start sending my girls to a good school in the fall." She straightened a bit, feeling better now. "I designed a new annex for Broadwell, and they gave me a break on the tuition."

"Your idea to barter . . . or theirs?"

Nola smiled. "I sort of nudged them in that direction."

"I can imagine." The diminutive woman seated before her gave a tinkling laugh. "You remind me of . . ." She stopped.

Now there was only the muffled, dignified ticking of a pendulum clock deep in the house, and the subdued whirring of the elderly air-conditioner. The music she'd heard earlier started up again, Schubert this time. Had Netta left a radio on?

Finally, Cordelia broke the silence.

"I have a picture Eugene took of a museum outside of Copenhagen that we visited the last time we were in Europe—he said, if he ever built his dream house, it would look like that." Cordelia wasn't looking at Nola, but at some point on the wall above her head. Her eyes seemed to glisten, but maybe that was only the light from the chandelier shining on her delicate-boned face.

"The Museum of Modern Art at Louisiana," Nola said, smiling at the thought of there being a Louisiana in Denmark as well. "Jörgen Bo was the architect. It's one I've always wanted to visit."

"It's really quite marvelous. . . . I hope you *do* get to see it someday. Because that's what I thought of when I saw your design. Not the Louisiana itself, mind you, but the *spirit* of it. I think you'll see that tomorrow, when you visit our library."

Our. The word seemed to hang in the air between them.

"I should be going," Nola said. "It's getting late. And I ought to check in at my hotel."

She rose awkwardly, feeling as if the ottoman, the Oriental carpet at her feet, even the walls themselves were tugging at her with their own gravity.

And then something *was* pressing her down, a small hand, soft as a moth's wing, yet surprisingly forceful.

"Don't go," Cordelia said, and for the first time her smile was genuine, lighting her whole face with a kind of incandescence that Nola, in her whole life, had seen in only one other person: her father.

She felt her throat catch, then a sharp stinging behind her eyes.

"There's someone I'd very much like for you to meet," Cordelia went on. "A dear friend of mine, the gentleman I spoke of earlier. Gabe Ross." She lifted her cordial glass as if in a toast. "He should be arriving at any moment. I know he'd love to meet you, too. You *will* stay for supper, won't you?"

"Hannah, I'm so glad you could come." Cordelia put her hand out, and was favorably impressed by the firmness with which Hannah grasped it. Not at all what she would have expected from the way Hannah was dressed, like one of those hippie folksingers Grace had been so enamored of at that age—jeans and a baggy black cotton top, her long dark hair draped about her narrow, scrubbed face.

"They couldn't find a baby-sitter."

For a moment, fooled by Hannah's deadpan expression, Cordelia felt flustered; then she realized it was Hannah's idea of a joke, and she laughed. Grace, standing beside her, laughed, too, and gave Hannah a playful nudge.

The ice was broken.

As they trooped in her front door, Hannah and Chris, followed by Grace and Jack, Cordelia had a sense that this was going to be easier than she'd feared.

Chris, at sixteen, was even taller than when she'd seen him last summer. He'd filled out some, too . . . but she prayed he'd brought something to wear to tomorrow's dedication ceremony other than the shorts and T-shirt he was sporting. Whisking his silky brown hair from his eyes with a practiced sideways jerk of his head, he offered her his outstretched palm, croaking in his recently acquired baritone, "High five, Nana."

Grace looked as if she'd filled out some, too—not the way Sissy had—merely a new flattering softness, the sharp bones in her face not so prominent, her tomboy figure a bit more rounded. And was that actually a *dress* she had on? It'd been so long since Cordelia had seen her in anything but jeans, on occasion dressy slacks, that she could hardly believe her eyes.

She kissed Grace's cheek, and smelled . . . green apples. She must have washed her hair with one of those fancy shampoos that had come in the ribboned basket of toiletries that Cordelia had sent as a housewarming gift for their new apartment. She felt touched, and allowed herself the luxury of patting her daughter's hair.

"How was your flight?" she asked.

"Not bad. We were delayed for a half-hour or so in Charlotte, but after that it was smooth sailing."

"You should have let me meet you at the airport."

"Heavens, no, Mother . . . Could you just see all of us squeezing into your old Buick with our mounds of luggage, sitting on top of you and Hollis? We rented a station wagon at the airport. That way I could drive around town and give Hannah and Jack the ten-dollar tour."

"Don't let her fool you, she just likes to be in control." Jack laughed, squeezing his wife about her waist. He made Cordelia think of a baker she used to buy bread from, a huge man with great floury hands who handled his loaves with the delicacy of a surgeon. "Grace in command, and the rest of us taking up the rear."

Cordelia stood on tiptoe as he bent down from what seemed like an impossible height to kiss her cheek.

"Well, come in, come in," she chimed, feeling unusually lighthearted as she ushered Grace and Jack into the sunlit front room while Chris took off upstairs with Hannah to show her the rest of the house. "I'll have Netta bring us a pitcher of iced tea. I hope you're hungry, that you weren't forced into eating any of that dreadful airplane food. We're having an early supper, fried chicken and mashed potatoes."

"Yes, Mother, a masked gunman held a Ruger to my head and said, 'Eat the stuffed ziti or die.' " Grace kicked off her high heels, and sprawled onto the chintz sofa below the bay window, exactly as she had been doing since she was fourteen.

"Poor nutrition is no laughing matter." Cordelia sniffed, but was unable to resist giving into the smile playing at her lips.

"I'll second the motion," Jack said. "All I've been hearing since Charlotte was how Netta was going to fatten us all up—as if I need any more." He patted his gut.

"Daddy! You've gotta come see this!" Hannah's glowing face appeared in the doorway. "A real turret, with a spiral staircase and everything, just like something out of *Wuthering Heights!*"

Jack, who was heading back outside to carry in the luggage, allowed himself to be led off up the stairs.

Now Cordelia was alone with her daughter for the first time since Grace's wedding. Grace had kept *saying* she was going to visit, but then something would come up and she couldn't get away. So she'd send Chris by himself, always a joy, but not quite the same as all of them being together.

There was so much she wanted to tell Grace, how much she'd missed her, and how happy she was for her and Jack . . . but all of a sudden she felt strangely awkward and even a bit shy.

"Sissy's sorry she couldn't be here," Cordelia told her. "The boys had Little League practice, and it was her turn to carpool. She'll be here for supper, though, and she said to tell you she's making your favorite ambrosia salad."

"*My* favorite?" Grace laughed. "I don't think I've touched the stuff since I was ten years old. I'll probably go into cardiac arrest from all that sugar."

But Grace wasn't saying it to be mean, Cordelia could tell. And Lord knew, if there was one thing on this earth Sissy could do well it was that ambrosia salad of hers, which she herself had been pretending for so long to love she'd almost convinced herself of it.

"Well, you know your sister—she has a tendency to cling to the familiar. And you've been away for so long. . . ."

"Does Sissy still make it with those itty-bitty colored marshmallows?"

"Mercy, yes," said Cordelia, and, before she realized what she was doing, she was rolling her eyes. "If anyone were to sneak a white one in there, she'd probably call it health food."

Grace giggled, holding her hand over her mouth. "Oh, Mother! I never thought I'd be saying this . . . but I'm actually glad to be here. It's the way I remember it from when we used to visit Gramma when I was a kid, before . . ." She paused.

"Before all the trouble between you and me started—isn't that what you meant to say?" Cordelia finished.

Grace was staring at her, one leg hooked over the other, her bare, hoisted foot jiggling like it had a life of its own. "You've changed, Mother."

"Well, I stopped putting those highlights in my hair. It was starting to turn that funny violet you see on old ladies, so I just let it go natural." She touched the ends of her silvery pageboy, which curled under just below her chin.

"You look absolutely beautiful. And you know perfectly well that's not what I meant." She swung her foot down, planting it squarely on the old but hardly worn Tabriz carpet in front of the tulipwood coffee table. Leaning forward with her elbows on her knees in a most unladylike fashion, she added, "I meant that you're a lot more relaxed . . . more direct. Could it have anything to do with a certain man in your life?" Her eyes sparkled.

"Well, if being direct is a disease, it is certainly catching." Cordelia felt herself flush. "And, if you must know, it's not serious."

"What, the disease, or Gabe Ross?"

"You're making fun of me now."

"Oh, Mother, I'm not making fun of you. I'd be delighted if you were half as happy with Mr. Ross as I am being married to Jack. And from what I've gathered, it *does* sound pretty serious."

"My letters, you mean?" Cordelia was surprised. She'd thought she was so discreet—only mentioning Gabe from time to time, commenting on the work he was doing in the garden, or some new innovation in his teen program at the hospital.

"I'm good at reading between the lines," Grace told her.

"He's asked me to marry him." Cordelia, with an even deeper sigh, settled back against the deep cushions of the burgundy plush chair—the one that had been Eugene's favorite.

"That's wonderful!"

"No, it isn't. Because I'm telling him no."

"You haven't turned him down yet?"

"No, but . . ."

"Oh, Mother, what's the matter?" Grace jumped to her feet, throwing her hands up in exasperation. "Does he pick his teeth after supper? Leave the bathroom door open when he takes a whiz? Wear navy socks with brown shoes?"

Cordelia felt a dart of annoyance. "There's no need to get sassy with me, young lady. . . ." She stopped, as if somehow she'd tuned into a radio channel and heard her old self talking, one of those dreadful Bible-thumping shows urging sinners to come to Jesus. She let her wagging finger fall back to her side. "Oh, Grace, it's nothing like that. Well, I suppose it *is,* but in a different way. I just can't see the two of us . . . What I mean is, we're nothing alike."

"Oh, Lord, that's exactly what *I* used to say about Jack." Grace's eyes sparkled. "And look where it's gotten us. I've never been happier."

"It's not just that we're different," Cordelia argued. "It's that . . . we move in such different circles."

"You mean Blessing wouldn't approve of your marrying Gabe Ross?"

"*I* don't care what anyone thinks, but we can't seal ourselves away. What would my life be like without my old friends?"

"Your *real* friends would want you to be happy. And, besides, Gabe Ross isn't the only one around here who sticks out like a sore thumb. Don't you think it's time you recognized what an extraordinary woman *you* are? Who among all your friends has accomplished half what you have? Just think of all the gossip and back-stabbing that'll come of you marrying Gabe as just one more mountain you've got to climb."

Cordelia, taken aback by Grace's praise, startled herself by admitting, "He's the only man I've known besides your father who sees things as they really are. But with Gabe it's not just . . . the big picture. He understands about the little things, too. And he . . . he would never lie to me. I *know* that somehow, just like I know that Sissy will be stuffing that awful ambrosia salad down our throats from here to kingdom come." She gave a short, dry bark of a laugh, feeling herself dangerously on the verge of tears.

"Then *marry* him, for God's sake."

Cordelia was silent for a long while. She watched Grace get up and restlessly roam about, picking up a cloisonné box here, the Lalique ashtray there, that silver-framed photo of Sissy and the boys atop the cherry console next to ones of all of them back when they were a family. She wanted to cry out, *Stop! Stop putting my life under a microscope . . . and let's just be a family again, like we were once before.* But what kind of family *had* they been? The one in that snapshot of her and Gene squinting into the camera, each with an arm about the sunburned shoulders of a pigtailed little girl, the summer they'd rented that house up at Lake

Kinawasha? Self-consciously holding a pose that was never real to begin with. A family that had been her ironclad *idea* of it more than anything else.

A kind of fuzziness crept over her, like the thick layer of dust under the beds that Netta was too arthritic these days to get to. She felt more confused about Gabe than before, yet she found herself wanting more than anything at this moment to see her life as Grace obviously did, with its achievements, and the promise it still held.

"I'll think about it," she said softly.

*T*his day is a gift from heaven, Cordelia thought as she mounted the steps of the platform that had been erected on the lawn in front of the library. Poised on the edge of the dais, she looked out over the crowd gathered for the occasion, and felt her heart swell. Oh, if only Gene could be here!

But, in a way, he *was* here. Cordelia's gaze traveled up the soaring stone façade of the library, with its staggered row of story-high windows, its angled recesses and gently sloping slate roof. The sun, backfiring off all that glass, seemed to bathe the faces below her in a kind of supernal glow, and from the grass, mown just that morning, drifted a smell she associated with everything that was good about summer— warm weather, and green, growing things. A few hundred feet away, sheltered by majestic old English oaks and catalpas, the Gothic-style brick-and-stone buildings of Latham University appeared almost to be bowing down in homage.

She marveled at the miracle of it—not just the way it had turned out, but that it had gotten built at all.

Little thanks to Dan Killian, standing over there, where they'd strung a gold ribbon between the cedar fence posts, shaking hands like a barnstorming politician with everybody who was anybody. And old Cyrus Gledding, chairman of

Latham's board, whom she'd had to fight tooth and nail against every cost-efficient shortcut he'd wanted to make—look at him now, his arm around Norwood Price, Latham's president, posing for that *Newsweek* photographer, all puffed up like he'd not only supported her but had built the library with his own hands.

What did it matter now, though? It was here, real . . . and now what looked like the whole country had come to celebrate. On one of the folding chairs set up on the dais under a canvas awning sat Coretta King, erect and queenly in an emerald suit and a black hat. Next to her, the Governor—he'd be the first to speak, after her own brief introduction. Then Senator Wirth. And Dexter Hathaway, pastor of Blessing's largest Baptist church.

And yet all those people out there—there had to be a thousand or more—were watching *her,* waiting to hear what she would say about her brilliant, courageous, beloved . . . and faithless husband. The television crews, with their vans ringing the newly landscaped grounds like so many covered wagons, armed with minicams and headphones and walkie-talkies. The old guard of Blessing, which had turned out in force. Her daughters and their children. Nola Emory, in a crisp copper-colored suit and green silk blouse, deep in conversation with Ed Karimian, the general contractor with whom she, Cordelia, had been at loggerheads for the better part of the past eighteen months. The Eugene Truscott High marching band, from nearby Macon, in their crimson-and-gold uniforms, so young and fresh and eager, their playing making up in vigor what it lacked in musicality.

And Gabe.

He stood off to one side, half hidden by one of the weeping cherries that flanked the bluestone path sloping up to the library's vaulted entrance. Wearing an old blue serge suit that had probably fit him better back in his teaching days, and a necktie she recognized, even from this distance, as the one Netta had given him last Christmas. A bit on the garish side, but he'd been so touched by Netta's thoughtfulness, he wore it every opportunity he got.

He saw her looking at him, and nodded, clearly not wanting to call attention to himself.

Now, as Cordelia crossed to the center of the platform under the clear summer sky, a mild breeze blowing strands of silver hair across her cheeks, she knew it was more than the triumph of this moment that was making her heart pound and her throat feel dry. She glanced down at the words neatly printed on the index cards she held clutched against the bottom button of her periwinkle suit jacket. As the band finished its enthusiastic, if slightly off-key, rendition of the national anthem, and the crowd began to applaud, Cordelia decided that the speech she'd written wasn't at all what she wanted to say. She slipped the laboriously printed cards into her pocket, and stepped up to the microphone.

She feared that she would have to struggle to find the right words . . . but when she opened her mouth, they quite unexpectedly were already there, inscribed in her heart, maybe where they'd always been.

"I don't believe my husband needs any introduction, but I'd like to say a few words about what brought us all here today," she began, hearing her voice bounce back at her in a chorus of echoes. "I started out some years ago wanting to erect a memorial to a man who stood for everything that's good about this country of ours. Equality, the right of every human being to stand up and be counted. But somewhere along the way, I discovered that I wasn't doing this just for my husband. . . ." She paused, now hearing only ringing silence and the rustling of the wind in the trees. Somehow, at this moment, she felt closer to dear Gene than she had since the years of their marriage.

"I think I needed to prove to myself," she went on, "that the man I'd so cherished was above reproach in *every* way. I'd clung to that belief, in the face of my doubts . . . even going so far as to condemn those who tried to tell me otherwise. I was afraid, you see. Of discovering that everything I'd believed in was a lie. Then, one day, I realized I was creating, not a memorial, but a . . . prison."

It was almost as if it wasn't her speaking, but someone reading aloud a familiar passage from some ancient book, the unrehearsed words flowing from her as if they'd been spoken many times before. She saw before her an ocean of faces stunned into absolute immobility. It was almost eerily quiet—the only sounds the persistent whirr of minicams and the muttering of the wind. She took a deep breath, and continued, "I know now that it is only when we open our minds that we can we truly memorialize our great men, our ideals. Because we will have learned that the human heart is an instrument, most of all, of forgiveness. And that true understanding can only come from allowing those we most esteem and hold dear to be human. I hope *that* is what you'll think of when you look upon this memorial built in my husband's name . . ." She smiled, waiting for the tightness in her throat to subside. ". . . and designed by his daughter Nola Emory Truscott, whose contribution I would like to acknowledge on this important day."

The crowd's collective gasp was like an ocean wave swelling toward her. She caught a glimpse of Nola's face, shocked, and then seeming to shimmer, a proud joy rising from her like waves of heat from parched ground.

Cordelia stepped back from the microphone, feeling a kind of horror mixed with relief. Had she really said all that? At the same time, she *felt,* as well as heard, the applause that began low to the ground and then seemed to swell, lifting her up like the beating wings of a hundred thousand eagles.

She saw, as if from some spiraling height, the pale valentine that was Grace's face, shining with tears . . . and, beside her, Sissy, in a polka-dot shirtwaist, looking vaguely bewildered, as if not quite sure whether she ought to be pleased or scandalized.

But Nola, *she* had grasped it all . . . and if two people who had started out with nothing in common but bitterness and resentment could ever be reconciled, then they had just come within a hair's breadth of it.

But she wasn't finished yet. The hard part was still ahead of her. Yet, strangely, it took no effort on her part at all to move in that direction.

She descended from the platform as if propelled by nothing more than the force of her longing . . . past the curtain of people and reporters and cameras on either side of her . . . past Lucinda Parmenter in a flowered hat staring slack-mouthed at her . . . past Sissy, now struggling to subdue that little monster of hers, Beau, who'd just kicked the bejesus out of his brother . . . past all the reasons that she had ever believed mattered, and which she now knew were as inconsequential as yesterday's weather.

When she reached Gabe, she wavered for a moment, unable, or unwilling—she didn't know which—to take that very last step. Then he smiled and reached out, and while cameras clicked and whirred and flashed, and a low buzz of voices cut through the waning applause, Cordelia accepted the callused hand of the man she intended to marry, come hell or high water.